Praise for Mary Balogh:

'One of the best!'
Julia Quinn

'Today's superstar heir to the marvellous legacy of
Georgette Heyer (except a lot steamier)'
Susan Elizabeth Phillips

'Ms Balogh is a veritable treasure, a matchless storyteller
who makes our hearts melt with delight'
Romantic Times

'Balogh is truly a find'
Publishers Weekly

'Balogh is the queen of spicy Regency-era romance,
creating memorable characters in unforgettable stories'

By Mary Balogh

Mistress Couplet:

No Man's Mistress
More Than a Mistress

The Secret Mistress
(prequel to the Mistress
Couplet series)

Huxtables Series:

First Comes Marriage
Then Comes Seduction
At Last Comes Love
Seducing an Angel
A Secret Affair

Simply Quartet:

Simply Unforgettable
Simply Love
Simply Magic
Simply Perfect

Bedwyn Series:

One Night for Love
A Summer to Remember
Slightly Married
Slightly Wicked
Slightly Scandalous
Slightly Tempted
Slightly Sinful
Slightly Dangerous

Survivors' Club Series:

The Proposal
The Arrangement
The Escape
Only Enchanting
Only a Promise
Only a Kiss
Only Beloved

The Westcott Series:

Someone to Love
Someone to Hold
Someone to Wed
Someone to Care
Someone to Trust

MARY BALOGH

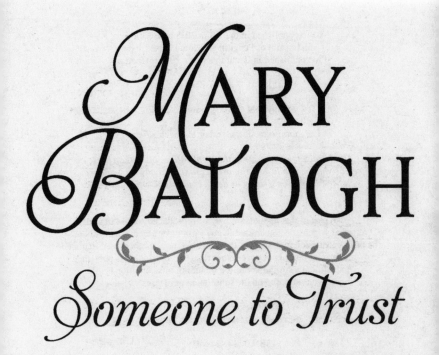

Someone to Trust

piatkus

PIATKUS

First published in the US in 2018 by Berkley,
an imprint of Penguin Random House LLC
First published in Great Britain in 2018 by Piatkus

1 3 5 7 9 10 8 6 4 2

A CIP catalogue record for this book
is available from the British Library.

ISBN 978-0-349-41922-0

Printed and bound by CPI Group (UK) Ltd, Croydon, CR0 4YY

Papers used by Piatkus are from well-managed forests
and other responsible sources.

Piatkus
An imprint of
Little, Brown Book Group
Carmelite House
50 Victoria Embankment
London EC4Y 0DZ

An Hachette UK Company
www.hachette.co.uk

www.littlebrown.co.uk

Someone to Trust

The Westcott Family

(Characters from the family tree who appear in *Someone to Trust* are shown in bold print.)

Stephen Westcott m. Eleanor Coke
Earl of Riverdale   (1704–1759)
(1698–1761)

George Westcott m. **Eugenia Madson**
Earl of Riverdale   (b. 1742)
(1724–1790)

Andrew Westcott m. Bertha Ames
(1726–1796)   (1736–1807)

David Westcott m. **Althea Radley**
(1756–1806)   (b. 1762)

Matilda Humphrey Westcott Louise Westcott m. John Archer Mildred m. Thomas Wayne
Westcott Earl of Riverdale   (b. 1770)   Duke of Netherby   **Westcott**   Baron Molenor
(b. 1761)   (1762–1811)   (1755–1809)   (b. 1773)   (b. 1769)

m. **Viola Kingsley**   m. Alice Snow   m. Ava Cobham
(b. 1772)   (1768–1789)   (1760–1790)

Jessica
Archer
(b. 1795)

Boris   Peter   Ivan
Wayne   Wayne   Wayne
(b. 1796) (b. 1798) (b. 1799)

Marcel Lamarr
(b. 1770)

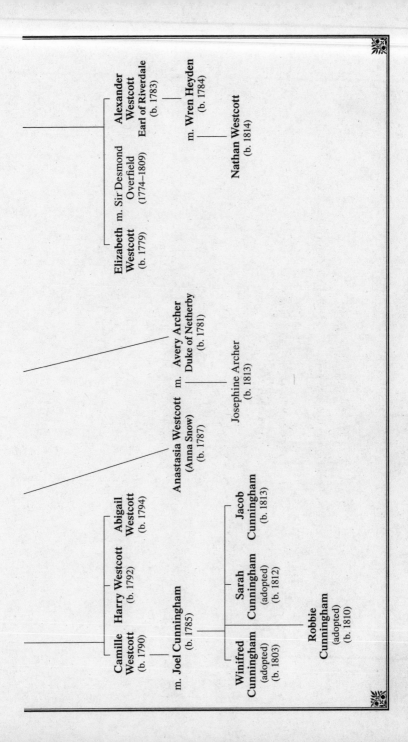

One

There was nothing like a family Christmas to make a person feel warm about the heart—oh, and a little wistful too. And perhaps just a bit melancholy.

Brambledean Court in Wiltshire was the scene of just such a gathering for the first time in many years. All the Westcotts were gathered there, from Eugenia, the seventy-one-year-old Dowager Countess of Riverdale, on down to her newest great-grandson, Jacob Cunningham, the three-month-old child of the former Camille Westcott and her husband, Joel. They had all been invited by Alexander Westcott, the present Earl of Riverdale and head of the family, and Wren, his wife of six months.

The house had been unlived in for more than twenty years before Alexander inherited the title, and had been shabby even back then. By the time he arrived it had grown shabbier, and the park surrounding it had acquired a sad air of general neglect. It had been a formidable challenge for Alexander, who took his responsibilities seriously but did not have the fortune with which to carry them out. That problem had been solved with his marriage, since Wren was vastly wealthy. The fortune she had brought to their union enabled them to repair the damage of years and restore the house and park on the one hand and the farms on the other to their former prosperity and glory. But Rome was not built in a day, as the dowager countess was not hesitant to remark after her arrival. There was still a great deal to be done. A very great deal. But at least the house now had a lived-in air.

There were a few other guests besides the Westcotts and their spouses and children. There were Mrs. Kingsley from Bath and her son and daughter-in-law, the Reverend Michael and Mary Kingsley from Dorsetshire. They were the mother, brother, and sister-in-law of Viola, a former Countess of Riverdale, whose marriage of upward of twenty years to the late earl had been exposed spectacularly after his death as bigamous. There had been many complications surrounding that whole ugly episode. But all had ended happily for Viola. For on this very day, Christmas Eve, she had married Marcel Lamarr, Marquess of Dorchester, in the village church. The newlyweds were at the house now, as well as Dorchester's eighteen-year-old twin son and daughter.

And Colin Handrich, Baron Hodges, Wren's brother, was here too. For the first time in his twenty-six years he was experiencing a real family Christmas, and after some feeling of awkwardness yesterday despite a warm welcome from everyone, he was now enjoying it greatly.

The house was abuzz with activity. There had been the wedding this morning—a totally unexpected event, it must be added. The marquess had burst in upon them without any prior warning last evening, armed with a special license and an urgent proposal of marriage for Viola a mere couple of months after he had broken off their engagement in spectacularly scandalous fashion during their betrothal party at his own home. But that was another story, and Colin had not been there to experience it firsthand. The wedding had been followed by a wedding breakfast hastily and impressively thrown together by Riverdale's already overworked staff under Wren's supervision.

This afternoon had been one of laughter-filled attempts to add to yesterday's decorations. Fragrant pine boughs and holly and ivy and mistletoe, not to mention ribbons and bells and bows and all the other paraphernalia associated with the season, were everywhere, it seemed—in the drawing room, on the stairs, in the hall, in the dining room. A kissing bough, fashioned under the guidance of Lady Matilda Westcott, unmarried eldest daughter of the dowager countess, hung in the place of honor from the center of the drawing room ceiling and had been causing laughter and whistles and blushes ever since yesterday as it was put to use. There had been the Yule log to haul in today and position in the large hearth in the great hall, ready to be lit in the evening.

And all the while as they moved about and climbed and perched, pinned and balanced, pricked fingers and kissed and blushed, tantalizing smells had been wafting up from the kitchens below of Christmas puddings and gingerbread and mince pies and the Christmas ham, among other mouth-watering delights.

And there had been the snow as a constant wonder and distraction, drawing them to every available window far more often than was necessary to assure themselves that it had not stopped falling and was not melting as fast as it came down. It had been threatening for days and had finally begun during the wedding this morning. It had continued in earnest all day since then, until by now it must be knee deep.

Snow, and such copious amounts of it, was a rarity in England, especially for Christmas. They did not stop telling one another so all afternoon.

And now, this evening, the village carolers had waded up the driveway to sing for them. The Yule log had been lit and the family had gathered and the carolers had come against all expectation, exclaiming and stamping boots and shaking mufflers and slapping mittens and rubbing at red noses to make them redder—and then quieting down and growing self-conscious as they looked around at the family and friends gathered in the great hall to listen to them.

They sang for half an hour, and their audience listened and occasionally joined in. The dowager countess and Mrs. Kingsley were seated in ornately carved and padded wooden chairs close to the great fireplace to benefit from the logs that flamed and crackled around the Yule log in the hearth. It gave more the effect of cheerfulness than actual warmth to the rest of the hall, but everyone else was happy to stand until the carolers came to the end of their repertoire and everyone applauded. Alexander gave a short speech wishing everyone a happy and healthy New Year. Then they all moved about, mingling and chatting and laughing merrily as glasses of spiced wassail and trays of warm mince pies were brought up from belowstairs and offered first to the carolers and then to the house guests.

After a while Colin found himself standing in the midst of it all, alone for the moment, consciously enjoying the warm, festive atmosphere of the scene around him. From what he could observe, there appeared to be not one discordant note among the happy crowd—if one ignored the impatience with which the dowager was batting away the heavy shawl Lady Matilda was attempting to wrap about her shoulders.

This was what family should be like.

This was what Christmas should always be like.

It was an ideal of perfection, of course, and ideals were not often attained and were not sustainable for long even when they were. Life could never be unalloyed happiness, even for a close-knit family such as this one. But sometimes there were moments when it was, and this was surely one of them. It deserved to be recognized and enjoyed and savored.

And envied.

He smiled at the three young ladies across the hall who had their heads together, chattering and laughing and stealing glances his way. It was not altogether surprising. He was not unduly conceited, but he *was* a young, single gentleman in possession of a title and fortune. Single gentlemen above the age of twenty were in short supply here at Brambledean. Indeed, he was the only one, with the exception of Captain Harry Westcott, Viola's son, who had arrived back from the wars in the Peninsula two days ago—also unexpectedly—on recruitment business for his regiment. Unfortunately for the three ladies, however, the captain was the brother of one of them and the first cousin of another. Only Lady Estelle Lamarr, the Marquess of Dorchester's daughter, was unrelated to him by blood, though she had become his stepsister this morning.

When they saw Colin smile, they all ducked their heads, while above the general hubbub he could hear one of them giggling. But why would he not look and be pleased with what he saw—and flattered by their attention? They were all remarkably pretty in different ways, younger than he and unattached, as far as he knew. They were all eligible, even Abigail Westcott, Viola and the late Earl of Riverdale's daughter, whose birth had been declared illegitimate almost three years ago after the disastrous revelation concerning her father's bigamy. Colin did not care a fig for that supposed stain upon her name. Lady Jessica Archer was half sister of the Duke of Netherby and daughter of the former duke and his second wife, the youngest of the Westcott sisters.

It had not been easy during the six months since Wren had married Alexander to sort out the complex relationships within this family, but Colin believed he had finally mastered them, even the step and half connections.

He was about to stroll across the hall to ask the three young ladies how they had enjoyed the carol singing when his sister appeared at his side and handed him a glass of wassail.

"You are going to have to stay here tonight after all, thanks to the snow, Colin," she said, sounding smug.

"But you already have a houseful, Roe," he protested, though in truth he knew it would be impossible to go home tonight and even more impossible to return tomorrow. Home was Withington House, nine miles away, where he had been living since the summer. It belonged to Wren, but he had gladly moved in there when she had offered it, rather than stay in London, where he had lived throughout the year for the past five years.

"*Roe,*" she said softly and fondly. She had been christened Rowena as a baby. *Roe* had been Colin's childhood name for her, and he still called her that when in conversation with her, even though her name had been legally changed to Wren. "One more guest will cause no upheaval, and it will make us all a lot happier. Me in particular. Was not the carol singing wonderful?"

"Wonderful," he agreed, though the singers had been more hearty than musical.

"And the wedding this morning was perfect," she said with a happy sigh. "And the wedding breakfast after it. And the snow and putting up more decorations and . . . oh, and *everything*. Have you ever lived through a happier day?"

He pretended to think about it, his eyes raised to the high ceiling of the great hall, his forefinger tapping his chin. He raised the finger. "Yes, I have, actually," he said. "The day Alexander came to call at my rooms in London and I discovered that you were still alive, and I went with him to meet you for the first time in almost twenty years."

"Ah. Yes." She beamed at him, her eyes luminous with memory. "Oh yes, indeed, Colin, you are right. When I looked at you, and you spoke my name, and I realized you were that little mop-haired boy I remembered . . . It was indeed an unforgettable day."

He had been told when he was six years old that ten-year-old Rowena had died shortly after their aunt took her away from Roxingley, supposedly to consult a physician about the great strawberry birthmark that swelled over one side of her face, disfiguring her quite horribly. In reality there had been no physician and no death. Aunt Megan had taken Rowena from a home in which she had been isolated and frequently locked in her room so that no one would have to look at her. Aunt Megan had married Reginald Heyden, a wealthy gentleman of her acquaintance, soon after, and the two of them had adopted Rowena Handrich, changed her name to Wren Heyden, and raised her as their own. Colin, meanwhile, had grieved deeply for his beloved sister and playmate. He had discovered the truth only this year, when Alexander had sought him out soon after marrying her.

Wren was lovely despite the purple marks down the left side of her face where the strawberry swelling had been when she was a child. And she was looking more beautiful than ever these days. Alexander had lost no time in getting her with child.

"Was Christmas a happy time for you when you were a boy, Colin?" Her face turned a little wistful as she gazed into his.

He had grown up as part of a family—there were his mother and father, an elder brother, and three older sisters. Roxingley Park was a grand property where there had always been an abundance of the good things in life. The material things, that was. His father had been a wealthy man, just as Colin was now. Christmases had come and gone, even after the supposed death of Rowena, the youngest of his sisters, and the real death of his brother Justin nine years later. But he did not remember them as warm family occasions. Not like this one. Not even close.

"I am sorry," she said. "You are looking suddenly melancholy. Aunt Megan and Uncle Reggie always made Christmas very special for me and for each other. Not like this, of course. There were just the three of us. But very lovely nevertheless and abounding with love. Life will get better for you, Colin. I promise. And you will be staying tonight. You will be here all day tomorrow and probably all of Boxing Day too. *Definitely*, in fact, for we will press ahead with the plans for our Boxing Day evening party even if some of our invited guests find it impossible to get here. This is going to be the best Christmas ever. I have decided, and I will not take no for an answer. It already is the best, in fact, though I do wish Aunt Megan and Uncle Reggie were still alive to be a part of it. You would have loved them, and they would have loved you."

He opened his mouth to reply, but Alexander had caught her eye from his position behind the refreshments and she excused herself to weave her way back toward him in order to distribute more of the wassail to the carolers before they left.

Colin looked about the hall again, still feeling warm and happy—and a bit melancholy at having been reminded of the brokenness that was and always had been his own family. And perhaps too at the admission that, though he was now Baron Hodges himself and therefore head of his family, and though he was twenty-six years old and no longer had the excuse of being a mere boy, he had done nothing to draw its remaining members together—his mother and his three sisters and their spouses and children. He had not been to Roxingley since he was eighteen, when he had gone for his father's funeral. He had done nothing to perpetuate his line, to create his own family, something more like this one. The Westcotts had suffered troubles enough in the last few years and no doubt before that too. Life was like that. But their troubles had seemed to strengthen rather than loosen the bonds that held them.

Not so with the Handrich family.

Could it be done? Was it possible? Was he ready at least to try? To do something positive with his life instead of just drifting from day to day and more or less hiding from the enormity of what doing something would entail? His eyes alit again upon the group across the hall. The young ladies had been joined by the three schoolboy sons of Lord and Lady Molenor. Winifred Cunningham, Abigail's young niece, was with them too, as were a couple of the younger carolers. They were all merrily chatting and laughing and behaving as though this Christmas Eve was the very happiest of days—as indeed it was.

Colin felt suddenly as though he were a hundred years older than the oldest of them.

"A penny for them," a voice said from close by, and he turned toward the speaker.

Ah. Lady Overfield.

Just the sight of her lifted his mood and brought a smile to his face. He liked and admired her more than any other woman of his acquaintance, perhaps more than any other person of either gender. For him she lived on a sort of pedestal, above the level of other mortals. He might have been quite in love with her if she had been of an age with him or younger. Though even then it would have seemed somehow disrespectful. She was his ideal of womanhood.

She was Alexander's elder sister, Wren's sister-in-law, and beautiful through and through. He was well aware that other people might not agree. She was fair haired and trim of figure and had a face that was amiable more than it was obviously lovely. But his life experiences had taught him to look deeper than surface appearances to discover beauty or its lack. Lady Overfield was perhaps the most beautiful woman he had ever met. There was something about her manner that exuded a seemingly unshakable tranquility combined with a twinkling eye. But she did not hoard it. Rather, she turned it outward to touch other people. She did not draw attention to herself but bestowed it upon others. She was everyone's best friend in the family, the one with whom all felt appreciated and comfortable, the one who would always listen and never judge. She had been Wren's first friend ever—Wren had been close to thirty at the time—and had remained steadfast. Colin would have loved her for that alone.

He had liked her since his rediscovery of his sister, but he had felt particularly warm toward her since yesterday.

He had felt a bit awkward being among the members of a close family, though everyone had made him welcome. Lady Overfield had singled him out, though, for special attention. She had talked with him all evening from her perch on the window seat in the room where they were all gathered, drawing him out on topics he would not normally have raised with a woman, talking just enough herself to make it a conversation. He had soon relaxed. He had also felt honored, for to her he must appear little more than a gauche boy. He guessed she must be somewhere in her mid-thirties to his twenty-six. He did not know how long she had been a widow, but she must have been quite young when she lost her husband, poor lady. She had no children. She lived with Mrs. Westcott, her mother, at Alexander's former home in Kent.

She had asked him a question.

"I was trying to decide," he said, nodding in the direction of the group of young people, "which of the three ladies I should marry."

She looked startled for a moment and then laughed with him as she glanced across the room.

"Oh, indeed?" she said. "But have you not heard, Lord Hodges, that when one gazes across a crowded room at the one and only person destined to be the love of one's life, one feels no doubt whatsoever? If you look and see *three* possible candidates for the position, then it is highly probable that none of them is the right choice."

"Alas," he said. "Are you quite sure?"

"Well, not *quite*," she admitted. "They are all remarkably pretty, are they not? I must applaud your taste. I have observed too that they are not indifferent to your charms. They have been stealing glances at you and exchanging nudges and giggles since yesterday—at least Abby and

Jessica have. Estelle came only today after the wedding, but she seems equally struck by you. But Lord Hodges, *are* you in search of a wife?"

"No," he said after a slight hesitation. "Not really. I am not, but I am beginning to feel that perhaps I ought to be. Sometime. Maybe soon. Maybe not for a few years yet. And how is that for a firm, decisive answer?"

"Admirable," she said, and laughed again. "I expect the young female world and that of its mamas will go into raptures when you do begin the search in earnest. You must know that you are one of England's most eligible bachelors and not at all hard on the eyes either. Wren is over the moon with delight that you will be staying here tonight, by the way. She was disappointed last evening when you insisted upon returning home."

"I believe the snow is still coming down out there, Lady Overfield," he said. "If I tried to get home, there might be nothing more than my eyebrows showing above the snow when someone came in search of me. It would appear that I am stuck here for at least a couple of days."

"Better here than there even if you could get safely home," she said. "You would be stuck there and all alone for Christmas. The very thought makes me want to weep. But will you call me Elizabeth? Or even Lizzie? My brother is, after all, married to your sister, which fact makes us virtually brother and sister, does it not? May I call you Colin?"

"Please do, Elizabeth," he said, feeling a bit awkward at saying her name. It seemed an imposition. But she had requested it, a particular mark of acceptance. What a very happy Christmas this was turning out to be—and it was not even Christmas Day yet. How could he even consider feeling melancholy?

"You ought to be very thankful for the snow," she said. "Now you will not have to waste part of the morning in travel. Christmas morning is always one of my favorites of the year, if not my *very* favorite. Is it not a rare treat indeed to have a white Christmas? And has that been remarked upon a time or two already today? But I cannot remember the last time it happened. And it is not even a light dusting to tease the hopes of children everywhere, but a massive fall. I would wager upon the sudden appearance of an army of snowmen and perhaps snowladies tomorrow, as well as a heavenly host of snow angels. And snowball fights and sleigh rides—there is an ancient sleigh in the carriage house, apparently. And sledding down the hill. There are sleds too, which really ought to be in a museum somewhere, according to Alex, but which will doubtless work just as well as new ones would. There is even a hill, though not a very mountainous one, alas. It will do, however. You will not be sorry you stayed."

"Perhaps," he said, "I will choose to spend a more traditional Christmas in a comfortable chair by the fire, eating rich foods and imbibing spiced wine and napping."

She looked at him, startled again. "Oh, you could not possibly be so poor spirited," she said, noticing the twinkle in his eye. "You would be the laughingstock. A pariah. Expelled from Brambledean in deep disgrace, never to be admitted within its portals again even if you *are* Wren's brother."

"Does that also mean none of your young cousins would be willing to marry me?" he asked.

"It absolutely means just that," she assured him. "Even I would not."

"Ah," he said, slapping a hand to the left side of his chest. "My heart would be broken."

"I would have no pity on you," she said, "even if you came to me with the pieces in your hand."

"Cruel." He sighed. "Then I had better be prepared to go out tomorrow and make a few snow angels and hurl a few snowballs, preferably at you. I warn you, though, that I was the star bowler on my cricket team at school."

"What modesty," she said. "Not to mention gallantry. But I see that two of the footmen are lighting the carolers' lanterns. They are about to leave. Shall we go and see them on their way?"

She took the arm he offered and they joined the throng about the great doors. The noise level escalated as everyone thanked the carolers again and the carolers thanked everyone in return and everyone wished everyone else a happy Christmas.

He *was* happy, Colin decided. He was a part of all this. He was an accepted member of the Westcott family, even if merely an extended member. Lady Overfield—Elizabeth—had remarked that they were virtually brother and sister. She had joked and laughed with him. Her hand was still tucked through his arm. There was surely no greater happiness.

There were a snowball fight and sledding to look forward to tomorrow.

And gifts to exchange.

And goose and stuffing and Christmas pudding.

Yes, it felt very good to belong.

To a family that was not really his own.

Two

Elizabeth Overfield had been fighting melancholy for the past few days and was taking herself severely to task over it. This was surely going to be the happiest of Christmases. She was spending it with her mother and brother and sister-in-law and the whole of the Westcott clan. The Radleys, her mother's side of the family, would have been here too if they had not had a prior commitment, but they had already agreed to come next year.

It was nothing short of a miracle that all the Westcotts were assembled here at Brambledean. The great upset of two and a half years ago could so easily have driven them apart into angry, bitter factions. But that had not happened. Rather, the family had pulled together and held together. Viola, the dispossessed Countess of Riverdale, had married here this morning. Her three children, officially illegitimate, were all here too. So was Anna, Duchess of Netherby, the late earl's only legitimate child. None of them seemed to resent in the least Elizabeth's brother, Alex, who had inherited the Riverdale title.

It was illogical, then, to be wrestling with depression.

After the carolers had finished singing, Elizabeth looked about the hall and tried to feel the mood of unalloyed happiness everyone else seemed to be feeling. Then her eyes had alit upon Lord Hodges, standing temporarily alone in the midst of the throng, a wistful, almost bleak expression on his face. And her heart had reached out to him as it had yesterday, when she had sensed his discomfort at being here among a family of virtual strangers. She had taken him under her wing then and found herself unexpectedly enchanted by his quiet charm and smiling blue eyes and by his tall, slim, youthful figure and blond good looks. Spending a couple of hours of the evening talking with him had been a great pleasure, but had done nothing to lift her general mood of depression. For she had found herself wanting to be young again as he was young now and filled with the youthful vitality that had once been hers until the passing of time and a disastrous marriage had sapped it out of her.

It would perhaps have been wise to stay away from him this evening. She did not want to develop any sort of tendresse for him, did she? That would be mildly pathetic. She had approached him anyway and been rewarded by his smile and his warm sense of humor. But she had sensed a certain loneliness in him, as she had last evening. This was not *his* family, after all. Only Wren belonged to him.

Loneliness could feel a bit more acute in circumstances like these, when one was surrounded by friends—and family in her case—but none of them was that particular *someone*, that love of one's life she had spoken of a few minutes ago. She had thought once upon a time she had found him. She had even married him. But it had turned out that despite his protestations to the contrary, Desmond Overfield had preferred alcohol to her, and her love for him had died an aching death even before he literally passed from this life. Or perhaps it never had quite died. Could love die if it was real?

Her lone state had felt even more acute today with the marriage this morning of Viola and the Marquess of Dorchester, a match she believed was going to be a happy one, though nothing in this life was ever certain.

Lord Hodges's situation—Colin's—was quite different from her own, of course. He was still very young, only in his middle twenties, she would guess. She watched him as he shook hands with some of the carolers and commended them on their singing and wished them a safe return home through the snow. Some young lady was going to be fortunate indeed when he really did set his mind upon marriage. She felt suddenly very middle-aged, if not elderly. Had she ever been young like the three girls he had been joking about marrying a few minutes ago, eyeing the young gentlemen with self-conscious awareness, all of life and hope and happiness ahead of her? But of course she had.

"What a wonderful day this has been," Anna said from beside her. "Do you think tomorrow will be an anticlimax, Elizabeth?"

"When there are the gifts to give and receive and the goose to be consumed and the Christmas service at church to look forward to?" Elizabeth said. "And the snow beckoning us to come outside? I think not."

Avery, Duke of Netherby, Anna's husband, sighed and shuddered. "You are not by any chance going to try forcing us to go out there to frolic, are you, Elizabeth?" he asked.

"Ah, but she is," Colin assured him. "She has threatened to have me permanently banished from Brambledean if I try insisting upon napping by the fire as any civilized gentleman ought on Christmas Day. And she has power, Netherby. She is Riverdale's sister."

Elizabeth smiled at the teasing.

Avery raised his quizzing glass to his eye and surveyed her through it, his expression pained. She twinkled merrily back at him, and they all turned their attention back to the departure of the carolers, who were stepping out onto newly swept steps but descending into deep white snow, their mufflers up about their ears, their hats and bonnets pulled low, their lanterns held high. A blast of cold air and even some swirling snow invaded the great hall while farewells and thanks and Christmas wishes were called back and forth yet again.

"Since there is plenty of wassail left in the bowl," Alex said, raising his voice above the slightly diminished hubbub after the doors had closed behind the departing villagers, "and since it must be six or seven hours since we last toasted the health and happiness of the Marquess and Marchioness of Dorchester, I suggest we do so again before we all retire for the night. Wren, where are you? You may pass around the glasses as I fill them, if you will."

Viola, once the Countess of Riverdale, now Viola Lamarr, Marchioness of Dorchester, was looking remarkably happy. Indeed, she glowed like the new bride she was. And the marquess was looking down at her with a gleam in his dark eyes that left Elizabeth feeling slightly breathless and . . . jealous?

But no, not that. She would never begrudge Viola her happiness. Envy, then. She was envious. And lonely again.

There had been a number of marriages in the family during the past couple of years or so, beginning with Anna's to Avery. Anna had lived with Elizabeth for a short while after she came to London from the orphanage where she had grown up, unaware that she was the daughter of the Earl of Riverdale—the legitimate daughter. Elizabeth had lived with her to help her adjust to her new life and feel less bewildered and alone. She and Avery's secretary had been the lone witnesses at their wedding. Then Camille, Viola's elder daughter, had married Joel Cunningham in Bath, and Alex had married Wren in London. Now Viola, who was in her forties, had married the marquess here at Brambledean. And the four family marriages appeared to have one thing in common, as far as Elizabeth could judge from the outside. All four were love matches. All four stood a good chance of remaining happy on into the future.

"Ladies?" Colin said. He had gone over to the wassail bowl with Wren and had returned with a glass in each hand, one for Elizabeth and one for Anna. "But no drinking before everyone has been served and the toast has been proposed."

"Tyrant," Elizabeth said. "Not even one tiny sip?"

"Not even," he said, but his eyes twinkled at her. "Alexander's orders. Lord of the manor and all that."

"I wonder what the penalty would be for disobedience," Anna said.

"You would not want to know," he told her, and winked before moving back to the bowl to help distribute the glasses.

"How very glad I am that Lord Hodges and Wren found each other again," Anna said. "Families really ought not to be kept apart for long years."

Elizabeth smiled sympathetically at her and noticed that Avery had slipped an arm about her waist. And envy assailed her again. And loneliness. It was something she really must do something about. She was thirty-five years old. Not young, but certainly not old. And she had prospects. During the past two Seasons, which she had spent in London with her mother, she had met a few gentlemen, both new acquaintances and old, who had shown signs of interest. It was possible she could marry again. She had been adamantly against remarriage after Desmond's death. Marriage to him had given her a healthy respect for freedom and independence. But not all men were like him. Not all marriages were unhappy or worse. And there were attractions to marriage.

One of those gentlemen, indeed, had expressed a very definite interest. Sir Geoffrey Codaire had first proposed marriage to her many years ago, just after she met Desmond. He had renewed his acquaintance with her during the past two years. He was as solid of build and of character as he had always been, neither particularly handsome nor especially vibrant of personality, but—well, solid and worthy. He was someone with whom she could expect a quiet and comfortable companionship. He was someone upon whom she could depend. More and more lately she had considered accepting the offer he had made again back in the spring. She had said no, but when he had asked if he might renew his addresses sometime in the future, she had hesitated, and he had insisted upon taking that as a hopeful sign and urged her not to answer his question. She had not done so, and they had left it at that. Perhaps this coming spring, if he asked again, she would say yes.

Maybe next Christmas she would no longer be here alone. Perhaps that core of melancholy she could not quite shake off would be banished by a new marriage, her own this time. She might even be with child, as Wren was this year. Sometimes she ached for the experience of motherhood.

The Reverend Michael Kingsley, Viola's brother, had been called upon to propose the toast, and silence descended upon the great hall as Alex tapped the ladle against the side of the wassail bowl.

Colin had joined the young people, Elizabeth could see, and stood with Jessica on one side and young Bertrand La-marr, the Marquess of Dorchester's son, on the other. His free hand, the one that was not holding his glass, was resting upon ten-year-old Winifred's shoulder—the youngsters had been allowed to stay up late tonight. He was looking happy. He was where he belonged.

The Reverend Kingsley cleared his throat, and Elizabeth turned her attention to the toast he was about to propose.

Christmas Day began early with breakfast and gift giving, most of the latter done in small, individual family groups. Colin was invited to join his sister and brother-in-law and Mrs. Westcott and Elizabeth in Wren's private sitting room, where he received an exquisite multicolored glass mug from Wren's glassworks, engraved with his name, and a new fob for his watch from Mrs. Westcott, and a muffler of soft, bright red wool from Elizabeth. He had bought matching leather-backed blotters and pen holders for Wren and Alexander, a paisley shawl for Mrs. Westcott, and a leather-bound notebook with a small attached pencil for Elizabeth. Exchanging gifts really was a delight, he discovered, accompanied as it was with exclamations of delight and effusive thanks and even hugs. It was something new to him. He had brought gifts for the children too.

Most of the family ended up on the nursery floor, where the children opened their presents and displayed them for adult admiration and played with them, though young

Jacob, it was true, was more interested in flapping his hands at his mama and papa's smiles than in appreciating the new stuffed animals they waggled before his face and the rattle about which they curled his fingers. One-year-old Sarah Cunningham, on the other hand, dashed about the nursery, shrieking with joy as she placed her new doll on her mama's knee before snatching it off in order to hug it and pet it before placing it upon someone else's knee. Winifred Cunningham thanked everyone solemnly for hair ribbons and muff and bracelets and rings and then dived into one of her three new books and was lost to the world. Josephine Archer bounced on the Duke of Netherby's knee and tried to bite one paw off a stuffed dog.

Lord Molenor's three sons, who were all in their teen years and therefore ought not to qualify for gifts from everyone, according to their father, exclaimed over cricket bats and balls and boots and mufflers and telescopes and books—which last items did not tempt any of them to dive in immediately. Boris obligingly rocked Sarah's doll and was rewarded by a hug and a kiss before she snatched it away, hugged it herself, and thrust it upon her grandmama.

Everyone convened in the drawing room after that for the distribution of gifts to the servants, the first such ceremony for many years. And, amazingly when one considered the apparent chaos of the morning and the depth of the snow, which was still falling intermittently, they all trekked to church in the village in time for the eleven o'clock service.

The ancient sleigh, spruced up to look almost respectable and decked with bells, which jingled when it was in motion, made two journeys to take the older folk. Everyone else walked—or waded. Any horseplay—Lord Molenor's term—was strictly forbidden on the way there. He bellowed with terrible ferocity when one of his sons slid a handful of snow down the back of his brother's collar and the victim spun about with a roar to retaliate. There was no further incident beyond an inelegant skid that sent Lady Estelle Lamarr sprawling in the snow. When her twin hauled her to her feet she looked like a living snowlady. Captain West-cott helped brush her down while she giggled in embarrass-ment and her cold-flushed cheeks turned surely a brighter shade of scarlet.

Colin walked with Camille and Joel Cunningham and carried young Sarah and her doll most of the way, Cun-ningham's arms being occupied with his infant son while Winifred clung to Camille's hand. He sat with them at church, which he was surprised to find full of parishioners. He could not recall any Christmas when his own family had attended church. They had thereby missed perhaps the most heartwarming service of the year with its emphasis upon birth and hope and love and joy and peace. On Christ-mas Day one could believe in them all, or at least in the possibility of them. Camille held Sarah, who was soon snuggled against her, doll and all, asleep, while Winifred leaned against her mother's arm with utter trust in the power of her family to love and protect her. Joel jiggled young Jacob gently on his knee when the baby began to fuss and was rewarded with a toothless smile and gradually closing eyelids.

It was surely time, Colin thought, to trust the idea of fam-ily. Or, rather, to trust his own ability to create one and per-haps even draw into it the members of the family with whom he had grown up. Wren was already a part of it. So were his sister Ruby and her husband, Sean, and their four children, even though they lived in Ireland and he did not see a great deal of them and Ruby was not the world's most prolific letter writer. But there were still his mother and his eldest sister, Blanche, and her husband. He would not think of them today, however. He did not want his heart to grow heavy.

He walked between Lady Overfield and Mrs. Althea Westcott, her mother, on the way home, the latter leaning rather heavily on his arm lest she slip and fall and make a cake of herself—her words. But she was taken up by the sleigh on its second journey from the church to the house, and Elizabeth took his arm when he offered it, first drawing her gloved hand free of her muff. She looked very fetching in her red cloak and red-brimmed bonnet, a vivid contrast with the whiteness of the snow and the hoarfrost on the branches of the trees.

"Fashionable half boots are woefully inadequate in all this snow, I am discovering," she said ruefully. "One can only hope they will dry out by this afternoon."

"You are still dreaming of snowball fights and sled races and other outdoor horrors, then, are you?" he asked. "Even though we are about to have our Christmas dinner and are almost bound to overindulge?"

"For that precise reason," she said. "I suppose you are still dreaming of a quiet fireside and a comfortable chair."

He laughed. Her eyes were sparkling with pleasure at the anticipated delight of freezing herself with snow frolics. "Have you ever considered marrying again, Elizabeth?" he asked.

She turned her face sharply toward him, her eyebrows raised.

"I do beg your pardon," he said. "That was probably a hideously unmannerly question, not to mention abrupt. But Christmas puts one in mind of family and children and togetherness, and—well, forget I asked, if you please. I have embarrassed myself. And doubtless you too."

But she laughed again. "I am not embarrassed," she said. "And, yes, I have considered remarrying. For a long time I did not. I thought I would be content to live out my life as a dutiful daughter to my mother in her old age. Alas, she will have none of it. And I must confess to feeling a mite relieved. I have started to look about me."

Two of Molenor's boys had made a chair of their interlaced hands, Colin could see, and Winifred was riding on them, her arms about their shoulders. She was laughing—something that was surely rare with her. She was a serious, studious, somewhat pious young girl, who had grown up in an orphanage in Bath before Camille and Joel adopted her along with Sarah last year when they married. Colin wondered if she realized she was bound to be dropped into the snow accidentally on purpose before they reached the house.

"With any success?" he asked Elizabeth.

"Yes, I believe so," she said after hesitating. "A gentleman I have known a long time made me an offer earlier this year. I said no at the time, but he asked if he might renew his addresses at some future date, and I did not say no."

"It sounds like a grand love story," he said, turning his head to grin at her. But really, why would she marry for any other reason than love? She was surely made for love with a man who would adore her and count his blessings for the rest of his life

"Well, it is not, of course," she said. "Perhaps I am a little too old for romantic love. Or perhaps I do not trust it as much as I once did."

"Now, that sounds purely sad," he said. And he meant it. *I do not trust . . . ?* Had love let her down? Perhaps because it had let her husband die? "And too old for romance? Tell that to those two."

He nodded ahead to the Marquess and Marchioness of Dorchester. Abigail Westcott was at Dorchester's other side, Lady Estelle Lamarr on his wife's. The four of them walked with their arms linked. There had been a look about the newlyweds this morning that had made Colin feel a little hot under the collar, though there had been nothing remotely improper in their behavior, just a glow about her person and an intensity about his eyes that could not be put into adequate words but spoke volumes.

"They do look happy," Elizabeth agreed, "after all of twenty-five hours of marriage. And yes, they are both over forty."

"I have always thought that I need not consider anything so drastic as marriage for years yet," he said. "I have only recently turned twenty-six, after all."

"Drastic?" She chuckled. "Leg shackles and tenants for life and all the other clichés you gentlemen like to use?"

"And establishing a family," he said, "and setting the tone I would want it to have. Taking up residence somewhere and making a home of it. Deciding where that would be. Making a choice of bride, knowing that I must live with my choice for the rest of my life—and that she would have to live with hers for the rest of her life. Being head of my family. Taking on the responsibility for it. Becoming a man."

He stopped in sudden embarrassment, especially at those final words. And she had not missed them.

"Do you see yourself as less than a man now, then?" she asked.

"I do not know quite what I meant," he said. "Becoming decisive, perhaps. Setting down my feet and taking a firm stand, perhaps. Knowing who I am and where I am going.

Where I want to go. Where I ought to go. You will be think-ing me an utter idiot. And you will probably be right."

"I think no such thing," she protested. "Many young men, and young women to a lesser degree, believe they know it all and blunder onward through life reinforcing their opinion of themselves with every ignorant action and never achieving their full potential as men and women and human beings. I think there are definite advantages to knowing early that really one knows very little and must be ever open to learning and changing and adjusting. Oh good-ness, listen to me. Or, rather, ignore me, please. Do you have anyone in mind now that you are perhaps maybe beginning to turn your thoughts toward matrimony? Or is it to be a case of tossing a coin to choose among the three you were considering last evening?"

"I have never yet seen a three-sided coin, alas," he said. "There was someone last Season, the sister of a friend of mine. She was shy and did not take well with the *ton*. I of-fered her my company on a few occasions and found I liked her. I believe she liked me. But I had a letter from her brother just a week or so ago in which he informed me that her betrothal to a gentleman farmer she has known all her life and apparently loved for years is to be announced over Christmas. So mine was no grand love story, either."

"Oh dear," she said. "Were you hurt?"

"I am almost ashamed to admit I was not," he said. "I was pleased for her and relieved for myself, to be perfectly honest, since I had never intended my attentions to be mis-construed as courtship. Obviously they were not, however. We are a sad, pathetic pair, Elizabeth. Perhaps we should put ourselves out of our misery and marry each other."

He said it as a joke. Even so, he felt instantly embar-rassed at his own presumption. He and *Elizabeth*?

"Now there is an idea worth considering," she said, all good humor. "You said you are twenty-six? I am thirty-five. Only a nine-year difference. No one would even remark upon it if it were the other way around—if *you* were nine years older than I, that is. But I fear it would very certainly be remarked upon this way around. I had better not take you up on your kind offer immediately. I will, however, put you on a list with a few other remote possibilities. I may even use my new leather-bound notebook and pencil for the purpose."

"Remote?" he said. "Ouch."

They looked at each other sidelong and both laughed. And oh, he *liked* her.

"Of course, I was fully aware of the age difference," he said. "I offered you my arm only because you are old and doddering. All of nine years older than I am. Oh, and I offered my arm because I enjoy your company too. There are certain people with whom one feels an instant affinity, a total comfort, an easy ability to talk upon any subject, even absurdities, without having to resort to the weather and the health of all one's acquaintances."

"And I am one of those people?" she asked.

"Yes," he said. "In all sincerity, Elizabeth."

"I am touched," she said. "In all sincerity, Colin."

They laughed again, but the wonder was that both of them did mean it. He had never had a female friend before. Friendly acquaintances, yes, but not . . . Well, there had been no one like Elizabeth.

He wondered if she had always been as she was now. Serenity seemed to hover about her. Even when she was joking and laughing it was there. Perhaps she had been born this way, able to weather the storms of life without succumbing to disillusionment or despair. Even as he thought it, however, he remembered her saying just a few minutes ago that perhaps she did not trust romantic love as much as she once had. And he thought of what she had just said about living and learning and changing and adjusting. Perhaps she had had to earn that inner peace she seemed to have achieved. But how? What disturbing experiences were in her past, apart from the loss of her husband, that was? How had she learned to cope with them?

He had never learned to cope with his own. He had learned only how to bury them deep inside himself. How to run and hide.

"It is heartening to see a mingled family begin to form, is it not?" she said of the four people walking abreast ahead of them. "Note that it is Abby walking at Marcel's side, while Estelle is on Viola's."

"Do you think Dorchester will do something for Abigail Westcott now that she is his stepdaughter?" Colin asked. "Draw her into society, perhaps, and force the *ton* to overlook her illegitimacy? Help her find a husband worthy of her upbringing?"

"I am sure he would," she said. "*If* she wishes it, that is."

"You think she may not?" he asked.

"I think it very possible," she said. "We have all tried, you know, and most of us have considerable influence, Alex and Avery most of all. There is really no reason for her to be ostracized, even though the highest sticklers will doubtless always consider her birth tainted. But I am not sure Abby is willing to allow others to help her slip and sidle into a life that would be very nearly like her old one but never identical. She is Viola's daughter. She is sweet and quiet and dignified. But I do believe she has a spine made of steel."

"Ah," he said. And she was also a lovely girl.

"Oh, oh," Elizabeth said suddenly. "That was thoroughly predictable."

A shriek and shouts of laughter came from up ahead and the bellow of Molenor's wrathful voice, and Bertrand Lamarr was hauling Winifred out of the snow while Molenor's boys quelled their laughter and made excuses to their father for dropping her. Molenor was obviously not convinced. He grabbed each boy by his coat collar and marched them at a brisk trot toward the house. Winifred meanwhile was gazing rather worshipfully at Lamarr.

Colin laughed. "I love this family," he said. "I really do, Elizabeth. And I love this place, shabby as it still is at present. And I am loving this Christmas. It is the only real Christmas I have ever experienced, you know."

"Is it?" she asked. Then her eyes grew mischievous. "Since it is also a white Christmas, I must see to it that you come to love it even more. But later. I want to get inside and take these boots off before my feet turn to blocks of ice."

"*Later* meaning games in the outdoors, I suppose," he said. "Hmm. We will see about that, Lady Overfield. I can fight quite fiercely when I am provoked, you know."

"Empty bravado," she said, laughing as they climbed the steps to the house and stamped their feet and shook off the hems of their outer garments.

"I can also fight dirty," he said.

"With snow?" She preceded him into the house, smiling an acknowledgment to the footman who held the door open. "Impossible, Lord Hodges. It is a contradiction in terms."

Three

Elizabeth had never quite understood why snow could turn grown adults into children as no other weather condition could. They all did indeed overeat at dinner, or if they did not exactly stuff more into themselves than usual, it still felt like overeating because of all the rich foods—the goose, the stuffing, the gravy, the Christmas pudding and custard, to mention just a few. And they did indeed feel a bit lethargic afterward and would doubtless have adjourned to the drawing room and drifted from there up to their rooms for what would euphemistically be called a rest—if, that was, there were not the snow outside, making a vast and sparkling white playground in the sunshine that had broken through the clouds, if only temporarily. It beckoned with a quite irresistible allure.

Everyone went outside, with the exception of the babies, Josephine and Jacob, who were both sleeping in the nursery, and the dowager countess and Mrs. Kingsley, who were flanking the fireplace in the drawing room, and Lady

Matilda Westcott, who felt it incumbent upon herself to keep an eye upon her own mother and Viola's in order to make sure they were not sitting in any draft and had taken no harm from their dinner.

Elizabeth was standing with Anna and Viola on the steps outside the front doors, looking at the scene below with some satisfaction and the anticipation of being a participant soon. She had been delayed when her maid had had to dash downstairs to retrieve her boots, which had been set to dry before the kitchen range. They had been toasty warm when she put them on.

"How lovely it is to see Harry looking healthy again," Anna said.

"It is," Viola agreed, sounding wistful as she gazed at her son, who had only recently recovered from serious injuries incurred in battle. "I just wish this recruitment business could take a year or more, though that is very selfish of me when so many other men are exposed to grave danger out in the Peninsula, the French as well as the Allies. And he is very eager to return to his regiment. He would go today if he could. Sometimes I wonder if the wars will ever be over or if anyone but the female half of the population wants them to be."

"But how well blessed you are, Viola, and how well blessed we all are, that he came home so unexpectedly in time for your wedding," Elizabeth said.

Captain Harry Westcott was attempting to direct Mildred and Thomas's teenage boys in the building of a snow fort, complete with battlements, dungeons, and tunnels. Oh, and apparently the obligatory maiden in distress. Ten-year-old Winifred had been volunteered for the role—though that seemed something of a contradiction—by one of the boys, and she was looking rather pleased at the prospect of being locked up in a tower with nothing but dry bread and water for sustenance while she waited for her prince to ride to her rescue. No one had yet volunteered for that role. Harry was trying, not too successfully, to inject some engineering sense into the builders and tunnelers, while Bertrand Lamarr stood with folded arms watching him, and Jessica and Estelle called out contradictory words of advice and encouragement.

The sisters Abigail and Camille were strolling along the driveway, which had been partially cleared since the morning, arm in arm with Colin. Avery and Joel were taking young Sarah and Mary Kingsley, the Reverend Kingsley's wife, for a sleigh ride. Sarah was laughing with glee and reaching for the jingling bells. Alex and Wren had gone out to the hill behind the house to make sure it was ready for the sleds when the action should move that way. Marcel and the Reverend Kingsley had gone with them. Thomas and Mildred—Lord and Lady Molenor—were watching the action a short distance away with Mildred's sister Louise, the Dowager Duchess of Netherby.

"I am indeed well blessed," Viola said in answer to Elizabeth's last words. "Camille is happily settled and Harry is safe and sound, at least for the present. And Abby . . . She has been lonely. Perhaps now that I am married she will be less so. Estelle is ecstatic to have a stepsister and is determined that they be bosom friends. I think Abby is touched by her eagerness."

Elizabeth was watching the three walkers, who had turned back toward the house. They looked to be in good humor with one another. She tried to imagine Colin and Abby as a couple. They would certainly make an extraordinarily handsome pair. And they would surely be compatible in character and disposition. But . . . Too compatible? Was that possible?

Perhaps we should put ourselves out of our misery and marry each other.

She smiled a little wistfully at the memory of his saying those words to her on the way home from church. It had been an absurdity, of course. But even so it was good to know that she was still young enough and personable enough to draw such a jest. And *why* was thirty-five feeling almost elderly these days?

There was a shriek from the direction of the fort—from Winifred or Estelle or both—followed by a bellow from Thomas, Lord Molenor.

"I hate to say I told you so, lad," Harry was calling out cheerfully to a sputtering Peter, who was digging his way out of a collapsed tunnel, "but I told you so. Just be thankful the roof was built of snow, not bricks."

Bertrand was laughing and slapping snow off the boy. "If I were you," he said, "I would listen very attentively when an infantry captain deigned to offer me advice. He is almost bound to know what he is talking about."

"He is extremely handsome, is he not?" Anna said.

"He is, indeed." Elizabeth assumed she was referring to Bertrand Lamarr, who was an outstandingly good-looking young man, very much like his father. But then she saw that both Anna and Viola were looking at Colin.

"He is an amiable young man too," Viola said. "It was unbelievably wicked of his mother to tell him when he was a child that Wren was dead. I am so very glad Alexander went in search of him after he married Wren."

"And look, Aunt Viola, at how he and Abigail are smiling at each other," Anna said. "Perhaps . . . Do you think . . . ?"

"I think Christmas is making you sentimental, Anna," Viola said. "Nevertheless, perhaps . . ."

They both laughed rather gleefully.

"What do *you* think, Elizabeth?" Anna asked. "Would they not make a lovely couple? And suit each other?"

He had just turned his attention the other way and was laughing over something with Camille.

"I think Abby can be trusted to choose the man best suited to her when she is ready, regardless of what we may think or hope—or fear," Elizabeth said. "I believe she will choose love or nothing. And I believe Lord Hodges is young and charming and very probably not even considering matrimony yet." Though she knew he was.

"You are very right, Elizabeth," Viola said. "About both of them."

Elizabeth turned her attention back to the fort building, in which Harry and Bertrand and even Winifred were now actively engaged with the three boys. But, against all reason, her thoughts continued to dwell upon Colin. She did not know much about his family situation, but she did know that Lady Hodges, his mother, was a difficult person to deal with and had made childhood insupportable for Wren with her disfiguring birthmark. And she sensed that life had been difficult for the other children too and that they had not had a happy home life. The fact that Colin now lived at Withington House, Wren's property, instead of in his ancestral home, and that he had rooms in London instead of living in his own town house there, told its own story. So did the fact that he was spending Christmas here instead of with his own family. And he had mentioned to her that he'd never experienced a Christmas like this one.

She was so *glad* he was here. He had been right this morning on the way home from church. They *did* have an easy rapport with each other. She felt as comfortable with him as she did with her own brother. Except that there was an added dimension to her friendship with Colin. She ought not, but she found him—

Suddenly her world turned cold and white and wet, and she gasped and lifted her arms helplessly to the sides as she heard laughter.

"I warned you I was a star bowler," a voice called cheerfully to her as she clawed snow out of her eyes and spat it from her mouth and tried to prevent it from trickling beneath her collar. Ugh. Oh, ugh!

"Oh, poor Elizabeth," Anna was saying, laughter in her voice.

"That was remarkably unsporting of you, Lord Hodges," Viola scolded, though she was chuckling too. "Elizabeth was not even looking."

Camille and Abigail were laughing merrily. So were the fort builders—and Louise and Mildred.

"A barefaced attack upon my sister," Alex's voice called from somewhere to the right. "And I returned in time to witness it. This calls for retaliation."

"A bigger, better snowball, Alex?" Harry suggested.

"Are you threatening my brother, Alexander?" Wren was laughing merrily with everyone else. "I cannot allow that, you know, even if you *are* my husband. Blood is said to be thicker than water."

"You also warned me that you are a dirty fighter," Elizabeth said, blinking away some snow clumps from her eyelashes and looking into the handsome, laughing face of Colin a short distance away. "You have just proved your point, sir. Well, war has been declared. Name your team, and I shall name mine. As the aggrieved party, I have first choice, I believe. I pick Alex."

"Wren," Colin said without hesitation.

Joel had carried a sleepy Sarah inside for an afternoon

nap but was back in time to join Colin's team after Elizabeth had chosen Cousin Louise's daughter Jessica.

"Thomas," Elizabeth said.

"Winifred."

"Camille."

"Bertrand."

"Boris."

"Lady Estelle."

And so the teams were formed. And Elizabeth suddenly felt young and invigorated and wildly happy despite her thirty-five years. Colin was laughing and gathering his team about him.

And the fight was on.

His team would have won handily, no question about it, Colin protested when the fight was over, to shouts of agreement from his own troops and jeers of derision from Elizabeth's. Her team had not played fair, he explained, for they had employed *strategy* of all the nasty underhanded things they could have done, probably because they had Captain Harry Westcott on their side. They had delegated two members of their team—the Dowager Duchess of Netherby and Lord Molenor—to the exclusive task of rolling snowballs and stockpiling them so that the rest of the team had merely to pick them up and hurl them. And their two snowball rollers had fast hands.

As it was, Lady Molenor, who had early designated herself judge and jury and had thus avoided having to be a participant, declared after ten minutes or so of vigorous action that the fight was a draw.

It was a verdict that was popular with neither side, though all of them were breathless and laughing as they hurled insults this time instead of snowballs. All of them were snow caked.

And then young Sarah Cunningham put an end to the altercation by coming back outside, wrapped to the eyeballs in warm clothing. Immediately ten people coaxed her down the steps by demonstrating to her how to make a snow angel. She came down and toddled among them, shrieking merrily at this new game and showering them with mittenfuls of snow. She made no angels herself, Colin observed. Not even a snow cherub.

It was the turn of the hill and the sleds then, and they trekked out there to find that Alexander, together with the Marquess of Dorchester and the Reverend Kingsley, had smoothed out a wide run. There were five sleds, all looking a bit ancient but still serviceable with their newly honed runners and brand-new ropes. Soon there were sledders zooming down the hill in ones or twos or—in one case— threes. But Molenor's boys came to grief during that particular run, the sled shedding the middle boy during its descent and then the other two while their father closed his eyes, shook his head, and refrained from bellowing.

Colin was having the best time he had had for a long while—well, perhaps ever. If he had been half serious about spending the afternoon quietly in the drawing room, toasting himself before the fire, nibbling upon more rich Christmas baked goods, and even dozing, he was no longer even thinking about it. Snow of this depth and consistency was too rare a phenomenon in England to be wasted. And by tomorrow it would probably be turning to slush.

He took Lady Jessica Archer down the slope and then Lady Estelle Lamarr after trying it once alone to be sure he could control the sled without making a thorough ass of himself. He relinquished the sled to someone else for a while and then offered to take Lady Molenor down, though she protested that she was far too elderly for such frolics.

"And there is definite danger," she said with all the air of resignation one might expect of the mother of three rambunctious boys. "Just look at that, Lord Hodges."

That was Camille Cunningham riding down with Winifred while her husband zoomed down behind them with a screaming Sarah and avoided crashing into them only after some fancy maneuvering and much laughter and shrieking from both sleds.

But Lady Molenor climbed on the sled anyway and laughed all the way down.

"I hope," Colin said later when he was standing at the bottom of the run watching the action and Elizabeth had just come down with the Reverend Kingsley, "I did not offend you with the snowball in the face?"

"Oh, let me see," she said. "Was that the first one or the fourth?"

"Numbers two, three, and four were part of a fair fight," he said. "The first one was not. I hope I did not offend you. Actually I meant to hit you on the shoulder."

"What?" she said. "You are not such a star bowler after all, then?"

"As for numbers two, three, and four," he said, ignoring the jibe, "you really need to learn how to duck, Elizabeth."

"The third time I *did* duck," she said, "and got it in the face anyway."

Her cheeks were bright red and glowing. So was her nose. Her hair beneath the red-brimmed bonnet was wet and pulling free of its pins. Her eyes were sparkling, her lips curved into a smile. She looked really quite beautiful with animation to add to the usual smiling serenity. She appeared young and vibrant. But she ought to be offended. He had concentrated most of his attack during the fight upon her, perhaps because she was concentrating most of hers upon him and had been so very obviously enjoying herself. She had missed by a mile with every snowball but one, and that had shattered harmlessly against his elbow.

"Yes. Thank you," he said when Dorchester offered him the sled he had just ridden down with his wife. The two of them wandered off together, hand in hand. Colin turned to Elizabeth. "Shall we?"

"But can I trust you?" she asked.

"Always." He clapped one gloved hand over his heart and they trudged up the hill side by side.

They did two runs together. The first was flawless. Colin's only regret was that the slope was not longer, but this was the highest hill in the park and it really was not bad. The second run was not so successful. Bertrand Lamarr, on his way down with Abigail, swerved to avoid colliding with his twin and Boris, Molenor's eldest boy, and Colin had to swerve to miss them both. He was on the outer edge of the run and hit soft snow before reaching the bottom. He tried to correct their course, but the sled had other ideas and went plowing farther in, veering wildly from side to side before upending its occupants into deep snow close to the bottom.

There were shouts from outside their cocoon of snow, though none sounded deeply concerned. Elizabeth was laughing and sputtering—from beneath Colin. He was laughing too as he raised his head and brushed foolishly and ineffectually at the snow covering her bonnet and shoulders.

"I will never live that one down," he said.

"I forgot to ask in what ways I might trust you," she said. "Foolish of me."

"With your life, ma'am," he said, grinning at her. "Behold yourself unharmed and only snow caked. At least, I *hope* you are unharmed." It occurred to him that his weight might be squashing her.

And then the most ghastly thing happened.

He thought about it afterward—he could not stop thinking, in fact—and squirmed with intense discomfort every time. What the devil had possessed him? And what the devil must she think even though she had assured him that she would not think about it at all.

He kissed her.

Which would not, perhaps, have been quite so bad if it had been a brief, brotherly smack on the lips—or, preferably, the cheek—to apologize for spilling her into the snow. Though even then . . . even then it would have been disrespectful to the point of . . . He could not think of a suitable word with which to complete the thought.

But this was not a brief kiss, or at least not very brief. And there was nothing brotherly about it. It was indeed on the lips, or, rather, it was all heat and moisture and mouths more than just lips, and for a fraction of a moment—or forever, he was not sure which—he felt as though someone had wrapped him in a large blanket that had been heated before a roaring fire. Except that the heat was inside him as well as all about him. And for that fraction of a moment—or that eternity, he was not sure which—he wanted her.

Elizabeth. The widowed Lady Overfield. A woman in her mid-thirties. Poised and mature and serene and inhabiting a universe so far beyond his own inferior world of uncertainty and immaturity that . . .

What the devil would she think?

When he raised his head, it did not look as if she was thinking much of anything at all. Her eyes were closed and she seemed a bit dazed.

"Oh, the devil," he said. Which was a marvelous way of

groveling and apologizing. The snow seemed to have frozen his brain. *Disrespectful* did not even begin to cover what his behavior had been.

"Do we have a few broken legs and heads in here?" Alexander's voice called, cheerful enough when one considered his words.

"That was a spectacular landing," Harry said, offering his hand to Elizabeth as Colin scrambled to his feet.

"If we were giving prizes," Wren said, knee deep in snow as she brushed at Colin's greatcoat, "you two would win the trophy for the most spectacular disaster."

"But alas," Harry said, "you get only the glory."

"You look dazed, Lizzie," her mother was saying. "You did not hurt yourself, did you?"

"Oh, not at all," Elizabeth assured her, laughing. "Not even my pride is dented. I was not the one steering."

"I might have known I would be blamed," Colin said. "Well, heap it on. My shoulders are broad."

"I say," one of Molenor's boys called from a short distance away, "I have never seen anything so funny in my life."

The boy was obviously given to hyperbole—as was Wren.

"Ah," Alexander said. "Perfect timing. The sleigh is coming with something to warm us."

It was indeed, and it was a very welcome distraction. A couple of servants, bundled up and smiling cheerfully, had arrived with two large containers of steaming chocolate and one of hot punch as well as a jar of sweet biscuits and a covered dish of warmed mince pies. They all tucked into the repast as though they had been fasting all day and warmed their gloved hands about their steaming mugs, ignoring the handles.

"We must have feathers for brains," the dowager duchess

said, "spending the afternoon shivering out here when we could be warm and comfortable indoors. And dry."

"I would not have missed this for all the comfort in the world, Mama," Lady Jessica cried, though she was breathing in the steam from her chocolate as she spoke. "This is the best Christmas ever. Is it not, Abby? And there is still the party to look forward to tomorrow evening and some fresh faces."

"It is the best," her dearest friend agreed. "Gentlemen as well as ladies, I hope. Tomorrow, that is."

"Oh, to be young again," the dowager duchess said. "I am returning to the house. Althea, will you come too?"

"I will indeed, Louise," Mrs. Westcott said. "Though I do agree with Jessica. A family Christmas is always a lovely thing, but a family Christmas with snow—and a Boxing Day party to look forward to—is unsurpassable."

She left Elizabeth's side and Colin took her place before he could lose his nerve completely. In which case he would have found himself in the impossible situation of having to avoid both her person and her eye for the rest of his life.

"Elizabeth," he said, "will you forgive me?"

She did not pretend not to know what he was talking about. "For the kiss?" she said, smiling at him. "There is nothing to forgive."

"I do not know what came over me," he said. "I did not . . . Well, I did not mean any disrespect. Whatever will you think of me?"

"I will think nothing," she assured him, "except that you were quick enough to know that a dumping in the deep snow was preferable to a collision with another sled. And that you comforted me afterward with a kiss. It was both appreciated and flattering. And it will be forgotten from this moment on."

"Well," he said. "I have rarely embarrassed myself more."

She laughed and removed one hand from about her mug to set on his sleeve. "I hope I have not spoiled your day," she said, patting his arm. "My mother was quite right about a family Christmas—with snow. I hope you feel we are in some way your family too."

"Thank you," he said. "I do. It has been a joy to come here, though I love my home too. Have you seen where I live—Withington House? It is a lovely place."

"I saw it last year when Wren still lived there," she said, "before she married Alex. I went there the day after I first met her in the hope of making a friend of her, and we have been friends ever since."

"I hope you will come there again before you return home," he said. "Maybe with Alexander and Wren and your mother. I believe you intend to stay on for a while after everyone else returns home."

"We do," she said. "Do you intend making Withington your permanent home?"

The house belonged to Wren, but she had offered it to Colin back in the spring when she discovered that he lived in London, even during the summer, when most of the *ton* deserted it for their country homes. He had wanted to purchase it from her, but she had insisted that he be her guest there for a year, at which time he would be able to make a more informed decision.

"I am inclined to say yes," he said. "But I am not sure it would be the right thing to do."

"Oh?" She raised her eyebrows.

"No," he said, taking the empty cup from her hands. "I am going to have to think about it."

It would be easy to hide there forever, in a house that was just the right size for him, with Wren and Alexander close by and friendly neighbors all about. But *hide* was the key word. He was Baron Hodges. He was head of his family. He had duties and responsibilities. If Justin, his elder brother, had not died, he would be free to hide to his heart's content. Indeed, there would be nothing to hide from. But Justin had died, and three years later so had their father. Colin had been left with a mother and three sisters—and the title and all that came with it.

"I will be delighted to visit with Alex and Wren," Elizabeth said. "So will my mother, I know."

There did not seem to be anything else to say. Had she really forgiven him? Not been disgusted? Was she really willing to step inside his own home? Had he really *kissed* her? Colin looked down into his cup and swirled the thick residue of chocolate at the bottom of it. He was not sure he could forgive himself. Not for *wanting* her anyway. Good God!

Fortunately Alexander suggested at that moment that they return to the house to warm up properly, and Elizabeth moved away to walk with Abigail and Anna. Colin hung back a few moments to return with Camille and Harry, who was carrying Sarah.

She was so terribly beautiful. Elizabeth, that was.

Four

The perfect Christmas Day concluded with a light evening meal, charades, a few card games, and singing about the pianoforte. No one was late to bed. It had been a busy day, much of it spent outdoors, and they all admitted to being tired.

"If you do not take care, Alexander," Louise, the Dowager Duchess of Netherby, warned, "you will be starting a family tradition and be stuck with us all every year."

"It is our fondest hope that that is exactly what will happen," he said. "Is it not, Wren?"

"Indeed it is," she agreed. "We can almost certainly promise a somewhat less shabby house by next year, Cousin Louise. I am not so sure about the snow, though. But there is still tomorrow to look forward to—a somewhat more relaxed day, perhaps, with the neighborhood party coming in the evening. If people can get here, that is."

"The carolers came last night," Thomas, Lord Molenor, reminded her. "Why not everyone else tomorrow?"

"We cannot promise a wedding every year either," Wren added, smiling at Viola and Marcel.

It had been a very nearly perfect Christmas Day, Elizabeth agreed as she climbed the stairs with her mother and Mrs. Kingsley. It really had been, she assured herself after she had bidden them a good night and shut the door of her room firmly behind her.

Very nearly perfect.

Except that she was quite unable to forget the dreadful embarrassment of the afternoon. She had had to call upon all her inner resources for the rest of the day to be her usual cheerful, sensible self. Her reaction was very silly, for it was *Christmas* and they had been *sledding* and laughing after being tipped into a snowbank. It was really not surprising that they had ended up kissing each other.

Was it?

The last man to kiss her, apart from a few familial pecks on the cheek, was Desmond, and that had been so many years ago she could not say precisely when it had been. But, goodness, he had been dead for six years, and she had left him a year before that. She was thirty-five years old, and this afternoon she had kissed a gorgeous boy. No, she was exaggerating, even belittling him. He was not a boy. He was twenty-six years old, very definitely a man. But he *was* gorgeous. And she had kissed him just as much as he had kissed her. She hoped not more. Oh, surely she had not done anything to provoke that kiss. How humiliating if she had— or if he thought she had.

She set her candle down on the dresser, avoided her image in the glass, and was very thankful that she had given her maid the afternoon and evening off. It was a relief to be alone at last.

She had reacted to that kiss with sexual awareness. She

had wanted him as she had not wanted any man since Desmond in the early years of their marriage. Certainly she had never felt it with Sir Geoffrey Codaire, though she had almost made up her mind to marry him if he asked her again in the spring.

The rest of her day had been fairly ruined. She had kept her distance from Colin, as far as that was possible in a family gathering and without being too obvious about it. But she had watched him covertly. He had been reserved and a bit shy yesterday. Today he had been at ease and enjoying himself. He had thrown himself with open enthusiasm into the charades. He had sung with everyone else, standing beside the pianoforte and watching Cousin Mildred play. He had kissed Mary Kingsley under the kissing bough when they found themselves beneath it at the same moment—and neither had seemed consumed by embarrassment or guilt. Indeed, they had smiled and laughed and he had even executed a mock bow as family members applauded and whistled.

He had fair hair that was thick and wavy and always slightly unruly even when it had obviously been brushed recently. He had blue eyes and white teeth, which were ever so slightly crooked at the front on top—an imperfection that somehow only enhanced his attractiveness. He was tall and slender and lithe, and . . . Oh, and *young*.

Elizabeth shivered as she cast aside her shawl and dress and then her stockings and undergarments and pulled on her nightgown before eyeing the water in the jug beside the washstand with some misgiving. The water would, of course, be cold. She was tempted to go to bed with an unwashed face, but finally found the courage to wash both it and her neck as well as her hands and arms to the elbows.

She dried herself briskly and huddled inside her dressing gown.

The truth was that she had allowed herself to become a little infatuated with Colin Handrich, Lord Hodges, and it just would not do. Good heavens, she was very close to being middle-aged. Some would say there was no *close* about it. How pathetic, not to mention horrifying, it would be if anyone guessed. Well, no one would guess because she would be more herself tomorrow.

She carried the candle to the small table beside her bed, slid reluctantly out of her dressing gown, and got into bed after snuffing the candle. She made a cocoon of the blankets, pulling them up about her ears while she warmed up.

Sleep eluded her.

It did not snow again, but it would take a few days for all that had come down to melt. The roads would be slushy and muddy and treacherous for quite a while. Colin resigned himself to at least another day and night spent at Brambledean. It was not difficult. He was enjoying himself.

He spent the morning of Boxing Day outside building snowmen, only to have his most artistic creation knocked down and trampled upon by young Sarah Cunningham while everyone else's snowmen were left intact. He snatched her up and held her, giggling, above his head before setting her down and chasing her with a snowball, which he finally hurled deliberately to miss.

He spent much of the afternoon in the drawing room, talking with Harry Westcott and the Duke of Netherby about the wars and watching Joel Cunningham, sitting slightly apart from everyone else, sketch first the dowager countess and then Lady Matilda Westcott without their knowing it. He was amazingly skilled. Both subjects were not only perfectly recognizable in the resulting drawings; their very essence seemed to have been captured too.

"It must be gratifying to have such talent," Colin commented when Joel closed his sketching book.

Cunningham looked back over his shoulder at him. "Well, it is," he agreed, "though I take no credit for it, only for making the effort to use it. But we are all talented, and in more than one way. Unfortunately, many people do not recognize their talents or consider them commonplace or inferior to other people's."

"Now you will have us wondering for the rest of the day," Harry said, laughing, "what *our* talents are. Are you sure we all have them, Joel?"

Colin wondered what the realization of his illegitimacy and the resulting loss of his title and properties and fortune had done to Captain Harry Westcott. His world had been turned upside down and inside out. Yet he seemed as cheerful now as Colin remembered him from the slight acquaintance he had had with him before it happened. Except that there seemed to be a core of hardness in him now, carefully hidden from his family, that had surely not been there when he was a carefree, wealthy young earl, sowing a few fairly harmless wild oats.

Colin's eyes came to rest upon Elizabeth, who had been avoiding him if he was not mistaken. He deeply regretted that brief, unguarded kiss in the snowbank yesterday that must have caused her reserve. Although she had been gracious about accepting his apology, she must despise him, or at the very least wish to make it clear that such disrespect was not to be encouraged.

She caught his eye even as he thought it and smiled

warmly at him. She made no move to come closer, however, and he kept his distance from her.

Bertrand Lamarr and his twin, Lady Estelle, had set up a game of spillikins with Lady Jessica Archer at the far end of the drawing room and were calling for someone else to join them so they could form two teams. Colin got obligingly to his feet. Lady Estelle was apparently to be his partner. She was an attractive combination of shyness and vivacity. And she was really very pretty. Also very young. Too young. She was eighteen, eight years younger than he. She smiled at him and blushed.

Lady Jessica was beaming at him too. But she was also not immune to the charms of young Bertrand, he had noticed.

"I was spillikins champion of my school class," Colin said with a grin. "Be warned, you two."

Lady Estelle laughed while the other two jeered.

Wren and Alexander had decided to use the ballroom for the Boxing Day party even though they admitted it was probably too large and was really the most shabby room in the house.

"And *that* is saying something," Alex had added with a rueful chuckle.

But they had invited almost everyone in the village and surrounding countryside, not only the members of the gentry, and the drawing room would simply not be large enough even if only half of those invited came. So one third of the ballroom had been set up with tables for refreshments, while chairs had been set about the perimeter of the remaining two thirds, and the whole room had been decorated with more greenery and ribbons and bows. It was to be lit with dozens of candles, and really who cared that the room would have been looked upon askance by the highest sticklers of the *ton*? Their Christmas party did not pretend to be a *ton* ball.

Fires had been kept burning for a couple of days in the two fireplaces that faced each other across the midpoint of the ballroom. They had taken away the worst of the chill. The fires would be kept going through the party, and the presence of a largish number of people would add more warmth.

A trio of musicians who played for the village assemblies had been engaged to provide music for the entertainment of the guests and perhaps even for some dancing if anyone seemed so inclined.

It all looked rather cozy to Elizabeth when she stood in the doorway early in the evening, her fine wool shawl—a Christmas gift from her mother—drawn snugly about her shoulders. Most of the family was already present, and the musicians had begun to play soft music. The two punch bowls had been filled as had some of the large food platters. And the outside guests had begun to arrive.

They came in surprisingly large numbers, considering the weather, and they came early. There was no concept here of being fashionably late. They arrived on foot and by sleigh, and in a few cases, by carriage, bringing with them hair-raising tales of slithering wheels.

"An entertainment at Brambledean is a rare treat for the people hereabouts, my lord," Elizabeth overheard the vicar say to Alexander as he wrung his hand. "Most do not remember anything so grand in their lifetimes. You cannot expect a little snow to keep them away, you know."

"I am delighted to hear it," Alexander told him. "And delighted to see it." He gestured about the ballroom.

Many of the new arrivals were apple-cheeked and a bit disheveled after walking all the way huddled inside coats and scarves and hats. Many were dressed in nothing like the sort of finery one would expect to see in a London drawing room, though all were clearly wearing their very best attire. None of it mattered. Everyone had come to be delighted, and delighted they all seemed to be. So did the Westcott family, who set out deliberately to welcome the newcomers, many of whom were feeling a bit shy and intimidated. They circulated about the room, talking to everyone who was not already part of a group, making sure everyone who wanted a seat had one, fetching food and drink to the older people.

And after a while there was dancing.

Most of it was country sets, performed with skill and enthusiasm by all and filling the space so that Elizabeth thought in some amusement that Wren would be able to boast afterward that the evening had been a sad squeeze—the greatest compliment any London hostess could be paid after a ball during the Season.

Elizabeth danced with the vicar and two of Alexander's tenant farmers.

It was the son of one of the tenants, a young man who had spent a few months in London earlier in the year and clearly fancied himself a man of the world, who begged for a waltz. He did so after a short lull in the dancing for them all to catch their breath and revive themselves with punch and sausage rolls and Christmas cake and other delicacies. Alexander conferred with the musicians, who indicated their knowledge of a suitable tune. Most of the guests were content to remain on the sidelines with their refreshments while a few brave couples stepped onto the floor to perform the steps of a dance not yet much performed in the country. The young tenant's son had Jessica in tow.

Alexander was looking about, Elizabeth could see, but Wren was busy filling plates for an elderly couple that was seated by one of the fires.

"Lizzie," he said, turning to her, "we cannot allow the waltz to proceed undanced, can we? Let us show everyone how it is done."

She willingly set her hand in her brother's. They had learned the steps together a number of years ago, and they waltzed well with each other. She could recall the two of them demonstrating the steps for Anna soon after she had arrived in London from Bath, though it was Avery who had finally taken her from the clutches of the fussy dancing master and persuaded her to relax and enjoy waltzing. The two of them were on the floor now, waiting for the music to begin. So were Viola and the Marquess of Dorchester and Camille and Joel and several other members of the family. Alexander led her onto the floor and they smiled warmly at each other.

"It is a wonderful evening," she said. "Everyone will remember it for a long time to come, Alex. But that means you will have to do it again."

"Of course," he agreed. "I cannot think of many things Wren and I will enjoy more in the coming years than putting on merry entertainments for our neighbors."

They both turned to look expectantly at the musicians. But someone clasped Alexander's shoulder before the music began.

"Why should we each have our sisters for partners for such a romantic dance, Alexander, when there is a simple alternative?" Colin asked. He had Wren by the hand.

"Why, indeed?" Alexander agreed and released Elizabeth in order to clasp his arm about his wife's waist.

"I hope you do not mind," Colin said half apologetically

to Elizabeth. "But Wren looked quite forlorn when she saw that your brother already had a partner."

"I am perfectly delighted," she assured him. "I will be waltzing with the most handsome young man at the ball."

He laughed. "*Is* it a ball?" he asked her. "But whether it is or not, it is a cracking good party. It was an inspired idea of Wren and Alexander's to invite virtually everyone. It is the way parties should be, especially at this time of year. Christmas ought to be for everyone. I mean for everyone to enjoy together."

There were, of course, the servants who must work. But no system was perfect. And Elizabeth had heard that Alex was paying them double their normal wage for the past two days and today and was giving them four paid days off as well.

The music began then, and Colin set an arm about her waist and took her right hand in his while she set her other hand on his shoulder. And oh dear. Oh dear, she had to think very firmly about her resolution while trying not to cling to his hand and shoulder. She concentrated for a few moments upon her steps, but he obviously knew how to waltz, and she soon relaxed and followed him into a wide twirl about one corner of the room.

. . . such a romantic dance . . .

Oh, indeed it was. She had always thought so. She had always thought that waltzing with someone special—with *the* someone special—must be the most romantic experience in the world. Colin surely was the most handsome young man at the party. His hair glowed almost golden in the candlelight and his blue eyes smiled into hers. She could feel the warmth of his hands and his body heat. She was aware of the light spicy smell of his cologne. And she was aware too after a few minutes of something incongruous—

of hands that clapped in time with the music, of feet that thumped on the wooden floor to add rhythm to the lilting waltz tune. She was aware of someone whooping, and she laughed. The guests gathered around the dancing area were watching with appreciative pleasure, she could see.

"So much for the romance of it all," she said.

"I am not at all sure it has not been enhanced," he said, grinning back at her. "Just listen. The waltz is usually a stately, solitary pleasure—solitary for each couple dancing it, that is. These people have made it into a communal pleasure. Feel the joy of it, Elizabeth."

And she did.

He twirled her with more enthusiasm than before, not changing the rhythm so much as taking it into himself and bringing it into her and sharing it with the room. She was not sure anyone would notice it as she did, but someone whistled, and they both laughed. And it was not just the two of them. Avery and Anna, Alex and Wren, Thomas and Mildred, the young tenant's son and Jessica—*all* the dancers had caught the joy of a Christmas dance that just happened to bear a close resemblance to the waltz.

She had never enjoyed it more. Colin's eyes laughed into hers as they danced. There were boisterous cheers when the waltz drew to a close, and Elizabeth, absurdly perhaps, felt that surely she had never been happier in her life.

"How fortunate I am," Colin said, tucking her hand through his arm as he led her in the direction of the refreshment tables, "to have had the loveliest lady in the room with whom to perform such a memorable dance. The waltz is going to seem quite flat when I next perform the steps at a very proper *ton* ball."

"What a flatterer." She smiled at him.

"Oh, but I did not call you the most beautiful lady here

merely because you called me the most handsome man," he told her.

"Well, then," she said, "I am much obliged to you, sir. And yes, please."

He was offering her a glass of punch.

"Your tone suggests that you do not for a moment believe me," he said, regarding her with his head tipped slightly to one side as she took a sip from her glass. "But you are. You are poised and beautiful from the inside out and I feel honored that you agreed to waltz with me. Did I offend you terribly yesterday?"

"No, of course you did not," she hastened to assure him. "It was of no more significance than any of the kisses I have seen you give beneath the mistletoe."

"Was it not?" he said. "You wound me. I still think you ought to marry me and save us both from the chore of having to go shopping separately at the marriage mart during the coming Season."

"How absurd you are," she said, wondering what would happen if she tried to take another sip of her punch. Would her hand be steady? She decided not to risk it. "For one thing, I am not going to be going shopping, as you so indelicately describe it. If someone should ask, I may say yes. Or I may say no and continue my life as it is. I shall be quite happy to do so, you know."

"And if I should ask?" he asked her. "In London during the Season, that is? On bended knee? With a single red rosebud in hand?"

"I should call you absurd again," she said. "Before taking the rosebud."

"Would you?" he asked her. "Call me absurd, that is?"

"Yes, indeed I would," she said, "for I would still be nine years older than you."

"And that is an insurmountable barrier, is it?" he asked.

"Of course it is," she said. "Colin, look what you have done to me. I cannot even drink my punch because you have made my hand unsteady with your absurdity."

"Is it the word of the evening?" he asked, taking the glass from her hand and setting it on the table beside them. *"Absurd? Absurdity?* Am I just a silly boy to you?"

"You are not a boy," she told him.

"Man, then," he said. "Am I just a silly man?"

"Yes, you are," she told him, "when you talk absurdly."

All the time he had been looking very directly into her eyes, his own smiling, perhaps with simple merriment, perhaps with something else. It was impossible to know. She was too agitated to read his expression. But if he *was* just teasing her, as surely he was, then someone ought to tell him that sometimes teasing could be a bit cruel. Perhaps *she* ought to tell him herself.

"Colin," she said. "Don't."

The smile faded, and he moved his head a little closer to hers for a moment, searching her eyes with his own.

"I am sorry," he said. "I really am, Elizabeth. I was merely teasing. I did not mean to embarrass you."

There. She had her answer. *I was merely teasing.* And did she feel any better?

"You did no such thing," she said, determinedly picking up her glass again and drinking from it. "Now, if you really wish to make yourself useful, sir, you may put two of those sausage rolls on a plate for me, since I would have to exert myself to reach for them myself."

"Yes, ma'am," he said.

"Alas," the languid voice of Avery, Duke of Netherby, said from beside them, "the waltz just sank to an ignominious near demise, I fear. Do you agree, Elizabeth, that you may never be able to dance it again without feeling that you are . . . *frolicking*?"

She laughed. "I thought it was quite delightful," she said.

"Quite so," he said with a sigh.

"Which is *exactly* what I said, Avery," Anna told him.

"You did indeed, my love," he said. "But I thought you were commenting upon the diamond stud you gave me for Christmas."

"It is heart shaped," Elizabeth said, peering at it nestled in the folds of his neckcloth. "How did you ever find it, Anna?"

"I daresay," Colin said, "the duchess had it specially made."

"How clever of you to have guessed, Lord Hodges," Anna said. "Did *you* enjoy the waltz?"

"But of course," he said. "My only complaint is that Lady Overfield has probably spoiled me for all other waltzing partners."

"Oh dear," she said. "Well, you must get her to promise to reserve a waltz for you at every ball during the coming Season."

"What a splendid idea," he said.

"Lady Overfield, ma'am," a gentleman said, approaching Elizabeth, who turned to smile at him. She recognized him as someone to whom she had been introduced on her first visit to Brambledean last spring. She could not recall his name. "May I have the honor of dancing the next set with you?"

"But of course," she said, setting down her glass. "It would be my pleasure, sir."

And she turned away from the table to engage in a

vigorous country dance in which once more almost everyone below the age of fifty—and a few above—participated.

And so the party continued until almost midnight, an unheard-of late hour according to a number of guests, who claimed that none of the village assemblies ever continued beyond half past ten. But it had been wonderful, wonderful . . .

The compliments came from all sides as coats and boots and hats and mufflers and gloves were pulled on and the sounds of sleighs and a couple of carriages drawing up outside the doors penetrated to the great hall. It was half past twelve by the time the last of the stragglers disappeared down the driveway, walking in a huddled group, a lantern swaying above their heads.

Elizabeth made her way to bed soon after, not sure if she was happy because it had been a lovely party and the perfect culmination to a memorable Christmas, or if she was sad because she had been teased and had been unable to take the teasing as lightly as it had been intended.

But no. She positively refused to be melancholy and to be such a killjoy that she could not take a teasing. It had been a lovely party, and the very best part of it had been the waltz—oh, and standing at the refreshment table afterward being teased. The teasing has been the best part of the evening and the worst.

How could it possibly be both?

But she was too tired to work out the problem in her head. And in her head was all it was. Why lose sleep over a muddled head?

She did not lose sleep.

She drifted off to the memory of the waltz tune and the thumping feet and clapping hands of those who watched.

And the smell of his cologne.

And his words . . . *You are poised and beautiful from the inside out and I feel honored that you agreed to waltz with me.*

Absurd, absurd, absurd.

But she fell asleep with a smile on her lips.

Five

Colin was able to leave Brambledean the following day even though the roads were still not ideal for travel and it took his carriage almost an hour longer than usual to cover the nine miles to Withington House.

It felt good to be home. He read a great deal over the next week and wrote letters to various friends and to his sister Ruby in Ireland. He also wrote a careful reply to one of his neighbors at Roxingley, a man he could not remember ever meeting in person, who had complained, not for the first time, about the nature of the house party that had been held at his home over Christmas *in his lordship's absence*. Those four words had been heavily underlined.

He called upon some of the neighbors close to Withington, and a few called upon him. He accepted an invitation to dine at the home of one family on New Year's Eve and was touched to find that his attendance was much appreciated by both his hosts and their guests. Dinner was followed by an informal dance, and he was careful to lead out each of the young ladies in turn. It felt good to be an accepted member of a neighborhood, even a favorite.

And it gave a lift to his spirits to be at the start of a new year. There was never any real difference between the last day of December and the first day of January, except that twenty-four hours had slipped by, but New Year, spelled significantly with capital letters when written down, was a symbolic occasion upon which one could readjust one's thinking and habits and believe that one's life could change and proceed in newer and better ways. There was always that extra awareness, that new blossoming of hope and resolve at New Year.

He could, if he really wanted to, take charge of his life during the coming year. He could become Lord Hodges in fact as well as just in name. Though that was not entirely fair to himself. He did take his responsibilities as a peer of the realm seriously. He had taken his seat in the House of Lords five years ago and was more faithful than many others in his attendance when it was in session.

But that in itself was not enough. He should take up residence at Roxingley instead of here. He should make a home of it. He should make it something respectable and respected rather than something to be ashamed of, something that could cause a neighbor to complain. It had never felt like home when he was growing up there, but there was no reason that could not change. After all, it was his now, and there was nothing inherently wrong with the house or the park or the surrounding farms, as far as he recalled. He could, if he really wanted to take his courage in both hands, confront his mother and Blanche, and make it clear to them that things must and would change. Though he winced somewhat at his mental choice of verb. Would it have to be *confrontation*?

He very much feared it would.

He could do something even more decisive, something he had already been considering. He could take a wife and set up his nursery and establish a family of his own. He could work at shaping it into the entity he dreamed of, something more like the Westcott family than his own had been. All the rest would be far easier to accomplish if he were a married man.

Or so he imagined. Perhaps the opposite would be true.

But did he really *want* to live at Roxingley? He was happy here. Did he want to be a married man? He liked being single.

Why were duty and inclination so often at odds?

He sent a note to Brambledean, inviting Wren and Alexander to come for tea two days after New Year. He included Mrs. Westcott and Elizabeth in the invitation, on the assumption that they were still there. He had ambivalent feelings about Elizabeth's coming, though. On the one hand he liked and admired her and even sometimes feared that he was a bit in love with her when it really was not that at all. He just *loved* her, as though she were his sister. Though whenever his mind reasoned that way he knew that was not it either. He yearned for her friendship, her approval, her smiles, her jokes, her exuberance, her serenity. For *her*. He felt totally at ease in her company. He could talk with her upon any subject that came into his head—or hers. He had missed her since coming home.

On the other hand he had blundered horribly with her—*twice*. As if the kiss after sledding were not enough, he had offended her, made her uncomfortable, even perhaps hurt her with his teasing at the Boxing Day party when he had suggested that she marry him. Though, to be perfectly honest with himself, he had been feeling a bit wistful too after that joyful waltz and *almost* wished it were possible to be serious. But she was a lady he respected more than any other, and he had embarrassed her, curse him. But she *liked* joking and laughing. Dash it all, life could be very complicated at times.

He half hoped that she had already returned home to Kent. The other half of him hoped she had not.

Yes, very complicated indeed.

Elizabeth went to Withington since she and her mother had stayed on at Brambledean after the New Year. She looked forward to seeing Colin again despite some leftover embarrassment at how she had allowed her genuine liking for him to stray into forbidden territory. Fortunately no one seemed to have noticed any sign of indiscretion. She was, of course, an expert at pushing feelings deep and smiling upon the world.

He was at the open door of the house to greet them on the appointed afternoon, despite the blustery chill of a January day. He hugged and kissed Wren. He hugged Elizabeth and her mother and shook Alex's hand.

"I would say welcome to my home if it were not in fact Roe's—Wren's," he said, laughing as he helped Elizabeth's mother off with her heavy cloak. "But welcome anyway. My cook has been excelling herself if the smells wafting upstairs all day are any indication. I intend to send you home too stuffed to eat any dinner tonight. Come into the drawing room and warm yourselves. I have just had more coal put on the fire."

The room looked cozy and a bit masculine. There was a pile of cushions on a chair in the corner. They had once been arranged decoratively over the rest of the furniture in the room. The small table beside the chair next to the hearth was covered with a stack of books, which looked as though it might topple over at any moment, an untidy pile of papers, and even an ink bottle and a quill pen balanced precariously close to the edge on one side. The rest of the room was tidy.

Elizabeth examined Colin and her feelings on this first meeting since Christmas. He looked relaxed and cheerful. He had hugged her without any apparent self-consciousness. He had not avoided her eyes. He had forgotten both the kiss and the awkwardness at the party, then. That was a relief.

"Do sit down," he directed them all. "Mrs. Westcott, come and sit by the fire. Here, let me move this stuff. I intended to do it before you arrived and forgot." And he swooped books and papers, pen and ink off the side table and deposited them, after a look around, on the floor in the corner beside the cushion-piled chair. "Now where did I put the doily that belongs on that table?"

Tea was brought in soon after. It was a veritable feast of sandwiches and jellies and cakes, though they did not go to the dining room to partake of it.

"I hope you do not mind," he said by way of explanation. "It is far cozier in here, especially on such a gloomy day."

"I am quite happy to have tea by the fire here, Lord Hodges," Elizabeth's mother said. "I am sure we all are."

Wren poured the tea while Colin served the food and insisted that they sample some of everything. "My cook will be offended if we send back anything more than a few crumbs," he said. "She is a tyrant. Is she not, Roe?"

"And an excellent cook," she said, "whether of savories or sweets "

"Why is it that a cold winter day seems less cold when the sun shines?" Elizabeth's mother complained later. "Alas, that rarely seems to happen in January or February. Certainly not today."

"But there are the spring flowers and the budding trees to look forward to in March," Wren said. "Sometimes even sooner for the snowdrops and primroses."

"You showed me the daffodils the second time I came when you were living here, Wren," Alexander said. "You called them yellow trumpets of hope."

"You will never let me live down that particular flight of fancy, will you?" she said, wincing.

"I have not yet seen the daffodils," Colin said, "but I look forward to it. That corner of the park is lovely, though, even without them. There are the woods and the stream and bridge and then the long slope down to the fence at the outer border of the park."

"Aunt Megan preferred her rose garden," Wren said. "But I always loved the daffodils more than anything else."

"Would you like to take a walk there?" Colin asked, setting down his empty cup and saucer on top of his plate and getting to his feet.

Alexander groaned. "Another day, perhaps?" he suggested. "When the daffodils are in bloom and there is some warmth in the sun?"

"The wind makes today a particularly raw day," Wren said. "And you have just had the fire built up again, Colin. Why waste it?"

"Cowards," he said, grinning.

"Guilty," Alexander said.

"I must confess that I am enjoying this cozy corner you have given me," his mother said. "The journey home in the carriage will be chilly enough."

"Elizabeth?" Colin turned to her with laughing eyes. "Are you a coward too?"

The question could have more than one meaning. She had no wish whatsoever to go tramping about the park in this weather merely to look at a daffodil patch without daffodils. And she had no real wish to be alone with Colin. Not yet. Not this close to the Christmas blunders. She had merely to repeat what everyone else had said. He doubtless would not even be offended or disappointed. He surely could not really want to go out walking. But . . . she had missed him and their private conversations.

"I am not," she said. "Lead the way."

"You will catch your death, Lizzie," her mother protested.

"No, she will not," Alexander said. "She has always liked to tramp about in the outdoors in all weathers, Mama, and she has always remained stubbornly healthy."

"I raised a monster," she said. "A healthy monster."

"I hope I am not going to be held responsible for your death by icicles," Colin said a few minutes later while Elizabeth was fastening her cloak in the hall and tying the ribbons of her bonnet beneath her chin and winding the heavy wool muffler he had lent her about her neck—the bright red one she had given him for Christmas. "How would I live down the shame?"

"Perhaps you will share my fate," she said, "and neither of us will have to feel shame or anything else."

"A distinct possibility," he agreed, opening the front door while she drew on her kid gloves and then slid her hands into her warm muff.

The presence of her muff prevented her from taking his arm. They walked side by side across the lawn to the west, past the house and the trellises beside it that were part of the rose garden in the summer, past the stables and carriage house and onward in the direction of the trees. It was not a large park, though it definitely earned its title. It was bigger than a garden.

"This is a pretty property," she said. "I am glad Wren did not sell it when she married Alex."

"I believe it holds many happy memories for her," he said. "She lived here with our aunt and uncle, who gave her all the love and security and sense of family she lacked during her first ten years. I wish I had known them. I did see Aunt Megan when she came to take Wren away, but I cannot remember either her face or her voice. And I never met my uncle. She married him after she left with Wren."

"I think part of the appeal of Withington," she said, "is that it has a happy feel to it."

She did not know a great deal of Wren's story. Neither Wren nor Alex had been forthcoming about it. But she knew enough to make her unutterably sad for a child who had lived through her early childhood without the close family ties Elizabeth herself had taken for granted.

"It does." He smiled at her. "And I agree with my sister that this is the loveliest part of the park. I spend quite a lot of time here. There is a sense of peace. I do not know if it is nature itself that creates it, or if Wren had some part in it by being happy and secure and consoled here."

They were walking among the trees, bare now for winter. Soon they were through them and standing on the bank of the stream, which was still flowing, though there was the rime of ice on the outer edges. There was a single-arched stone bridge spanning it to their left.

"Are you horribly cold?" he asked as she withdrew one hand from her muff in order to lift the muffler over her mouth and earlobes.

"The muffler helps," she said. "No, not horribly cold." Just freezing.

"Just freezing," he said in unison with her thought.

"How did you know?" she asked.

"Because I am too," he said, and they both laughed.

"Since we have come this far," he said, "shall we at least cross the bridge and look at the daffodil bank so that you can imagine it later even if you are not at Brambledean when they bloom?"

"Lead on," she said, sliding her hand back into the warmth of her muff.

"We do not have to go down," he said when they stood at the top of the grassy slope.

"Having come so far?" She slipped a hand free of her muff again in order to hold up the hems of her dress and cloak and ran down to the bottom, gaining speed as she went. She was laughing when the fence stopped her momentum, and turned to watch him come down after her.

Oh, why did a man in a caped greatcoat and shining top boots and tall hat pulled low on his brow always look so virile? Well, perhaps not all men did, or even most. But Colin Handrich, Lord Hodges, certainly did.

"You see?" he said, gesturing toward the hill. "It is very bare of anything but weary-looking grass."

"Ah," she said, "but I have an imagination." And she could picture it carpeted with nodding daffodils, the trees coming into bud at the top of the bank, the sky blue overhead. "We need winter if only that we can have spring."

"That sounds like a philosophy for life," he said, coming to stand next to her at the fence. "Have you known winter, Elizabeth? Ah, but that was an insensitive question. Of course you have. You lost your husband. Were you very much in love with him?"

"Yes," she said. "Very much indeed when I married him."

"But not later?" He chuckled.

"You did not know I was living apart from him when he died?" she asked. She was surprised he had not heard it from Alex or Wren, but they were not tattlers, those two.

His smile disappeared. He leaned back against the fence and crossed his arms over his chest. "I am sorry," he said. "No, I did not."

"I loved the man he was at heart," she said. "I still do. I am convinced he had a sickness that was incurable, though not many people share my view. Why is it, Colin, that ninety-nine men—or women, I suppose—out of a hundred can drink to their heart's content and even to excess on occasion without their very character being affected? Why can they take the liquor or leave it depending upon the occasion? Why does it not destroy their lives and those of their loved ones? And why is it that the remaining one out of a hundred is consumed by the very liquor he thinks *he* is consuming? Why must he drink it against his better judgment and even against his own will? Why does it possess him like a demon and sometimes banish the person he was and ought to be? Why does it make him vicious, particularly with the very person he loves most on the dwindling occasions when he is sober?"

His head was turned toward her. She had the feeling he was looking intently at her, though she did not turn her own head to look.

"Did he hurt you?" he asked after a lengthy pause.

"Oh, I am so very sorry," she said, stricken. "I do not know where all that came from. I never talk about such things, even with my family any longer. At least, I must make that *almost* never. Forgive me, please. This is a wretched way to thank you for inviting me for tea."

"Did he hurt you?" he asked again.

She sighed. "Usually I could hide the scrapes and bruises,"

she said. "Occasionally I invented head colds or headaches that kept me at home if a bruise or cut was visible. Twice I fled home to Riddings Park. My father sent me back the first time, when Desmond came for me, and I did not argue. He was sober and abjectly penitent and swore most convincingly that no such thing would ever happen again. It was easy to believe him even though I had heard it before. For the thing was that he really meant it, and I still loved him. Or, rather, I loved the man he was when he was not drinking. The second time was after my father died, and Alex refused to send me back even though Desmond came once alone and then with a magistrate. Alex hit him—Desmond, that was, not the magistrate. It was the only time I have known him be violent. I had a broken arm and one very black and bloodshot eye among other things. I have lived at Riddings ever since. Desmond died the year after—in a tavern fight."

Colin had moved, she realized. He was standing directly in front of her. "I am so sorry for the terrible pain you had to suffer," he said. "And I do not mean just the broken arm or the eye. But how do you do it, Elizabeth? How do you show . . . springtime in your demeanor? Almost constantly. Contentment, serenity, maturity, good sense, kindness—I could go on. How do you do it when you have lived through such a nightmare?"

Was that the appearance she gave? If so, she was glad. She had taken a long time cultivating it. And it had been worse even than he knew.

"Is it just an outer armor?" he asked. "Do you still suffer inside?"

She withdrew her gloved hands from her muff and set them against his chest, slipping them beneath the capes of his greatcoat. It was probably unwise, but she needed the human contact and sensed that perhaps he did too. It could not have been a comfortable story to listen to, and it was wrong—and uncharacteristic—of her to have inflicted it upon him.

"We all suffer, Colin," she said. "It is the human condition. No one escapes, even those who may appear to others to live charmed lives. But we all have the choice of whether to be defined by the negatives in our lives or to make of our present and future and our very selves what we want them to be. Although I am convinced Desmond was in the grip of a terrible sickness, I also believe that he succumbed to it without trying hard enough to fight back. Perhaps I do him an injustice. Perhaps there was no way out for him. I do not judge him and, yes, I did mourn him and still do, though I doubt my family is aware of that. I loved him, you see. But I refused to get sucked into the dark whirlpool of his descent into darkness. Oh, it was touch and go for a few years, for I blamed myself when his rages came upon him and did all in my power to change myself. I became a cringing creature who tried desperately not to provoke him. But after I left him, I chose to be my own person, the one I wanted to be. It took a while. A long while. I had vowed to love him in sickness and health, yet I had abandoned him. Guilt is a powerful force. But ultimately my will proved stronger." She thought so, anyway. Perhaps it was just that her will had not been tested. She shivered.

His gloved hands were covering hers against his chest and he took a half step nearer to her. She could feel the warmth of his hands and the comforting strength of them. She could feel his closeness.

"I wish I had your firmness of character," he said, his face very close to her own, and she had the fanciful thought that there was pain in the very heartbeat she could feel faintly with her right hand.

"Have you known winter, then?" she asked, raising her eyes to his.

He closed his own briefly and dropped his chin.

"There was Roe—Wren," he said. "She had that great unsightly strawberry birthmark covering the side of her face. No one could bear to look at her. Certainly no one could bear the thought of anyone else—anyone from outside the house—seeing her, and there were always visitors. She spent most of her childhood in her room, often locked in lest she wander. She was not even allowed into the schoolroom because . . . no one could bear to look at her. I suppose servants took her food and other necessities, but I was the only one who spent time with her in her room. I loved her and enjoyed taking my toys to her and playing with her. I used to read to her after I learned how. I thought she was sick. I used to kiss the strawberry mark better every time I left her. But the strangeness of her situation, the horrible injustice and cruelty of it, did not occur to me at the time. It was just the way things were. If Aunt Megan had not come . . . But she did come, and Roe's winter was over, or at least it began to turn toward spring."

"And did your winter also turn to spring?" Elizabeth asked. But she sensed it had not. The pain in his voice was not just for Wren.

"It had not felt like winter before she left," he said. "I was told she had gone away to be made better, and was unutterably sad because I had lost my playmate. I hoped and hoped she would be home soon, healed and able to run about outside with me and play with me. And then I was told she was dead and I cried until I was empty of tears. How is it possible for a child to be so deeply hurt that he cannot be consoled? I had kissed her better a hundred times or more but she had not got better. Our aunt had taken her away so that a doctor would make her better, but she had died. The injustice of it struck me then, at the advanced age of six. Not the injustice of the way she had been isolated, but the injustice of . . . fate. I might have called it God if we had been a godly family. We were not. I asked my nurse why there was no funeral. I knew somehow about funerals. She told me not to be troublesome, so I was not. But I mourned Roe for the rest of my childhood. Mourning her became a part of me. She had not had a chance to live, yet I seemed to have no choice but to live."

Elizabeth listened to him, aghast. One child in his family had been locked away because she had an unsightly deformity, and another—himself—had had his emotional needs ignored or perhaps not even detected. And why had they lied to him?

He was looking into her eyes, frowning. "Why did they lie to me?" he asked.

Oh, God. What answer was there? "She had been taken to another home," she said, "where she was the only child and could be given the full care and attention of your uncle and aunt. Your parents probably thought you would forget about her more easily if you thought her dead." It was a ridiculous answer. The real answer was obvious. When Wren had been taken away, they had been happy to consider her dead.

"I am sorry," he said. "I ought not to have asked such an unanswerable question. For a few minutes I reverted to that little boy. Why do so many people uphold the myth that childhood is the happiest time of one's life? It is not true, is it?"

"Not for everyone," she said.

"Was it for you?" he asked.

She nodded. "Yes, it was. I was fortunate."

"And then you married a bounder," he said.

She drew a slow breath. "I do not like to hear him called that," she said. "He was ill. I am convinced he was ill. I loved him." And hated him for the unforgivable—which she had not yet confronted and perhaps never would.

"I am sorry," he said. "And I do understand. My brother was a drunk too. Life is not simple, is it?" He grinned suddenly and looked boyish again. "Maybe I ought to write a book. A profoundly philosophical work entitled *Life Is Not Simple*."

Elizabeth laughed. "But remember the original analogy," she said. "Winter *does* turn to spring, Colin, and spring turns to summer. Wren speaks with the warmest affection of her aunt and uncle and her years with them. She became a strong and independent woman even if she *did* hide behind a veil until last year. And then she met Alex and is clearly happy with him. Best of all, as it relates to your story, she did survive and you found out about it. You found each other again and have a close and loving relationship."

It was not a happily-ever-after situation, of course. There was still the rest of his family, or its surviving members at least, who had treated both Wren and Colin so cruelly. And who knew what else had happened during his boyhood that had led him now to live in rooms in London when he owned a town house there and to spend Christmas with the Westcott family rather than his own?

He was smiling into her eyes, his face still close to her own. "You have a very soothing presence, Elizabeth," he said. "Thank you. But I have kept you standing here too long. You must really be feeling like a block of ice by now."

Strangely, she was not.

"Not quite," she said. "I believe I still have the use of my limbs." He was so close. He was smiling. He was very . . . lovely.

"You are very beautiful," he said. His eyes dipped to her mouth and his head moved a fraction of an inch closer to hers. But instead of kissing her, he looked back into her eyes and smiled again. And she was relieved and disappointed. "If it is indeed your intention to choose a husband during the Season this year, some man is going to be very fortunate indeed."

She had never been beautiful or even more than ordinarily pretty, but the compliment warmed her anyway. And it was not the first time he had paid it.

"Thank you," she said.

"But at every ball you attend," he said, his lips almost touching hers, "I must ask that you reserve one set of dances for me."

As if her dance card would be crowded to capacity. "It is a promise," she said.

"Preferably a waltz, as the Duchess of Netherby suggested on Boxing Day," he added, and something happened to both her breathing and her knees at the thought of waltzing again with Colin. "In fact, definitely a waltz."

"That can be arranged too," she said. She was almost whispering, she realized. "But I believe there will be plenty of young ladies in London to compete with me for your attention."

"Ah," he said, "but none of them will be Elizabeth, Lady Overfield."

He might have kissed her then. She sensed that it was about to happen. She drew away sharply from him and busied herself pulling up the muffler to cover her mouth before she dug her hands into her muff.

He had taken a step back and watched her, his hands clasped at his back. "I'll race you up," he said.

"I do not for a moment doubt it," she agreed, but she took the slope at a run anyway and arrived at the top, panting and laughing, only just behind him. He stretched out a hand to haul her up the last few feet.

They walked back to the house without talking, but it was a companionable silence.

Almost.

Oh no, it was not companionable at all. It resonated with a kiss that had not happened and with words that had been spoken.

But at every ball you attend, I would ask that you reserve one set of dances for me.

Preferably a waltz . . . In fact, definitely a waltz.

Six

Colin returned to London after Easter, reluctantly admitting to himself that he would not make his permanent home at Withington after all. He definitely needed to settle at Roxingley. While he had been neglecting it, his mother had had the run of it, and if the complaints of his one neighbor were anything to judge by, that was not a good thing.

His mother had always liked to host lavish house parties, but while Colin's father was still alive, perhaps there had been some check on what happened at them and even upon who was invited. Now there was no such restraint. He knew that his mother held parties in the London house too during the Season. *Sleazy* was one way they had been described in his hearing on one occasion before someone had shushed the speaker.

It was more than time he did something about the situation.

If only Justin had lived . . . But he had not, and the repetition of that thought was becoming tedious.

He left Withington after Wren's child was born—a chubby, healthy, dark-haired little boy, whom they named Nathan Daniel Westcott, Viscount Yardley. Mrs. Westcott had returned to Brambledean to help Wren through the final weeks of her confinement, but Elizabeth had remained at Riddings Park. The father of a friend of hers was dying, and she had stayed to give help where she could. Colin was disappointed and hoped she would be free to go to London for the Season as she had planned. Perhaps he ought not to hope for it, though. He really ought to turn his mind to the serious task of choosing a bride from among the eligible young ladies who would be brought to town in search of husbands at the annual marriage mart that was the Season.

He wondered if Elizabeth remembered promising to waltz with him at every *ton* ball they both attended.

He settled in his old rooms close to White's Club. Until last summer he had lived there year-round since coming down from Oxford at the age of twenty-one, though most members of his social class fled the heat of summer to return to their country estates. He had stayed even during the winter when company was sparse.

He resumed the life with which he was familiar. There were his parliamentary duties and the regular communications with his bailiff at Roxingley Park and his man of business in town. There were his clubs and conversations with his peers. There were his close friends of long standing. There were his boxing and fencing clubs. There were rides in the various parks.

But this year he was going to have to give closer than usual attention to the numerous invitations that were delivered to his rooms daily. He had always attended a variety of entertainments—private concerts, soirees, garden parties, Venetian breakfasts, among others. He had generally avoided balls whenever possible, however. He enjoyed dancing. He even liked mingling with crowds. But it had always seemed to him that balls, more than any other type of social event, were for courtship. It was to the grand balls of the Season that hopeful mamas took their daughters in search of husbands. He was a baron, a peer of the realm. He was also young and wealthy, and his glass told him, all vanity aside, that he was passably good-looking. He had always been unwilling to take the risk of somehow being snared by a young lady determined to land herself a titled husband or, more likely, by her even more ambitious mama. He knew men who had been the victims of such aggressive husband hunting.

He would avoid the grand balls no longer.

He lined up four such invitations on his writing desk one morning, considered them carefully, and found himself wondering—of all things—which of them, if any, *she* would attend. Elizabeth Overfield, that was. He knew she was back in London with Mrs. Westcott. Wren had mentioned the fact in her last letter. But he had no idea how many *ton* balls she was in the habit of attending. Probably not very many. She was no young girl fresh upon the marriage mart, after all. And she already had her beau, the man with whom she was considering marriage this year.

He just hoped the man was worthy of her—if there was such a man. He hoped the man would appreciate her, at least, and cherish her. And love her. And make her laugh. And take away the remnants of her winter. And . . .

Well. It was none of his business really.

He looked from one invitation to another, not really seeing them, but seeing Elizabeth sputtering and clawing snow out of her eyes and then challenging him to a snowball fight and setting about choosing her team. He must give her lessons sometime in how to throw accurately. Oh, and he had lied when he had told her that particular snowball had been intended for her shoulder. It had not. He had made the snowball deliberately soft, and he had aimed it just where it had landed. He wanted to dance with her again—to waltz with her, as he had on Boxing Day. He wanted to waltz with her at every ball of the Season.

Would she be married by the end of the Season?

Would he?

He dipped his quill pen into the inkwell and set about accepting all four invitations.

Mr. Scott died just before Easter—one week after Wren and Alex's baby was born, in fact. Araminta Scott, his daughter and Elizabeth's friend, was free to recover both her health and her spirits after tending him with great devotion through a lingering illness. Araminta had insisted, when Elizabeth offered to postpone her visit to London and stay at home longer, that her friend get on with her own life.

"You have already missed the birth of your nephew on my account, Lizzie," she had said. "I will not have you also miss your second—no, third—marriage proposal from Sir Geoffrey Codaire."

Elizabeth had protested that she was expecting no such thing, but Araminta had threatened to bar her door against her friend if she insisted upon staying.

So here she was in town soon after the start of the Season. She and her mother were staying at the house on South Audley Street that had belonged to the late Earl of Riverdale and now belonged to his daughter, Anna, Duchess of Netherby. She had inherited her legitimate father's wealth even as Alexander had inherited his title. Anna had persuaded Alexander to live there whenever he was in town, though she had been unable to convince him to accept it as a gift.

Wren and Alexander would be coming to town a bit later, after Wren had fully recovered from her confinement and it was safe for the baby to travel. Elizabeth could hardly wait to see him. Alex's son! Her nephew. The first child of the next generation of their family. Neither of the two children she had conceived during her marriage to Desmond had reached birth.

Nathan's arrival in this world made her more aware than ever of her advancing age, of the limited term of her fertility. She simply must at least try to make it possible to have a child of her own. There had been those few gentlemen last year, in particular Sir Geoffrey Codaire with his steady fidelity to her down the years, his proposal of marriage last year, and his expressed intent to renew his addresses at some future time. The future was now. She must hope that he would make his offer again, and this time she must not hesitate. He was a good man. He was someone she could trust with her person and her loyalty and affection. He was someone with whom she would feel happy to have a child before it was too late.

Elizabeth always enjoyed being in London. It gave her a chance to visit family and friends who lived far from her most of the year. And there were the shops and theaters, the galleries and libraries. There were concerts to attend and private dinners and parties, and sometimes grander entertainments, like garden parties and soirees. And there was the occasional ball, though Elizabeth did not attend many of them. Balls were intended for those very young ladies in search of husbands.

This year, however, she looked more closely at those

invitations. Perhaps there was someone new to meet. Or perhaps . . . Well, perhaps he had not forgotten the promise he had extracted from her to reserve a set of waltzes for him at each ball. *He* being Colin, Lord Hodges, young and vibrant and achingly good-looking. How laughable that a woman of her age should be dreaming of dancing with him at a *ton* ball. And why did she always think of herself as a woman of advancing years when she thought of Colin? She resented it.

She wondered if he had made a definite decision to begin a serious search for a bride this year. If so, he would almost certainly have forgotten about an impulsive commitment made to her at Christmas.

It did not matter.

Maybe she would meet Sir Geoffrey Codaire at a ball. She really must hope to meet him somewhere this year.

Colin *was* in London. Alex had told her so in a letter from Brambledean. Would she be a little disappointed if he had forgotten the promise he had extracted from her?

How lowering that the answer was yes.

She spread out four invitations to balls as she sat at the escritoire in the morning room one day soon after the post had been delivered. All were sure to be well attended. Which would he attend? All of them? Some? One? None?

She sighed.

"Are there any interesting invitations we ought to accept?" her mother asked, looking up from her knitting. She was making Nathan a pair of booties.

"There are no fewer than four balls in the next two weeks," Elizabeth said. "I cannot decide which we ought to attend. Perhaps all four?"

"Indeed?" Her mother raised her eyebrows. "Are you on the lookout for a husband in earnest at last, then, Lizzie?"

"Oh goodness," Elizabeth said. "At my age, Mama?"

"My love," her mother said, "if I were your age, I might well be shopping at every available ball myself."

They both laughed, and Elizabeth picked up her quill pen to accept the invitations. All four of them. It felt a bit reckless.

Sir Randolph Dunmore's house on Grosvenor Square was the site of the first grand ball of the Season—or so declared Lady Dunmore to a group of her friends, who passed on the word to their friends until they had collectively squashed the pretensions of any minor hostess who had tried to lay claim to the honor with any ball that had preceded it.

Lady Dunmore had a daughter to introduce to society and marry off—the second daughter. The first had married a wealthy baronet within three months of her come-out ball, and Lady Dunmore expected no less of Lydia, the accredited beauty among her five daughters. No expense had been spared. The ballroom floor had been polished to a high gloss. The chandeliers sparkled even before the candles were lit. Banks of flowers and hanging baskets made the room look and smell like an indoor garden. A small army of cooks hired for the occasion had been at work for three days producing every conceivable delicacy, both savory and sweet. An eight-piece orchestra had been engaged to provide the music.

Colin attended the ball in company with Ross Parmiter and John Croft, two of his closest friends. John had two sisters to provide for as well as a mother to support, all on a very moderate fortune, but he was nevertheless always ready and willing to add a wife to the household—if, that was, he should happen to fancy some young lady sufficiently and the same young lady should fancy him. He was ever hopeful of finding her, but his friends had noticed that he fell in and out of love with dizzying regularity and never did actually fix his interest upon any one candidate. Ross liked dancing and female company and could enjoy both without any great fear of being caught unawares in parson's mousetrap. Though his father was well born and not by any means impoverished and made his only son a generous allowance, there was no grand fortune or ancestral property there, or even a title.

Colin Handrich, Baron Hodges, of course, fell into a different category altogether.

Lady Dunmore smiled graciously upon all three gentlemen when they passed along the receiving line, for they were all personable and single and prospective dancing partners for her daughter and the other young ladies present. No hostess wished to see even the least of her young female guests remain a wallflower all evening. But she showed a particular preference for Lord Hodges as she introduced him to her blushing daughter, smiling from one to the other of them as though picturing to herself how they would look together at the altar rail of a packed church on their wedding day.

Colin had expected it and took it all in stride. She was a pretty girl, Miss Lydia Dunmore, dark haired, very slender, with a delicate complexion that suggested she had spent most of her life so far in the schoolroom. She wore a white gown, as most very young ladies did during their first Season. She looked barely eighteen, even perhaps younger than that. He could not see the color of her eyes. She peeped only briefly at him through her eyelashes before directing her gaze at his dancing shoes.

"Dare I hope, Miss Dunmore," he asked because her

mother clearly expected it, "that your dancing card is not yet full and I can secure a set with you sometime this evening?"

"Oh," her mother declared before the girl could do more than peep up at him again and open her mouth to speak, "apart from the opening set, which Lydia is to dance with Viscount Fettering, who is her cousin, she has promised no set to any gentleman. It would not have been fair to fill her card before the ball, as she could have done three times over, and so disappoint a number of her guests. Lydia, my love, Lord Hodges has asked you a question." She beamed from one to the other of them.

"I would be happy to dance a set with you, my lord," the girl said.

"The second," Lady Dunmore said.

"I thank you for the honor," Colin said to her daughter, and followed his friends into the ballroom.

It was crowded and buzzing with the collective sound of a few dozen conversations. The musicians were tuning their instruments, an indication that it must be almost time for the dancing to begin. Colin recognized people wherever he looked, as was to be expected when he had lived in London through every spring Season for the past five years. There were a few unfamiliar faces too, however, most of them belonging to young men newly down from university or up from the country without having furthered their education, or to young ladies recently released from the schoolroom and come to town to acquaint themselves with the *ton* and acquire husbands during their first Season if they should be so fortunate.

It was all much as usual, in fact.

"It looks as if there is a pretty decent crop this year," John Croft said cheerfully and a bit disrespectfully, his quizzing glass in his hand though not held to his eye as he gazed upon all the young ladies.

"You are in love already, John?" Ross Parmiter asked, winking at Colin.

"Not quite," John said with a laugh, dropping his glass on its ribbon. "But the brown-haired girl with the topknot is a looker, and she seems to be with Baker. She must be one of his sisters or cousins. There are said to be at least a dozen of them. Ha! A baker's dozen. Funny, that. I believe I will take a stroll over there and get Baker to introduce me."

The topknot, Colin guessed, had been constructed to give the girl some height. She was unusually small otherwise. But John was right about her looks. She had a pretty, animated face and, if he was not mistaken from this distance, dimples. Dimples were always appealing.

"I'll come with you," Ross said.

Colin would have gone too, but his glance had just alit upon Mrs. Westcott across the room, her hair plumes nodding as she talked with a group of older ladies. She spotted him at the same moment and smiled and inclined her head. Beside her, Elizabeth, Lady Overfield, was in conversation with a tall, stocky gentleman. She was neatly dressed in a primrose-colored gown with short, puffed sleeves, a modestly scooped neckline, a fashionably high waistline, and a scalloped hem. Her hair was dressed prettily but without any noticeable topknots or ringlets or excessive curls—or plumes. She had made no attempt, it seemed, to make herself look either glamorous or younger than she was. She never did, in fact. It was ironic, then, that the very simplicity of her dress gave her a youthful appearance. And beauty, though she did not need the dress to give her that.

She had not seen him. But her mother touched her arm even as he watched and said something to her, and she looked across the room until she saw him. He raised a hand in greeting, and she smiled. She looked like the springtime, or she made him feel like the springtime or some such poetic nonsense. The gentleman too turned his head. Colin knew him. He searched his mind for a name but could not immediately recall it. The man was a worthy citizen, however, one of a set of dull fellows who hung together at White's and talked endlessly and knowledgeably about crops and drainage and livestock and other such farming subjects. Colin stayed out of earshot whenever he could. Was he by any chance the man whom she . . . ?

But surely not.

Oh, Elizabeth, no.

A couple of people had moved in front of them and Colin, looking away, spotted the stately figure of the Dowager Duchess of Netherby close by with Lady Jessica Archer, her daughter. He strolled toward them as they finished talking with another couple. Both ladies seemed pleased to see him, and he was able to secure Lady Jessica's hand for the third set, the first having already been promised.

"Your cousins are not in town yet?" Colin asked her.

She made a face. "Nor will they be," she said. "Abby remains irritatingly stubborn. Avery and Anna have offered to bring her out. Mama has offered. Alexander and Wren have offered, though they are not in town yet either. Even Uncle Thomas and Aunt Mildred have offered. And now she has the Marquess of Dorchester for a stepfather, and he has suggested bringing her out with Estelle. His own daughter, Lord Hodges! Abby's *stepsister*. Estelle is eighteen years old and you would think, would you not, that she at least would be all eagerness to be here? But no such thing. She would rather postpone the pleasure until next year. She wants to enjoy one full year at home with her father and her new stepmother, if you please. It is all very provoking for me. Not that Abby would come anyway, I daresay, even if Estelle did. She is my dearest friend in the world, Lord Hodges, but sometimes I could shake her until her teeth rattle."

Flushed and animated as she was, Lady Jessica Archer looked very pretty indeed. And she was no milk-and-water miss.

"I brought Jessica to London kicking and screaming, Lord Hodges," the dowager told him, shaking her head as she regarded her daughter fondly.

"Hardly, Mama," Lady Jessica said with a sigh. "I am nineteen years old. I cannot stay at home forever, can I? Yet forever it might turn out to be if I wait for Abby. Perhaps we could grow old together as sad spinsters in a remote country cottage somewhere." She caught Colin smiling and laughed, a girlish peal of glee.

Yes. Very pretty indeed. And a duke's daughter. But perhaps his own baron's title would be considered too lowly . . .

They were interrupted by the arrival of her partner for the opening set, and Colin looked around the immediate vicinity for a partner of his own. There were invariably more ladies than gentlemen at such affairs, and it would be unmannerly to stand on the sidelines and thus doom one of them to stand there too. He saw Miss Cowley, a young lady with whom he had a slight acquaintance, nearby with her mama and smiled as he moved toward them. The girl smiled back with almost open relief.

John Croft was already out on the dance floor with the girl with the topknot, Colin saw as he led his partner to the line of ladies before taking his place in the line of gentlemen opposite. Ross had a partner too, a tall girl, who was giggling with the lady next to her.

The stocky gentleman was joining the end of the line

with Elizabeth. She was going to dance the opening set, then. Colin was glad of that. She was far too young and attractive to spend the evening sitting or standing with the mothers and chaperones. He would solicit her hand for a waltz later in the evening—he assumed there would be a few on the program despite the presence of a number of very young ladies who would not be allowed to participate until they had been approved, probably later in the Season, by one of the patronesses of Almack's.

He looked forward immensely to holding her to her promise. For the moment he felt that he had come this evening for no other purpose but that.

He had another partner now, however, and was neglecting her. He smiled reassuringly at her. This was not her first Season. He was not even sure it was her second—it seemed to him he might have known her longer than two years. She looked as though she was feeling some doubt, even some anxiety about her eligibility. Life could be cruel to girls who did not find husbands within a year or two of their release from the schoolroom. They could so easily be flung upon the shelf and left there to gather dust. And what a ghastly image that was. Perhaps . . . But, no. He felt no real attraction to Miss Cowley, and it would surely be a huge mistake to marry any woman just because he felt sorry for her and wished to save her from being doomed to go through life as a spinster, dependent upon her male relatives.

Now that he thought about it, he felt no real attraction to Lady Jessica Archer either, though she was a very pretty, lively girl and he really did like her. He felt a moment's amusement as he remembered seeing her on Christmas Eve with Abigail Westcott and Lady Estelle Lamarr, their heads together as they looked him over self-consciously and giggled. He had liked all three. He had not felt the pull of any special attraction to any of them. And to be fair, he did not believe he had left any of them lovelorn and brokenhearted after Christmas.

He glanced along the line to catch Elizabeth looking at him. She raised her eyebrows, amusement in her eyes, and he realized he had been smiling at nothing—except the memories.

Miss Lydia Dunmore, looking both nervous and excited, joined the head of the line with Viscount Fettering, and the orchestra struck a chord. Miss Dunmore was an interesting prospect—very pretty and modest, if her behavior in the receiving line was an accurate indication of her character. He looked forward to dancing the second set with her.

He turned his attention back to Miss Cowley as he smiled and bowed to her and she curtsied to him.

The dancing began.

Seven

A short while earlier Sir Geoffrey Codaire had arrived at the Dunmore ball not long after Elizabeth and her mother. After passing the receiving line and looking purposefully about the room, he made his way directly toward them. He paid his respects and explained that he had arrived in London the day before yesterday and had come to the ball tonight when he discovered that they were to be here.

"But however did you find that out, Sir Geoffrey?" Elizabeth's mother asked.

"Lady Dunmore is a second cousin, ma'am," he explained. "I made a particular point when I called upon her yesterday of asking if you and Lady Overfield were to be among her guests tonight. She assured me you were."

"That is very flattering, I am sure," she said, and chatted amiably with him for a few minutes before resuming her interrupted conversation with her sister-in-law and a few other ladies of her acquaintance.

Elizabeth meanwhile looked critically at him. As she

remembered, he was a fine figure of a man. She felt relieved to see him, though she could wish her mind had chosen a different word. It made her seem desperate. She was also pleased to learn that he had come just because she was to be here. His interest in her had not cooled since last spring, then.

"I was delighted to discover you were to be here this evening," he said, turning his attention to Elizabeth. "I know you do not attend many balls. I hope I have not arrived too late to engage you for the first set."

"You have not," she assured him. She had not exactly been besieged by would-be partners since her arrival, and it looked as though she would not even have a waltzing partner this evening. Colin had not come.

"Then I beg you to consider the first set of dances mine," Sir Geoffrey said—and at that very moment she caught sight of Colin in the receiving line with two other young gentlemen.

He *had* come.

It seemed absurd, watching him bowing to the very young and lovely Miss Lydia Dunmore while her mother glanced fondly and speculatively from one to the other of them, to imagine that he would even *think* of dancing with her, Elizabeth. The ballroom was full of very young ladies, more than usual, surely, for the beginning of a Season. In his black and white evening clothes, his fair hair almost golden in the candlelight, he looked youthful and really quite dazzlingly attractive. And, of course, hugely eligible.

"I will indeed," she told Sir Geoffrey. "Thank you."

He remained at her side. He asked after her brother and sister-in-law and the baby before telling her about some innovations he had implemented on his farms during the past summer despite contrary advice from his neighbors and even his own steward. The yield on his fields had increased significantly as a consequence while that on his neighbors' had not. And his pastureland . . .

"There is Lord Hodges, Lizzie," her mother said, nodding across the room, her hair plumes indicating the direction.

And Elizabeth saw him again. The two gentlemen with whom he had arrived were moving away from him, and for the moment he stood alone, looking across the room at her. She smiled at him and felt inexplicably breathless. And for some absurd reason she recalled telling him—as a joke— on Christmas Eve that when one looked across a crowded room and one's eyes alit upon that certain someone, one instantly *knew*.

Knew *what*, for heaven's sake?

"Hodges?" Sir Geoffrey said. "But, ah, yes. Lady Riverdale is his sister, is she not?"

"She is indeed," Elizabeth said. "He spent Christmas at Brambledean with our family, and we were all very happy he did. He is a personable young man and good fun." Even when he was hurling a wet snowball into one's face—she had not for a moment believed his protestation that the first snowball had been intended for her shoulder.

Two ladies, strolling arm in arm about the outer edge of the dancing floor, stepped into her line of vision, and after they had passed he had turned away to join Cousin Louise and Jessica, who were both smiling at him with obvious pleasure. Poor Jessica. Last year she had cut short her very successful debut Season because she was upset that Abigail could not be with her. Yet this year Abby still refused to come to London even though Marcel, Marquess of Dorchester, her new stepfather, had assured her his influence would gain her entrée to all the most select entertainments of the Season. Jessica was going to have to learn to live for herself and not worry so much about the injustice life had dealt her very best friend, especially because at this point some of it seemed self-inflicted. Abby would find her own way, whatever it turned out to be.

Life could sometimes be cruel to the very young. And to the not-so-young too.

Perhaps Jessica and Colin . . .

But the dancing was about to begin. The members of the orchestra had finished tuning their instruments, lines were forming for the opening set, and the receiving line was breaking up. Lady Dunmore was presenting her daughter with her partner for this all-important first public dance of her young life.

"Shall we?" Sir Geoffrey extended a hand, and Elizabeth set her own on top of it. Colin had a partner—not Jessica. He had already led her to the line of ladies and taken his place opposite her. He was smiling, but not at his partner or anyone else, it seemed. It was not just a sociable smile. There was genuine amusement in it. Had she been close, Elizabeth would have posed the question she had asked when she joined him in the great hall on Christmas Eve—*a penny for them.*

He turned his head and caught her looking. She raised her eyebrows as though she really were asking the question, and his smile faded to leave him looking a bit sheepish. But Lydia Dunmore had reached the head of the line with her partner, and a chord sounded to herald the start of the dancing.

Elizabeth curtsied to Sir Geoffrey Codaire.

There were to be only two waltzes, Colin discovered after the first set. It was understandable, of course. The evening was in honor of a young girl who would not be able to dance it for a while yet, and there were many other such young girls in attendance. Yet the ball would have been frowned upon if the program had not included any waltzes at all. The new dance had rapidly gained in popularity since being introduced to polite ballrooms not so long ago.

The first waltz was to be just before supper, the other sometime after. Colin thought about pushing the pleasure as far forward into the evening as possible and waiting until after supper. A few considerations made him decide otherwise. What if Elizabeth left early? Or what if he appeared at her side to claim her for the second waltz only to discover that someone else had got there ahead of him? And why waste the fact that the first waltz was also the supper dance? He would enjoy having Elizabeth's company at supper. He hoped she would not dislike his company. But she had agreed to waltz with him at every ball they both attended.

He approached her as soon as the set before the waltz had ended and he had returned his partner to her mother's side. He sensed that Codaire—the man's name had popped into his head earlier when he was not even trying to recall it—was making his way toward her too and quickened his pace to reach her first. It occurred to him as he did so that she might be disappointed if it was indeed Codaire she hoped to marry. But he did not slow down. The man could waltz with her after supper.

She was looking flushed and bright-eyed.

"Lord Hodges," Mrs. Westcott said. "You have not missed one set all evening. You must be the most sought-after young man here tonight."

"I can only be thankful, ma'am," he said, "that there are enough ladies here willing to dance with me."

She rapped him on the arm with her fan. "Their mamas

would line them up to dance with you if it were not an un-genteel thing to do," she said. "And their daughters would be only too happy to stand and wait. I may be slightly partial since you are my daughter-in-law's brother, but I do believe you are the most handsome young man in the ballroom. Is he not, Lizzie?"

Colin laughed and hoped he was not blushing.

"You look very distinguished in black and white," Elizabeth told him, her eyes twinkling.

"Which is a tactful way of saying I am not the most handsome man here?" he said. She had called him just that at the Boxing Day party, he recalled.

"I have seen two or three who might give you some competition," she told him. "Lady Dunmore is certainly going to be able to boast tomorrow that she hosted the first grand squeeze of the Season so far, is she not?"

"Who would dare contradict her?" he asked. "She has been declaring it so, apparently, for the past week. The next set is to be a waltz. Will you dance it with me, Elizabeth?"

"Oh, do, Lizzie," Mrs. Westcott urged. "You know how you love the waltz above all other dances. And poor Lord Hodges may be doomed to being a wallflower if you refuse, for most of the very young ladies will not be allowed to dance it."

"You have exposed my worst fear, ma'am," he said, and she laughed and tapped him on the arm again and turned her eyes upon her daughter.

"It would appear that I must do my charitable deed for the day and waltz with you, then," Elizabeth said.

She had not told her mother about their private arrangement? He wondered why not. The two of them seemed close.

"It is the supper dance," he reminded Elizabeth as he led her onto the floor.

"Is it indeed?" she said. "Does that mean we are going to have to converse for all of half an hour over our supper? I hope you have enough observations about the weather to keep awkward silences at bay."

"If I have not," he said, "I can always resort to assassinating the characters of a few of our fellow guests."

"Ah, a man of infinite resources." She laughed, and he felt instantly happy. He loved her laughter.

They stopped on the dance floor and stood face to face, smiling at each other. He set one hand behind her waist and held up his other hand for hers. She took it and set her left hand on his shoulder. She smelled good—of a lightly floral scent with hints of something more spicy. He was not good at identifying perfumes, only at appreciating them—or not. Most girls he had danced with emphasized the floral a bit much.

"I wonder," he said, "if there will be hand clapping and foot stamping and a few exuberant whoops tonight."

"Poor Lady Dunmore would swoon quite away and never lift her head in public again," she said.

The music began at that moment, and he twirled her into the steps of the waltz, noting, as he had on Boxing Day, how light she was in his arms, how her spine arched inward beneath his hand, how she followed his lead without faltering and without causing him to fear that he would tread on her dancing slippers or that she would trip over his shoes.

There were other couples waltzing, though not as many as for the other dances. Most of the very young people stood on the sidelines watching and trying not to look wistful. Ross Parmiter was waltzing with Lady Jessica Archer, John Croft with Miss Cowley, Colin's first partner of the evening—and looking at her, interestingly enough, rather as if he was falling in love. The ballroom smelled like a garden. There was cool air wafting through the open French windows along one side of the room. Candlelight from the chandeliers overhead seemed to swirl with the rhythm of the dance.

But after a minute or two Colin stopped noticing his surroundings. He even forgot the ease with which they danced together, he and Elizabeth. He felt only the exhilaration of waltzing with a partner who loved the dance as he did and moved in his arms as though she fit there. As though she belonged there. She danced with a slight smile on her face, more dreamy than deliberate, a sort of Mona Lisa smile. And this was how dancing should always be, he thought. It could go on for all of the rest of the evening as far as he was concerned. The circle of their bodies and the space between were a warm and private world within a larger world of color and music and dance.

But inevitably the music drew to an end.

"We did agree, did we not, Lady Overfield," he said as they stopped dancing but did not immediately let go of each other, "that we would waltz at every ball of the Season?"

"We did indeed, Lord Hodges," she replied, the dreamy smile fading to be replaced by her more habitual twinkle. "And I shall hold you to the promise. You waltz better than any other partner I have ever had. But do not tell my brother that, if you please."

"My lips are sealed." He offered his arm to lead her into the supper room and was very glad he had chosen this waltz rather than the one later. He felt happy and lighthearted, as he had not felt since he left the country. For a while he could forget about the weight of his self-appointed task of reordering his life and simply enjoy the company of a poised, beautiful woman.

And I shall hold you to the promise. He felt flattered. No—he felt *honored*.

"Let us make it the *first* waltz at each ball, shall we?" he said.

Her eyes were smiling warmly when they met his. "The first it shall be," she agreed.

Lady Dunmore must be feeling very gratified indeed, Elizabeth thought as they entered the supper room. Chairs were close packed on either side of the two long tables, and every one was occupied, as far as she could see. Several smaller tables had had to be arranged about the perimeter of the room to accommodate the remaining guests. Colin seated her at one of them, and she was secretly glad.

"I have never particularly enjoyed waltzing at London balls," he said, shaking out his linen napkin and spreading it on his lap.

"Yet it is the very dance you have engaged to perform with me at each ball of the Season," she said.

"Oh." He looked at her, startled, and then laughed. "I have never much enjoyed it—before tonight. It has always been such a chore. One feels obliged to remember the steps and execute them with precision and elegance, to guide one's partner without either treading upon her dancing slippers or crashing into another couple with her, and—as if all that were not enough—to converse with her too."

"But you did not converse with me," she pointed out as she set a collection of savories and sweets on her plate from the selection in the middle of the table.

"I did not, did I?" he agreed. "You see? I am an abject failure. But I felt comfortable enough with you simply to enjoy the dance. I knew I would, though. It is why I asked you to waltz with me at every ball."

Comfortable. There was not much romance in the word, was there? But why should there be?

"And you did not once tread upon my feet," she said.

He grimaced. "I did it once," he told her. "The very first time I waltzed in public. My partner was a true lady, though. She brushed off my profuse apologies with the smiling assurance that it was nothing at all, but for all of the following half hour I could see that she was gritting her teeth in mortal agony."

They both laughed as he filled his own plate. But they were interrupted before he had finished when Lady Dunmore came hurrying up to their table.

"Lord Hodges," she said, sounding mortified, "you really ought not to be sitting at one of these tables, removed from our other guests. There is an empty place close to the head table. Do let me seat you there."

Colin glanced at Elizabeth. "I am quite content to be here with Lady Overfield, ma'am," he assured her.

She turned to Elizabeth, as though noticing her for the first time. "Ah," she said. "Now where can we place you, Lady Overfield? Perhaps closer to Mrs. Westcott?" She looked along one of the long tables.

"Please do not exert yourself, ma'am," Colin said, a firmer note in his voice. "Lady Overfield and I are perfectly happy with each other's company. We are, after all, almost siblings. My sister is married to her brother."

"Ah, yes, of course," she said. "Very well, then, but you really ought to have been more appropriately directed when you stepped into the room." She moved away, clearly vexed with her servants.

"I do believe," Elizabeth said, "you have been approved as a suitor for Miss Dunmore's hand. Are you happy about it?"

He thought. "She seems to be a sweet young lady, though a little on the shy side," he said. "Getting her to contribute more than a monosyllable here and there to a conversation is a bit like pulling teeth."

"But she is very pretty," she said.

"She is," he agreed. "Exceedingly."

"You are doing what you were thinking about at Christmastime, then?" she asked him. "You are looking for a bride?"

"I suppose so," he said. "It seems cold-blooded. But I daresay one cannot have a wife if one does not first seek one." He looked at Elizabeth.

For a moment she felt a stabbing of envy. If she were only ten or fifteen years younger . . . But even as a girl she had not been renowned for her good looks. She would have been no competition for someone like Miss Dunmore. She had actually been surprised when Desmond began to court her, for he had been a handsome man, much sought after by other ladies.

"And what of Sir Geoffrey Codaire?" he asked. "He was your partner in the first set, and I cut him out for the waltz. He was making his way toward you, and I broke into a run to reach you first."

"Oh, you did not," she protested, laughing. "What a spectacle you would have made of yourself."

He always looked particularly boyish—and impossibly attractive—when he grinned, as he did now. Then he was serious again. "Is he the one you are going to marry?" he asked.

"Goodness," she said. "There is no offer on the table." She glanced to where Sir Geoffrey was sitting, talking with

Sir Randolph Dunmore at one of the long tables. By chance she caught his eye and smiled.

"But there has been and will be again?" Colin asked. "Is he the one who offered for you last year? And do invite me to mind my own business if I am being offensive."

"He was indeed obliging enough to ask me last year," she admitted. "Whether he will repeat the offer this year remains to be seen. It is altogether possible he will take me at my word and content himself with being my friend."

"And would you be disappointed?" he asked.

Would she? She did not know what other prospects she might have. One of the other gentlemen who had shown some interest last year seemed to have lost it this year. He was here tonight and had not come near her. The others were not here at all and might not even be in town. Besides, none of them had entered into anything that might honestly be described as a courtship.

"He is a worthy gentleman," she said.

"And worthiness matters to you," he said. It was not a question.

"Yes, of course," she said. "It is of primary concern, in fact. If I remarry at all, it must be to someone I can trust."

"Trust to do what?" he asked, leaning back so that a servant could pour their tea.

Elizabeth waited until the man had moved on to the next table. "To remain worthy for the rest of our lives," she said. "I cannot be more specific than that, I am afraid."

"You want your life to be predictable, then," he said.

"Yes, I do." She sighed. "It sounds dreadfully dull, does it not? But dull predictability has its attractions, Colin, when one is thirty-five years old and has experienced all the perils of unpredictability. I would know what I was getting into with Sir Geoffrey and what to expect."

"You do not want any laughter?" he asked her. "Or any joy?"

"Does worthiness preclude them?" she asked. Though she could not actually imagine laughing with Sir Geoffrey. Or feeling joyful with him.

"You were made for joy, Elizabeth," Colin said. "Remember Christmas?"

She remembered it all too well. It stood apart from everything else in her life for years past—perhaps ever.

"Not every day can be Christmas," she said.

"Perhaps it ought to be," he said, and she thought wistfully of snowball fights and sled runs and kisses in the snow.

"What of you?" she asked. "You have danced every set so far this evening, each time with a different partner. Have you met anyone else in addition to Miss Dunmore in whom you feel any particular interest?"

"I have enjoyed dancing with them all," he said, "though with you most of all. I have not felt Cupid's arrow penetrate my heart, if that is what you mean, not even over Miss Dunmore. The only time I looked across the ballroom and found myself gazing transfixed upon a special someone, she was you."

His eyes were smiling, and Elizabeth laughed. It was a lame joke. Even so, she felt sad, for the same thing had happened to her when she spotted him in the receiving line and realized he had come after all. As though his attendance was all on account of her and his promise to waltz with her. As though she had come here for no other reason.

She was supposed to be thinking of Sir Geoffrey tonight and of her future. She was supposed to be thinking of security and trust and good sense, not lamenting that she had been born fifteen years too soon.

"What qualities are you looking for?" she asked. "Beauty and sweetness of character?"

"More strength of character, I suppose," he said. "Being my wife will not be easy."

"You plan to be a bad-tempered tyrant, then?" she asked.

"I hope not," he said. "No, what I meant was that being my baroness will not be easy. Not under the circumstances."

The circumstances being his mother, she supposed, and the fact that he had not yet really taken up his inheritance and put the stamp of his own character upon it.

"I have not even been to Roxingley in eight years," he said. "My mother lives there."

Yes. The girl he chose as his bride would have a difficult time of it. She would need great strength of character. She was not to be envied—except in her bridegroom.

"Elizabeth." He leaned forward slightly across the table, the smile gone from his eyes. "Tell me how I am to find a woman just like you."

Her heart turned over. Her stomach too. His eyes, gazing into hers, were as earnest as she had ever seen them. She set down her cup in its saucer, careful not to rattle it. She was thankful she had not drunk much or eaten anything.

"Well, let me see," she said. "For one thing, there is no one *just like* me. There is only me." What did he see when he looked at her? A mature woman who had all of life's answers? "For another, I have years of experience of life that the young ladies among whom you are seeking a bride cannot be expected to have. They will learn, however. None of us can escape the ups and downs of life, and we all gain far more from experience than from any advice we hear from loved ones or read from any book."

He gazed at her for long moments before saying anything.

"Girls are raised for marriage, are they not?" he said. "For being wives and carrying out wifely duties, including the running of the marital home."

"Yes," she said.

"Why do they not all rebel?" he asked.

"Because we are raised to believe that is what we want," she said.

"And is it?" He frowned. "What did *you* want, Elizabeth?"

"Marriage." She smiled. "And happily-ever-after."

"I am sorry it did not work out for you," he said, searching her eyes with his own. "And now you want marriage again with a dull, solid fellow?"

It did seem a bit like madness when there were such things as laughter and joy in the world. But they were fleeting things and not always available. Solidity of character was dependable.

"I want my own home," she said. "I want to be part of a couple so that I do not have to feel lonely at events like family Christmases. I want—I hope for—children."

"Your need is emotional," he said, "yet you look for safety and dependability. My need is practical, yet I dream of love. I would like to be in love with the woman I marry. But there are so many other considerations that I suppose are more important. I dream of perfection, Elizabeth. You do not dream at all."

She felt stricken. Of course she dreamed. Oh, *of course* she did. Did he not understand that even her modest hopes might be beyond her grasp if no one offered for her? No one upon whom she could depend, anyway.

"I am being an insensitive lout, am I not?" he said when she did not reply. "I daresay you would prefer to be head over heels in love with Codaire if it were possible. I have made you look unhappy in the middle of a ball, when I should be making you smile. Let us talk about something else. I had a letter from Roe this morning—from Wren. She tells me Alexander keeps insisting that the baby smiles at him when she knows very well it is merely wind."

"Ah," Elizabeth said. "That is sweet. I so envy them."

"Because they are married and in love?" he asked her. "Because they have a child? I was supposed to be changing the subject."

"I had two miscarriages during my marriage," she told him. And goodness, she was not in the habit of talking about *that*. Never that. Even with her mother.

"Perhaps," he said after a brief silence, his voice low and gentle beneath the hubbub of conversation at the long tables—and he reached out a hand to cover the back of one of hers—"you will have better fortune with Codaire or whichever of your suitors you choose to marry. You have had a number of dancing partners this evening. All the single ones among them must realize what a perfect treasure you are."

"Indeed?" She smiled at him.

"Yes, indeed," he assured her. "I am single and I danced with you. And *I* realized it."

"You are both kind and gallant, sir," she said lightly, still smiling, though it felt as though her heart was breaking.

"What I am," he said, "is in awe of you, Elizabeth. The more I learn of you, the more I respect and admire you. You have incredible strength of character. I still think I ought to marry you. And that you ought to marry me. It would solve both our problems. We could trust each other, could we not?"

His eyes were twinkling, she saw when she looked into them, holding her own smile in place. "I believe the last time you told me I could trust you, you spilled me into a snowbank," she said.

"And did you take a deadly chill or break every bone in your body?" he asked. "Or any bone at all?"

"No."

"Well, then."

They gazed at each other across the table, smiling and . . . Was there some undercurrent to the brief silence? Or was it only on her side? It was something achingly tempting. Something unmistakably sexual. And something unthinkable. Good heavens, his *older* sister was married to her *younger* brother.

"I shall keep your offer in mind," she said, "while I wait to see if I have a better one before the end of the Season."

"Well, that is a death knell to my self-esteem," he said, removing his hand from hers and sitting back in his chair. "I shall have to continue waltzing with you and using all my charm upon you until I can convince you that I am the only one for you. Confess, Elizabeth. Did you not feel it when you looked across the ballroom earlier at your mother's bidding and saw me? Did you not feel the earth move? Did you not hear violins play?"

"Well, goodness," she said. "Do you mean that the earth did not *really* move? Do you mean the violinist was not really playing a romantic melody on multiple violins?"

But everyone about them was moving. The dancing must be about to resume. She had taken one bite out of a lobster patty during the past half hour and had drunk one third of a cup of tea. He had not done any better. He stood and offered his hand.

"Allow me to escort you back into the ballroom," he said.

Lady Dunmore was awaiting him in the doorway. She

linked an arm through his. "I am sure you have done your duty by your sister's family for one evening, Lord Hodges," she said, nodding graciously to Elizabeth. "Come. There is a young lady to whom I must present you before the next set begins."

Colin was about to protest, Elizabeth could see. She slipped her hand from his arm.

"Do go," she said. "My mother is just a few steps away." As though at her age she needed the constant presence of a chaperon.

She watched as he was led away to meet the rather plain girl who stood with Miss Dunmore.

I still think I ought to marry you. And that you ought to marry me. It would solve both our problems. And we can trust each other, can we not?

Oh, Colin.

Eight

It did not take long, Colin soon discovered, for word to get out that Lord Hodges was in search of a bride. During the two weeks following the Dunmore ball, he felt almost as though he were constantly interviewing candidates, most of them pressed upon him by their mothers. It was really quite dizzying and not a little disconcerting, for the more he thought about marrying, the more he came to believe what he had told Elizabeth at the ball. His baroness would have to be a young woman of extraordinary strength of character, for his mother would be no ordinary mother-in-law. She would not take kindly to having either her name or her position as mistress of Roxingley and the house on Curzon Street usurped.

And he, of course, would have to be an extraordinary husband in order to prevent her from overpowering his wife. He would have to be a stronger man than his father had been—or than he himself had been at the age of eighteen.

At a garden party in Richmond he took one young lady strolling through the hothouses on the suggestion of her mother, who could not stand the heat herself. He sat in an open summer house for a while with another young lady, whose mother needed urgently to have a word with their hostess. Later, on the terrace outside the house, he found himself left alone for all of ten minutes with a young lady whose mother had spotted an old and dear friend she had not seen in ages.

Soon after the mother returned, he was introduced to Miss Madson and took her out on the river in one of the boats. She was a pretty, auburn-haired girl, who seemed both intelligent and sensible. She did not seem to believe, as many other young ladies did, that it was unfeminine to talk about current affairs or the books she had read. Colin, pulling on the oars, relaxed and enjoyed her company and even kept her out a bit longer than he ought, given that there was a small queue of people awaiting their turn in the boats. He liked Miss Madson and wondered if she liked him. Her elder sister, who was sponsoring her come-out, was waiting for her on the bank and gave Colin a long and speculative look.

The following evening at a soiree he twice found himself spending several minutes tête-à-tête with young ladies before he ended up turning pages of music for Miss Dunmore as she played on the pianoforte. Miss Dunmore was a real beauty, and he found her quietly charming now that she had recovered from her shyness at her come-out ball. Her mother watched from a distance, clearly gratified that he was appreciating her daughter's accomplished playing.

Ross Parmiter's sister—the newly betrothed one Colin had befriended last year—was in London with her mother and Miss Eglington, her future sister-in-law, to shop for bride clothes. Colin accompanied them all to a portrait gallery one afternoon and then to Gunter's for ices. Miss Eglington was an amiable, modest young lady. The ladies were expecting to be in town for a few weeks, she told him when he asked. He looked forward to seeing her again.

He attended a couple more balls during those two weeks and waltzed with Elizabeth at each. He enjoyed those sets more than any others. She was lovely to dance with, and she was lovely to *be* with. He could converse with her—or not—without any self-consciousness or mind-searching for a suitable topic. Since neither waltz was the supper dance, though, he did find himself missing the chance to converse with her at greater length.

On the afternoon following the second of the two balls, he walked around to the house on South Audley Street, hoping to find the ladies at home, though he knew Wren and Alexander had not arrived in town yet. They were there, though Mrs. Westcott was busy entertaining Mrs. Radley, her sister-in-law, and two other older ladies. When Colin asked Elizabeth if she would like a walk in Hyde Park, she seemed happy to oblige.

"I could see a beautiful afternoon waste away beyond the window," she said after they had stepped outside and she had taken his arm.

They strolled along the bank of the Serpentine—they and what seemed like a hundred other people. The sunshine sparkled off the water, and children were at play on the bank, some of them sailing toy boats, a few being called away by anxious nurses, others trailing their hands in the water.

"Hoping to catch fish," Colin said.

"Or fascinated by the way their hands change size and shape underwater," she said. "How much fun children have exploring their world." She smiled as she watched, and it seemed to Colin that she looked wistful.

"What happened to your own?" he asked her, and wished he could recall the question even before she turned her head and looked at him with raised eyebrows. "You told me you miscarried twice."

Drat his unguarded tongue—something that seemed to happen only with her. It was a horribly intimate question to have asked. He could feel himself flush. They had stepped off the main path to be closer to the water. Fortunately there was no one really close by. Even so . . .

"The first time was quite soon after I discovered I was with child," she said. "The second time was different. He came early. Too early. He could almost live on his own but not quite. He died. Or he never lived. Not outside the womb, anyway. He had lived inside me. I felt him all the time."

"He?" he said softly.

"Yes," she said. "He."

He tried to frame an apology, but it was eras too late by now. She was not visibly agitated. Indeed, she was almost uncannily controlled. But there seemed to be a world of pain in her chosen pronoun—*he*, not *it*.

"They were both accidents," she said.

But there was something in the way she said it that chilled him. Something defensive. There was something worse in her choice of word—*accidents*.

"Were they?" he said.

"The second one certainly was," she said. "I fell downstairs. I broke my arm and lost my child."

She . . . broke her arm. How many times had she broken it, for the love of God?

"And went home to your mother and brother," he said softly.

"Yes," she said. "I lost the child there a few days later."

"Elizabeth—"

"Don't," she said, drawing him onto the path and turning to walk back in the direction of home. "It *was* an accident, the falling downstairs. I was trying to get away from him and I was going too fast. He did not push me."

And the first time?

"You went home to your father the first time?" he asked.

"Yes," she said. "But he did not know about my . . . condition. No one did but the two of us. It was too early. I had only just found out."

She did not explain exactly when her first miscarriage happened or how closely connected it was to her reason for running home. But she did not need to. There obviously *was* a connection. Oh dear God, Elizabeth!

"I am so sorry I pried," he said. "And how inadequate any sort of apology is. I have no right to know."

"And I had no right to say anything," she said, frowning. "And to a near stranger, and a man at that. I do not know why I did. Forgive me. The second time everything was explained as a tragic accident—as indeed it was. I saw a physician in London after I had recovered, and he assured me that I could still have children. That was seven years ago. But . . . Oh, this is *such* an inappropriate conversation. Let us talk about something else. You must know that you have become the most eligible bachelor in town."

"I do feel a bit besieged," he admitted. "And a bit humbled. There are many very sweet young ladies in town, Elizabeth."

"But who is special among them?" she asked. "Your name is often coupled with Miss Dunmore's. *Is* she special? And who else?"

"Miss Madson is more sensible," he said. "And Miss

Eglington is more modest. And . . . Well, I could go on. No one feels special to the exclusion of all others. Perhaps I am too difficult to please, which would suggest a horrible arrogance in me. I do not suppose I am particularly special to anyone either." He paused and sighed. "I have a dream, Elizabeth, of having a family like yours. I want to celebrate a Christmas like last year's with my own family, even though it is much smaller. I have a mother and three sisters, each of whom has a spouse. There are children. Yet it does not function like a family and I am not sure it ever can. Indeed, I am pretty sure it cannot. Certainly it cannot if I do not work very hard at bringing it about. And that involves choosing the right wife. But what young woman fresh from the schoolroom could possibly deal with . . . well, with my mother."

She drew breath to speak but did not do so, perhaps because there was nothing to say.

"But enough of me," he said, "How about you? Codaire seems to be a definite beau. He has a proprietary air when he is close to you. Is he special, Elizabeth?"

"He is very attentive," she said. "It is flattering."

But she had not said he was special.

And then he saw the carriage that had just driven through the park gates onto the main driveway—white and gold and ornate and pulled by four white horses. Like a fairy carriage conveying a fairy queen to and from her fairy palace.

"Lady Hodges," Elizabeth said.

"Yes," he said. His mother—just as though his words of a few moments ago had summoned her.

They were some distance away, and there were plenty of other conveyances and pedestrians to hide among. There were four outriders, two on each side of the carriage, black horses ridden by young men clad in black. Good God. Oh good God. It was like a circus parade. He could die of embarrassment. And the whole entourage was attracting attention, as it always did. Though he understood that her public appearances were rare these days.

Colin had seen his mother occasionally during the past five years since she always spent the months of the Season in London. It had always been from a distance, however. He had not come face to face with her or spoken with her since just after his father's funeral when he was eighteen. He had decided then that he never wished to see her or speak with her again. He had tried to cut all ties with her, to forget her, to carry on with his own life without her. It could not be done indefinitely, of course. Not when he was the only remaining son, Baron Hodges of Roxingley, head of the family, owner of all the property and possessor of the fortune. And there was always gossip, some of which inevitably reached his ears—as in that letter of complaint after Christmas. There was also his conscience, which whispered to him that she was his *mother*, and a son ought to honor his parent.

His mother had always been sociable to the exclusion of all else in life. She had always loved to surround herself with people, mostly young, mostly men, who admired her and paid lavish homage to her beauty. There had been rumors of lovers—Lord Ede, for example, who was still a faithful member of her court though he was no longer young—but Colin had never known, or wanted to know, the truth of the matter. She had always loved to amuse herself with large house parties in the country, and sometimes he and his brother and sisters—with the exception of Wren— were brought down from the nursery floor to be displayed for the admiration of the guests. The guests themselves,

Colin had understood after he grew up, were not always or even often chosen from among the most respectable elements of society.

Times had changed, of course. She now avoided balls and any entertainments at which she would be exposed to the raw and unflattering light of chandeliers. Rather, she chose places and occasions at which she could be staged in dim and flattering light and keep herself at some remove from those who gazed upon her. The theater and the opera were among her favorite venues. There she could arrive late, after everyone else was already seated, make a grand entrance, and sit in her private box, where she would be seen from some distance. She was always accompanied by young men who vied with one another for the privilege of waiting upon her. And almost always she had Blanche attendant upon her—Colin's eldest sister—with Sir Nelson Elwood, her husband. Blanche was an essential part of the tableau—blond and exquisitely lovely, but not more lovely than her mother. And, from a distance, often looking the older of the two.

On one occasion Colin had witnessed the spectacle before fleeing. She had caused a stir. For though she must now be close to sixty or even past it, she had looked like a girl. Even from a distance, however, it had been obvious to him that the blond hair, puffed and curled and ringleted, was not her own, and that the youthful color in her cheeks and on her lips and the dark luster of her long eyelashes owed more to cosmetics, heavily applied, than to nature. Even the eyelashes themselves had been noticeably fake. The notice she had inspired, mostly from men in the pit—cheers, whistles, catcalls, courtly bows, and kisses blown from fingertips— had held as much mockery as genuine homage. Or so it had seemed to her mortified son. For she had looked like a caricature of a young girl rather than the real thing.

And on rare occasions, as today, she rode in her carriage in the park at the fashionable hour, sumptuously clad all in white, her face veiled as she wafted a hand in greeting to acquaintances and even received a favored few at the open window. Blanche was usually at her side.

He did not know if she was today. The carriage drove on by without slowing, and Colin drew a deep breath of relief.

"You are entirely estranged?" Elizabeth asked.

"We have not spoken or come face to face for eight years," he said. "Soon after the guests had left the house following my father's funeral, at which she had been swathed in black, she appeared in the drawing room in her customary white, demanding that I help her write invitations to a house party. She needed cheering up, she told me when I protested. And when I asked her how it would look if she held one of her house parties so soon after my father's death, she patted my cheek as though I were still a child and told me I was a sweet innocent. It was what everyone would expect of her, she told me. She was certainly not going to lose a year of her life and her youth dressed in black and going about with a long face and living in a silent house. I tried to lay down the law, but the law, it seemed, was not on my side. I was Lord Hodges of Roxingley, possessor of all that went with the title, but I was also a minor. Three guardians would see to it that for the following three years I lived my life wisely—according to what my mother considered wise, I understood. So I did what an eighteen-year-old would do. I washed my hands of the whole thing and left home, never to return."

"Except that now you intend to do just that," she said as they crossed the road and made their way along South Audley Street.

"It will not be easy," he said.

"Will you come in?" she asked when they reached the house.

"I will not, thank you" he said. "I have taken enough of your time. I am sorry if I upset you by stirring up old memories. And there is no *if* about it, is there? I ought to have used the word *that*. I am sorry that I upset you. And I am sorry I ever made the mistake of thinking your serenity indicated a woman who had never known any great trouble in her life. I have much to learn. I wonder you put up with me."

She set her hand in his and he raised it to his lips.

"I do it because you care," she said. "You could so easily be arrogant, Colin. You have everything from which arrogance often springs. But you care for others. Even, I think, your mother. You cannot simply ride roughshod over her and impose your will now that you are able, can you? Instead, you look for a solution that will suit everyone, your mother and your future wife included."

"I suppose it really cannot be done, can it?" he said ruefully. "Are some problems just without solution, Elizabeth?"

"I do not know," she said. "That is too hard a question. Thank you for the walk. Thank you for listening. Colin . . ." She hesitated. "Choose someone you can *really* care for. Someone you can love. Not just someone you believe capable of filling the role of baroness."

"And yet," he said, smiling at her, "you would choose with your head only and no reference to your heart."

"My case is different from yours," she told him.

"Because you are elderly and past the age for love and romance?" he asked.

She laughed softly. "Something like that," she said.

"You can be so foolish sometimes," he said, "despite your experience and superior wisdom. You are not elderly or even close. And you were made for love. And probably even romance."

"And laughter and joy?" she said, and he remembered using those two words with her at the Dunmore ball.

"Yes, and those too," he said. "Please do not do something you will forever regret just because you believe life has passed you by."

Surely she would regret marrying Codaire. He was a dry old stick, to say the least. Though perhaps he was just the man for her. What did he know? All he did know was that he wanted her to find and experience all the good things life had to offer. If *he* were Codaire, he would spread the moon and stars and everything that was bright in the universe beneath her feet.

He kissed the back of her hand again and took his leave of her. He waited until she had been admitted to the house and then made his way back along the street. If Overfield were still alive, he thought, it would give him the greatest pleasure to confront him. His uncontrollable drinking had been a sickness, Elizabeth believed. Perhaps it had. But she was too kind in her judgment. Nothing—*nothing*—could excuse him for his abuse of his wife. Nothing could excuse him for killing her two children while they were still in her womb.

Good God almighty. Elizabeth!

He was not worthy to kiss the hem of her garments.

"I was unfortunately mistaken," Lord Ede said, flicking open the lid of his snuffbox and preparing to take a pinch. "I was off by one day."

"Wrong is wrong, Ede," Lady Hodges said, her sweet voice sounding a little petulant. "And now I will have to go out two days in a row. It is very inconvenient. And it will be remarked upon."

"But of course it will. The *ton* will be in raptures," he said. "How often are you seen twice in as many days?"

She gestured away with a slender white hand the fan one young gentleman was wafting before her face. "You are quite sure it is tomorrow, Ede?"

"Quite," he said. "Weather permitting, I daresay. The delectable Miss Dunmore. At the fashionable hour. In his curricle."

"*Is* she delectable?" she asked. "Quite flawlessly beautiful? The most sought-after beauty of the Season?"

"It is being said," he told her, one hand hovering over his snuffbox while he appeared to concentrate upon its contents, "that she is more lovely than anyone else this Season or last Season or indeed any Season all the way back to . . . When was it you made your own come-out?"

"A few years ago," she said.

"All the way back to a few years ago, then," he said before setting a pinch of snuff on the back of his hand and sniffing it up each nostril.

"Everyone said when I made my come-out that my beauty was unsurpassed in living memory," she said. "Some said it would remain unsurpassed for many years to come."

Lord Ede sneezed into his handkerchief. "They were right," he told her.

The young man with the fan and the one on the other side of her chair who held her lace-edged handkerchief lest she have need of it murmured agreement.

"But she is beautiful, this Miss Dunmore?" she asked. "And he has been seen paying court to her a number of times? And is to take her driving in the park tomorrow? And he really, truly is in search of a bride, Ede?"

"Let me see," Lord Ede said. "Four questions, all with the same answer. A simple yes. Would I make a mistake or tell a lie?"

"You were mistaken today," she reminded him. "He was in the park. I caught a glimpse of him. Did I not, Blanche? But not with anyone who could possibly have been Miss Dunmore or any other eligible young lady. I recognized her. She was that faded creature. Riverdale's sister. Blanche?"

"Lady Overfield, Mother," Blanche said.

"Lady Overfield," Lady Hodges repeated. "Why would he so waste his time when he is in search of a bride?" She drummed the perfectly manicured fingers of one hand on the pink velvet arm of her pink velvet chair and looked about her pink-hued drawing room with dissatisfaction. "No company today when there might have been after all. And now tomorrow's gathering will have to be canceled. Because my son is choosing a bride and must be steered in the right direction. He must pick the most beautiful girl there is. I can allow no less. It would be too lowering. And after he marries her, Blanche, we will be a trio of beauties and hold court here and at Roxingley. I daresay we will be famous."

"You must mean *more* famous," Lord Ede said. "If that is possible."

"I daresay I do," Lady Hodges agreed sweetly. "And I suppose people will flatter me, as they always do, and pretend to believe that Miss Dunmore must be my sister."

"Indeed," his lordship agreed.

"Your *older* sister," the young man with the handkerchief murmured.

"And my dearest Colin will be back in the fold at last," she said, her eyes dreamy. "He was always more handsome than Justin. But more wayward. I have given him rein, but now he will return. How lovely it is going to be. A late spring wedding at St. George's and a grand summer house party at Roxingley."

"Are they not all grand?" Lord Ede asked. "With you presiding?"

"Grander," she said. "This will be a party everyone will talk about for years, Ede, and everyone will know it in advance and clamor for invitations."

"It is to be hoped," he said, "that I will be the recipient of one of them without having to clamor?"

"You ought not," she said, turning her eyes upon him and looking at him critically. "You are growing old, Ede—lined face, white hair. I wish you would color your hair and use some discreet cosmetics. However, you are still handsome. *Distinguished* is the word I believe people use."

"We are not all ageless as you are ageless," he said, making her a mock bow.

"True," she said. "You must go away now. I am tired of you. And I must go and rest before dinner. I would not wish to look hagged even though I am not entertaining tonight."

"Hagged?" The young gentleman with the handkerchief sounded shocked.

"Impossible," his counterpart with the fan muttered.

Lord Ede took his leave.

Nine

Sir Geoffrey Codaire was attentive whenever he and Elizabeth met. Sometimes they did so by chance, as on Bond Street one afternoon when she and her mother were shopping and he persuaded them to join him for tea and cakes at a nearby tearoom. Sometimes they met by design, as when he escorted her to a dinner one evening with a neighbor of his from the country who was in town for a few days with his wife. He was at all the balls she attended and danced with her at each.

Elizabeth always found him courteous, and predictable. He never made a nuisance of himself. He did not keep her and her mother longer than half an hour at the tearoom, since he knew they had more shopping to do before they returned home. He came for her promptly on the evening of the dinner and returned her at a timely hour. He never asked for a second dance at a ball, though sometimes he came to stand with her when she was not dancing with someone else. More and more she felt that marrying him would be the sensible thing to do if he asked again.

She did meet someone else. One evening Aunt Lilian, her mother's sister-in-law, introduced her to Mr. Franck at a private concert, and he sat by her and engaged her in conversation between performances. He fetched her refreshments during the intermission while her mother and aunt went to talk with mutual friends on the other side of the room. He was a widower of three years with two boys away at school. The younger had joined his brother there just this year, leaving his father feeling restless. Hence his decision to spend a month or two in London, something he had not done for a number of years. He was a pleasant-looking man about her own age, Elizabeth estimated, with an amiable disposition and an unassuming air.

He called on her two afternoons later, the day after she went walking with Colin. Mr. and Mrs. Latchwick, neighbors from Kent, were there too, and Mr. Franck made himself agreeable to them all until Sir Geoffrey Codaire was announced. Soon after that Mr. Franck rose to take his leave after inquiring if Lady Overfield intended being at Lady Arbinger's ball that evening and asking, when she had replied in the affirmative, if she would do him the honor of reserving the opening set for him.

Sir Geoffrey took tea before asking Elizabeth if she would drive in the park with him later, during the fashionable hour. She hesitated, as there was the ball during the evening and it had already been a bit of a busy afternoon. But it was a beautiful day again and she had not set foot out of doors all day.

"That would be pleasant," she said. "Thank you."

He returned promptly at the appointed hour and handed her up into his curricle outside her door.

"What a lovely day it is," she said as they set out for the park close by.

"It is," he agreed. "The Latchwicks appear to be an amiable couple."

"They are," she told him. "We are very fortunate in all our neighbors at Riddings Park."

"Having friendly neighbors is indeed important," he said. "I am also fortunate in that regard. Franck seems a pleasant enough fellow too. I understand he has been lonely since the death of his wife and is a bit fragile."

"Fragile?" She raised her eyebrows.

"It is the very word with which he was described to me by the wife of an acquaintance of mine," he told her. "It would be regrettable if any lady were to toy with his feelings, since he fancies himself in need of a new wife. The lady who spoke of him is of the firm belief, however, that he is not ready for remarriage yet, if he ever will be, poor man. Apparently he doted upon his wife."

Elizabeth frowned as they drove toward Hyde Park and turned between the gates. Why had he said that? As a warning? So that she would not hurt Mr. Franck? So that she would guard against his hurting *her* since he did not have a whole heart to offer? So that she would not marry another man and leave *him* disappointed?

He turned his head and looked sharply at her, perhaps alerted by her silence. "I have just been listening to the echo of my own words," he said. "They made me sound like a jealous fool. I do beg your pardon. I am no such thing. At least, I am not *jealous*. You must decide if I am a fool."

"That is the last word by which I would describe you," she said.

"Thank you," he said. "That is a relief to hear."

She laughed.

They spent the next twenty minutes or so driving slowly about the circuit that was always crowded with carriages and horses and pedestrians at this time of day, greeting acquaintances and friends, stopping to exchange more than just a few words with some of them, listening to tidbits of news and gossip. Elizabeth promised two more sets for the evening's ball.

"If I do not speak up promptly," Sir Geoffrey said as he drew his curricle away from the crowds, "I may discover this evening that your card is too full to accommodate me. Will you keep the first waltz for me, Lady Overfield?"

She hesitated for only a moment. "I am afraid I promised it a while ago," she said.

"Ah," he said. "The second, then?"

"Yes," she said. "I shall certainly reserve that one for you and will look forward to it."

He sighed. "I wish I did not always have to come second even in waiting to waltz with you," he said. "Is it to young Hodges you have promised the first tonight? He seems to enjoy waltzing with you. I suppose there are not enough young ladies who have been approved to dance it."

But he was distracted at that moment, and she was rather startled to see the distinctive white coach and horses with the black outriders approaching. Sir Geoffrey was forced to pull his curricle almost right off the roadway. Elizabeth caught a glimpse of the white-veiled figure of Lady Hodges. What? Two days in a row?

"For one moment," Sir Geoffrey said when the carriage and its entourage had passed, "I thought it must be the prince regent approaching."

"No," she said. "Just Lady Hodges."

"Ah," he said. "The famous eccentric. And mother of Lady Riverdale. And Lord Hodges."

"Yes," she said.

He turned the curricle onto a quieter avenue, though she was in a bit of a hurry to get home with the ball to prepare for this evening. He slowed his pace and she understood what was coming. She was not sure she was ready. But when would she be if not now?

"I asked you last year if I might still dare hope," he said. "You did not answer me then and I chose to believe that I *could* hope. Tell me now if you would prefer me not to continue."

The time had come, then, and there could be no more procrastinating. If she did indeed tell him she would prefer that he said no more, she must also add that her answer would never change. She could not keep him dangling forever. It would be vastly unfair to him. He deserved better.

And she had reasoned this out with herself all winter and more recently here in London after seeing him again and spending some time in his company. She could not do better. He was all she could ever ask for in a husband—except that there was no spark of romance in their relationship. No romantic love. There had been both in her first marriage, but look where that had got her.

You can be so foolish sometimes . . . you were made for love . . . do not do something you will forever regret. She could almost hear Colin say those words to her just yesterday.

"I shall not tell you not to continue," she said.

He turned to look into her face. "I may proceed, then?" he asked her. "*Will* you marry me? I have been devoted to you all these long years. I will remain devoted for the rest of my life."

It was the most ardent he had ever sounded, and Elizabeth felt a moment's panic. But she had gone too far now to retreat. And she knew that when she had time to think about it later, she would be satisfied that she had done the right thing. Her future would be settled. She would soon be a married lady again with her own home and the hope of a child of her own. Perhaps children. Life was offering her a second chance and she would be foolish indeed not to take it. And this time she would not be rushing into it, stars in her eyes and foolishness in her heart—despite what Colin had said.

"I will," she said. "I would be honored to be your wife, Sir Geoffrey."

He continued to gaze at her. It was a good thing the roadway ahead of them was deserted.

"You will not be sorry," he said. "You will be mine, and I will take good care of you, Elizabeth. *May* I have the privilege of calling you that?"

"Of course." She smiled at him. "And I shall take care of you . . . Geoffrey."

"I believe," he said, "we ought to return to South Audley Street without further ado to seek your mother's blessing. Will she give it, do you believe?"

"I do," she said. "She thinks well of you."

"And Riverdale?" he asked. "Will he give his blessing?"

She was not sure Alex would be delighted. He had a romantic soul. He had almost found himself having to renounce that a year ago when circumstances seemed to be compelling him to seek a wealthy bride at the cost of love. Fortunately—*very* fortunately—he had found both wealth and love with Wren.

Well, she too had had her chance at love and it had not served her well. Alex knew that. He would be pleased, she believed, that this time she would be assured of being treated well and would know security and contentment.

"Of course he will," she said. "He will trust the wisdom of my choice."

"Then I am the happiest of men," he said, seizing the first opportunity to change direction in order to take her home. "Even if I cannot have the first waltz with you this evening."

It was the closest she could ever remember his coming to making a joke. It endeared him to her.

But she hated the way her heart ached a little bit when she thought of the man with whom she would share that dance.

Colin had just driven into the park and joined the circuit, Miss Dunmore beside him, when he saw Codaire's curricle drive away in the opposite direction. Elizabeth was with him, and Colin regretted missing paying his respects to her. However, if she was at tonight's ball he would waltz with her and find out if he had seriously discomposed her by drawing out those confidences yesterday about the loss of her children. He had certainly discomposed himself. He had had bizarre dreams and even a few nightmares last night.

He drew himself back to the present in order to give his attention to his companion. They had come where they would see and be seen while they nodded and chatted with friends and acquaintances, and he was perhaps taking one step closer to making his choice. Perhaps it was just as well. Perhaps he needed a nudge in the right direction. The only trouble was—what *was* the right direction?

"Oh look," Miss Dunmore said, pointing to the road Codaire had just taken. "It looks like a fairy coach."

And Colin knew himself trapped. His mother was out

driving in the park for the second day in a row, and she was about to join the crowd. It was going to be impossible to avoid her. He could hardly spring his horses when other vehicles and people on horseback were close packed about them. And there would be no hiding in the crowd. It soon became clear to him and to a few dozen other people that the white carriage was making its deliberate way toward his curricle. Despite its size and the presence of four outriders accompanying it—or perhaps because of those facts—everyone gave way before it. It would have been quite extraordinary if it were not for the fact that this sort of thing happened all the time with his mother.

And so he came face to face with her for the first time in eight years. One slender white-gloved hand rested upon the window, which had been lowered. Her head and face were covered with a fine white lace veil. She was alone in the carriage.

"My dearest," she said in the sweet little-girl voice he remembered so well. "What a delightful surprise to find you here in the park on the very day when I came to take the air. You may present your young lady to me."

It was, of course, not a surprise at all. She had planned this. But how had she known? Foolish question. His mother always knew everything, though some mistake must have been made to bring her out yesterday.

"Miss Dunmore," he said with the greatest reluctance, "Lady Hodges, my mother."

Miss Dunmore was blushing and saucer-eyed—and looking lovelier than ever—as she acknowledged the introduction.

"Very pretty," his mother said, her eyes fixed upon the girl through the veil. "Exquisitely lovely, in fact. And the daughter of Sir Randolph Dunmore, whose lineage is quite impeccable as is that of his wife. You must bring Miss Dunmore to see me, dearest. Come for tea one day soon. It is gratifying to discover that you have an unerring eye for beauty, but it is only what I would expect of my son, of course."

Good God. Oh good God. He could think of not a blessed thing to say. And of course the crowds were packed closely enough around them that any number of people would have overheard every word—and would gladly share with those who had not. This would keep drawing room conversations lively for the next day or two.

"I will not keep you longer, my dears," she said when neither he nor Miss Dunmore spoke. "Young couples must be left to each other's company." She tapped her hand against the outside of her carriage, and it moved off, a path again opening like magic before it, with a little help from the outriders.

Colin closed his eyes briefly. His mother had come to this very public venue, then, to place her stamp of approval upon his courtship of Miss Dunmore. To force his hand. To raise expectations in her bosom and that of her mama when the incident was reported to her. His mother had always been expert at manipulating people in whom she had a certain interest, and she was doing it now, after having been seemingly content to live without him for eight years. She had decided to step into his affairs before he could step into hers.

"How beautiful she is," Miss Dunmore said, sounding awestruck as the carriage disappeared from sight. "But I do not understand how she can possibly be your *mother*. She must have been awfully young when she had you." She did not know, it seemed, about his four older siblings, three of them considerably older.

My dearest.

. . . your young lady.

It is gratifying to discover that you have an unerring eye for beauty.

And the voice. Oh, the youthful, honeyed voice.

The opening set had already begun when Colin arrived at the ball that evening. He was late, thanks to lively dinner conversation with friends at White's. Well, and perhaps there had been a bit of avoidance involved too. He had somehow managed when he took Miss Dunmore home earlier not to allow himself to be maneuvered into soliciting her hand for the first set and so sending an even more pointed message than he had already sent. He had left her excitedly recounting to her mama their meeting with his mother.

He danced the second set with a young lady introduced to him by Lady Arbinger, and the one after that with Lady Jessica Archer, who always seemed delighted to see him while it was clear she was in no way romantically attached to him—or to anyone else for that matter. She talked to him about the marriage mart with some disgust.

"I resent been looked upon as a commodity, Lord Hodges," she said. "And I am vastly relieved that you do not look at me that way. Or anyone else as far as I have observed. You are a true gentleman."

The first waltz of the evening came next. He had seen Elizabeth as soon as he stepped inside the ballroom, wearing her primrose ball gown again and looking as fresh as springtime, her cheeks flushed, her eyes sparkling as she danced with Codaire. Colin had felt a bit ashamed of expressing his doubts about her choice yesterday when he had taken her walking. It was really none of his business whom she married. How was he to know what or who would make her happy?

She was standing now over by the French windows with her mother and an animated group of people whom Mrs. Westcott introduced to him when he approached as her brother and sister-in-law and her niece and nephew with the niece's husband. He already had a nodding acquaintance with the latter two gentlemen. Elizabeth was still sparkling, though it seemed to Colin that some of her animation dimmed when he turned to her and asked if he might have the honor of the next set.

Perhaps he really had offended her.

"Yes," she said. "That would be lovely. Thank you."

"I have looked forward to this moment all day," he told her quite truthfully when they had stepped out onto the dance floor.

She smiled at him. But . . . was there a little restraint in the smile? Or was he reading something into it that was not there?

"Did I say anything to offend you yesterday?" he asked her. "Forgive me if I did. I am sure you know better than I what you ought to do with the rest of your life."

"I was not offended," she said. "But I apologize for what I said too. You must choose whom you wish to marry, Colin, without being besieged by advice from someone who presumes to think she knows better who will suit you."

"My mother came to the park again today," he told her. "She came deliberately to see me—and to express for my ears and those of a significant number of the *ton* her approval of my courtship of Miss Dunmore." Over her shoulder he could see that Codaire had joined Mrs. Westcott and her brother and sister-in-law. Presumably he did not intend to waltz himself. "How she knew about us or the fact that we were going to be there today, I have no idea. I wonder if she expected to find us there yesterday."

"Oh, were you there today?" she asked. "I saw Lady Hodges. I was with Sir Geoffrey Codaire."

"Yes," he said. "You were driving away as we were arriving."

"But are you courting Miss Dunmore?" she asked.

"I very much fear I may be now," he said.

"You fear?" She raised her eyebrows.

But the orchestra played a decisive chord at that moment and he took her in his arms and ignored the question. For the next several minutes he did not want to think about Miss Dunmore or marriage or his future as a more assertive Lord Hodges. They moved into the steps of the waltz.

"I have longed for this since the last ball," he said after a minute or two had passed. "Dare I hope you have too?" He was smiling, trying to recapture the usual comfort he felt with her. Somehow it was eluding him. She seemed a bit . . . absent.

She hesitated slightly before answering. "Yes, I have," she said. "You are lovely to waltz with, Colin."

"And would you miss our dance if ever you were at a ball and I was not?" he asked her, persisting in foolishness.

There was definite hesitation now.

"Colin," she said as he twirled her about one corner of the ballroom, "it is unofficial at the moment. No announcement will be made until after Alex and Wren arrive in town within the next day or two and a few letters have been written. But I am betrothed."

He felt a bit as though someone had taken a hammer to his heart. He actually lost his breath for a moment. But of course she was. This was why she had come to town for the

Season, and the Season was already a few weeks old. He had known. He had been expecting it.

"Codaire?" he asked.

"Sir Geoffrey Codaire, yes," she said. "He asked me this afternoon and I said yes."

This afternoon.

He forced himself to smile. "And you are happy?"

"Yes, I am," she said. "It is what I have wanted."

"Then I will wish you lifelong happiness," he said. "With a man you can trust to care for you as you deserve to be cared for."

"Thank you," she said. "I will wish you the same, Colin. With Miss Dunmore, if it is she whom you choose. Or with someone else. I hope you will find the happiness you deserve."

"Do we always get what we deserve?" he asked her before drawing her a little closer in order to avoid a collision.

"No," she said. "Life is not always so tidy. But Alex and Wren have the happiness they deserve, and now I have. I am confident you will too."

"You are able to foretell the future, then, are you?" he asked.

"Oh, by no means," she said. "Thank goodness. But I am ever hopeful for the people I love." An arrested look came into her eyes then, followed by obvious embarrassment and a deepening of the flush in her cheeks.

. . . the people I love.

"I do love you, you know," she said. "I could not love you more if you really were my brother, Colin."

Ah. He smiled at her a little ruefully, and she smiled back as they fell silent and enjoyed the rest of the waltz. Determinedly enjoyed. Did not really enjoy at all. Perhaps it was their last. He was not sure she would want to do this again. He was not sure he could.

I could not love you more if you really were my brother.

Why did the words hurt just a little bit?

Codaire was still with her mother and family group when the dance was over. Colin extended a hand to him. "I understand I am to congratulate you," he said. "You are a fortunate man."

Codaire took his hand but did not return his smile. "I am indeed," he said. "Our news is to be shared with just a select few, you will understand, until Lady Overfield's brother and my family have been informed."

Too late Colin realized he should have made no mention of the betrothal since he could not lay claim to being one of a *select few*.

"Your secret is safe with me," he said.

"Lord Hodges is Wren's brother," Elizabeth said simultaneously, "and therefore very nearly my brother too."

Codaire released Colin's hand.

"The announcement will be made soon, Lord Hodges," Mrs. Westcott said. "It cannot be soon enough for me. There must be a betrothal party, of course, and there will be the wedding to plan. I have already informed Sir Geoffrey that his preferences will scarcely be consulted. Wedding preparations belong exclusively to the bride's family." Her eyes were twinkling, and she looked for the moment quite like her daughter.

"And I have informed you, ma'am," Codaire said, "that you will hear no argument from me, provided Elizabeth will be my wife at the end of it all."

Colin felt distinctly out of place as the family members all laughed and gazed fondly from Elizabeth to Codaire and back again. He made his bow and walked away. Actually he did not stop walking until he was outside the ball-room, and then he paused only long enough to decide that he had no wish whatsoever to step back in there. He proceeded on his way downstairs, early though it still was, retrieved his hat and cloak from a footman, and left the house. He was thankful that he had walked here and did not have to wait for a carriage to be brought around.

So Elizabeth was betrothed to the man of her choice.

He was happy for her.

Miss Dunmore was at that ball. So was Miss Madson. He paused on the pavement for a moment. But no, he had not solicited the hand of either in advance for a set at tonight's ball and therefore was under no obligation to stay. There was a difference, of course, between obligation and expectation, and he was in no doubt that Lady Dunmore in particular expected him to dance with her daughter after what had happened in the park this afternoon.

Ought he to go back, then?

There was no reason on earth why he should not. Elizabeth had told him about her betrothal because he was a close family connection, and it was surely perfectly natural that he should congratulate Codaire after the set was over. The man's obvious annoyance was understandable, perhaps, but not something dire enough to send Colin scurrying away as though he had committed some unpardonable social faux pas.

So she was betrothed. He was happy for her. He really was.

And he had his own courtships to pursue. Plural? Or had they now become singular? What powerful beings mothers were—his own and Miss Dunmore's.

Yes, he really ought to go back.

He walked away.

Ten

Alexander and Wren arrived in town the following day, and for several minutes, as might be expected, all the focus was upon the baby, whom Mrs. Westcott had not seen since a week after his birth and Elizabeth had not seen at all. But finally he was taken up to the nursery for a well-earned rest and Elizabeth was able to tell her brother and sister-in-law of her engagement.

Wren, who had never met Sir Geoffrey Codaire, declared with a warm hug for Elizabeth that if he had won her heart, then she was going to love him as a brother. But Alexander remembered that his sister had rejected Codaire just last year and wondered why she had changed her mind this year.

"I was not at all sure at the time that I wished to remarry at all," Elizabeth explained. "But I gave it careful thought through the summer and over the winter, particularly at Christmas when all the family was together at Brambledean. And I decided that I did. I thought about Geoffrey then and his many good qualities. I thought I could not do better—*if* he renewed his addresses this year, that was. But he had told me he might."

"Then I am pleased for you, Lizzie," her brother said, though he still did not look quite convinced.

The official announcement of the betrothal appeared in the morning papers the next day, and it brought a stream of visitors during the afternoon—all of them family except for Sir Geoffrey himself. Elizabeth's Aunt Lilian and Uncle Richard Radley, her mother's sister-in-law and brother, came with Susan and Alvin Cole, their daughter and son-in-law, though they had all already heard the news at the Arbinger ball. The Dowager Countess of Riverdale came with Lady Matilda Westcott. Like Alexander and Wren, they had arrived in London only the day before. Thomas and Mildred, Lord and Lady Molenor, came—without their three boys, who were away at school. So did Louise, Dowager Duchess of Netherby, with Jessica, and Avery and Anna, Duke and Duchess of Netherby.

"I warned you the family would be in full evidence as soon as word was out," Elizabeth murmured to Sir Geoffrey when he arrived, the last to come. Her eyes twinkled in amusement.

"It pleases me," he told her, keeping his voice low too. "For your sake and for mine too. There is less likelihood that you will change your mind again."

Again? Had she changed it before, then? She supposed she had. Last year's no had changed to this year's yes. "Have I been so fickle?" she asked him.

"If you have," he said, his eyes looking very directly into hers, "those days are fortunately over."

They were permitted no more private words. The family took over, and Elizabeth sat back to listen. She had always been amused when the Westcott family gathered to plot and plan as she described it to herself. It had started with Anna three years ago, when she had arrived from Bath, summoned from the orphanage where she had grown up and then taught. She had been greeted by the announcement to both her and the entire Westcott clan simultaneously that she was not only the daughter of the recently deceased Humphrey Westcott, Earl of Riverdale, but was also his only legitimate child. He had, they all learned, secretly married Anna's mother and then left her, but she had still been alive when he married Viola. The rest of the family had heard the news that Viola's three children were all hence illegitimate at the same time Anna had.

Consternation on that occasion had quickly given place to numerous plotting and planning sessions as the family grappled with the twin gigantic questions of what to do about Anna and what to do about Viola and her children. Avery had solved the problem of Anna by marrying her, while Viola and her children had solved—or would solve— their own problems. But none of that deterred the family from gathering when anything new, either happy or potentially catastrophic, appeared on the horizon. For while they perhaps did not provide actual solutions for anyone, their mere assembly seemed to offer what everyone needed most in these situations, mutual support and understanding.

Now it was Elizabeth's turn, and the Westcott family numbers were swelled by her maternal relatives, who all had opinions too. She sat back to await developments. She did not particularly want a betrothal party, but she had no real objection either. She did not particularly want a grand wedding at St. George's, but if that was what would make everyone happy, then she was prepared to give them what they wanted. A large wedding did not seem quite appropriate, perhaps, when this would be her second marriage, but she must remember that it would be Geoffrey's first.

There was some discussion over whether the betrothal party would be a mere soiree or whether it would include some dancing. The drawing room would not be large enough for dancing, Cousin Susan pointed out.

"But the ballroom would," Wren said.

"Then it would not be a party but a ball," Cousin Matilda remarked.

Elizabeth turned her head to exchange a look of amusement with Geoffrey. At least, there was amusement on her part. He looked gravely back at her, and she wondered if he was feeling a bit overwhelmed. She regretted for one unguarded moment that there was not some spark of romantic love between them, or at least that instant understanding there sometimes was between two people who were very close.

As between her and Colin, for example.

But thinking about Colin made her feel inexplicably melancholy. She had the strange feeling she had hurt him last evening during their waltz when she had told him she was betrothed, though that was absurd, of course. Why *hurt*? He had known she was half expecting a proposal and that she intended to accept it. He himself was in search of a wife and had already singled out a number of potential candidates. He had definitely been embarrassed by Geoffrey's annoyance that he knew about the betrothal when they had agreed to keep quiet about it to all except close family members until after the official announcement. That had been her fault, of course.

Elizabeth's thoughts had wandered. Geoffrey caught her eye again, and he half shrugged as she picked up the drift of the conversation.

The betrothal celebration, predictably, was no longer a party but a full-blown ball. And it was not to be held here at South Audley Street, though both Alex and Wren seemed to have put up a spirited argument. They had only just arrived in town, the family had pointed out. Wren was still recovering from her confinement. They would have the wedding and the breakfast to plan, and those events would occupy all their time and energy. The wedding was to be held soon, it seemed. As soon as the banns could be read, in fact.

The betrothal ball was to be given by Anna and Avery at Archer House on Hanover Square—a grand venue indeed.

"We have given a number of balls there in the past three years, Cousin Althea," Avery was explaining to Elizabeth's mother with his characteristic sighing ennui. "I believe I could plan one in my sleep."

"Oh, you could not, Avery," the dowager duchess said indignantly. "You raise one weary eyebrow and your secretary does everything for you, down to the finest detail. Even Anna and I become superfluous in the face of his efficiency."

"Quite so," he said. "Edwin Goddard plans and executes and I sleep."

Cousin Louise clucked her tongue and shook her head as she gazed in fond exasperation at her stepson. "But always with one sharp eye half open," she said.

"Archer House really is the perfect setting for a grand ball," Anna said. "And I want to host it for you, Elizabeth. You were so kind to me when I first arrived in London. You came to live with me right here in this house, and you kept me from rushing back to Bath and hiding my head beneath my teacher's desk in the schoolroom there."

"Do as you will, Anna," Elizabeth said, smiling at her.

"I recognize that I have no say in any of this. I am merely the bride."

"How do *you* feel about a grand ball, Sir Geoffrey?" her Aunt Lilian asked. "Men can be funny about such things."

Uncle Richard snorted.

"Provided no jot or tittle of my agreement with Mrs. Westcott is broken," Geoffrey said, "and I end up with Elizabeth as my wife, I will be happy to attend anything that is planned for us."

"He is a man after my own heart, Lizzie," her aunt said. "Do keep him."

"Splendid." Anna clasped her hands to her bosom. "A ball at Archer House it will be, then. If Alex and Wren and Cousin Althea will not be horribly offended, that is."

"I think it will be quite lovely, Anna," Elizabeth's mother said, "to be able to attend my daughter's betrothal ball without also having to plan it."

And so it was settled. There was to be a ball as early as next week and the wedding in less than a month's time—at St. George's. And then . . . And then the rest of her life would begin and she and Geoffrey would live happily ever after.

Well, probably not quite that.

Contentedly ever after, then. She could confidently predict that. And contentment would be good enough, even preferable to exuberant happiness, in fact. Happiness did not last. There was more stability in contentment. And stability was what she had craved ever since leaving Desmond.

Happiness—and the hope that it would last forever—was for young people.

Like Colin.

She hoped fervently for his happiness with the bride he would choose and felt quite depressed again.

* * *

Colin was feeling a bit low in spirits by the time the Archer House ball rolled around. For one thing, he feared Elizabeth was making a mistake and all the ebullient high spirits and sense of fun she had displayed at Brambledean over Christmas would be lost to the quiet decorum of marriage with a dull man. *Not* that it was any of his business. But he was fond of her. No, more than that. He had placed her on a pedestal at Christmastime and she had remained there ever since. He . . . What was an appropriate word? Worshipped? Adored? Cherished her? He very dearly wanted to see her happy in a second marriage, even if the thought made him selfishly despondent because it would set a distance between him and her that had not been there before.

He was a bit depressed too with the direction his own affairs had taken. He was being maneuvered. He could feel it happening, yet he seemed almost powerless to do anything about it. He did try. He escorted Miss Eglington to a concert one evening with Ross Parmiter and his sister. And he took Miss Madson for a drive to Kew Gardens and a picnic on the grass. Her sister and brother-in-law accompanied them.

But he feared he was fated to marry Miss Dunmore. Though *feared* was surely the wrong word. He liked her. She was beautiful and sweet and accomplished and appeared to have all the qualities any gentleman could ask for in a wife. If he did not know it for himself, he had her mother to tell him so—frequently. And that was the trouble. Left to himself, he might well fall in love with the girl, make her his offer after talking with her father, marry her, and live happily ever after with her. But he was not being left to himself.

She and her mother seemed to appear at every social event he attended. They were even at the concert, and Lady Dunmore looked very contemptuous as her eyes lingered upon Miss Eglington. He half expected to see them at Kew too, though that at least did not happen. He seemed forever to be finding himself sitting next to Miss Dunmore or fetching her food or drink or turning pages of music for her or escorting her out to her carriage or dancing with her.

And then there was the letter that had come from his mother. He almost had not recognized her handwriting. He had recognized the perfume that lingered about the paper, however. She wanted him to take tea with her at the house on Curzon Street. As soon as he had named a day, she would herself write to Lady Dunmore and invite her and her daughter to come too.

Miss Dunmore is very lovely, dearest, she had written. *You make a dazzlingly attractive couple. I will have to be very careful that you do not outshine me, though a number of people are saying that would be impossible. I tell them they are nothing but flatterers, but they keep saying it.*

Colin wrote back, breaking a long silence, apart from that brief meeting in the park. He was not formally courting Miss Dunmore or any other lady, he informed her. It would be inappropriate, then, to single out anyone to take tea with him and his mother and hers.

His letter was brief and, he hoped, clear. But he did not like the fact that his mother was edging her way back into his life and trying to do it on her terms. She had always surrounded herself with beauty—which she then proceeded to control and use to draw attention to herself and her own superior and everlasting loveliness.

He was *not* going to let it happen to him.

But did that mean he must stop considering Miss Dunmore

as a bride? It seemed unfair—to both her and himself. He believed she favored him, and not just because her mother did. And he still thought it possible that he might fall in love with her.

Determined as he was not to be manipulated, he still found that he was to dance with her twice at Elizabeth's betrothal ball—for the opening set and for the second waltz, since she had recently been approved to dance it. Her mother had seemed a little chagrined that it could not be the first waltz, but he had explained that Lady Overfield had already promised that one to him.

"Oh well," she had said grudgingly, "I daresay you feel obliged since she is the sister of your brother-in-law, Lord Hodges. However, I suppose you are sorry now that you know Lydia is permitted to waltz."

He was not feeling in a particularly cheerful mood, then, when he arrived at Archer House and made his way upstairs to the receiving line and the ballroom, John Croft at his side.

Archer House on Hanover Square was indeed the perfect setting for a grand ball, the ballroom being large and spacious and luxuriously decorated and situated at the head of a wide, sweeping staircase. Elizabeth had attended balls here before—for Anna when she was being introduced to society, for Jessica at her come-out last year. But this ball was for her.

She and Geoffrey stood in the receiving line with Anna and Avery on one side, closest to the door, and her mother and Alex and Wren on the other. And she was hit by the reality of it all. Invitations had gone out to almost everyone of any social significance in London, and it seemed that almost everyone must have come—as was to be expected, of course, when the ball was hosted by the Duke and Duchess of Netherby.

It felt very real now, her betrothal. There was no going back. Not that there had been from the moment she had said yes. And not that she wanted a way back.

She was standing in the receiving line, feeling vivid and rather dashing in her new high-waisted ball gown of gold lace over bronze silk with deep and elaborately embroidered scallops at the hem and the edging of the short sleeves. She usually favored pastel shades, but Wren and Anna, who had accompanied her to the modiste on Bond Street to choose among fabrics and patterns for the ball and her wedding, had insisted upon this for her betrothal ball, and Elizabeth had meekly acquiesced.

"You are as much the tyrants over my clothing as Mama is over my wedding plans," she had told them.

"The thing is," Anna had said, "that you cannot be allowed to fade into the background at your own betrothal ball or at your wedding, Elizabeth. We will not allow it. Will we, Wren?"

"And you are very good at fading into the background after making sure that everyone else steps forward," Wren had said. "Now it is your turn to bask in the warm rays of the sun. Those colors are going to look *gorgeous* on you."

Well, they *felt* gorgeous, Elizabeth had to admit now as she shook one more hand and submitted to one more kiss on the cheek while guests passed along the line and wished her well and congratulated Geoffrey. She turned her head to smile at him. He looked stiff and large and imposing in his formal evening clothes. He had confided to her earlier that he had never expected such a public fuss over their decision to marry.

She wished suddenly that she *did* love him, that this moment, this event, was colored with the aura of romance. A foolish thought. She could wish too that she was eighteen years old again, but wishing it would not bring it about. Anyway, she would not really want to be eighteen again. And she would not want to be painfully in love again. Besides, there were many different kinds of love. She would continue to cultivate an affectionate respect for Geoffrey, and that would be a good kind of love. Perhaps the best.

She turned back to greet the next guest in line and found herself gazing at Colin. For a moment he seemed like a stranger, and she saw his tall, slim figure and all the golden glow of his youth and good looks. Then he was simply Colin again and she felt a rush of warm affection as she held out a hand toward him.

"Colin," she said. "I am so glad you came." She had been half fearful that he would not come after the embarrassment he must have felt at the Arbinger ball when Geoffrey had shown his displeasure that she had told Colin of their betrothal.

He took her hand in his and raised it to his lips. "You look very fine indeed, Elizabeth," he said. "I could not possibly have missed this of all balls, could I? I do hope you have not been engaged for the first waltz."

"I have kept it for you," she assured him. "As always." Ah, but *always*, she supposed, must end after tonight. Perhaps it ought to have ended before tonight. He withdrew his hand from hers and held it out to Geoffrey.

Elizabeth turned to greet Mr. Croft, Colin's friend.

And then, just minutes later, it was time for the dancing to begin. Elizabeth and Geoffrey led it off with an old-fashioned quadrille. She smiled at him and settled into a conscious enjoyment of the evening. It felt like the official beginning of something, as indeed it was. It was the beginning of the rest of her life, and this time she had planned it wisely and well. Good sense was a far better guide than . . . well, than romance.

"I will lay claim to the *second* waltz of the evening since the first is already taken," Geoffrey said as the dance came to an end. "At least, I *hope* the second is still open."

"Of course it is and it will be yours. I shall look forward to it," she told him in all sincerity. "It is a bit of a joke between Colin and me, you know, left over from Christmas. We danced together at a Boxing Day party in what can only be described incongruously as a jolly waltz. Since we were both planning to be in London for the Season, we agreed to waltz together at each ball we both attended."

"A justification is not necessary, Elizabeth," he said. "You may dance with whomever you choose."

She expected to see a smile on his face, but there was none. And it struck her as it had once before that he did not smile often. Or laugh. He was too serious minded perhaps to indulge a strong sense of humor. There was nothing wrong with that. He was a good man.

He stood beside her until her next partner came for her before going to claim his own. Colin had danced the quadrille with Miss Dunmore, who looked at him with something of a proprietary air, as did her mother, who watched from the sidelines, her hair plumes nodding graciously in their direction. Now he was leading out the auburn-haired Miss Madson.

The first waltz came almost an hour later. Elizabeth was standing with Geoffrey and Wren and Sidney Radley, her maternal cousin, when Colin approached.

"Why is it that you are so favored, Hodges?" Sidney asked, sounding deliberately aggrieved. "I came with five minutes to spare to solicit Lizzie's hand, but she had already promised the waltz to you."

"It is my good looks," Colin said with a grin. "Not to mention the fact that I am Wren's brother."

"Lord Hodges has the unfair advantage, Radley, of having reserved a waltz at every ball of the Season with Elizabeth as long ago as Christmas," Geoffrey said. "I see I will have to put my foot down quite firmly after we are married."

Everyone laughed except Geoffrey himself. And Elizabeth, turning her head to look into his face, wondered if he *had* been joking. But surely he had.

"I will reserve the third waltz for you if you wish for it, Sidney," she said. "I will be dancing the second with Geoffrey. I am basking in all the novelty of being besieged by partners at my betrothal ball." And she set her hand on Colin's sleeve and stepped out onto the dance floor with him.

"You are happy, Elizabeth?" he asked while they waited for other couples to gather about them before the music began.

She was. Oh yes, she was. But she wondered again if this was the last time she would waltz with Colin, and the thought that it might well be saddened her. He raised his eyebrows. She had not answered his question.

"Of course I am," she said. "But beginnings always make me a little melancholy, for they imply endings too. The end of what came before."

"Am I to expect to see you in floods of tears on your wedding day, then?" he asked.

"I sincerely hope not," she said with a laugh. "Will you be there?"

"But of course," he said. "I have already answered my invitation."

"Have you?" She had not looked at the list of acceptances for a couple of days. But why had she doubted he would come? And why had she half hoped he would not? "I will return the compliment and come to yours."

"Will you?" he said.

"If I am invited, that is," she added.

"You will be at the top of the list," he told her.

"Are you making progress?" she asked him. "Is Miss Dunmore the one? She is extremely pretty. Or Miss Madson? She looks sensible and . . . nice. Or even Miss Eglington perhaps? Or . . . someone else?"

"I think you and I ought to elope," he said, and they both laughed.

But she looked searchingly into his eyes. Despite the laughter, he did not look quite the carefree young man she had known at Brambledean. He was not finding it easy, then, to make the changes in his life he had decided were necessary. But she suddenly remembered Christmas Eve and the family and the carolers, and Colin standing among them, looking bleak. Her heart had reached out to him then, as it did now.

"I believe the waltz is about to start," he said. "Let us enjoy it, shall we?"

Yes, she would savor it to the full.

They danced without talking for a while, and Elizabeth focused her full attention upon a conscious enjoyment of the occasion, of this particular dance, of this particular partner. He was smiling, his eyes on hers. And how precious, oh how utterly precious was this moment. This now.

And how . . . desperate.

"I shall miss waltzing with you," he said, echoing her thought of a few minutes ago.

"You are not going to dance with me after this evening, then?" she asked.

"I do not believe Sir Geoffrey would approve," he said.

"Oh, but he was joking just now," she protested.

"Was he?" He was still looking at her. His eyes yet held traces of his smile.

"Yes, of course he was," she said. "But perhaps you are tired of waltzing with me, which might be just as well. For soon I will be an old married lady, and you perhaps will be a . . . young married man."

"It is not a possibility," he said. "It is a definite impossibility, in fact. I could never grow tired of waltzing with you, Elizabeth." And he swept her into a double twirl, causing them both to laugh while she concentrated upon her steps. Not that it was necessary. He was a superb dancing partner. He proceeded deliberately to show off for her with fancy footwork, drawing her with him and laughing down into her upturned face. And she was reminded, as she so often was when she was with him, of Christmas Day and all the carefree, joyful outdoor activities he had pretended to resist while she had somehow been set free by the snow to revert to girlhood exuberance.

Ah, it had been a good time, a precious little cameo to last a lifetime, for it could never be repeated.

She felt like weeping.

"That snowball *was* intended for my face, was it not?" she asked.

He looked startled for a moment and then grinned in comprehension and chuckled outright. "I would not confess to such a dastardly deed even under torture," he said. "Would a gentleman deliberately hit a lady in the face with a snowball when she was not even looking?"

"But are you a gentleman?" she asked.

He answered with another grin and some eyebrow waggling and twirled her again.

She must stop looking back. She must look forward instead.

"You are still planning to make Roxingley Park your home, are you?" she asked him.

"It is time I confronted a few ghosts," he said. "Perhaps when I go there I will discover that after all they are without substance."

"Perhaps," she agreed. "But ghosts can exert a powerful influence."

"Say it is not so." He smiled, but his eyes searched hers. "Have you not rid yourself of yours entirely, then, Elizabeth?"

"I am not sure one ever does," she said. "One accepts them, makes peace with them, and stops paying attention to them."

She still could not believe she had told him about her miscarriages. She *never* spoke of them. She guarded her thoughts so that she never thought of them either. Even her dreams had been ruthlessly purged of them. But she had spilled it all out for Colin, or enough anyway for him to fill in the missing pieces. Her son would have been seven years old now, the other child three years older.

"And how does one make peace?" Colin asked.

"By . . . forgiving oneself," she said. If that was the right word.

"Even when one was not in any way to blame for whatever happened?" His smile had turned to a puzzled frown. His head had moved closer to hers.

"Yes," she said. "For we always *do* blame ourselves even when we know we are innocent. Instead of hoarding a secret sense of guilt, it is better to forgive ourselves. And to forgive the guilty one too, or at least recognize that except in very rare circumstances we were not the victims of pure evil, only of wrongs done against us by people who were themselves hurting when they hurt us. I do not mean we must excuse those wrongs that were done us, only that we must . . . understand why they were done and then forgive. We must do it for our own sakes. Resentment and hatred and grudges are a poison that harms the person who harbors them far more than it harms anyone else."

And oh goodness—it was only as she finished speaking that she realized how very inappropriate was the sudden turn the conversation had taken. In just a couple of minutes they had gone from warm laughter to . . . this. It was at the same moment that she realized they had stopped dancing. Everyone had, in fact, and moved off the floor, for the waltz had ended. But the two of them still stood a little way onto the dance floor, holding each other in waltz position, their heads almost touching, totally absorbed in their conversation.

But there was no chance to smile, even to laugh off their earnestness. There was no chance to move apart and leave the floor as everyone else had done. A voice spoke from just behind Elizabeth, pitched—surely unintentionally—at a volume that drew instant attention from numerous guests standing nearby.

"Forgive me for interrupting such a touching tête-à-tête," Sir Geoffrey Codaire said, "but you have spent quite enough time with my affianced wife, Hodges. Enough for tonight and enough for a long time to come. I would be obliged if you would unhand her so that I may escort her to her proper place at her mother's side."

Eleven

G ood God!
   Colin released his hold on Elizabeth and looked
incredulously at Sir Geoffrey Codaire, who was standing a
couple of feet behind her, solid and righteous.

"For God's sake, will you keep your voice down, sir," he
said softly and urgently, though he was aware of a sort of
hush falling upon the people close to them and a few shush-
ing noises from others farther away. He took a step back as
he smiled and bowed to Elizabeth. "Thank you for honor-
ing me with a dance, Lady Overfield."

He would have turned and strolled away, though he realized that considerable damage had already been done.
Within minutes almost everyone in the ballroom would
have learned of that brief exchange. It would be the subject
of drawing room conversations and endless speculation tomorrow. He was prevented from moving away, however,
when Sir Geoffrey spoke again.

"Am I to be subjected to censure by a mere puppy for

admonishing him when he has subjected my betrothed to unwanted attention?" he asked, his voice vibrating with barely leashed fury. "It was indeed an honor that was granted you, Lord Hodges, one you have abused by making a spectacle of the lady."

"Geoffrey." Elizabeth had turned to set a placating hand on his arm. She too spoke softly, but by now it was far too late to prevent a major scandal. There was a spreading ocean of silence surrounding them, and more and more heads were turning their way to see what had caused it. "You are embarrassing Lord Hodges, and you are embarrassing me. Do let us go and join Mama."

"And you think *you* have not been embarrassing *me*?" he asked, turning his glare upon her.

Colin saw Elizabeth close her eyes and opened his mouth to speak.

"A slight misunderstanding, is there?" a languid voice asked almost on a sigh, and all attention turned—as it always did when he spoke—upon the Duke of Netherby, who was resplendent in silver and dove gray and white, rings upon almost every well-manicured finger, jeweled quizzing glass in hand and halfway to his eye. He was neither a tall nor a husky man, and Colin had never known him to raise his voice or become agitated upon any provocation. He had once overheard a gentleman describe His Grace as a man too lazy to step out of his own shadow. But he had a presence more magnetic than Colin had known in any other man. The three of them and everyone else within earshot turned to gaze upon him.

"I must confess," he continued, "that I too thought you were about to monopolize the company of Lady Overfield for another set, Hodges, and I was a trifle put out for the next dance is mine, I believe, Elizabeth?"

She stared at him for an uncomprehending moment. "So it is, Avery," she said.

"Quite so," he said. "But of course I realized my mistake the moment I thought it. You were merely finishing your conversation with Lord Hodges."

"Netherby—" Colin began.

"My betrothed—" Codaire said.

"I was," Elizabeth agreed. "And—"

They all spoke simultaneously.

His Grace moved the quizzing glass an inch closer to his eye. Light from the candles overhead winked off the jeweled handle.

"Lizzie?" Alexander too had appeared on the scene. "What—?"

"And I believe her grace is waiting for you to partner her in the next set, Hodges," the duke said. "Elizabeth, Codaire, let us forget about dancing the next set and take a stroll into one of the salons to partake of a glass of wine, shall we? Dancing is thirsty work. Riverdale, will you join us? And your mother too, perhaps?"

And thus he brought a precipitate end to a scene that had been on the brink of turning ugly. Or uglier. It was already ugly. Even Netherby could not work miracles. There could be no erasing what had been seen and heard. Nothing could prevent the gossip that was sure to follow. *Had* he made a spectacle of himself during that waltz? More important, had he made a spectacle of Elizabeth?

But even as the conviction grew on him that indeed he must have, he remembered her saying that we tend to blame ourselves for bad things that happen even when we know we are innocent. Neither of them had done anything deserving of Codaire's disastrous outburst.

Colin turned away abruptly as Elizabeth moved off on

the arm of her brother and Codaire followed while Netherby strolled toward a dismayed-looking Mrs. Westcott and led her off in the same direction. Good God, he wished a large hole would suddenly appear in front of him to swallow him up. He had not been invited to go too, and he supposed Netherby had been wise to exclude him. But he would dearly like to plant Codaire a facer. How dared he so publicly humiliate Elizabeth?

As he turned, he came face to face with a smiling duchess.

"I wish the next set were a waltz too," Anna said as she slid one hand through his arm. "You dance it so very well, Lord Hodges."

She drew him unhurriedly away from where he had been standing, and conversation began again behind them, though there was surely an extra buzz of excitement about it. Colin smiled.

"I have been informed by His Grace that I reserved the next set with you," he said. "But will you mind terribly if I leave you standing, so to speak?"

"In order to rush away never to be heard from again?" she said. "Yes, I am afraid I do mind, Lord Hodges, unless you have already reserved the set with someone else. Sir Geoffrey Codaire has caused dreadful embarrassment for Elizabeth. I do not know what got into him. It seems so unlike him. Jealousy, perhaps? You are a very good-looking man, you know, and years younger than he." Her eyes laughed into his. "Come. Join the set with me for the Roger de Coverley. I must insist. I will not be a wallflower at my own ball."

He danced with her. It was one of the hardest things he had ever had to do, aware as he was at every moment of speculative eyes upon him. He knew it was difficult for the duchess too. This was her home and her ball. Her husband was at this very moment trying to quell possible scandal, an impossibility even for him. Neither he nor any of the other four people who had left the ballroom had reappeared.

What the devil had he done? *Had* any of it been at least partly his fault? What could he do now to put things right? Continue to dance and smile? Leave? But he had not yet danced with Miss Eglington, and he had told both her and Ross when he met them this morning on Oxford Street that he would. But would she still want to dance with him? Would Ross want it? And he had reserved the second waltz of the evening with Miss Dunmore. Would her mother still want him to honor his promise? Would Miss Dunmore?

Good God, this was all dashed nightmarish.

And it was hideously unfair to Elizabeth. In a few weeks' time she was going to *marry* Codaire. And she had such high hopes about it. What sort of a marriage was it likely to be? Was it going to be any better than her first marriage? Was it going to be worse? If the man was capable of losing his temper and humiliating her publicly as he just had, what might he be capable of in private?

It was really none of his business.

Except that somehow it was. He was the one who had been the inadvertent cause of a scene that would be played and replayed in fashionable drawing rooms for days to come. And the gossip had already begun. A single glance about the room made that perfectly obvious. Everyone was careful to avoid his eye.

He danced from instinct, without giving the steps and the figures any conscious attention. He horribly neglected his dancing partner. Though he was smiling, he realized when he checked.

"Thank you, Lord Hodges," the duchess said, taking his

arm at the end of the dance and leading him in the direction of Wren, who had also been dancing.

Colin fixed his eyes upon the sister he loved, tall and beautiful and elegant. But when he was still a short distance away from her he switched his perception and saw also the purple birthmark all down the left side of her face. Most of the time he was unaware of the blemish, as he believed all those who loved her were. He looked at her and saw only Wren. But he wondered now if she still had to muster all her courage every time she stepped outside the safety of her own home to face people who might stare or grimace or outright turn away from her.

It was terrible to feel conspicuous.

"Ought I to stay?" he asked his sister after the duchess had moved away.

"Yes, I am afraid so," she said, slipping an arm through his. "And so must I. Take me to the refreshment tables, Colin."

"*Was* it my fault?" he asked her. "Was I embarrassing her? Was I making a spectacle of her?"

"Absolutely not to your first two questions," she assured him. "Though I was not really watching. I was waltzing with Alexander. But Elizabeth *is* a spectacle tonight—in the best possible way. It is the whole point. This is her betrothal ball, and it would be strange indeed if all eyes were not upon her. Anna and I persuaded her to wear the gold and bronze gown because it draws attention to her beauty. Now I wonder . . . Colin, is it wise for her to marry Sir Geoffrey? I have been a little concerned since meeting him, I must confess. Or perhaps *disappointed* would be the better word, for he seems to be staid and serious and . . . well, dull. I have understood why Elizabeth chose him, but I have thought that maybe she ought to have chosen someone with more . . . What word am I looking for? Light? Joy? Humor? Someone who can bring out the sparkle that is there at the core of Elizabeth and shows itself all too rarely. I have thought that perhaps she deceives herself when she believes that a life of quiet decorum is what will suit her best. Only she knows what will make her happy, of course, but . . . But *now*, Colin? What did he mean by going after you like that, and so publicly?"

He took two glasses of punch off a tray and handed one to her.

"I don't know," he said, but his sister's words only underlined his own uneasiness for Elizabeth. "But if Netherby had not arrived on the scene when he did, I might have forgotten myself sufficiently to slap a glove in Codaire's face. It does not bear thinking about, does it? But he accused *Elizabeth* of embarrassing him. How? By smiling and even laughing as she waltzed with me? By openly enjoying herself?"

"I am very glad, then, that Avery *did* arrive on the scene," she said.

The dancing had resumed, Colin saw, but still none of the five absentees had reappeared. But he did notice his friend Ross was dancing with Miss Eglington.

"What is happening out there, Wren?" he asked. "Ought I to go and find out? Apologize? But to whom? It would go much against the grain to apologize to Codaire, but if it will make things easier for Elizabeth, I—"

But now he spotted Netherby strolling into the ballroom and stopping to look languidly about him for a few moments before moving off to mingle with some guests who were not dancing. Alexander appeared a few moments later, saw them almost immediately, and came briskly toward the refreshment tables, smiling cheerfully.

There was no sign of either Elizabeth or Mrs. Westcott. Or of Sir Geoffrey Codaire.

Avery directed them past the salons that had been opened for the use of guests and on downstairs to the library. Two footmen hastened inside ahead of them to light candles, then closed the door behind them as they left.

Avery offered Elizabeth's mother one of the comfortable leather chairs beside the fireplace before crossing the room to seat himself in the far corner, as though to distance himself from the confrontation he had set up. Alexander took a stand before the unlit fire. Elizabeth stood inside the door, having shaken her head when Avery indicated the chair across from her mother. Sir Geoffrey strode to the middle of the room. He held up a hand before anyone else could speak.

"I have something to say," he said. "It is for Elizabeth, but I am happy to say it in front of the present company, since Mrs. Westcott and Riverdale are personally concerned and this is Netherby's home, and he and the duchess have been good enough to host this event in celebration of our betrothal."

He paused, though no one seemed inclined to interrupt him or to offer to leave him alone with Elizabeth.

"I am deeply sorry," he said. "I was concerned about appearances and was unfortunately unaware that I was speaking loudly enough to be overheard by other people in addition to the one I was addressing."

"And yet," Elizabeth's mother said, "Lord Hodges asked you to keep your voice down, Sir Geoffrey, but you did not."

"I was overwrought, ma'am," he said. "But however it is or was, I apologize most sincerely to you, Elizabeth." He turned to look at her, a frown between his brows. "What I said was unpardonable. I do, nevertheless, beg you to forgive me."

"Is there any good reason why she should?" Alexander asked when Elizabeth did not immediately respond.

Sir Geoffrey rubbed one knuckle across his forehead as though to erase the crease line between his brows. "None whatsoever," he said. "I have held you in the deepest regard for many years, Elizabeth. Last year I hoped you might be prepared to reward my long patience. I was bitterly disappointed when you refused my offer, but I was encouraged too by your hesitation when I asked if it was your final answer. When I offered again this year and you said yes, I was overjoyed at the realization that you were to be mine at last. My wife. My own treasured possession. But the delay until we marry, even though only as long as it takes for the banns to be read, has been irksome. I am afraid that tonight I tried to claim what was my own before I was entitled. In doing so, I have offended your family and caused you distress and embarrassment. I do assure you that it will never happen again, even after we marry. I will never again expose you to a public spectacle."

"Only, perhaps, to a private one?" Avery wondered quietly from his corner.

Sir Geoffrey wheeled about to face him. "You misunderstand, Netherby," he said. "I set great store by proper decorum. I try at all times to conduct myself as a gentleman ought. Occasionally—rarely, I hope—I fail. And for my failure this evening I ask pardon. Of you because I caused a scene in your ballroom, of Mrs. Westcott because I caused her daughter distress, of Riverdale as Elizabeth's brother, and of Elizabeth herself for accusing her of inappropriate behavior as she danced with a younger man." He turned back to her. "I beg you to forgive me. If you wish, I shall make my apology to Lord Hodges too, given the fact that he is Lady Riverdale's brother. And if you wish, or if Netherby wishes, I shall make some sort of public apology in the ballroom."

He stood in the middle of the library, his feet firmly planted a few inches apart, his hands clasped at his back, the frown still on his brow. He seemed to have finished what he had to say.

"That is very handsome of you, Codaire," Avery said. It was unclear if he meant it or if he was speaking ironically.

"Making a public apology would be quite the wrong thing to do," Elizabeth's mother said. "It would merely cause mass discomfort and provide far more food for gossip than there already is. The only thing to do is brazen it out, return to the ballroom smiling, and proceed to enjoy the evening as though that horrid incident had not happened at all. Are you able to do that, Lizzie?" She too was frowning and looking none too happy with her own suggestion.

"Elizabeth?" Sir Geoffrey took a step toward her, one hand outstretched.

"I will not return to the ballroom," she said. "I am sorry, Avery, for the ruination of your ball."

"Think no more of it, Cousin," he said, wafting one beringed hand in her direction. "Our ball will be the talk of the Season. What more could any host ask? There will surely be no other to match it." This time he did not appear to be speaking with any irony.

"Elizabeth—" Sir Geoffrey began.

"There is no betrothal," she said. "And there will be no wedding."

"Elizabeth?" He dropped his arm and looked rather as though she had slapped his face. "For one small mistake?

No, forgive me. It was not small. But just one mistake nevertheless. You would cause the massive disaster of a ruined ball, a broken engagement, and a cancellation of wedding plans that are already well advanced? All for *one* mistake?"

She felt too weary to engage in any argument or explanation. There was nothing to say. Except one word.

"Yes," she said.

"You would dare suggest that *my sister* is the cause of the disaster this evening?" Alexander asked.

Sir Geoffrey's frown disappeared. His jaw hardened. He showed no sign of having heard. "I was sadly mistaken in you, I see, Elizabeth," he said. "I believed that at your age you had long ago put aside the frivolous side of your nature that drove your first husband to drink and had acquired the level of maturity that one ought to be able to expect of a lady past the first blush of youth. And perhaps the second."

Elizabeth did not see her brother move. But she did see him fell Sir Geoffrey with one blow to the jaw.

Her mother stifled a shriek.

"Well done, Riverdale," Avery said softly.

Elizabeth did not move.

Fortunately there had been no furniture to add danger to Sir Geoffrey's fall, which had nevertheless been a heavy one. He lay on the carpet dazed for a few moments but not unconscious. He rubbed a hand along his jaw and got awkwardly to his feet, ignoring the hand Alexander held out to assist him. He shook his head as though to clear it.

"You wish for satisfaction, Riverdale?" he asked stiffly.

"I have already had it," Alexander said curtly. "It is a pity this is not my house. It would give me even more satisfaction to tell you to get out."

"That pleasure falls to me," Avery said, leaving his

chair. "But it would be inhospitable to send a guest on his way without his hat and cloak and carriage."

He strolled to the door, stepping around Elizabeth, who seemed incapable of moving, and instructed someone in the hall outside to call up Sir Geoffrey Codaire's carriage if it was within hailing distance or a hackney cab if it was not. Sir Geoffrey brushed past Elizabeth too without looking at her and then past Avery and strode out into the hall to take charge of his own departure.

Avery closed the door.

"It is my turn to apologize," Alexander said. "I ought not to have done that in your presence, Mama, or in yours, Lizzie. Or in your library, Netherby."

"I was only disappointed that you got to him before I could," Avery said.

Elizabeth's mother had hurried across the library to gather her daughter in her arms. "I am so glad, Lizzie," she said. "*So glad* that you refused to accept his apology. But oh, my poor girl. My poor dear."

Elizabeth's mind was numb. From the moment she had heard Geoffrey's voice behind her after the waltz ended, she had not been able to think with any clarity at all. Except for the one point, upon which she had been perfectly clear from that first moment. She was not going to be able to marry him after all. She had not wavered from that conviction while she listened to his apology, though she had not spoken until a couple of minutes ago.

What a spectacular disaster.

By tomorrow, long before any official notice could appear in the papers, everyone would know that her betrothal had ended not even halfway into her betrothal ball. Even tonight everyone would know, or guess at least.

This had turned into a horrible embarrassment for Anna

and Avery, who had been so kind to her. And for her mother and Alex and Wren, who had been so pleased for her.

And for Colin.

She had determinedly kept her mind away from him until now.

He was seriously looking for a bride this spring so that he could begin the new phase of his life he had been planning since last Christmas and New Year. Half the *ton*—at least!—were here tonight and would have witnessed the debacle. She wondered how the story would play out in fashionable drawing rooms tomorrow. She wondered who would have seen what or heard what and if those accounts would bear any resemblance to the truth. Through absolutely no fault of his own, Colin was in danger of being seen as a heartless wrecker of a formally declared betrothal.

They had waltzed together, perhaps a bit overexuberantly with their fancy footwork and exaggerated twirls, smiling into each other's eyes and laughing. But what had been so very wrong about that? And ultimately they had been talking so earnestly with each other, their heads almost touching, that they had missed the end of the set.

What on earth had they been talking about? She could not even remember. But how would their absorption in each other be construed? Would she be seen as an older woman toying with a young man's affections? Would he be seen as a young man deliberately goading an older man by dallying with his fiancée? And would anyone remember who his mother was and decide they were not surprised by his behavior? Would anyone seem to remember that she had driven Desmond to drink and a premature death?

Geoffrey had thought it. All these years later he had thought it.

"I am quite all right, Mama," she said, drawing away from her mother's arms. "Avery, I am more sorry for this than I can possibly say."

"Let me see." He tapped his quizzing glass against his chin and looked upward. "For which of your many sins are you expressing regret, Elizabeth? I cannot think of a single one, and quite frankly I have no wish to listen to any confession of imaginary wrongdoings."

"*Was* I behaving inappropriately?" she asked. "*Was* I, Mama?"

"Absolutely not, Lizzie," her mother assured her. "Everyone knows that you and Lord Hodges are exceedingly fond of each other. He is Wren's brother and the only relative of her own with whom she is close now that her aunt and uncle are deceased. You have nothing with which to reproach yourself. Nothing whatsoever."

"We have been gone from the ballroom for a long time," Alex said, flexing his right hand. "Mama is quite right, Lizzie. You have nothing over which to hang your head. Neither does Colin."

"I am not going back up there," she said. "I am sorry, Avery."

"I will take you home, Lizzie," her mother said, as though Elizabeth were a child again.

"I shall rejoin my guests," Avery said, "and drive them all to distraction by behaving as though nothing of any moment has happened. As nothing has that is any business of anyone except you, Elizabeth, and your immediate family. Riverdale? Will you step into the lion's den with me?"

"I shall see my mother and Lizzie on their way first," he said.

But their mother dismissed him as soon as he had sent for the carriage. "Wren will be anxious," she said. "Go to her, Alex. And I daresay Lord Hodges may be with her. Assure him that none of this is his fault and he is not to talk himself into taking any blame."

It seemed forever before their carriage arrived and they had been handed inside and the steps put up and the door shut to hide them away in the darkness of the interior.

"Lizzie," her mother said, taking her hand in a warm clasp.

"I cannot talk yet, Mama," Elizabeth said, resting her head against the cushion behind her and closing her eyes. "I am sorry."

Her mother squeezed her hand.

And it struck Elizabeth like a tidal wave. There was no more betrothal. There would be no wedding, no marriage, no home of her own. No children. For she would not now remarry. How could she? She had chosen Desmond for love, and he had loved liquor more than her. She had chosen Geoffrey for his steady character, and he had revealed himself as a possessive, jealous man almost before the word *yes* had passed her lips.

My own treasured possession, he had called her.

He had seen her as a *possession*.

There was after all no one to trust.

Not even herself and her own judgment.

Loneliness lunged at her and took what felt like a death grip on both her throat and her stomach. Each breath was difficult to draw and even harder to release.

Twelve

The evening was interminable.

Colin stayed and smiled without ceasing. He answered questions. Lady Overfield had a headache and had gone home with her mother. He did not know where Sir Geoffrey Codaire was; perhaps he had accompanied the ladies. He danced. Not with Miss Madson—when he returned to claim a second dance with her, her elder sister, a formidable chaperon, informed him that her card was full for the rest of the evening. Her tone implied that it would be full for the rest of the Season too. He danced with Miss Eglington after exchanging a measured glance with Ross Parmiter. She was gravely quiet through the set, though she did look up at him during one almost private moment and told him quite earnestly that she did not believe a word of any of it. He thanked her, though he could only imagine what *any of it* was. And he waltzed with Miss Dunmore. Her mother nodded graciously to him when he went to claim his partner, more than half expecting to be snubbed.

"It was most obliging of you, Lord Hodges," she said, "to waltz with Lady Riverdale's widowed sister-in-law on the occasion of her betrothal. I hope she was suitably gratified. It is really too provoking that you were drawn into that vulgar scene by Sir Geoffrey Codaire, who would surely have been beneath your notice and that of the Earl of Riverdale and the Duke of Netherby if Lady Overfield had not been desperate enough for a husband to accept an offer from him. If anyone should try to hint in my hearing that you behaved with anything less than the strictest propriety, I shall set that person right in no uncertain terms, you may be sure. Now off you go with Lydia or you will miss the start of the waltz."

Lydia Dunmore herself seemed only too pleased to be waltzing. She was flushed and smiling as they danced and made no reference to the last waltz he had performed. She was slender and light on her feet and followed his lead without any missteps. She seemed to have grown even prettier since her come-out ball a few weeks ago. Her complexion had gained color. Her eyes sparkled as she conversed with him. But he could not find the energy to feel any great admiration for her, let alone fall in love with her. His heart was heavy with other matters.

Her engagement was off—Elizabeth's, that was. He could not feel as sorry about that as perhaps he ought, for he had not liked Codaire even before that bizarre episode earlier. But what was going to happen to her now? There was certainly going to be gossip. There already was. She was thirty-five years old. All she had wanted was contentment in a marriage with a worthy gentleman. It had not been a lofty dream. Now it was shattered.

. . . if Lady Overfield had not been desperate enough for a husband to accept an offer from him.

Could he really bear to have Lady Dunmore as a mother-in-law?

He walked home later that night with a growing sense of guilt even though he had been assuring himself for the last few hours that he was guiltless, and others had borne him out. He had known Codaire did not like him and disapproved of Elizabeth's dancing with him. So what had he done? He had waltzed with her anyway, and with the same sort of exuberance with which they had danced at the Boxing Day party. He had laughed and enjoyed himself with her. And then they had plunged unexpectedly into a conversation so intense that they had remained on the dance floor after everyone else had left it. What the devil had they been talking about? He could not even remember.

He wondered how she was feeling now. He doubted she was sleeping. And it was all so monstrously unfair. She had been looking radiant and happy. It had been *her* night. And she had done nothing wrong.

He felt no doubt whatsoever that gossip was going to erupt into outright scandal tomorrow. And gossip was always at best an exaggeration of the truth, at worst a total distortion of it.

He would have liked to remain at home the following morning. To hide. But if he hid now, it would be progressively difficult to show himself later. And word of what was being said out there would inevitably reach him—through his valet, through his friends, through the gossip columns of the papers. There was no hiding, in other words.

He went to White's Club, which was just a stone's throw away from his rooms, and met, purely by chance, both the

Duke of Netherby and Lord Molenor on the threshold. At least, he thought as they stepped inside and relinquished their hats and gloves to a waiting servant, he had some moral support.

A group of men gathered in the reading room, as they regularly were in the mornings to read the papers and exchange news and views, were busy talking, their voices carrying beyond the open doors of the room.

". . . a fortunate escape," someone was saying.

"You have my deepest sympathies," someone else said.

"They were actually embracing on the dance floor after everyone else had left it?" a third man said in the form of a question. "Surely nothing quite as vulgar, Codaire."

Colin pricked up his ears, and his companions fell still beside him.

"It is as true as I am sitting here," Sir Geoffrey Codaire said. "Overfield used to say she was a slut and I never believed him. I ought to have. I should have slapped a glove in that young puppy's face last night, but he actually did me a favor. In three weeks' time I would have been married to the woman. It scarcely bears thinking of."

"You would not have put up with . . ." someone was saying when Colin stopped listening.

The Duke of Netherby, armed with his quizzing glass and his most haughty manner, had stepped into the doorway. Colin clamped a hand on his arm and stepped past him. Codaire saw him come and cocked an eyebrow.

"And speaking of the devil," he said without much originality.

The group of men, some of them elderly, all of them surely older than Codaire, gawked.

"I will hear an apology, Codaire," Colin said, keeping

his voice down in deference to the purpose of the room, though he doubted anyone in it was trying to read. "For the lie about what the lady and I were doing after the set of waltzes was at an end. And for the insult to the lady."

"You are suddenly her father or her brother, are you, Hodges?" Codaire asked him.

"I am the brother of her sister-in-law," he said. "More important, I am a gentleman."

There was a collective sound from all the other men somewhere between a gasp and a sigh.

"You are implying that I am not?" Codaire asked.

"I will make it more than an implication," Colin said. "You are no gentleman, sir. And I will hear your apology."

"Or . . . ?" Codaire looked at him with raised eyebrows.

"Or the word will doubtless spread via the gentlemen gathered here that you are not of their number," Colin said. "And I will ask you to name your seconds."

Again that collective gasping sigh.

Codaire stared at him. His face had turned a dull red. "I am not a violent man, Hodges," he said.

"There is an easy way to avoid violence," Colin told him.

There was a rather lengthy silence, during which two gentlemen cleared their throats.

"It certainly *looked* like an embrace," Codaire said.

"It was not," Colin said curtly.

"Then my apologies," Codaire said. "Though I daresay I am not the only one who saw it that way."

Colin said nothing. He wondered if the Duke of Netherby and Lord Molenor had stepped into the room behind him. He did not turn his head to look.

There was another uncomfortable silence, during which the cheerful voices of new arrivals wafted in from beyond the door.

"It was Overfield who called her a slut," Codaire said. "I was merely repeating what he said. He is deceased."

Colin waited.

"I have never called her that myself," Codaire added. "These gentlemen are my witness that I did not do so today. If I implied . . ."

He paused, but no one came to his rescue.

"I am sorry if I seemed to imply that I concurred in that description of the lady," he said handsomely.

"Lady Overfield waltzed with me last evening because I asked in the hearing of her mother and other relatives," Colin said. "We danced, we conversed, and we were a little slower than the other dancers clearing the floor because we had not quite finished our conversation. Are those the facts as you observed them, Codaire?"

"I believe—"

Colin held up a staying hand. "Are those *the facts*?" he asked.

"I suppose so," Codaire said.

"You suppose?"

"Those are the facts," Codaire said. "But—"

"But?"

"But nothing. I believe some of the gentlemen in this room are trying to read."

"I am sure they will recount the details of this exchange accurately after they leave here," Colin told him. "We all hear things, Codaire. Word gets around. If I should hear that you have spread any other untruths about last evening or about Lady Overfield herself, I shall find you. And next time I will not offer you the easy way out of making an apology. My advice to you would be to leave town for a while— perhaps for the rest of the Season. I shall not insist upon it, but I would not be pleased to encounter you personally during the next few months. I would be even less pleased to learn that you had encountered Lady Overfield."

He turned to leave the room. Lord Molenor was standing in the doorway, nodding his approval when he caught Colin's eye. Netherby was seated in one of the deep chairs not far inside the door, looking sleepy. He got to his feet and followed Colin out.

"I was very much hoping," he said, "not to be named as your second, Hodges. One never knows quite what to wear to affairs of honor."

"Well done," Lord Molenor said meanwhile, closing his hand about Colin's shoulder and squeezing. "Poor Elizabeth. She has had a very fortunate escape, but this is going to be a wretched disappointment for her. Mildred is huddled with her sisters this morning. They are discussing strategy. One always needs to keep one's distance when women plot and plan. Come and have breakfast. I worked up an appetite just listening to you. Netherby? You will join us?"

Colin preceded them into the dining room even though he had worked up just the opposite of an appetite. "By God," he said, "the man is a coward. He must outweigh me two to one, and he would have had the choice of weapons."

"Ah," the Duke of Netherby said softly, "but he is not a violent man, Hodges."

The Westcott family, or at least that part of it that was in London, did what it did best. It gathered about its own in a time of crisis. It gathered to comfort and commiserate. And it gathered to consider the problem and offer a practical solution. It descended in a body upon the house on South Audley Street on the afternoon following the betrothal ball.

She might have expected it, Elizabeth thought when it was too late to escape to her room and lock herself in. Would she have done so if she *had* thought about it, though? It would have been very ungracious. And ungrateful. She knew very well that if it had been another member of the family who was in trouble, she would have been among the first to rally.

She was sitting in an armchair to one side of the fire in the drawing room when they arrived. And yes, the fire had been lit because the day beyond the windows looked appropriately gray and cold. It was only surprising it was not actually raining. She had been sitting there for some time, refusing the drinks and food both her mother and Wren had been trying to press upon her and assuring them that she was quite all right, thank you, that there was really nothing to fuss about, that she was actually looking forward to returning to Riddings Park tomorrow. For that was what she had decided to do. She had always been happy there. She would be happy again. No one need *worry* about her.

Inside she felt dead. Or at least too weary either to feel or to think. She did not want to be fussed over. She did not want sympathy. She did not want the concerned looks with which her family was regarding her. She just wanted to be left alone. If only she had the energy, she would screech just that message at them. If she had the energy, she would have gone up to her room and shut the door long before the rest of the family arrived.

But she had not found the energy and so she was trapped. It was her own fault. It served her right. She ought not to have thought of marrying again. Her life had been perfectly decent as it was. Now everything was ruined. Again. She ought not to have accepted the offer of a man she not only did not love but did not even like particularly well. It was shameful to admit that truth now. She had always found Sir Geoffrey Codaire a bit of a bore. She ought not to have waltzed with Colin. She ought to have ended that foolish arrangement as soon as she was betrothed. She ought not to have laughed with him and allowed him to twirl her about the ballroom with such lack of restraint. She ought not to have got involved in that wretched conversation. She *still* could not recall what it had been about. Something about . . . forgiveness? She ought not . . .

She ought not, she ought not, she ought not.

Was there nothing she *ought* to have done? Or ought to do? Just because she wanted to, perhaps? She wanted to scream and have a massive tantrum, but she did not have the energy. Perhaps that was fortunate for everyone who would have been at the receiving end of it.

It was not only the Westcotts who came. The Radleys arrived too—Uncle Richard, her mother's brother, and Aunt Lilian; Susan and Sidney, her cousins; and Alvin Cole, Susan's husband.

Only last week they had all gathered here upon the announcement of her betrothal. They had discussed how it and her wedding were to be celebrated. She had been amused at the time and content to let them talk and have their way. She had not wanted a betrothal ball but had allowed one to be arranged—with disastrous consequences. She had not wanted a grand wedding at St. George's, but she had acquiesced in the plan. She had felt the warmth of family, the joy of it then. Now her betrothal had ended, there was to be no wedding, and they had come to discuss how they were to prevent her from being destroyed by scandal. They had come because they cared.

It was burdensome to be cared about.

If only she cared too.

But *why* was there a scandal?

She had done nothing wrong. Neither had Colin.

That made no difference to anything, of course. She had been an adult member of the *ton* long enough to understand that a person could be destroyed by gossip even when there was little or no truth to any of it. Was there truth to any of this? Had she somehow dishonored Geoffrey with her behavior? Had his outburst been in any way justified? But even if it had been . . .

Oh, she was too weary either to assume any of the blame or to repudiate it.

She just wanted to go home—as she had wanted to go home after that last beating by Desmond and her accidental fall down the stairs and the dreadful aftermath of it all. Had nothing changed in her life? Had she made no progress?

"We need to discuss what is to be done," Cousin Eugenia, the Dowager Countess of Riverdale, announced after she had settled herself in the armchair on the opposite side of the hearth from Elizabeth's and everyone else was variously disposed about the room. "Elizabeth is clearly incapable of deciding anything for herself. She looks quite dazed and pale, poor dear. And Althea and Alexander and Wren are too distressed for her sake to have been able to offer much practical advice, I daresay. So the rest of us will have to do it for them."

"Quite right, Mama," Cousin Louise, the Dowager Duchess of Netherby, said. "I daresay Elizabeth is wanting to withdraw to Riddings Park and is planning to do it without delay. Am I right, Althea? It would, of course, be exactly the wrong thing to do."

"Then what is . . ."

Elizabeth stopped listening. She gazed into the fire while her mother perched on the arm of her chair and patted her back as if by so doing she could make everything better.

By the time Colin arrived at the Earl of Riverdale's house on South Audley Street, it was the middle of the afternoon and the weather was threatening to turn nastier than it already was. Gray clouds hung low and billowed across the sky at the mercy of a wind that was unseasonably chilly and was using the street as a funnel. It was almost but not quite raining.

There were no fewer than three carriages drawn up before the house, a sure sign that the Westcotts were rallying around one of their own. He did not hesitate anyway. If he did not call now, he never would, and he would forever have to live with a guilt he knew he had no need to be feeling. Unfortunately, one could not always control guilt. It took up house at the very center of one's being and simply refused to budge even when one informed it that it had chosen to occupy the wrong host.

They were all there in the drawing room—all the ones who were currently in town, anyway. The Dowager Countess of Riverdale sat to one side of the fire that had been lit against the chill of the day with Lady Matilda Westcott predictably hovering over her, a bottle of something in her hand—probably smelling salts held at the ready should her mother do something as uncharacteristic as succumb to a fit of the vapors. Lord and Lady Molenor sat side by side on a love seat. The Dowager Duchess of Netherby occupied a sofa, Lady Jessica Archer on one side of her, Wren on the other. The Duchess of Netherby was seated on a chair beside them, the duke on a chair in the far corner of the room. Alexander stood with his back to the fire, his feet slightly apart, his hands at his back. Elizabeth was sitting on the chair across the hearth from the dowager countess with her mother perched on the arm, one of her hands patting her daughter's back. And some of Mrs. Westcott's family were there too—her brother and sister-in-law, their son, and their daughter with her husband.

Colin could not have felt more like an outsider if he had tried after he had been announced and had stepped into the room. And he was not at all sure anyone was glad to see him, except perhaps Wren, who got immediately to her feet and came toward him, both hands outstretched.

"Colin," she said, taking his hands and kissing his cheek. "It is so good of you to have come. The weather is turning wretched, is it not?"

"It is probably going to start raining at any moment," he said, squeezing her hands before releasing them. Elizabeth, after one brief incurious glance, was not looking at him or at anyone else for that matter. She was sitting with straight spine, not quite touching the back of her chair, her hands clasped in her lap. She was dressed simply and neatly. So was her hair. She was pale, her face expressionless.

"I am sorry—" he began, but his words were met with a chorus of protests.

"You were one of the victims of that shocking episode last evening, Lord Hodges," the dowager duchess said. "You have *nothing* for which to apologize."

"We were all agreed upon that long before you came," her sister, Lady Molenor, said. "You did nothing amiss."

"But it was indeed good of you to come today, Lord Hodges," Lady Matilda added. "I said you would. *Mark my words,* I said, *Lord Hodges will do the correct and courte-ous thing."*

"No one argued with you, Matilda," her mother said sharply. "I suppose, young man, you have been blaming yourself for waltzing with Elizabeth. Such a shocking thing to do at a ball. I just wish someone had invented the dance when I was a girl."

"Codaire behaved very badly, Hodges," Mr. Radley, Elizabeth's maternal uncle, told him. "And I do not hesitate to say so aloud in Lizzie's hearing since she has broken off her engagement to him and doubtless agrees with me. And Molenor has been telling us what happened at White's Club this morning. Well done."

"We *all* agree with you, Papa," Radley's daughter assured him. "But poor Lizzie is suffering anyway. We have been discussing what is to be done for her, Lord Hodges. She is determined to go back home to Kent, to Riddings Park. But we are united in believing that it is quite the worst thing she could do, almost like an admission that she has committed some unpardonable offense, whereas in reality she is the wronged party as anyone with any sense must see. She would do far better to remain in town and go about as usual with her head held high. It is not as though she will be forced to do it alone. We will all stand by her. *Both* sides of her family."

"Not all of us are in full agreement on the solution, Susan," Mrs. Westcott said. "I can understand Lizzie's desire to go home for a while. It is not because of the scandal, which of course is not her fault in the slightest, but because her heart has been bruised."

"Come and sit here, Lord Hodges," the Duchess of Netherby said to Colin as she got to her feet. "I shall move over with Avery. You really must not blame yourself, you know, though I am sure you have been doing just that. You are Wren's *brother*, and what could be more natural than that you should dance with Elizabeth during her betrothal ball? No one in their right mind would think you guilty of anything other than a very proper familial courtesy."

"Come," Wren said, slipping an arm through Colin's to draw him toward the chair the duchess had vacated.

"No," he said. "Thank you. I am not staying. I came to ask Lady Overfield if she would take a walk in the park with me. Will you, Elizabeth?"

"It would be most unwise. It is going to rain at any moment," Lady Molenor said.

"And it is blowing a gale out there," the dowager duchess added.

"You would need a closed carriage to venture into the park with any comfort today, Lord Hodges," Mrs. Radley said. "I believe you must have come on foot? No one heard a carriage stop outside."

"You would catch your death of cold, Elizabeth," Lady Matilda warned her. "If you did not already do so last night, that is. You are not looking at all the thing today. Not that you can be expected to do so under the circumstances."

"Lizzie needs a rest, Lord Hodges," her mother said kindly, patting her shoulder. "All this attention is proving too much for her, much as she appreciates everyone's having come to show their sympathy and support. I am going to take her upstairs—"

"It seems to me," the Duke of Netherby said softly, and everyone fell silent to hear what he had to say, "that the question was directed at Elizabeth."

"And Elizabeth's family has a perfect right to answer for her when she is not up to answering for herself, Avery," the dowager countess told him. "Yes, Althea, do go on up with her. We will excuse you both."

"Thank you, Lord Hodges." Elizabeth had raised her eyes to look at Colin, still without any expression on her face. "I shall go and fetch my outdoor things."

"Elizabeth," Lady Matilda protested, "do you really think you ought?"

"My love—" Mrs. Westcott said.

"Take an umbrella," Alexander advised.

Thirteen

They walked the short distance to Hyde Park in silence, though Elizabeth did take Colin's arm when he offered it. She had been very tempted to allow her family to manage her life, at least for this afternoon, and have herself hustled off to bed to be tucked in warm and safe. As though she were still a child. Sometimes she wished she were. But they planned to go home to Kent tomorrow or the next day, she and her mother, and if she had her way, they would never leave there again. Or she would not, at least. It seemed only fair, then, to allow Colin to have a private word with her since he had been horribly and unfairly involved in what had happened last evening. He had been decent and courageous enough to come inside the house today even though it must have been obvious to him as he came along the street that he was not the only visitor. It could not have been easy.

The wind was behind them while they walked along the street. It smote them from the side as they crossed the road and turned to enter the park. It was what her father had used to describe as a lazy wind—too lazy to go around a person, it blew right through clothing and skin and bones instead until it came out the other side. It was a saying of his that had always amused her. Not today, though. It was a gray and cheerless day, a perfect match for her mood.

The park looked almost deserted when they entered it, unlike the day when they had strolled by the Serpentine and she had told him about her miscarriages and they had seen his mother's carriage pass by. Today there was not another pedestrian in sight and most of the vehicles on the main driveway were closed carriages. Rain threatened, though it had not yet begun actually to fall. They turned off the road to walk diagonally across the grass toward a distant line of trees.

"Elizabeth," he said, speaking to her at last, "I am so sorry—"

"No." She cut him off. "You did nothing wrong, Colin. *Nothing.* I will not have you blame yourself. And if part of your concern is over the fact that I will not after all be marrying Sir Geoffrey Codaire, then it is misplaced. I am only thankful that I discovered a pertinent truth about him while I was still engaged to him, not after we married. He is not the man I thought he was. I am not at all sorry Alex knocked him down."

"*Did* he?" He turned his head sharply toward her. "I wish I could have done it, but the ballroom was not the place for it, was it? I could not bear the way he insulted and humiliated you before so many people."

"You would have fought a duel with him," she said. "Cousin Thomas told us about it this morning. I am very glad it did not come to that. As for what happened, it is best forgotten." Foolish words. Neither of them was likely ever to forget.

"While we danced I found myself wanting to recapture the spirit of that absurd waltz at the Boxing Day party," he said. "But I ought not to have done it at your betrothal ball of all places. I ought not to have made you laugh in that joyful way you have when you are really enjoying yourself while your betrothed and half the *ton* were looking on. I just did not *think*, and for that I must blame myself. And then to make matters worse we got into that intense conversation— I cannot for the life of me remember now what it was about. Can you? I just did not notice when the music ended."

"Colin," she said as they turned to walk parallel to the trees rather than passing through them to the woodland path beyond. "You really must *not* torture yourself any longer with such foolish self-accusations. It was not you who behaved badly. *At all.* Neither was it me. It was Sir Geoffrey Codaire. People are supposed to enjoy themselves at a ball. We were doing just that. They are supposed to be sociable and converse with one another. It is what we were doing. The whole incident was dealt with quite satisfactorily downstairs in Avery's library. I put an end to our betrothal, Alex knocked him down when he turned spiteful, and Avery ejected him from the house, though not bodily. He left on his own feet. There will be a notice in the papers tomorrow to announce what everyone knows anyway. My mother and Wren have written to everyone who was invited to the wedding, all the wedding arrangements have been canceled, my mother and I will return to Riddings Park tomorrow or the day after, and . . . Well, and there is the end of the matter. I only hope all this does not have negative repercussions for you, but I do not expect it will. Men and women are usually judged by very different standards. I daresay your matrimonial prospects have actually been enhanced, if that is possible."

They walked onward in silence for a while, the wind in their faces now and a strong suggestion of dampness in the air. It was not a pleasant day at all. Even so, it felt good to be outside and walking. It felt good too, she admitted to herself with a twinge of guilt, to be away from her family for a short while, even Wren and Alex and her mother.

But this was good-bye to Colin. Oh, not forever, she supposed. There would doubtless be family occasions that would draw her away from Riddings eventually—the birth of another child for Alex and Wren, for example. She would almost certainly see him again. But not soon and not often. She would never waltz with him again—an absurdly trivial thought that brought a soreness to her throat and a gurgle she disguised by swallowing.

"Not all men are as Codaire is," he said. "Or as your first husband was."

She turned to look at him, tall and good-looking and very serious. "Are you suggesting that I try again?" she asked him. "I know not all men are villains, Colin. Or all husbands. There are Alex and Avery and my Uncle Richard and Joel Cunningham and . . . and Alvin Cole to disprove any such silly notion. The problem is not with all men, but with the men I choose as husbands. I was sure Desmond was the one for me. I loved him with my whole heart. But he was weak and sick and something in him hated me and turned that hatred to viciousness. All these years later I was sure Geoffrey was the man for me—solid and steady and loyal and patient and a whole host of other good things. But he is possessive and autocratic and jealous and something in him has hated me all these years—for being frivolous enough to choose Desmond instead of him when I was young, perhaps, and then driving my husband to drink."

"If he said that last night," he said, "then he deserved to be knocked down."

"It is not men I do not trust as much as it is myself," she told him. "I am obviously a terrible judge of character. And there is something in me that . . . that men hate."

"I do not hate you, Elizabeth," he said, sounding almost angry. They had stopped walking, she realized. "I like and respect and admire and honor you."

"I *was* sounding self-pitying almost to the point of hysteria, was I not?" she said, smiling ruefully at him. Her lips felt a bit stiff as though they had not smiled for a long time. "But thank you, Colin. You are kind. And it was good of you to come today, when I know it must not have been easy, and even to maneuver matters so that you could have this private word with me. I do appreciate it."

He turned away slightly in order to raise the large black umbrella of Alex's he had taken from the hall stand. It had started to drizzle slightly, she realized. He raised it over both their heads but made no move to walk onward.

"Do you trust *me*?" he asked.

"Of course I do." She smiled again. "But I am not considering marriage with you, Colin."

"I thought perhaps you might," he said, "if I asked."

And she realized with a rush of dismay what this was all about—this call at the house, this invitation to come walking, this desire to speak privately with her. She set a hand on his arm and moved half a step closer to him.

"Because of last night?" she said. "Because you still fear you somehow compromised me and owe me marriage? Oh no, Colin. But I do thank you most sincerely."

"Because you need someone to trust and I think I am that man," he said. "We both know I am not solid and firmly established in life. You know I have problems to solve, an identity to establish, a future to carve out, changes to make—I could go on and on. I am not someone you can ever have considered as a husband, but by your own admission your choices have not worked well. I *can* be trusted, Elizabeth, and I can offer the security of name and fortune. I would never let you down. I would always care for you. No. Let me rephrase that. I would always care *about* you. I would never ever behave as though I own you no matter what church and state may say to the contrary. I would always respect you and hold you in affection. I would always seek out your companionship. *Will* your trust me? *Will* you marry me?"

Elizabeth blinked several times. If the umbrella had not been firmly over their heads and tipped slightly into the wind, she would have chosen to believe it was the rain that was moistening her cheeks.

"Don't cry," he said softly. "Have I made you cry?"

"Colin." She set a hand flat against his chest. "My dear. You have been developing an interest in several eligible young ladies. Perhaps you have even singled out one as the favorite. Miss Dunmore, perhaps? It would hardly be surprising if you had fallen in love with her, and she would be an excellent choice."

"No," he said. "The number is still plural, surely an indication that I am not in love with any of them, whatever being in love means. I really do not understand the term. I care for you more than for anyone else I have met this spring."

"You are very kind," she said again with a sigh. "But Colin, I am almost ten years older than you."

"Always it comes down to that, does it not?" he said. "Codaire is older than you are, Elizabeth. That is perfectly obvious. How much older?"

He had told her the day he proposed and she accepted his offer. The irony had struck her even at the time. "Nine years," she said. "He is forty-four."

"And when you accepted his marriage offer," he said, "did you protest that you were almost ten years younger than he?"

"No," she said.

"Did it even occur to you to do so?" he asked her. "Did you feel any unease at all about the age gap?"

"No," she said. "But—"

"*I* feel no unease about the age gap between us," he said. "I feel even less now than I did at Christmas. Then I thought your serenity was bone deep, or soul deep. I thought you had reached that pinnacle of maturity that I imagine we all dream of reaching but never actually do achieve. I thought you were beyond my reach, to be admired, even worshiped from afar. But I suppose there are always more changes to adjust to, more growing to do, more doubts and insecurities to be wrestled with. You are still on a journey to somewhere, are you not, Elizabeth? Just as I am? Just as everyone is? Perhaps—no, probably—that somewhere does not really exist. Not in this lifetime anyway. Though it is to be hoped we can pick up some wisdom along the way. As you have. And as I perhaps have begun to do. But we are not the universes apart I once thought we were. Only a few miles, in fact."

"Nine miles?" she suggested.

"It is not so very far," he said. "Is it? Nine miles is the distance between Brambledean and Withington. It can be traveled just to take tea. Nine years are all that separate us.

They are surely not an insurmountable barrier. Unless I appear so young and gauche to you that I am quite beneath your notice."

"Colin." She patted her hand against his chest and looked into his eyes, shaded by the brim of his hat and by the umbrella and the heavy clouds. They gazed steadily back into her own. And she was horribly tempted. She was weary and wanted to lay her cheek against his shoulder and . . . surrender.

It felt almost like a death wish. A giving up of herself because she was weary to the very depths. Weary of living, of struggling, of hoping, of making dreadful mistakes, of losing hope. And trust. Somewhere, however, she found a shred of strength.

"I will not allow you to do this," she said. "Something this . . . monumental would need long and careful consideration even if it should be considered at all. It cannot be done just because you are a gentle, kind, and conscientious man."

"My God, Elizabeth," he said, and suddenly his eyes were blazing at her and his voice was sharp with anger. "You do not understand, do you? You do not know me at all. You *do* think I am an insecure, untried little boy. You think I must be protected from my own weakness and frailty. I may be nine years younger than you, but I am a man."

And his free arm came hard about her waist and hauled her against him. Even as her hands splayed over his chest to brace herself he lowered his head and kissed her—urgently, ungently, and openmouthed, with all the passion with which he had kissed her on Christmas Day, except that this one did not end after a few brief seconds. Rather, it gentled and deepened as her hands slid up between them to grip his shoulders, and her mouth opened to admit his tongue. She leaned into him, feeling hard thigh muscles against her own as well as the firmness of his man's body pressed to hers. All was heat in contrast to the chill of the weather. And yearning. And a desire too painful for pleasure.

They must be in full view of the carriage drive, she realized when rational thought began to return and she felt rain on her face. He still held the umbrella, but it had dipped to one side, the lower edge of it almost touching the ground. But she could not hear much traffic, only the distant clopping of a single set of hooves.

He was gazing into her eyes then, his arm still about her waist, the umbrella over their heads again. He still looked a bit hard-jawed and angry. Older than usual, the open, youthful eagerness missing from his face. She had never seen him like this before. She had offended him, it seemed, by holding his youth and good nature against him. Though she had not intended to belittle him, only to point out that she was a totally unsuitable choice of bride for him. Especially when that choice was being forced upon him by circumstances—or so he seemed to believe. It was horribly unfair.

He had been smiling and happy last evening as he danced with Miss Dunmore. They had looked stunningly attractive together.

She patted her hands against his chest.

"I did not ask on the spur of the moment, Elizabeth," he said. "I have asked you more than once before."

"Ah," she said, "but always as a joke."

"Perhaps to you," he said. "Not to me."

She tipped her head slightly to one side. Was it true? But no, he was deceiving himself. He was fond of her as she was of him, but he had never seriously considered her as a wife. Even that kiss at Christmas . . . Ah, that kiss. She relived it sometimes in her dreams when she could not control the memory and—yes, she might as well be honest—she relived it all too often in her daydreams too, when she was in control. And now he had kissed her again with real passion. Passion, though, was not love. Indeed, it had seemed to proceed more from anger.

She could not bear . . . "Colin—"

"We could replace all of today's vile gossip with something even more sensational but altogether brighter," he said. "We could marry tomorrow, Elizabeth. Or we could announce our betrothal tomorrow and plan our wedding with more care. We could marry at Roxingley if you wished or at Brambledean or at Riddings Park. Or here. Let us do it. Perhaps that ghastly incident last evening happened for a purpose. For this very purpose. Are we going to continue not even to consider each other with any seriousness just because of the matter of nine years?"

It was more than that. Oh, surely it was. He had come to London looking for a bride, and he had been looking— among the very young ladies who had only recently left the schoolroom. He was a great favorite with them. He could have almost any one he chose. And they were all at least fifteen years younger than she. That was a staggering fact.

But as she gazed into his eyes, she was horribly tempted not to overthink this decision, not to bring common sense to bear upon it. Common sense had never worked very well in any of the important decisions of her life. Perhaps it was time to give impulsiveness a try. It was a horribly dangerous and irresponsible way of making a huge, life-changing decision, of course, but . . . Perhaps it was time to do what she wanted to do rather than what she ought to do.

She had spent all last summer and winter and early spring thinking through her very wise, sensible decision to marry Geoffrey.

But perhaps she was still off balance after their kiss. Perhaps if she gave herself a few more minutes to recover and think clearly . . .

"No," she said. "No, Colin. I do thank you and I do appreciate what you are trying to do. But I cannot allow it. I care too much for you."

His jaw hardened again and he gazed at her for a long while without speaking. "You care for me," he said at last, "but not enough to marry me."

"I care for you too much to marry you," she said.

"That is nonsense," he told her. "It is such nonsense, Elizabeth. You accepted the offer of a man you did not care for at all, but you have rejected mine."

There was no answer that would not simply take them in circles. She drew a slow breath.

"Yes," she said.

He nodded, his eyes never leaving hers. "I thought," he said, "you would trust me."

As if trust could solve everything. Or anything. As if it could mend a breaking heart. Only love could do that. Perhaps.

Rain—not drizzle any longer—drummed on the umbrella. A gust of cold wind blew and cut through them.

He would not come back into the house with her. He would not take the umbrella with him either, even though the rain was coming down heavily. He stood watching her climb the steps and rap the knocker against the door and step inside when it opened almost immediately. But then there was an impasse. She closed the umbrella and stood looking down at him on the pavement. He turned and strode away, water already dripping from the brim of his hat.

Elizabeth watched him go until he was almost out of sight, even though she was being partially rained upon. And her heart ached. She wanted to call him back. She wanted to dash after him. She did neither. He was a young man with a young man's dreams, and she . . . She was past dreams. She was past even practical plans for her own future. She would endure. She had done it before and she would do it again. But she felt now that she would never be happy, that she *could* not. And she would not drag him down with her merely because he was kind and gallant and had persuaded himself that he really wanted to do what his conscience urged him to.

She was very tempted to walk right on by the drawing room and continue upstairs to her room. She stood for a moment outside the doors, drew a deep breath, smiled, and walked in.

"The heavens have opened up," she said, taking off her bonnet and fluffing up her hair, though it was really quite wet in front.

"Colin did not come in with you?" Wren asked, clearly disappointed.

"No," Elizabeth said. "I believe he felt too wet. He held the umbrella more over me than himself, and he would not take it with him." She crossed the room to warm her hands at the fire. There was a bit of a silence behind her.

"It was kind of him to come here and show some concern for you," Aunt Lilian said.

"Yes," Elizabeth said, and added what she had not intended to say. "He offered me marriage. It was extremely kind of him. I said no."

"Well, of course he did," Cousin Louise said. "And of course *you* did."

"He would have felt obliged to make you an offer," Cousin Mildred agreed, "especially after what happened at White's this morning. But it would have been absurd, to say the least. Lord Hodges did the right thing and so did you, Elizabeth."

"I am very sorry, Elizabeth," the dowager countess said, "that the two of you were put in such an awkward situation by Sir Geoffrey Codaire, who really ought to have known better. Young Lord Hodges is fond of you, as you are of him. I observed that at Christmastime. I only hope neither of you will allow the events of the past twenty-four hours— not even as long—to cloud your friendship. You are, after all, practically brother and sister."

"No such thing will happen, I assure you," Elizabeth said, smiling again as she turned from the fire and sat in the chair beside it.

Her eyes met those of Cousin Matilda, who was hovering as usual slightly behind her mother's chair on the other side of the hearth. Matilda was looking steadily back at her, and an unexpected understanding passed between them. One was so often inclined to dismiss Matilda as a sort of caricature of the aging spinster who had devoted her life to her mother's care. But family lore had it that as a young girl she had refused a number of eligible suitors her father had chosen for her because she had a romantic attachment to a younger son of a gentleman of no particular account and no fortune. Elizabeth did not know the truth of the story, but something in Matilda's expression inclined her to believe it.

Matilda poured a cup of tea, added two teaspoons of sugar, and brought it to Elizabeth.

"Matilda," her mother said. "That tea will be cold by now."

"Lizzie does not take sugar in her tea, Matilda," Elizabeth's mother said.

Elizabeth took the cup and saucer and smiled. "It is perfect," she said, "and just what I need after being chilled to the bone outside. Thank you, Matilda."

"Mama insists that you will wish to go to Riddings, Lizzie," Alexander said. "But if you would prefer, you may go to Brambledean and we will join you for the summer."

"We would love to have you," Wren added.

"I am not going anywhere," Elizabeth said after sipping the tea and schooling her face not to show her disgust at the oversteeped, lukewarm, horribly sweet beverage. "I am staying right here. And tomorrow I am resuming my normal way of life. Why should I not? The gossips may make much of me for a day or two, but they will soon grow tired of old news."

"Oh, Elizabeth," Anna said, clasping her hands to her bosom, "that is *exactly* what I would expect you to do. May I call on you in the morning and we will go shopping together?"

"I suppose," Avery said, sounding faintly pained, "I am about to be presented with a bill for another bonnet, am I, my love?"

"*You* will not be presented with anything, Avery," Cousin Louise said tartly. "Your secretary will."

"Quite so," he said agreeably.

"May I come too?" Jessica asked. "If you are going to have to pay for one bonnet, Avery, it might as well be two."

"I am proud of you, Lizzie," Uncle Richard said with a wink.

I thought you would trust me.

There had been a world of pain in his voice. As though

she had rejected him because she did not trust his motives or his ability to know his own mind or to be steadfast in his devotion to her if she married him.

Was there truth in what he had said? He could not possibly *want* to marry her. He could not possibly be happy with her. Not in the long term. He needed someone . . .

But what did she know of his needs?

Perhaps he *was* right. Perhaps she did not trust him.

Or perhaps she just wanted his happiness more than she wanted her own.

Fourteen

By the time Lord Ede arrived at the house on Curzon Street, he was wearing dry clothes—he had got soaked to the skin during his lone ride through Hyde Park, the rain having come on before he expected it and more heavily than he had anticipated. His valet had rubbed his silver hair with a towel until it was almost dry. By now it was entirely so.

He made his way upstairs and entered Lady Hodges's boudoir unannounced. He was the only male who was allowed to do so, though each time the lady herself complained about his presumption while her small army of maids and wigmakers and mantua makers and manicurists and cosmetics artists scurried about or bent to their task of making her presentable for the evening, which was to bring a group of chosen guests to the house to provide music and poetry and conversation and flattery.

"Ede," she said after delivering the expected scold in her sweet little-girl voice, "what have you discovered? Nothing is to come of that ridiculous threat of a duel this morning, it is to be hoped? And what of Lady Dunmore and her daughter? They have not spurned him? Though it is hardly likely when he is such a brilliant match for the daughter and she was allowed to waltz with him after that most ridiculous of ridiculous scenes. How could anyone, even a dolt like Sir Geoffrey Codaire, believe that my son was flirting with that aging widow?"

"He was in close embrace with the aging widow in the park not an hour ago," he told her.

"*What?*" She snatched her hand away from the young woman who was buffing her nails and turned her head sharply so that her wig slipped slightly askew and the wigmaker paused before gently repositioning it and continuing with her task of creating a perfect ringlet to curl over my lady's neck.

"You wish me to provide details?" he asked her.

"He is a fool," she said after staring at him for a few moments. "He must believe he owes her marriage after drawing attention to her on the ballroom floor last evening. Or after *she* drew attention to *him*. You may be sure that that is the way it was, and who can blame her for trying when she thought her only option was to ally herself with a dull and plodding farmer? But how dare she, Ede? *How dare she?*"

"Calm yourself, my love," his lordship said, flicking open his snuffbox with one thumb and examining the contents before helping himself to a pinch. "I daresay he will not be unwise enough to marry the woman."

"*Marry* her?" she half shrieked. "It will not be allowed to happen. Not when I am so close to having him back after all this weary time and a bride with him who is both beautiful and biddable. I will certainly not have him marrying an old and ugly widow merely because he feels obliged to play the gallant. What do we know of her, Ede?"

"Only what the whole world knows," he told her. "She was married to a drunk and left him after he had beaten her one too many times. He died in a tavern brawl a year or so later. She has lived a dull and blameless life since. Of course, Codaire did mention at White's this morning that her first husband called her a slut. And something or someone drove him to drink. And she did break her marriage vows in most scandalous fashion by running home to her mother and refusing to go back to him. But everyone knows these things."

"And everyone has probably forgotten most or all of them," she said. "That must all have happened years ago."

"It is always possible to refresh memories," he said. "And the *ton* is very ready to hear some titillating stories about the widow who danced and laughed indiscreetly at her own betrothal ball with a much younger man and even attempted to draw him into a public embrace when the dance was over."

"And actually *did* embrace him this afternoon in a public place," she said. "How dare she, Ede? Oh, how *dare* she? You will see to it?"

He returned his snuffbox to his pocket and strolled to the dressing table upon which her jewelry for the evening had been laid out. He fingered a diamond necklace he had given her for some forgotten birthday.

"Consider it done," he said.

"And what can I do to rescue my dearest Colin?" she asked. But she did not wait for his suggestion. "My heart is set upon Miss Dunmore for him. Where is Blanche?" She looked at one of her maids. "Fetch Lady Elwood." The maid scurried from the room. "I shall have her send an invitation to tea tomorrow. No. I shall have her send an invitation to the two ladies to ride with me in my barouche in the park tomorrow—provided the weather is better than it is today, that is. And Blanche will invite Colin to accompany us. No. Lady Dunmore will invite him. Will the sun shine, do you think?"

"For you?" he said, looking her over with lazy eyes. "For you even the sun can be persuaded to shine."

"Well, so it ought," she said. "I will wear my new Chantilly lace veil. It is quite exquisite. Of course everyone will say it is not more exquisite than its wearer, but I am accustomed to listening to flatterers. I do not believe half of what they say."

Colin spent the following morning at the House of Lords, trying to immerse himself in the nation's business rather than dwell upon his own. It was not easy.

He had seen the terse notice of the ending of the betrothal of Elizabeth, Lady Overfield, to Sir Geoffrey Codaire in the morning paper and found that he was feeling more sorry for himself than he was for her. Why had she accepted Codaire but refused him? *I care for you too much to marry you,* she had told him, and it seemed as much nonsense to him now as it had then. It was true, perhaps, that he had offered for her because he had not been able to shake the conviction that he must have compromised her and therefore owed her marriage. But the point was that he had *wanted* to do so too. The thought of actually being married to Elizabeth was a bit dizzying. Not to mention dazzling.

It had hurt him that she had said no.

He returned to his rooms in the early afternoon to find

the usual pile of invitations and other mail and a note from Lady Dunmore that had been hand delivered. He frowned at it before breaking the seal. Yes, there was still *that*, his search for a bride, which he was now free to resume. If he could find the heart to do it, that was. But life must go on. He broke the seal.

It was an invitation to take tea with the family and a few friends. Today. He looked at the clock on the mantel. In an hour and a half's time. *The family. A few friends.* It sounded a bit ominous, as though he were being admitted to some exclusive inner circle. Did he wish to be? Miss Dunmore was a sweet young lady and very beautiful too, though that fact was not of paramount importance to his choice. There was no one he liked better. Except . . . No. There was no one he liked better.

Ah, Elizabeth. He wondered if she had returned to Riddings Park today. It was depressing to know that she might prefer to incarcerate herself there than marry him.

He arrived at the Dunmore home promptly at the appointed time to discover that the family and friends referred to in the invitation appeared to consist of Lady Dunmore and her daughter. They were alone in the drawing room when he was announced. Lady Dunmore rose graciously to her feet and Miss Dunmore stood a moment later to make him a curtsy.

"Lord Hodges," Lady Dunmore said, "it is such a beautiful day after yesterday's wind and rain that it seemed a positive sin to waste the afternoon sitting indoors drinking tea. When Lydia and I received an invitation to drive in the park in an open barouche, we made the decision to accept and sent notes to our friends to wait until tomorrow."

"I cannot blame you," Colin said, wondering if his own

note had gone astray. "I will not keep you, ma'am. If I may, I will return tomorrow with your other guests."

"Oh, but the invitation to drive includes you," she said. "It will be a great pleasure to drive in the park with you and Lady Hodges."

Colin felt a slight buzzing in his head. "With my mother?" he asked. But he held out no real hope that he had misheard. This was exactly the way his mother manipulated the people around her, and clearly she had decided that it was time he returned to the fold with a bride who would become an ornament to her world of youth and beauty.

"She will be here in . . . five minutes," Lady Dunmore said, glancing at the clock on the mantel. "Perhaps you will escort us back downstairs, Lord Hodges, so that we may don our bonnets and gloves and be ready to step outside the moment the barouche arrives."

He really had no choice, Colin thought. And he wondered if there had ever been a planned tea with family and friends or if Lady Dunmore had been given her orders— disguised as sweet suggestions—by his mother. What he ought to do, of course, was step out of the house and stride off down the street before she appeared. He ought to establish right now that he was not to be manipulated, that he would take possession of the world of his birthright in his own time and on his own terms.

But this was not between just him and his mother, as she would very well know. There were two other ladies involved, most notably a sweet and innocent young girl.

He offered Lady Dunmore his arm and smiled at her daughter as they left the room and descended the stairs he had mounted in all innocence just a few minutes before.

His mother was dressed as usual in white, with a magnificent lace veil decorating the brim of her hat and covering her face. She was seated in a white and gold barouche drawn by the white horses that were also used for her closed carriage. She looked youthful and fragile and ethereally lovely. The four black-clad outriders were gathered a discreet distance behind the conveyance. It was really a quite extraordinary scene, and hideously embarrassing, Colin thought as he stepped outside with the ladies, who were gazing at the tableau with identical looks of awe.

"Mother," he said, nodding in her direction.

"Dearest." She moved over on the seat and patted it. "Lady Dunmore, do join me here, and the young people may share the other seat. Is it not a beautiful day?"

Colin handed the ladies in first and then climbed in himself after only a moment's hesitation, during which he entertained the thought once again of shutting the door and walking away. But he could not so humiliate Miss Dunmore, who was gazing at him with wide eyes and flushed cheeks.

And so he endured an hour's ride in Hyde Park, being viewed by the whole of the fashionable world and much of the unfashionable one too while his mother wafted one white-gloved hand rather like a queen condescending to acknowledge her subjects. She talked too, praising Miss Dunmore's beauty, telling her how much she would love Roxingley, urging Lady Dunmore to come and take tea with her one afternoon, congratulating Colin on his good looks and sense of style and on his kindness in dancing with the *aging Lady Overfield* at her betrothal ball.

"It is shameful that Sir Geoffrey Codaire was jealous of you," she said. "It was a shame for her since he cast her off and it is unlikely at her age that she will find anyone else. But I do understand that *you* were not flirting with *her*, dearest. Not that I needed to be told any such thing. The very idea is laughable in its absurdity."

Colin noticed the emphasis upon certain words, implying that Elizabeth had been flirting with him.

"Lord Hodges was indeed *not* flirting, ma'am," Lady Dunmore assured her. "It would have been preposterous. I saw the whole thing with my own eyes, and it was entirely the other way around. I heard last evening that Lady Overfield has a history of flirting once she believes she had secured a man, either through marriage or betrothal. It was just unfortunate for her that Sir Geoffrey was unwilling to put up with her tricks but confronted her with them. However, I do not wish to spread any gossip. I took no notice of it, you may be sure, once I understood that no untrue rumors were being spread about Lord Hodges, who behaved with perfect decorum."

Good God. Oh, good God.

I heard last evening . . . He had been perfectly well aware that there was gossip over that wretched ball, and he had fully expected exaggeration and distortion of the truth. But was all the blame being put upon Elizabeth while both Codaire and he were being exonerated?

And . . . *Lady Overfield has a history of flirting.* Who the devil was digging into her past and coming up with such a preposterous charge? *Codaire?*

"It ought to be mentioned," he said, "that it was Lady Overfield who broke off the engagement with Sir Geoffrey Codaire. And that at no time during my acquaintance with her has she *flirted* with me. Or with anyone else to my knowledge. I hold her in the deepest esteem."

"That is very much to your credit, Lord Hodges," Lady Dunmore assured him. "For the lady's brother is married to your sister, and loyalty to one's family and their connections is always admirable."

He could argue, proclaim, justify, lose his temper, correct misconceptions and outright untruths, but what would be the point? Rumor and gossip, once they got started, were like a raging wildfire, and whoever had started this one clearly understood that. He ought to have slapped a glove in Codaire's face after all yesterday morning, Colin thought. He might have to seek him out again if this sort of thing persisted.

He was scarcely aware of the sensation they were causing, especially after they had approached the circuit where the daily parade of carriages and riders and pedestrians congregated each afternoon of the Season. Here was Lord Hodges in an open conveyance, sitting shoulder to shoulder with Miss Dunmore while both their mothers sat opposite them, nodding graciously at all around them, conversing with the greatest amiability with each other, and smiling benevolently upon the dazzlingly beautiful tableau their offspring presented to the world.

He only knew as he set about making himself agreeable to Miss Dunmore that he was seething with an impotent fury and feeling as helpless as he had at the age of eighteen when his mother had planned one of her grand house parties the very day after his father's funeral. He could feel himself being sucked into his mother's web—if that was not a hopelessly mixed metaphor.

When the barouche finally returned to the Dunmore home, Colin descended from the carriage to help the two ladies alight, but he declined Lady Dunmore's invitation to accompany them inside.

"No, ma'am, thank you," he said. "I will escort my mother home."

"As a good son ought," she said, beaming approval upon him.

"How kind of you, dearest," his mother murmured.

He sat beside her for the journey to Curzon Street and exchanged the smallest of small talk with her even when she tried to draw him out upon the subject of Miss Dunmore's charms. He was not about to engage in any sort of conversation with her when there were all of five sets of ears—the coachman's and those of the four outriders—within hearing distance.

He handed his mother down from the carriage outside the door of his house and entered it for the first time in many years. He waited in the hall while she lifted back the veil from her face, removed her hat with slow care, and turned to take his arm while they climbed the stairs to the drawing room. Without the veil, her face revealed itself as a skillful work of cosmetic art. Together with the carefully curled blond wig, it somehow set her at one remove from reality, more like a life-size doll than a live woman.

They stepped into the drawing room, and Blanche rose from a chair and came toward them while Sir Nelson Elwood, her husband, set down his book and got more slowly to his feet.

"Blanche." Colin took his sister's hand in his and bowed over it. She was still very beautiful, he thought, her face free of cosmetics and flawless, though no longer youthful, her blond hair thick and healthy. Beautiful but lacking in animation.

"Colin," she said.

Nelson was helping their mother to her chair at the other side of the room, a remarkable piece of furniture, all pink velvet in a pink room from which all raw daylight was ruthlessly kept at bay by pink curtains that filtered in a light that was flattering to the mistress of the house. Her chair was higher than the others in the room and was reached by two steps that served as a footrest once she was seated. It gave her the advantage of seeming to dominate the room and all that was in it.

The four outriders, having divested themselves of their outdoor garments, came hurrying into the room to serve her.

"Out!" Colin said, pointing to them and indicating the door behind him with his thumb.

Everyone froze and looked at him as though he had sprouted an extra head. All except his mother, who sat back in her chair and regarded him with a half smile on her lips. The four men, all young, all beautiful, turned to look inquiringly at her.

"I would remind you," Colin said, "that you are in my house at my pleasure. You may wait elsewhere in it until your presence is needed."

"The master of the house has spoken, my dears," his mother said, sounding amused, and the four men withdrew, passing close to Colin as they did so, eyeing him as though to intimidate him.

"Mother," he said when he heard the door close behind them, "I daresay word has spread that I have begun to consider taking a bride. I have become acquainted with several ladies since returning to London this year, in some of whom I have an interest. Perhaps some of them have an interest in me. I have not made my choice yet. I do not feel anywhere close to doing so. Until I do, I will be careful not to raise expectations where they may not be fulfilled or to give marked attention where it may cause hurt. Miss Dunmore is an amiable young lady. It would be strange indeed if I did not enjoy her company and if it did not cross my mind that she might make me a good wife. I do not know her feelings on the subject. I do not have a close enough acquaintance with her to have asked, and she is a properly brought up lady who does not wear her heart on her sleeve. Lady Dunmore, on the other hand, clearly has ambitions, for which she cannot be blamed since she has several daughters to settle. Today my life was made considerably more difficult even as her hopes have been raised and her daughter has been made more vulnerable. I resent the fact that without any invitation to do so you have chosen to interfere in my affairs and play matchmaker. It must and will stop."

"Colin," Blanche said reproachfully.

Nelson returned to his chair, picked up his book, and apparently began reading it.

"Such masterful behavior, dearest," his mother said. "I knew you would turn into a fine young man as well as an extraordinarily handsome one. But sometimes young men, just like young ladies, do not know their own minds and fritter away their lives in indecision and procrastination unless they are given a little help. Miss Dunmore is clearly the one for you. She is the loveliest of this year's crop of young hopefuls, and my son cannot demean himself by choosing anything less than the best. How shameful it would be if someone more decisive were to snatch her from under your very nose—as your father did me. I had other prospects, you know, many of them, in fact, and several would have led to more dazzling matches than the one I made. But your father took one look at me and knew what a treasure was within his grasp. He grasped it without waiting for someone else to forestall him."

"I am not my father," Colin said. "And I have no claim upon Miss Dunmore, lovely though she is. If she chooses to encourage someone else, she may do so with my blessing. I will not have my hand forced, Mother. Not with her and

not with anyone else. I will not have you take over my life
and organize it to suit your interests. I shall marry when I
am ready to do so, and I shall marry a woman entirely of
my own choosing. I shall take her to Roxingley, and she
will be mistress there. It will be run as she and I see fit. I
hope you understand this. I do not want any unpleasantness
between us. I do not want total estrangement either. But I
am more than just your son. I am a man in my own right. I
am a person. I am Lord Hodges."

"Dearest," she said, taking up an ostrich feather fan from
the table beside her and fanning her face with it, "do sit
down and have a quiet talk with me. It has been so long. Far
too long. Blanche, ring the bell for tea."

"I will not stay, Mother," he said. "I have another ap-
pointment."

It was not true, but he could not remain here any longer
in this dim, feminine light.

"You must come back another time, then," she said, offering her hand.

He crossed the room to take it and kiss the back of it,
feeling curiously like a courtier upon whom his queen was
conferring a special favor.

"Do send my men in as you leave, dearest," she said. "It
is wearying to have to fan my own face. Did you hear Lady
Dunmore tell me how very handsome you are and how very
much you resemble me? You may not have heard. You were
conversing with Miss Dunmore at the time. And the mother
added that she was convinced you must be my brother
rather than my son. People are such flatterers, are they not?
Do you think I look old enough to be your mother?"

"I know that you *are* my mother," he said, turning away
and taking a brief leave of Blanche and Nelson, who looked
up from his book to nod at him.

A minute or so later he was hurrying along Curzon Street, trying to outpace his memories of the afternoon. *His mother.* That very public display in the park of an apparently well-advanced courtship. *His mother.* Miss Dunmore's mother. Miss Dunmore herself, sweet and lovely and very possibly in daily expectation of his making a formal call upon her father. *His mother.* Her voice. Her endless vanity. Her way of maneuvering people and events so that she almost always got her way.

Elizabeth.

The viciousness of rumor and gossip was passing him by, it would seem. And Codaire too. Instead, it was all focusing upon Elizabeth. Her vivid appearance and exuberant behavior at the ball, particularly during their waltz, was being turned against her. Her past, real and imagined, was being dredged up and turned against her. Was the *ton* satisfied with whatever nastiness had been flying about yesterday? If she had gone to Riddings Park, would it die down now from lack of fresh fuel?

Had she gone?

A London without Elizabeth in it was going to be a bleak place.

He thought of yesterday's kiss in the park and his depression deepened. He could very easily fall in love with her. Perhaps in a way he already had. But it was not an inclination he could indulge. She was not for him. Yet—

I care for you too much to marry you.

Oh no, Elizabeth. If you cared, you would have said yes.

Fifteen

Elizabeth's day began with the announcement in the morning papers of the ending of her betrothal. It made her stomach turn over a bit and robbed her of any appetite for her breakfast. It was all so very public and embarrassing. Yet it was not nearly as upsetting as she had expected it to be when she saw it so starkly set out in print. It had been a huge mistake to accept the proposal of a man to whom she had felt no real attachment except gratitude. She almost deserved the embarrassment.

There was to be more than she expected, however. A letter from Viola, Marchioness of Dorchester, came with the morning post. She had written from her home at Redcliffe Court in Northamptonshire primarily to congratulate Elizabeth on her betrothal to Sir Geoffrey Codaire with whom she had a slight acquaintance going back a number of years. She remembered him as a worthy gentleman of steady character and wished Elizabeth well. But the letter continued beyond mere congratulations. It was, in fact, brimming over with exuberant happiness, for not only had Viola heard, as everyone else in Britain had by now, that Napoleon Bonaparte had been captured and exiled to the island of Elba, thus ending the long wars, but she had also discovered just the day before that Harry had survived the last great bloody battle of the wars at Toulouse in southern France. She had given in to Marcel's persuasions and was coming to London to celebrate the wonderful news by attending Elizabeth's wedding.

You more than anyone else in the Westcott family deserve happiness, Elizabeth, she had written. *How could I not come to celebrate your great day with you as you helped celebrate mine on Christmas Eve?*

Oh dear. But it would surely be too late now, even if she wrote without delay, to stop Viola from coming—and presumably Marcel too and Abigail and Marcel's twins. They would have to find some other way of celebrating.

The morning continued when Alexander joined her and their mother at the breakfast table and asked Elizabeth if she had read the paper.

"The notice about my betrothal?" she said. "Yes. I am glad it is there for all to see, though everyone knew anyway, of course. Now the gossip, which I am sure was rife yesterday, will have a chance to die down."

"Not the notice," he said, setting the paper down beside her plate. It was folded to display one column of the social pages. "I believe I am going to have to have another word with Codaire."

She picked it up and read. A reliable source had reported that Lady Overfield was conspicuously absent from a certain well-attended soiree last evening, too embarrassed no doubt to show her face after humiliating her betrothed and rendering many of the most respectable elements of the *ton* aghast when she had set her cap quite outrageously at a far younger man, who would remain anonymous out of deference to his good name. Her affianced husband, the reader would be gratified to know, had broken off the engagement without further ado.

Oh. Well, she had known it would not be good. Gossip by its very nature was vicious and not always accurate.

"Please do not confront Geoffrey," she said. "It will only make things worse, Alex, and prolong this whole ridiculous episode. I will doubtless survive the injustice."

"Do you wish to change your mind and go to Riddings or Brambledean after all?" he asked. "I will give the order if you want."

"It might be best, Lizzie," their mother said. "Viola will understand."

"No," Elizabeth said. "I am going to stay. And I must go and get ready. Anna and Jessica will be here soon, and Anna is always on time."

It was obvious which way the wind was blowing, of course, and would probably continue to blow for a while. As in so many cases of scandal, the woman was at fault and the man blameless. In Colin's case it was a good thing. In Geoffrey's it was not. But perhaps he would gain some satisfaction from being painted as some sort of wronged, martyred hero. The only thing she could do was wait it out until the gossip died down, as it inevitably would after a few days.

In the meantime, she had a mission to accomplish. She had to find that one bonnet on Bond Street that she would not be able to resist.

By the following morning more stories about Elizabeth had been dredged up from somewhere in the realm of fancy and

embellished with rumors and half-truths and outright untruths as they were bandied about in almost every fashionable drawing room and ballroom and gentlemen's club in
London. Many members of the *ton*, though not by any
means all, were quite happy to forget that just a few days
earlier they had held Lady Overfield in the highest esteem
as a dignified, modest, amiable widow. Some even claimed
to recall that they had accepted their invitation to her betrothal ball with a certain misgiving since they remembered her flirtatious ways during her first marriage and
feared she would make some sort of unseemly exhibition of
herself at the ball. A few professed to have felt a similar
unease at accepting their invitation to her wedding, upon
the conviction that poor, respectable Sir Geoffrey Codaire
was almost certainly going to rue the day before the summer was out.

There were those who were quite happy to recall that
Lady Overfield had made herself ridiculous after the
marriage of her brother last year by setting her cap at her
sister-in-law's far younger brother in a quite unseemly display of flirtation. It was she, rumor had it, who had insisted
that he be invited to spend last Christmas at Brambledean
when all the other guests were members of the Westcott
family. And it was she who had maneuvered matters this
spring so that the amiable and long-suffering—and very
handsome—Lord Hodges waltzed with her at every ball.
An unidentified source had even claimed to have seen her on
the day following the disastrous betrothal ball hurl herself
upon him in Hyde Park, where she had persuaded him to
walk with her in the rain. It was very fortunate for him that
he had not taken a chill. He had repulsed her advances, of
course.

Colin heard it all in one way or another during the

course of the morning and was appalled. But the trouble with gossip and slander was that it was almost impossible to stop once it had started. He felt all the helplessness of his situation. He thought he should go about everywhere denying everything on her behalf, but knew very well that it would do no good. He would merely add fuel to the flames.

The fact that the whole thing was ridiculous and would soon die down and be virtually forgotten within weeks did nothing to soothe his agitation. He hoped she had gone home to Riddings Park and would not hear the worst of what was being said about her, but it was not so. Alexander told him when they met at the House of Lords that she had decided not to go but was trying to carry on with her life as though nothing had happened to disturb it.

"I find all this hard to believe," Alexander said. "We are all familiar with gossip. It can be sickening. But I do not remember anything quite as vicious and relentless as this. Where is it coming from?"

"Codaire?" Colin said, tight-lipped. "I am going in search of him. Enough is enough."

"Save your efforts," Alexander said. "He left town the very day you confronted him at White's."

Colin was left wondering if there was anything he *could* do. She had refused to marry him. He had no right to offer any sort of protection at all.

Then something else happened.

He arrived back at his rooms in the early afternoon to be informed by his disapproving valet that two visitors awaited him in his sitting room and one of them was *a lady*. He gave the impression that he would not have admitted her to what were strictly bachelor rooms had she not had her husband with her and had she not happened to be Lord Hodges's sister. They had been here for longer than an hour.

Blanche? And Nelson? Here? What the devil?

Colin let himself into the sitting room and closed the door.

His sister was seated straight-backed on the edge of a chair, her hands folded in her lap. Nelson was standing over by the window. He had probably seen Colin returning home.

"Blanche?" Colin said. "Nelson? To what do I owe the honor? Have you been brought no refreshments?"

"We did not want any," Blanche said, getting to her feet. "And we will not be here more than a minute or two longer. There is something you ought to know, Colin, and I have come to tell you. Mother has sent a notice to appear in tomorrow morning's papers. It is an announcement of your betrothal to Miss Lydia Dunmore."

"What?" He stared at her blankly.

"You did hear correctly," she said. "It is all I have to say. Come, Nelson."

"Wait." Colin held up one hand. "My betrothal? But there is no such thing. I have not even offered for Miss Dunmore. I am not even . . . What . . . Did Mother send you? Does she know you are here?"

"Of course she does not," she said. "Nelson?"

His brother-in-law approached across the room, nodded to Colin as he passed, and opened the door for his wife. Blanche left without another word and Colin found himself staring at the closed door.

What the devil?

Until a few days ago he had not exchanged a single word with Blanche for eight years. They had never been close. The twelve-year gap in their ages had been virtually insurmountable while they were growing up. She had never seemed to like him, and he could not pretend ever to have felt particularly fond of her. For reasons of her own she had chosen to stay loyal to their mother and to be her virtual shadow even after her marriage to Nelson. She had no children and no sense of humor—strange that those two things seemed to go together in his mind. Yet now, right out of the blue, she had chosen to come here, where the presence of ladies was much frowned upon, to warn him that his mother was up to one of her manipulative tricks—though a particularly outrageous one even for her. She was about to have his betrothal announced and make it next to impossible for him to withdraw.

Good God!

Did Lady Dunmore know about it? But it seemed unlikely that his mother would have gone to these lengths without the lady having at least some inkling of what was in the wind. Did Miss Dunmore know? And approve? But Colin had the feeling that that young lady was not often consulted on her own future.

What the devil was he going to do?

And why had Blanche broken the silence of years and the indifference of a lifetime to come here to warn him? He assumed it *was* a warning. Had their mother finally done something to outrage even her? Did she not want the competition of a younger, very lovely sister-in-law to take attention from herself? Yet strangely he had never sensed any real vanity in Blanche.

Did it matter what her motive had been?

The notice was to be in tomorrow's papers? Was it too late to stop it? Surely not. But . . .

He had been pacing the living room floor. He halted in the middle of it now, his hands clasped at his back, his eyes closed. Suddenly he felt overwhelmed. Everything had slipped from his grasp. His resolutions of a few months ago were in tatters, his dreams transformed into nightmares. He had decided to step out into his own life and take charge of it, to make something meaningful of it, forge his adult identity, become the man he could be proud of being. He had hoped for a little happiness along the way. Perhaps a lot of happiness.

He might have known it would not be possible. He might have known that his mother, given the smallest chance, would shape his life as she wanted it to be—something that would reflect favorably upon her, something she could control and bring into her own orbit.

Except that . . . His arms dropped to his sides and he clenched his fists. His eyes were still closed.

Except that he did not have to let it happen.

As far as he knew, no one had ever fought against his mother and won. Was there any reason to suppose that he could be the one exception?

Was there any reason to suppose he could not?

At the same moment he knew very well what had been happening with Elizabeth—or rather with her reputation. Perhaps he had suspected it from the start and had known it almost for sure as soon as he had learned from Alexander that Sir Geoffrey Codaire had left town the very day of their confrontation at White's. Now he knew it for certain.

Was he going to go down in defeat without even a fight?

Was he going to allow Elizabeth to suffer the sort of vicious character assassination that was almost impossible to fight against because it was being orchestrated by an expert who never lost?

No, he was not. By God, he was not!

* * *

Elizabeth went out during the morning when Wren invited her to go with her to see the new display of her Heyden glassware at a shop that regularly sold it.

Elizabeth was glad of the outing. Despite her resolutions of the day before yesterday and yesterday morning, she was unnerved by the ferocity of the stories that were being told about her. She was bewildered too. Why was it happening? Who could hate her so much. *Geoffrey?* But despite his unexpected jealousy and the spite with which he had spoken to her in Avery's library, she could not believe he would so relentlessly set out to blacken her name and make it impossible for her to remain in London.

She had not been out since yesterday morning, when she and Anna had each bought a bonnet and Jessica had bought two. They went and looked and admired and were made much of by the shop owner—at least, Wren was. He assured her that her pieces were more sought after by his customers than any others. They met absolutely no one Elizabeth recognized. They arrived home late for luncheon and almost late for Nathan's feed.

"He is just beginning to think about being cross," Alexander said, bouncing the baby, who was cradled in the crook of one arm. He kissed Wren on the nose as she gathered Nathan in her arms and took him up to the nursery. Alexander turned to Elizabeth, frowning.

"What?" she asked. "There is more, I suppose."

"I do not know where whoever it is finds his material," he said, tight-lipped. "All sorts of stories from the years of your marriage to Overfield. Stories from last year and this year and even Christmastime. Some of them are even partially recognizable. Someone is finding these stories and twisting them quite maliciously."

"I really do not want to hear any more," she said. "I am sick of the whole thing. The very worst thing I ever did in my life was accepting Geoffrey's proposal."

"It is not him," he said. "He left town the day after the ball."

She was right, then. But who *was* doing it? Or was it a whole group of people who were feeding off one another's nastiness? But *why?*

"I suppose we can expect a family gathering this afternoon," she said.

"It would not surprise me," he said.

But soon after luncheon, before any of the family descended upon South Audley Street, Colin was announced.

Elizabeth was in the morning room, explaining in a letter to Araminta Scott, the friend of hers who had recently lost her father, that she was no longer betrothed and was very happy to be single again. She put her pen down in some haste and got to her feet. Colin was the last person she wished to see at the moment. Her emotions were ruffled enough without having to confront her painful feelings for him.

And he was not looking happy. Or boyish. Only very handsome and attractive to boot. She wanted him to go away.

"I beg your pardon," she said, smiling at him and clasping her hands at her waist. "I daresay you came to see Wren. I believe she is in the nursery with Alex."

"No," he said. "I came to see you."

"Did you?" she said. "I suppose you have heard all the gossip. It would be strange if you had not when all the rest of the world must have done so. You must not worry about me, Colin, if that is what you have been doing. Perhaps someone will be obliging enough to murder his grandmother soon and there will be another conversational topic to distract from me. In the meanwhile I will not run away. I positively refuse to do so. And you must *not* worry about me."

"I am so sorry, Elizabeth," he said, and for the first time she noticed how pale he was. "It is all my fault. At least, it is all on account of me. It is not Codaire. It is my mother. It has to be. Only she could do something like this."

She gazed at him, uncomprehending. *"Lady Hodges?"* she said. "But that is absurd. *Why?"*

"One thing you need to understand about my mother," he said, passing the fingers of one hand through his hair and turning away from her so that he would not have to look into her eyes, "is that she always has to have her own way. No matter what. And she always does get it. There is no standing up against her. Though I do intend to do just that. But what is going on now is that she has heard that I am in search of a bride this year, and she has taken it into her head that I must marry Miss Dunmore, whom she considers to be the most beautiful of the eligible young ladies making their debuts this year. My mother has always surrounded herself with beauty and she has decided to add my wife to her court—and me too. She will not compromise on that now she has decided on it. I have explained to her that I have not chosen anyone yet and that when I do, it will be someone who suits me. After what happened a few evenings ago, she is clearly afraid that I will marry you. She is doing everything in her power to prevent it. And she has considerable power. I have never quite understood it, but she does."

Elizabeth gazed at him, aghast. "She sees me as a threat?" she said.

He turned his head to look at her. "But she is right," he said. "I did ask you to marry me. And thus subjected you to *this*." He gestured with one hand as though all the gossip hung in the air about them. "It is not enough for her to nudge me in the direction she wants me to take or even to trick me. She has to destroy you to make doubly sure."

Elizabeth licked lips that were suddenly dry. "You must be exaggerating," she said. "You are speaking of *your mother*, Colin."

"And a son must speak no evil of his own mother," he said, striding across the room until he stood at the window, looking out. "Do you think it is easy for me to say these things to you or even to *think* them? She decided upon her campaign and is carrying it out with ruthless intent—but with no personal involvement whatsoever. No one would ever be able to accuse her of spreading even one word of the gossip. No one would ever find proof that she was behind it. But I know as surely as I am standing here that she *is* behind what has happened to you during the past few days."

"But how," she asked him, "would she know about things that happened during my first marriage?"

"Oh, she would know," he told her, turning his head to look at her over his shoulder. "And what she does not know she will make up. The truth and lies are all the same to her. There is only one unassailable truth in her universe. She is the center of it, and everything and everyone else exists to praise and adore her. Only the young and most beautiful are allowed to inhabit her inner orbit."

He turned his head sharply away again and tipped it back. She guessed his eyes were closed and that perhaps he was trying to hold back tears. She felt a bit as though she had walked into someone else's nightmare. But it was all so *ridiculous*.

"One thing she obviously does not know," she said, "is that you did indeed offer to marry me and I refused. She could have saved herself a lot trouble if she had discovered that. Perhaps I should simply write and tell her so."

"Good God, no!" he exclaimed, turning sharply from the window.

She moved closer to him. "What are you going to do about your courtship of Miss Dunmore?" she asked him. "Do you *want* to marry her, Colin?"

He closed the distance between them and took both her hands in his. He held them tightly, almost to the point of pain. "My mother, probably with some sort of acquiescence from Lady Dunmore, has sent a notice of our betrothal to the morning papers," he told her. "To be published tomorrow."

"Oh," she said, her heart plummeting to come to rest somewhere in her slippers. But—his *mother* had sent the notice?

"Blanche was awaiting me in my rooms when I returned from the Lords earlier," he said. "She had come to warn me. She has never done anything to help me like that before. I am not sure why she did it today. Perhaps she does not want the sort of competition Miss Dunmore would represent for herself. Or perhaps I do her an injustice. Perhaps she thought that this time our mother was going beyond the pale."

"You are going to be forced into marrying, then?" she asked him. "Oh, Colin. Are you sure it is what you want?"

"I am very sure it is what I do *not* want," he told her. "And there is time to put a stop to it. I will be doing that shortly. But what I really want to do, Elizabeth, is put another notice in the papers in its stead. I want to put in a notice of *our* betrothal."

He tightened his hold on her hands even further.

"Ours?" She stared blankly at him. "Yours and mine?"

"Yes," he said. "It is the only way, Elizabeth. You must see that. Only by marrying me can you put an end to the lies and the gossip. Only by marrying you can I protect you as I ought."

She frowned. "I do not need the protection of any man," she told him.

"I know," he said. "But I feel the need to offer you the protection of my name. And only by marrying you can I avoid the matrimonial traps my mother will keep on setting until I have married the woman of her choice and been brought firmly into the web of her influence. If I marry you, I will be free of her and break the pattern of a lifetime. I have evaded it for eight years, but this is the only way I can truly escape it."

He gazed at her eagerly and anxiously. He wanted to marry her so he could free her from his mother's spite and so he could free himself from her determination to choose a wife for him and dominate his life.

He was afraid, she realized. And she could rescue him. They could rescue each other. Oh, it was *not* a good basis for marriage. Not on either of their parts.

There had been no mention of fondness or love.

But she knew he *was* fond of her. And she, God help her, was far more than just fond of him. She could not do it, though. Could she?

She needed to *think*. But she had thought and thought about her decision to marry Geoffrey. She had thought about it for months. And where had thinking got her?

"I have brought that look to your face again," he said softly. "You are looking stricken, Elizabeth. Do you really, *really* not want to marry me? Because of my youth? My immaturity? *My mother?*"

"Oh, Colin," she said, and she had to blink her eyes so that she could see him clearly.

He released her hands in order to fold her in his arms, crushing her against him as he did so and holding her head against his shoulder, her face turned in toward his neck.

"I cannot *bear* what you are being made to suffer," he said, his breath warm against the side of her face. "I cannot bear that it is all on account of me. It makes me seem no better than Codaire. Forgive me, Elizabeth. Please forgive me."

"Colin," she said against his neck. "Oh, do not do this to yourself. There is nothing to forgive. You do not have to sacrifice the rest of your life as an apology to me."

"Is that what you think?" He took her by the shoulders and held her a little away from him. "That I see you as some sort of broken thing that can be mended only if I marry you? I do not know if you were broken for a while during your marriage to Overfield and after you had left him. I suspect you were. But you did what was incredible and mended yourself, and now you can be buffeted from all sides and made to suffer, but you cannot be broken. That has been evident in the past few days. And now you will continue to insist upon standing alone against all the fury and spite of my mother just because you do not want to be seen to lean on me in any way. I admire and honor you more than I can ever put into words. But I want to stand beside you. Not in front of you to shield you, despite what I may have implied a few minutes ago. I want to be *beside* you, Elizabeth."

She could feel his pain as an aura about him that engulfed her. She knew he cared. She knew he respected her as a person who could stand alone if she must. She knew . . .

Oh, she knew she could trust him.

But . . .

"Elizabeth," he said, and his eyes looked very blue as they gazed into hers from mere inches away, "*will* you marry me? Not for any other reason than that you want to? As I want to marry you?"

And he had spoken just the words that brought all her defenses crumbling down.

. . . for no other reason than that you want to. As I want to . . .

"Yes, then," she said, and watched his eyes brighten with tears.

"Thank you." She saw his lips form the words as his hands tightened on her shoulders but heard no sound.

God help her, what had she done?

"Yes," she said again. "I will marry you, Colin. Because I want to."

Sixteen

This felt all too familiar, Elizabeth thought a few minutes later as she stood outside the drawing room door, wondering if she should go in or escape to her room. She needed time to think. Or just to be cowardly. It was too late to think, if by *thinking* she meant reasoning out some question so she could come to a sensible decision. Far too late. And there was no point in hoping that Wren and Alex and her mother were up in the nursery with Nathan. She could hear voices from within. How many of them had come? The whole family? Were they not tired of trying to deal with her problems?

Anna and Avery were there, and Cousin Louise and Jessica. They must have all come together. And Josephine was there too, sitting on Wren's lap, playing with her necklace.

"Elizabeth!" Anna exclaimed, coming toward her with open arms. "We came to cheer you up if it can be done and to assure you that it is all nonsense. All of it. I cannot *be-*

lieve what is happening. You of all people. You are kindness itself and all that I aspire to be as a lady." She hugged Elizabeth and shed a few tears.

"A marvelous job you are doing of cheering her up, my love," Avery observed. "We brought Josephine with us, Elizabeth, so that you could bounce her on your knee and forget all your woes."

"We are going to organize a party to go to Vauxhall one evening," Jessica said. "One night when there is to be music and dancing and fireworks and we can all believe we are in fairyland. Well, I daresay Mama and Anna will organize it. And Avery's secretary. *Mostly* Mr. Goddard, actually. But you are to come with us and anyone else you would like us particularly to invite. Abby and Estelle and Bertrand may be here to come too. Mama mentioned that you may want to invite Mr. Franck. I have met him and like him."

"My love," Cousin Louise said. "Allow poor Elizabeth to get a word in edgewise. But really, Elizabeth, unless you have decided to go home to Riddings, as Althea thinks you ought, all you can do is carry on as if life were normal until it is. And we will all stand by you, you may rest assured. No one is going to say anything cruel in *my* hearing. And Avery has only to raise his quizzing glass halfway to his eye and any would-be gossiper will melt into an ignominious puddle at his feet."

"Dear me," Avery murmured. "I hope my boots will not be splashed. My valet would not be pleased."

Anna held Elizabeth's hand tightly.

"Did you finish your letter to Miss Scott, Elizabeth?" Wren asked. "I would not let anyone disturb you because I know you particularly wanted to write to her today."

"I did not," Elizabeth said. "I barely got started. Colin came."

"Colin?" Wren rescued the pendant of her necklace from Josephine's mouth. "He was here? While we were upstairs with Nathan? But why did you not tell him you were busy and send him up? And he has gone away without seeing us? How vexing of him."

"He had a rather urgent errand and could not stay," Elizabeth said. Her lips were beginning to feel a bit stiff.

Before she could say more there was a tap on the door behind her, and the butler opened it to announce the arrival of the Dowager Countess of Riverdale with Lady Matilda Westcott and Lord and Lady Molenor.

"We have come," the dowager announced rather unnecessarily. "I have never been more angry in my life. Well, rarely anyway. Who is spreading all these ridiculous stories? Of Elizabeth of all people. There is no one more worthy of respect and admiration. Elizabeth, who has long been the rock of cheerfulness and kindness for the whole family. Can a rock be cheerful? Or kind? Never mind. Matilda, if that is a vinaigrette you are withdrawing from your reticule, you may put it away again. When I am about to have a fit of the vapors, I will let you know."

She crossed the room to her usual chair as she spoke and seated herself. Everyone else, who had risen to greet the new arrivals, resumed their seats. All except Elizabeth, who stood in the middle of the floor feeling very conspicuous indeed.

"You missed Colin," Wren said. "We all did. He spoke to Elizabeth and then dashed off on some urgent errand. I wonder why he came at all. Did he say, Elizabeth?"

"Yes," she said. "He came to persuade me to marry him."

"Again?" Alexander frowned. "Can he not accept that he is in no way responsible for any of what has been happening? Must he keep on torturing himself with the conviction that he did something to compromise you when he waltzed with you? I hope you set him right this time, Lizzie."

"I said yes," she said.

There was a beat of silence in the room.

"Well, bless my soul," Matilda said, the first to break it. "You have followed your heart, Elizabeth."

"Matilda!" Cousin Louise said scornfully. "What utter nonsense you speak. There must be all of ten years between them."

"Nine," Elizabeth said.

"Elizabeth." Wren had a hand over her heart. Josephine was on her father's lap, trying without much success to get his quizzing glass into her mouth. "Oh no. No. I can understand his offering. But you cannot—Oh, surely you cannot have *accepted.*"

"My love," Elizabeth's mother said, hurrying toward her and setting an arm about her waist. "You have been horribly upset, and I hold Sir Geoffrey Codaire *entirely* to blame whether he has had any hand in this ugly campaign against you or not. I feel desperately sorry for Lord Hodges, for everything started while he was dancing and conversing with you. But for the two of you to *marry* . . . It is preposterous, as you will see when you are in a calmer frame of mind. You are four years older than Alex, Lizzie, and he is older than Wren, and she is four years older than Lord Hodges."

Yes. Nine years.

"We will send for him to call here later," Alexander said, getting to his feet and coming toward her. "We will settle this matter once and for all. We will persuade Colin that he does *not* owe you marriage, and in the meantime we will assure you, Lizzie—all of us will—that trying to set his mind at rest by marrying him is not the answer to anything. You would have a lifetime enmeshed together in a mismatch."

He drew her into his arms, and her mother's arm fell to her side.

"I am so sorry about all this," he told her. "I wish I could do more to protect you. Sometimes one feels so helpless. But I do agree with—"

"Not *all* of us will try to persuade Elizabeth to change her mind," Matilda said, interrupting. "Not all of us were blind over Christmas or have remained blind this spring. Nine years are nothing when the heart is involved."

"The heart!" her sister said impatiently. "Have some sense, Matilda. And what do you mean about Christmas? I suppose you sensed a budding romance that simply was not there. And you cannot romanticize what is happening here. Lord Hodges and Elizabeth, both acting with the best of intentions, are trying to console each other. It is quite admirable of them. But it would be a disaster if they tried to do it by *marrying*. You must not do it, Elizabeth."

"Elizabeth." The languid voice of Avery silenced them all. He had given his daughter his watch to play with. "Must you? Must you marry Hodges?"

It was not an admonishment. It was a question.

"No," she said. "There is no compulsion for either of us to marry the other. We have agreed to it because it is what we both want."

"Quite so," he murmured.

Anna, sitting on the arm of his chair and smoothing a hand over Josephine's very blond hair, smiled. "Then all has been said and nothing further needs to be added," she said. "Except heartfelt wishes for your happiness, Elizabeth."

"Nothing needs to be added?" Cousin Mildred said.

"With all due respect, Anna, *everything* needs to be said. You must consider, Elizabeth—"

But there was another tap on the door, and Aunt Lilian and Uncle Richard stepped in with Susan and Alvin, and the whole thing started again.

"Lord Hodges came here a while ago," Jessica told them before anyone else could. "He offered Elizabeth marriage again, and this time she said yes."

Elizabeth pulled on the bell rope for the tea tray to be brought in while the room erupted into sound about her and everyone weighed in on whether she ought to do it or not. And, in the case of the naysayers, what she ought to do instead and how she would extricate herself from the situation without hurting Lord Hodges's feelings. It would really be a shame to hurt them, they were agreed. He was such a pleasant young man with a tender conscience, though of course there was no need for his conscience to be feeling tender or otherwise over what was happening. He was as innocent as Elizabeth herself was.

"We will definitely have Colin here this evening," Alexander said, silencing the voices before the tray arrived. "Perhaps you will send a note around to his rooms, Wren. We will talk this over and persuade him that marrying Lizzie would not only be unnecessary but would also be the wrong thing to do—for both of them. You must not worry, Lizzie, about already having—"

"It is too late," she said, and everyone's attention turned her way. "He hurried off to make sure he could get the notice of our betrothal into the morning papers."

For a few moments only two persons moved. Josephine, who was standing on Avery's lap while he had a firm hold on her waist, bounced and beamed at him. Matilda, who was standing beside her mother's chair, clasped her hands to her bosom and beamed at Elizabeth.

Colin was in time to stop the announcement of his betrothal to Miss Dunmore, though only just. And it was not easy to convince the editor with whom he spoke that it should be withdrawn when he was not the one who had paid to have it published. However, when Colin explained that he *was* the one who would pay a lawyer to sue the paper for publishing information they knew to be false about himself, he was given no more argument. And his own announcement was accepted meekly in exchange.

He was not sure as he walked away from the newspaper offices whether it was relief he felt or panic. There was probably a bit of both. If all had progressed as it had been progressing a week or so ago, he might well have ended up marrying Miss Dunmore and living a reasonably happy life with her. But he certainly would not have been happy at being forced prematurely into marriage by his mother and hers, especially as his mother would without any doubt have proceeded to dominate her.

But—was his marriage to Elizabeth any less forced? Had he given himself, and her, time to properly consider what they were doing? It was all very well to have told her quite truthfully that he had offered because he wanted to marry her and for her to tell him that she had accepted because she wanted to marry him. But what did that *mean*?

Were they about to make the biggest mistake of their lives?

It was too late now, though, to do anything about it. And there was some relief in that thought too. He hated making decisions—the momentous ones that changed one's life when it was impossible to know if the change was going to be for the better or the worse.

Besides, the thought of actually being *married* to Elizabeth really was a bit dizzying. More than a bit.

He had planned to return to the house on South Audley Street during the evening since there was much to discuss with Elizabeth—with his *betrothed*. He did not doubt that her mother and Wren and Alex were going to have plenty to say to him. But he found his steps taking him that way as soon as he had finished his business.

He was curious to see if they had come again, her family, and was not at all surprised to see three carriages drawn up outside the house. The Westcotts and the Radleys were nothing if not predictable. Endearingly so in many ways. They really cared for one another. They would not have gathered to gloat. They would have come to comfort and support and to offer solutions.

Poor Elizabeth. He wondered how they were reacting to her news. Provided she had had the courage to give it, that was, but he would wager she had.

Dash it all, he ought not to have walked this way. Having done so, he would consider himself cowardly if he did not rap on the door knocker. Besides, these people would have to be confronted sooner or later. Another thing about the Westcotts and Radleys was that they did not go away.

Two minutes later he was being announced and admitted to the drawing room. Upon entering he was stared at for a silent moment.

"Colin," Elizabeth said then, looking quite her old self, poised and serene and smiling a warm welcome. She crossed the room toward him and slid an arm through his. "I am so pleased you were able to return so soon. Do come and sit down. I will pour you a cup of tea. It will still be hot. Everyone *does* know."

He could see Elizabeth's manner for what it was, a sort of armor that hid what was quite possibly a massive vulnerability. And he marveled that he had got to know her well enough since last Christmas to understand that about her more and more. Her serenity was self-imposed and held in place by willpower and the determination not to be at the mercy of her feelings—or other people's.

Everyone had recovered from any shock they must have felt. Wren came and hugged him wordlessly. Alexander wrung his hand and looked hard at him while he offered congratulations. Mrs. Westcott hugged him too and informed him that she was going to call him Colin since he was soon to be her real son-in-law rather than just an honorary one. Anna, Duchess of Netherby, hugged him as did—surprisingly enough—Lady Matilda Westcott. Everyone else offered words of congratulation and handshakes in the case of the men. Lady Josephine Archer blew a bubble at him.

And he sat on the love seat beside Elizabeth and wondered how they had all reacted when she told them. It was cowardly of him not to have stayed to face it with her, though he really had had a good reason for leaving.

"Mrs. Radley was just asking Elizabeth when," Lady Molenor said to him, "and where. She had not had a chance to answer before you walked in."

When and where?

"The wedding," she added.

Ah. If he had his way, they would simply go off and do it, the two of them, as the Duke and Duchess of Netherby had apparently done a few years ago, taking only Elizabeth and the duke's secretary with them as witnesses. He just wanted to be married to her. He wanted the nonsense over and done with.

"We have not decided," Elizabeth said, her voice as calm as usual. "Colin had to rush away earlier. We will need to talk about it." In private, her tone seemed to suggest, though no one else seemed to notice that.

Everyone proceeded to discuss the matter. It ought to be soon, some of them believed. As soon as the banns could be called. There was no hurry at all, others felt. It would be better, in fact, to wait until all the unpleasantness had blown over—and remember that it was going to be added to tomorrow with this new announcement appearing in the paper. And it took time to plan just the sort of wedding one wanted.

There was more division on the question of where. A quiet church in London, Lord Molenor suggested while others agreed—perhaps the very one where Anna and Avery had married three years ago; Brambledean, Alexander thought; Riddings Park, his mother believed; Roxingley, Lord Hodges's own home, would be splendid according to Lady Matilda.

Colin was growing a bit tired of being managed. Of feeling that control over his own life was slipping from him.

"There will be no banns," he said, and everyone stopped talking to pay attention to him, almost as though they had only just realized that the prospective groom was there in their midst. He glanced at Elizabeth beside him. "We will marry by special license within the next week or two." Not at Roxingley. Or at Brambledean or Withington either. Or at Riddings Park. "Here in London."

"At St. George's on Hanover Square," Elizabeth added just when he was about to take up the idea of the small church where the Netherbys had married. He looked at her in some surprise and saw that her chin was raised a little higher than usual.

"Oh dear," Mrs. Radley said. "Are you quite sure, Lizzie? Will you not feel very much exposed to public view there?"

"Of course she is sure," the dowager countess said. "They both are. They certainly don't want it to look as if they feel they are creeping off to do something clandestine and a bit shameful. Of course it must be St. George's. And the whole of the *ton* must be invited. Nothing else will do."

No. Not any of the people who were reveling in the cruel stories about her this week. "*Friends* will be invited," Colin said.

"And family," Elizabeth added. "On both sides."

His eyes were still on her. Her chin was still up. There was what looked distinctly like a martial gleam in her eye. Surely she was not thinking of . . . But when she turned her head to look back at him, he knew that she had indeed used that term *on both sides* deliberately.

It would be madness.

"The wedding breakfast will be held here," Wren said. "In the ballroom."

Colin was still looking at Elizabeth, and she was still looking back at him. He smiled suddenly. Indeed, he would have laughed outright if they had been alone.

She obviously felt no such inhibition. She laughed.

And suddenly she was the Elizabeth of Christmastime, a bright, merry star, a gleam of pure mischief in her eyes, a flush on her cheeks.

And he laughed with her.

"I have just had a very comical thought," Lady Jessica Archer said. "Aunt Viola and the marquess are on their way here with Abby and Estelle and Bertrand. They are coming for Cousin Elizabeth's wedding. And now they will be here in time for—Cousin Elizabeth's wedding." She laughed gleefully.

"They are going to be unspeakably confused when they arrive," Alvin Cole said with a guffaw of merriment. "They will wonder if they misread the name of the bridegroom."

Some of the laughter had gone from Elizabeth's face. Colin touched the back of her hand with his fingertips and she smiled just for him.

Good God, he was betrothed. To this woman, whom he respected, even revered above all others. She was going to be his *wife*. His lifelong companion and friend. Perhaps the mother of his children.

What the devil had he done?

Elizabeth was seated at the escritoire in the morning room again, quill pen in hand, when Colin was admitted the following morning. Her mother and Aunt Lilian had gone shopping, and Wren and Alexander had taken Nathan in his perambulator for an airing in the park. She smiled, feeling all the strangeness of the fact that they were betrothed. It was official now. The notice had appeared in the morning papers. He strode across the room and bent over her to kiss her on the lips.

How lovely, she thought. *How absolutely lovely.* His blue eyes gazed into hers when he raised his head. She set down her pen carefully without wiping off the nib.

"You saw it?" he asked.

"The notice?" she said. "Yes, I did."

He looked boyish and eager. "I am glad it is settled," he said. "I am glad you cannot have second thoughts."

Or was he glad that *he* could not? She had lain awake

half the night in a cold sweat of panic. The only thing that had calmed her in the end and allowed her at least a few hours of sleep was the fact that it was too late to do anything about it. She could hardly end two betrothals within a week, could she?

"What is amusing you?" he asked.

"The thought that even the notorious Elizabeth Overfield could not call off two betrothals within one week," she said.

"Have you been tempted?" he asked.

"Yes," she admitted. "Well, not tempted. But I have wondered what I would do if I had not so fully committed myself."

"And did you decide?" he asked. He straightened up, a curious half smile on his lips.

"Yes," she said. "I decided that I can only move forward in the conviction that I made the right decision. And that you did too."

"You did." He nodded slowly. "And I did. But I have interrupted you. Again. Are you still writing to the same person as you were yesterday?"

"Araminta Scott?" she said. "No, I finished that last evening. She is my closest friend, a neighbor from Kent. I have invited her to come to London for our wedding. I am writing now to Camille to invite her and Joel to come if they can gather their family together in time and have no other commitments they cannot break." She remembered something suddenly. "Oh, I had a letter this morning from Sir Geoffrey Codaire."

"Did you indeed?" He folded his arms and leaned against the side of the escritoire. He crossed one booted foot over the other. "An apology?"

"Yes," she said. "A thorough and humble one. I found it

a bit touching. He even admits that possessiveness and jealousy drove him on that evening and assures me he will cast them firmly and permanently aside if I will but forgive him and agree to resume our betrothal. He promises to do all in his power to restore my reputation, which he fears he may have tarnished quite unjustly."

"*May have?*" He took the letter she was holding out toward him and glanced quickly through it.

"If he returned home," she said, "I daresay he does not know just how badly my reputation has been tarnished."

"You are *touched* by this?" he asked, replacing the letter on the desk and recrossing his arms.

Everyone made mistakes. No one was perfect. But not all people were prepared to say they were sorry, to beg forgiveness and ask for another chance. Not everyone was willing to commit to a change of behavior and attitude. "I feel badly for him," she said.

Then she remembered that he had accused her of driving Desmond to drink with her frivolous behavior.

"Are you afraid you have acted a bit impulsively?" Colin asked.

"By agreeing to marry you?" she said. "No, indeed. Even if I had not done so, I would not go back to him. I do feel sorry, though, that he did something he now regrets but cannot reverse. He is not an evil man." But there had been the spite as well as the jealousy. And apparently he had been saying derogatory things about her at White's the morning after the ball. She really had never known him at all, had she? A disturbing thought when she had had such a long acquaintance with him.

"Do you believe," Colin asked her, "that he would never be jealous again if he were given a second chance?"

"Fortunately," she said, "I will never know." But she *did*

know. She closed her eyes suddenly and remembered Desmond and how time and again he had sworn to her that he would stop drinking, that he would never again abuse her either verbally or physically. People did not change so easily. "But I will write back, if you have no objection. I would rather there be no lasting hostility between us."

"If I have no objection?" He stood looking down at her, frowning. "Listen to yourself, Elizabeth. If I had an objection, I would be no different from him. Has no man ever really *trusted* you?"

"What does trust have to do with it?" she asked.

"If you were to write to him without my knowledge and I found out later," he said, "would I wonder what you had said to him? What you had said about me? Would I think that if you had gone behind my back on that, you might do it with bigger things? Would I begin to be suspicious of you and spy on you and demand obedience and total disclosure? That would be no marriage, Elizabeth. There would be no trust there. You may write to Codaire or not. It is none of my business. It is yours. You do not ever need to ask me to whom you may write. Or with whom you may waltz. Or converse. Or laugh. You are going to be my wife, not my possession."

He was angry, she could see. She reached out a hand to rub along one of his folded arms. "You make me understand why I said yes to you yesterday," she said. "I shall write to him and accept his apology."

He unfolded his arms and leaned down to kiss her briefly on the lips again.

"Tell me," he said. "Do you plan to hide away until our wedding?"

"I do not believe I will be allowed to," she said with a laugh. "Cousin Eugenia and Matilda are going to host an afternoon tea, as is Aunt Lilian. There is the suggestion of an evening at the theater with Anna and Avery and Wren and Alex. And possibly an evening at Vauxhall Gardens with Cousin Louise and Jessica and a party they will put together. There may be a soiree at Cousin Mildred and Thomas's. There will doubtless be more ways devised for dragging me out to face a carefully selected audience. In the meanwhile I daresay I shall go shopping and looking over a gallery or two with whoever wishes to accompany me, preferably with someone who does not desperately believe that I need *protection*."

"I love to see your eyes twinkle," he said. "You have lovely eyes, Elizabeth."

"But only when they twinkle?" She could feel herself blushing.

"You need to do something far bolder than gazing at paintings in some gallery," he said, "or taking tea with a group of matrons or sipping wine at a soiree. We need a ball to attend."

"Oh, I think not," she said hastily. "I do not feel too kindly about balls at the moment."

"I seem to remember accepting an invitation to a certain ball," he said. "For this evening, in fact. Given by the Ormsbridges. They married last summer after she had had a successful debut Season. There is no title in Ormsbridge's family, but he is enormously wealthy and of impeccable lineage. He is also a good fellow and a friend of mine since our days at Oxford. It is generally agreed that Mrs. Ormsbridge did brilliantly well for herself. It is his private opinion that he did even better for himself. They have organized a lavish ball, I understand, to show the world just how well they both did. I danced with the lady a few times last year and found her delightful and charming. Did you accept your invitation? I daresay you received one. Everyone did."

"Colin," she said, "you cannot possibly be suggesting that we attend it. *Tonight?*"

"Why not?" he asked. "Apart from the fact that you are not feeling too kindly about balls at the moment, that is."

"Because," she said.

"Hmm." He frowned in apparent thought. *"Because* is not a reason. Try again."

"Colin!" She looked at him in exasperation. "Just consider how the last ball ended. It was less than a week ago."

"Have you met Mrs. Ormsbridge?" he asked her. "Do you like her?"

"I have no personal acquaintance with her," she said, "though I recall that she was one of Jessica's friends last year when they made their debut together. I remember her as a pleasant, unaffected girl. I have seen her a few times this year. She seems happy."

"Make her happier, then," he said. "Make her ball the most successful, most talked about of the Season. It is bound to be just that if we attend, you know. We will be the sensation of the hour—probably of the week. Maybe of the month. After this morning's announcement, the *ton* will be agog for their first sight of us together as a betrothed couple."

"Oh dear," she said, and bit her lower lip before laughing despite herself. "I am very much afraid you are right."

"I often am," he said agreeably, and grinned down at her. "Are you going to attempt to make yourself respectable again by attending teas and soirees? Or are you going to face the music and dance to it?"

"Oh dear," she said again, and stared at him. And she had a sudden memory of Viola when she had come here last year for Alex's wedding and did not want to be seen by the *ton*. It had seemed too soon to her after her marriage to

Cousin Humphrey had been exposed as bigamous. And Wren did not want to be seen by the *ton* either because she had worn a veil almost all her life and had only recently begun to leave it off in private. But the two of them had challenged each other and went off to the theater together one evening, brazen and unveiled. What they could do, she could surely do.

"I will write to Mrs. Ormsbridge to ask if she would prefer that I stay away," she said. "The last thing I would want to do is ruin her ball."

His eyes were smiling into hers and he was looking despicably handsome.

"This is madness," she added.

"Will you reserve the first waltz for me?" he asked.

Seventeen

L ady Hodges's eyes were glittering with gaiety by the time the last of her guests had taken their leave. It had been a merry afternoon during which she had entertained numerous persons, including several young ladies whose mothers knew no better than to allow them to attend one of her afternoon teas without the proper chaperonage, and several young gentlemen who came to pay homage to the goddess and flirt outrageously with her and a little more suavely with the other ladies. Conversation had been lively and had involved much laughter from the men and blushing and tittering from the ladies. A young poet, whose hair was too long and too wild and whose coat was almost thread-bare at the elbows while his shirt points wilted from too little starch, had read aloud a sonnet to the curl that brushed my lady's cheek, claiming afterward that he had composed it upon the spot.

"I do not doubt it," Lord Ede had muttered, opening his snuffbox and examining its contents.

"Be kind, Ede," Lady Hodges had replied in her sweet voice, offering the back of her hand to the poet as a special favor and smiling graciously upon him.

She had participated in the conversation, moving among her guests, smiled sweetly upon the blushing young ladies and archly at the gentlemen who flirted with them. She had laughed lightly and preened herself and protested at all the compliments and flattery and protestations of adoration that were poured upon her. She had slapped a fan across the wrist of one gentleman when he recoiled and expressed astonishment after it was revealed to him that Blanche, Lady Elwood was my lady's daughter, not her elder sister, as he had assumed.

"You will apologize immediately to Lady Elwood for the insult," she had told him. "Though everyone makes the same mistake, or pretends to, when they meet her for the first time. Everyone is a flatterer. Come, admit she is lovely."

Lady Hodges sank into her chair when she was at last alone—apart, that was, from her usual retinue. Blanche sat close to her while Sir Nelson Elwood, who had been absent through much of the party, stood behind her chair. Lord Ede was over by one of the windows, though he could not see out since the pink curtains that covered them and filtered a dim and flattering light into the room were not on any account to be touched. Four young men, who did not live at the house and were not officially servants, though they were not considered guests either, hovered about her chair, one taking charge of her peacock fan, another holding a lace-edged handkerchief that she might conceivably need, a third fetching her a glass of lemonade, and the fourth merely hovering because there was nothing much else to do for the moment.

The lady's gaiety was brittle. All the occupants recognized that and awaited the outburst of sweetness that must inevitably follow.

"You read the notice of my son's betrothal in the morning papers, I daresay, Ede?" she asked.

But it was a rhetorical question. He could hardly *not* know about it. Someone had mentioned it earlier and congratulated Lady Hodges. She had smiled dazzlingly upon the speaker, called him kind, and tapped him on the cheek with her closed fan. Any possibility that someone else might join him in his congratulations had died when the other guests had noted the red mark left behind on the unfortunate gentleman's cheek.

"I did," Lord Ede said. "She is a lady to be reckoned with. She did not flee to the country as almost any other lady would have done."

"I am curious," she said. "Why is he betrothed to the widow instead of to Miss Dunmore?"

"Clearly someone talked who had no business talking," he said.

"Perhaps," she said, "it was you. Perhaps you were careless."

"I am never careless," he informed her. "Perhaps you have met your match in the widow."

She looked long and hard at him while the one young gentleman fanned her face. "We shall see," she said. "How many years older than Colin is she?"

"At least ten years, my lady," the hoverer with nothing else to do said.

She transferred her gaze to him. "You must be mistaken," she said sweetly. "I would have guessed at least twenty."

"At least that much, my lady," he said.

"The *ton* really ought to be made aware that it was she

who put that notice in the papers," she said. "Everyone ought to be able to trust that what the papers tell them is true and accurate. She is clever. It is how widows of no beauty acquire second husbands, I suppose. It is a little pathetic, is it not? But very dishonest. Dishonesty is something I cannot bear. My poor dear Colin. Could he possibly have known what today would bring him?"

Lord Ede looked at her, one cynical eyebrow raised. "He has been waltzing with her at balls," he said. "He was waltzing *and* laughing with her during the ball that put an end to her betrothal. And he was kissing her in Hyde Park the following afternoon."

"She is very clever," she said. "I will give her her due on that. Lady Dunmore, on the other hand, is very stupid and ill-bred, and I am happier than I can say that Colin will not be marrying her daughter. She is an insipid girl, would you not say, Ede? Her beauty is much overrated."

"I daresay Lady Dunmore was upset when she wrote you that letter," he said.

"And no wonder," she said, "when she was expecting to see in the paper this morning that her daughter—her *second* daughter, I might add—had netted the greatest matrimonial prize of the Season. She was presumptuous. And to blame *me*, Ede, was the outside of enough. I have never said anything to encourage her ambitions. Quite the contrary."

Lord Ede was accustomed to her blatant lies and scarcely blinked. So too apparently were the other occupants of the room, who did not blink at all.

"My dearest Colin is only betrothed to the dowdy widow," she said. "They are not married yet. I wonder . . ."

The hoverer with the handkerchief cleared his throat and she turned her attention upon him.

"It is said, my lady," he told her, "that Lord Hodges is a friend of Mr. Ormsbridge and has accepted his invitation to the Ormsbridge ball this evening. It is said that it will be one of the grand squeezes of the Season. It would seem possible, even probable, that he would take his newly betrothed with him."

"Oh, surely not, my lady," the hoverer who had fetched the lemonade said, sounding shocked. "Not when the lady is in such utter disgrace with the *ton.*"

"I believe," Lord Ede said, sounding faintly amused, "the lady has backbone."

"Indeed?" Lady Hodges said. "She has my compliments. But will she make such a bold move? And will Lady Dunmore and Miss Lydia Dunmore attend the ball too? It would seem more than likely when the Season is already well advanced and the poor girl has no suitor of any significance." She turned her head to contemplate her daughter, who was sitting silently nearby.

"Lady Overfield may prove a worthy opponent," Lord Ede said, drawing his snuffbox from his pocket again and flicking open the lid with his thumb. "So may Hodges."

"He is merely being stubborn," she said with a dismissive wave of one hand. "He is doing this to defy me, the foolish boy—if, that is, he knew about this morning's announcement in advance. He knows he has always been my favorite and so feels the need to assert his independence of me even if that means doing something as unutterably rash as affiancing himself to a woman twenty years his senior. *At least* twenty years. He will come to heel. He loves me."

He made her a mocking bow as he took a pinch of snuff and sniffed it up each nostril.

Lady Hodges was looking again at her daughter, who

had just been informed that she was not her mother's favorite.

"Blanche and Elwood, my dears," she said, "you must go to a ball tonight. The outing will do you good."

Wren and Alexander, returning from their walk in the park with the baby, thought her mad. And then Wren rushed at her and hugged her tightly and declared that it was *just* what she might have expected of Elizabeth.

"I have never known anyone more courageous," she declared, forgetting the enormous courage that had taken her last year from being a lifelong hermit to becoming the socially active Countess of Riverdale.

Alexander still thought her mad and blamed Colin for making such a reckless suggestion.

Elizabeth's mother, returning from her outing with Aunt Lilian, was aghast, but then caught her daughter up in a hug even tighter than Wren's had been.

"It is *just* the sort of thing you would do," she said. "Foolish, foolish Lizzie. We must let the family know."

Aunt Lilian nodded. "Richard and I did not intend to go even though we accepted our invitation," she said. "I must return home, Althea, to let him know we will be going after all. I am not sure about Susan and Alvin or Sidney, but I shall send notes around to them without any delay."

"It is still madness," Alexander said. "Even the full force of our two families may not be sufficient to save you from deep humiliation, Lizzie. Colin ought to have known better. I suppose it was his suggestion."

"Yes," she said, smiling at him. "And he held my arm behind my back and twisted it until I said yes."

He tutted and shook his head. "What did I do to deserve such a headstrong sister?" he muttered.

"Or such a reckless brother-in-law?" Wren asked ominously.

He sighed and shook his head.

Aunt Lilian left without further ado, and Elizabeth's mother disappeared into the morning room to write a few hasty letters.

She could expect a small army of supporters this evening, then, Elizabeth thought. That did not stop her from breaking out in a cold sweat several times during the afternoon, however, even after she received a short but warm and gracious note from Mrs. Ormsbridge in answer to her own, assuring her that she would indeed be welcome at tonight's ball.

She decided upon her turquoise evening gown for the occasion. It was three years old and everything about it spoke of simplicity as opposed to high fashion. The waistline was fashionably high, it was true, and the line of the skirt fashionably slender. The neckline was low enough to be in the mode, though not low enough to draw attention. But there was no scalloping or fancy trim or embroidery at the hem or about the edges of the short sleeves. Its appeal, she had always thought, lay in the expert cut. It hugged her curves to below the bosom and then swirled about her legs and hips in slim folds as she moved. The fabric caught candlelight without exactly shimmering. Her maid dressed her hair high with more curls than she wore in the daytime but not many more, and no ringlets or fussy tendrils to wave over her temples and neck.

She was satisfied with her appearance, even though her palms felt clammy as she brushed them over the skirt. One of her fears for tonight was that everyone who looked at her—and she was quite sure that everyone *would*—would be searching for signs that she was trying to appear younger than she was. She was thirty-five years old and was content to look every one of those years. Not more, though. She had been just as careful to avoid appearing in any way dowdy.

Oh, how could she think of her appearance as *one* of her fears as though there were only two or three more? There were so many, she could write a book. For several days now she had been painted as the blackest, most depraved of villains. And now, worst of all, she had snared the Season's most eligible bachelor, a gentleman who was rich and charming and handsome beyond words, and years her junior. Pins and needles were added to the clamminess of her hands. She could not seem to inhale fast enough to keep up with the beating of her heart.

Oh, how she *hated* this, she thought as she took up her shawl and fan and made her way downstairs to where her mother and Alex and Wren were waiting for her, looking, the three of them, as though they were steeling themselves to accompany her to the gallows. They all smiled as though on cue as they spotted her descending the stairs. She hated feeling as self-conscious as she had as a young girl making her debut into society. But she knew this evening would be many times worse than that had been.

No, it would not. She was thirty-five years old, a mature woman of experience who could face down any embarrassment or outright attack. She was Elizabeth Overfield, and her conscience was clear. She had done *nothing* of which she was ashamed. Oh, there would be those who would be only too eager to make much of the haste with which they had become betrothed, a mere few days after the ball to celebrate her betrothal to another man. Those people would argue that they had just proved Sir Geoffrey had been right about them. But they had *done nothing wrong*. Why should they wait a month or two months or a year before making their announcement just to give the appearance of a proper decorum? People must believe what they would. If the *ton* was about to give her the cut direct or worse, then that was *their* business. Hers was to attend a ball to which she had been invited with her betrothed—who had offered for her because he wanted to and whom she had accepted because she had wanted to. Not that those facts were anyone's business but their own.

She smiled her genuine, easy smile, though it cost her a great deal of effort to do so.

Just minutes later they were inside the carriage on their way to the Ormsbridge mansion, and very soon after that the carriage drew up before the house. A footman opened the door and set down the steps, and they descended onto the red carpet and entered the hall, which was all bustle and noise. The people lined up on the stairs to greet their host and hostess before passing into the ballroom turned almost as a body to gaze downward upon them.

Well, Elizabeth thought, it was not as though she had not expected it. And it was too late to change her mind and dash homeward to hide beneath the largest down bedcover she could find. She smiled instead and drew upon all her inner resources of serenity.

Colin was awaiting them in the hall, looking youthful and long-limbed and golden-haired and stunningly handsome in his black and silver evening clothes. He stepped forward, smiling, and took Elizabeth's hand in his, bowed over it, and raised it to his lips. There was an almost audible sigh from the direction of the stairs.

"It still astounds me," he said, his voice low, "that you are going to be my wife."

It was astounding to her too.

"Is that a compliment?" she asked, her eyes twinkling at him. "Please do not answer if it is not."

He straightened up, her hand still in his, and took his time about answering. She might have felt anxious if it had not been for his slow smile. "How can I find the right words?" he said. "There is something about you that is not just beautiful but is beauty itself. I can scarcely believe my good fortune. I realize that I would never have won you in a million years if circumstances had not allowed me to rush you off your feet."

Oh. And the wretched man looked quite sincere.

"How long," she asked him, "did it take you to rehearse those words? You are quite absurd."

"Agreed," he said. "Make it a million and a half years, then." He cocked his head to one side. "Nervous?"

"It is a good thing women wear long skirts," she told him. "My knees are knocking. And never tell me you are as calm and relaxed as you look."

He laughed softly and turned to kiss Wren's cheek—always the one with the birthmark, she noticed—and greet the other two before offering Elizabeth his arm and leading her toward the staircase.

The very young Mrs. Ormsbridge was flushed with a very obvious excitement as she stood in the receiving line at the first ball she had hosted. But when she caught sight of them as the majordomo was announcing their names, her face lit up with an even greater pleasure.

"Lady Overfield," she said, clasping Elizabeth's hand and proceeding to speak very quickly and breathlessly. "Michael and I were at the Duchess of Netherby's ball last week and I must tell you that I felt for you. What happened then and what has happened since has been unbelievably unfair to you. I hope you realize how many people agree with me on that. The people in the other camp do seem to make the most noise, but they are to be ignored, even despised, by anyone of sense. I was terribly pleased when Michael read me the announcement of your betrothal in this morning's paper. Pleased for you and pleased for Lord Hodges, whom I consider a friend." She flashed a smile at Colin. "And I was touched to receive your note this morning. It seemed so very like what I know of you to be so thoughtful. You are going to make my ball the most talked about of the Season, which is lovely for me but not so much for you, I would guess. It was very brave of you to come and I honor you. Michael, look who is here."

Mr. Ormsbridge bowed to Elizabeth and said all that was proper while his wife turned her attention to Colin and, after him, to Elizabeth's mother and Alexander and Wren.

And the moment had come. Colin offered his arm and Elizabeth took it, and they proceeded into the ballroom, where the hubbub of conversation noticeably changed tenor, first sinking to a near hush and then rushing back with renewed vigor. It was obvious to Elizabeth that word of their arrival had preceded them upstairs and everyone had been eagerly awaiting this moment.

It was, she thought, surely the most dreadful moment of her life. But even as she thought it, she knew how ridiculous that was. There had been far worse moments. And why should this be so dreadful? What had she done that she need feel this way? She turned her head toward Colin and found that he was looking back at her, his eyes steady on hers and very blue and smiling and filled with . . . what? Pride? His arm was firm beneath her hand.

And she realized something about him at that moment. She knew he could easily have avoided this. All of it. He had not needed to offer for her, either the day after the debacle of her betrothal ball or yesterday. He had done nothing to compromise her, nothing to make it necessary that he sacrifice himself for her sake. And, even having done so, having offered and been accepted, he had not needed to face the *ton* with her in quite such a public manner. It could not be easy for him, after all, to be seen with the most notorious woman in London, however unjust the charges. It could not be easy for him, after such an abrupt announcement in this morning's papers, to come here to face some of the young ladies who must have hoped he was beginning a courtship of them. If Miss Dunmore or her mother had had any inkling of what this morning's announcement might have been, and if they were here this evening, they might make things very difficult for him.

But he had done it all. For his own sake? Surely not. For hers, then. Because he was kind and honorable and a rock of stability and uprightness and kindness. When he had seen himself at Christmastime as an immature young man, he had been mistaken. She recalled his saying on Christmas Day that he needed to become a man. But he *was* a man. One of the very best. And he was utterly trustworthy. She had wanted, above all other consideration, to marry a man she could trust, and quite despite herself she had found him.

They smiled at each other, and if she had been resisting the knowledge ever since Christmas that she was deeply, irrevocably in love with him, well, she could deny it no longer. And why should she? He was to be her husband.

Her mother and Wren and Alexander had come to join them. But Colin moved his head closer to hers and spoke for her ears only.

"The Westcott and Radley families are about to close

ranks about us like an impenetrable shield," he said. "Shall
we wait for them? Or shall we stroll across to the other side
of the ballroom to talk with the group that includes Ross
Parmiter?"

She looked across the room to see his friend gazing back
at them and raising a hand in greeting. Why could they not
wait for *him* to come and speak with *them*? But that was not
the point, was it? And when had she ever been afraid to
walk across a ballroom floor?

"Let us stroll, by all means," she said.

And so the great ordeal of the evening was under way.
Everyone was, of course, fully aware of them almost to the
exclusion of all else, though many were too well bred to
stare openly. Normally Colin felt perfectly comfortable in
large gatherings in the sure knowledge that he was not fasci-
nating enough to draw more than his fair share of attention.
Even this year, after interest was piqued at the Dunmore ball
and word had quickly spread that he must be in search of a
wife, he had not felt unduly uncomfortable. For the extra
interest had meant that his search was made easier for him.
Eligible young ladies had been brought to him without any
effort on his part.

Tonight he felt distinctly uncomfortable. And conspicuous.

It helped to know that Elizabeth must be feeling worse
and that really tonight was all about her, not him. Her hand
was light and steady on his arm, and when they had smiled
at each other a few moments ago, he had found just what he
had expected to see—calm dignity, a smile of warm socia-
bility, slightly twinkling eyes, a woman perfectly at home
in her body. And he had felt a rush of affection for her, as

well as a great welling of pride that this woman was his betrothed and everyone knew it.

He understood now, as he had not at Christmas, how hard she had had to work over the years to achieve this poise, which was more than skin-deep, for there was nothing brittle about it. Yet for all that, there was a fragility deep inside her that he found endearing, for she was not a marble woman but one of deep feeling. He had always admired her serenity. Now, in her fragility, he saw the promise of a relationship. From a perfect, controlled Elizabeth he could only have taken. With a vulnerable Elizabeth, he could also give. The age gap between them had somehow narrowed. No, it had closed. It was irrelevant.

He concentrated upon giving and thus lost his self-consciousness.

They stopped a few times as they made their leisurely way about the ballroom to where Ross Parmiter was standing with his group, watching them. They spoke briefly with friends and acquaintances who made a point of speaking with them, congratulating him and offering their good wishes to her. No one openly denounced them, but he had gambled upon that. For though the *ton* could gossip quite viciously among themselves, its members rarely displayed open bad manners in public. That was why Codaire's words at the betrothal ball had been so shocking. Even some of the highest sticklers nodded formally to them as they passed and made no concerted effort to keep out of their way or give them the cut direct.

But how could anyone ostracize Elizabeth Overfield? Seeing her tonight, elegant, dignified, warmly smiling, surely all but a very small minority must realize how ridiculous the stories about her had been. Surely the vast majority must realize they had been deliberately set in motion by someone who meant her harm.

There was in some way more discomfort for him than for her. Miss Madson was at the ball, and his path about the ballroom floor with Elizabeth took them directly past her. She had a faction of relatives and friends and young gentlemen gathered protectively about her, all of whom were intent upon making it perfectly clear to him and everyone else in attendance that she had never been in any way interested in him. Colin did not hear more than a few stray remarks from the group, but it did not take any great effort of imagination to understand the intent of its members.

Miss Dunmore was also present and unfortunately close to Ross Parmiter's group. There was an even larger faction gathered about her, led by her mother, who ostentatiously turned her back upon them as they drew near and made a comment, just audible, that the nasty smell must be coming from the French windows, which were some distance away and were shut fast. Other members of the group raised their voices just sufficiently to be heard commenting upon the plainness of *someone's* gown and the unbecoming style of her hair, upon how she had driven one husband to the grave and would surely not be happy until she had done the same to a second. There were quips too about cradle snatchers. And on and on while Miss Dunmore herself looked pale and bravely tragic. It was interesting that they were all attacking Elizabeth rather than him. Unless, that was, the bad smell comment had been aimed at him.

At least Codaire was not present.

Ross looked curiously at Colin when they came up to

him, but he bowed to Elizabeth and wished her well and reserved a set of dances with her for later in the evening.

And then the opening dance was announced and Colin led Elizabeth off to join one of the lines. He smiled at her as he took his place opposite, and she smiled back. No one shunned them. Indeed, the lady next to Elizabeth, a plump young matron, turned to congratulate her and inform her, with a giggle, that she was the envy of all the unmarried ladies in town and very possibly some of the married ones too.

Michael Ormsbridge and his wife joined the head of the lines and the dancing began.

They had done this thing, Colin thought sometime later as he and Elizabeth reached the head of the lines and took their turn twirling down between them while the other dancers stood back and clapped their hands. And, wonder of wonders, they had survived intact. She was flushed and bright-eyed and looked as though she might be genuinely enjoying herself.

Mrs. Ormsbridge would have her wish. Her ball would surely be declared the grandest squeeze of the Season so far and the one most talked about for the whole of the spring. She dazzled her guests with her beauty and smiles, and Ormsbridge looked fair to bursting with pride and happiness. They did not really need the added allure of two notorious guests.

Radleys and Westcotts prepared to rally around them after the opening set was over. Colin was aware of Louise, Dowager Duchess of Netherby, stately in purple with tall hair plumes to add height to her already impressive figure, bearing down upon Mrs. Westcott and Wren and Alexander from one side and of Sidney Radley coming from the other direction with Susan and Alvin Cole. But Elizabeth, who seemed not to have noticed either group, caught his arm before they reached her mother and nodded in the direction of the door.

"Oh look, Colin," she said, and her face lit up with a warm smile.

For the second day in a row he found himself looking upon Blanche and Nelson. He could not recall ever seeing them at a ball before—or ever seeing them anywhere without his mother until they had appeared in his rooms yesterday. A quick glance assured Colin that she was not with them now.

"Do let us go and meet them," Elizabeth said, slipping a hand through his arm. "They must have come on your account."

His sister and Nelson watched their approach, both striking and elegant figures, neither of them smiling. Colin wondered if they had received a formal invitation.

"Lady Elwood," Elizabeth said when they were close, her voice warm and welcoming. "Sir Nelson. How lovely actually to meet you at last." She held out her right hand to Blanche as Colin realized the two had never been formally introduced.

"Lovely," Blanche murmured, her voice chill. "Mother said you would be pleased."

And of course there were a dozen or more people close enough to hear the brief exchange and only too eager to do so, and there were many more than a dozen who had a clear view of what was happening—Elizabeth smiling with warm charm and offering her right hand, Blanche cold-faced and ignoring it, Nelson poker-faced with his hands clasped at his back, Colin no doubt looking like a grinning idiot.

Was he grinning? He checked. No, actually he was not.

What the devil? Just yesterday they had come quite unexpectedly—and quite out of character—to warn him that his mother was about to trap him into an engagement to Miss Dunmore. Tonight they had come . . . why?

To embarrass him?

To embarrass Elizabeth?

Eighteen

Elizabeth understood almost immediately. Of course they had not come here to offer support for Colin's choice of bride, as had been her first thought when she spotted them standing just inside the ballroom doors. How naïve of her. They had gone to his rooms yesterday, unknown to Lady Hodges, to warn him about the way he was about to be trapped into marrying Miss Dunmore. But that did not mean they had come tonight to celebrate his betrothal to *her*. Indeed, they were probably as horrified by it as Lady Hodges must be.

Tonight they had come as her emissaries. They had come to cause trouble, probably in an effort to set Colin free to choose a bride more acceptable to his mother. Was she to be subjected, then, to two ballroom scandals within a week and the ending of two betrothals—to different men? It was too bizarre to contemplate. And *bizarre* was a benign word. Indeed, the whole situation would be worthy of farce if it were not also horrifying. How could all this be happening to her? She had been so very ordinary and nondescript until a few days ago, her life of no particular interest to anyone except her and her family. Yet now . . .

How was it possible to be so out of control of her life—again?

But the very thought of losing control of what happened to her, as she had when she was much younger and more foolish, stiffened her spine. It was simply not going to happen. She flatly refused to wilt and wither beneath the cold scorn of people who did not even know her.

Was every eye in the ballroom upon them? Normally it would be conceited to imagine such a thing, but these were not normal times. *Of course* everyone was watching, even those who went to some pains to pretend otherwise. Attention had been focused upon them even before the arrival of Sir Nelson and Lady Elwood. Now it must be riveted upon them. When had these two last appeared at a *ton* event? She could not remember ever seeing them. Had they even been invited to this ball? It must be as obvious to the *ton* as it was to her that it was the sudden announcement of Colin's betrothal in this morning's papers that had brought them here.

The only question that remained was what did they intend to do?

Mother said you would be pleased, Lady Elwood had just said.

"Lady Hodges was quite right," Elizabeth said, smiling warmly and returning her unshaken hand to her side. "Lady Elwood, do come and take a turn about the floor with me before the next set begins. We really ought to get to know each other since we are soon to be sisters-in-law." She slid her arm through Lady Elwood's, clearly taking her by surprise, and proceeded to lead the way in a stroll about the perimeter of the dance floor together.

It was a huge gamble, of course, for she was offering her future sister-in-law the perfect opportunity to do what she had come to do. Lady Elwood had but to create a scene, even something as slight as pulling her arm away and speaking a few cold and cutting words before returning to her husband's side. The flames of scandal would leap higher than ever and engulf Elizabeth. But in taking the initiative, she had the advantage, at least for the moment.

They were close in age, Elizabeth knew. They were of a height too, though Blanche was more slender. She was also blond and classically beautiful, her carriage erect and elegant. She was wearing a blue gown that was in the very height of fashion. *Ice* blue, Elizabeth could not help thinking, to match the woman who wore it.

"Lady Hodges was unable to come too?" Elizabeth asked politely.

"She is dining with Lord Ede," Lady Elwood said. "She considers balls generally insipid."

Elizabeth knew the gentleman slightly. He was an older man, tall and elegant and still distinguished looking despite distinct signs of dissipation.

"I am pleased that you and Sir Nelson came anyway," Elizabeth said. "I have never had the opportunity to meet you socially until now."

"I have never felt any wish to meet you," Lady Elwood said coldly, her arm stiff beneath Elizabeth's as though she had begun to realize how she had been outmaneuvered.

Eyes were almost openly upon them and ears straining to hear them as they passed.

"After Wren married my brother," Elizabeth said, "I must confess that I had no particular wish to meet you either. But circumstances have changed. I am about to marry Colin. I have a rather large, warmhearted family on both my mother's side and my father's. Colin dreams of having such a family of his own, albeit smaller. Colin and Wren are very close, and he has a good relationship with your sister, Ruby, and her family in Ireland, though he does not have a chance to see them as often as he would like. I know it grieves him that there is no closeness with his mother or with you and your husband. What grieves him necessarily grieves me. It would please me more than anything if the situation could be put right."

She smiled at Cousin Susan and Alvin Cole, who were beaming encouragement at her as she passed them.

"It is he who left at the age of eighteen as soon as we had buried our father," Lady Elwood said. "No one forced him to leave. Neither my mother nor I have sent anyone away."

"Except Wren," Elizabeth reminded her, perhaps unwisely. But she could not let the untruth pass unremarked upon.

"No," Blanche said. "Rowena was *taken* away by our aunt. Or sent away by my father. Whichever you prefer. Just as it was my father who sent Colin away to school as soon as he was old enough to go and then to Oxford. That was not Mother's doing. It was done as a deliberate cruelty to her."

Elizabeth turned her head to look at Blanche. She knew almost nothing about Colin's father. She had never asked and he had never volunteered any information. Was there any truth in that last remark?

The sets were beginning to form for the next dance, she could see. They had almost completed the circuit of the floor. Now what? So far she had averted disaster, but was it enough?

"You must love Colin," she said, "to have gone to his rooms yesterday morning to warn him of the trick that was about to be played on him. With your help he was able to evade it and betroth himself to me instead. Is there any possibility of peace between us, Blanche? And *may* I call you that since we will soon be sisters-in-law? I care deeply for your brother. I am not your enemy. Or your mother's."

"What you are," Blanche said, "is a clever opportunist. We all know—the whole of the polite world knows—why you are about to marry my brother, *Lady Overfield*. And you know nothing about my feelings for him or my reasons for calling upon him yesterday. My mother will never recognize you as his wife. If you marry him, she will make your life hell. It is no idle threat. My mother does that sort of thing superlatively well, and she does not like you. That is, in fact, a massive understatement."

Her words were chilling. But Elizabeth continued to smile. Colin was still standing with Sir Nelson. Uncle Richard Radley and Cousin Sidney were with them.

"Blanche," Colin said, reaching out a hand toward his sister as they drew near. "You have returned just in time to join the set with me. Elizabeth must join it with Nelson."

Elizabeth was not sure exactly how the two of them had planned to cause trouble tonight. Probably they had intended very publicly to give her the cut direct and to say something suitably nasty in the hearing of a sufficient number of ball guests that everyone would be sure to hear of it within minutes. It would not have taken much. Her name had already been very thoroughly dragged through the mud. They had surely been hoping to make it impossible for her to continue with the betrothal or even to remain in London. But whatever their intention had been, it was thwarted, partly by Elizabeth's presence of mind in linking her arm with Blanche's and walking and conversing with her before Blanche could realize how she had been outmaneuvered, and partly by what followed, courtesy of the Westcotts and Radleys. No sooner had that particular set come to an end than Alvin Cole solicited Blanche's hand for the next and Cousin Louise and Elizabeth's mother and Aunt Lilian arrived together to converse with Sir Nelson while Elizabeth danced with Mr. Parmiter and Colin danced with Jessica.

Blanche Elwood did not have the skill of her mother, Elizabeth thought, and her husband seemed to lack sufficient interest to take any initiative. At the end of that set, they left the ball. Elizabeth watched them go from her mother's side and wondered how their appearance here tonight would be interpreted. As a stamp of approval upon Colin's marriage, perhaps, acting on behalf of his mother? Quite the opposite of what they had intended, in fact?

"Well," her mother said, "that was interesting. Did they come to wish you well, Lizzie? But poor Wren."

Wren had stayed well away from her sister. The appearance of the Elwoods in the ballroom must indeed have been distressing for her. She approached now with Alexander. She was smiling.

"Did they come to make trouble?" she asked. "If they did, you handled the situation superbly, Elizabeth. So did Colin. Let us hope they will cause no further trouble. You two have had enough unpleasantness to last a lifetime. Yet you bear up so well beneath it all."

"I am quite determined," Elizabeth assured her, "to have some sort of amicable relationship with your sister, Wren, and with your mother too. I must. For Colin's sake, since his position as head of the family and owner of the homes where your mother lives compels him to try to make peace with them. But I do understand how disloyal that forces us to be to you. Is there any possible way—"

But she was interrupted by a touch on her shoulder, and she turned to find a gentleman of her acquaintance standing there.

"Lady Overfield," he said. "Is it too much to hope that you are free to dance the next set with me?"

"Thank you," she said. "I am, and I would be delighted."

Colin, she saw, was leading a young lady whose name she could not recall onto the floor.

Could they relax now? Was the worst over?

Would the evening *never* end?

Time must have slowed, Colin thought as the ball proceeded. He had never known such a long evening. It had been worth coming, however. They had used the endless time productively. Elizabeth had employed her poise and charm to show people that the caricature of Lady Overfield with which they had been presented during the past few days was nothing but nonsense. She had walked and danced and conversed and smiled and at no point clung to her family, as she might have been forgiven for doing. And he had been awed at the way she had handled Blanche and averted what might well have spelled disaster for her return to society.

He had spent the evening mingling with as many fellow guests as possible, shamelessly charming the ladies and chatting with the men. When some of his friends expressed amazement over this morning's announcement, he laughed and told them he had been trying since Christmas to persuade Lady Overfield to marry him and had finally succeeded. It was very nearly the truth. He added that he was the most fortunate of men, and that really was the truth.

Long before a waltz was announced, however, depression threatened to sneak in under his guard. His mother had tried to trap him into a marriage to which he had quite explicitly not consented merely because she had wanted Miss Dunmore as her daughter-in-law and minion. Having failed at that she had sent Blanche and Nelson this evening to destroy the betrothal he *had* chosen and publicly announced this morning. It did not matter to her that she could do it only by destroying Elizabeth, who had done nothing to deserve such cruel treatment. His mother would not approve of Elizabeth because she was thirty-five years old and not beautiful in the only sense that was important to her, and because she must sense that she could not dominate Elizabeth as she would have been able to do with Miss Dunmore or most of the young girls who were currently in search of husbands. And Blanche, though for reasons of her own she had defied their mother yesterday, had come to do her bidding tonight.

They were *his mother* and *his sister*.

He thought about Mrs. Westcott and Alexander—Elizabeth's mother and sibling. But the comparisons—or, rather, the contrasts—were too painful to dwell upon.

He ought perhaps to have encouraged Elizabeth to withdraw to Riddings, her home in Kent, until the scandal had blown over, as it inevitably would as soon as his mother had believed she had won and did not need to expend any more energy on finding truths and half-truths from her past with which to blacken her name. Perhaps he had done Elizabeth no favor by persuading her to marry him.

Perhaps it had been selfish of him.

One thing he knew for certain. He was going to call upon his mother tomorrow and have a proper confrontation with her. She was difficult, almost impossible to deal with, as everyone who had ever crossed her path had discovered. She always had her own way. But it could be allowed to happen no longer. And merely turning his back upon her and ignoring her existence would no longer serve either. Tomorrow he would assert himself once and for all and . . . Well, his mind could not quite grasp what might be accomplished.

He was just going to do it. There was no alternative.

He was bowing to Elizabeth then as couples made their way onto the floor. "This is my waltz, I believe, Lady Overfield," he said.

She smiled at him in that twinkling way that always warmed him from his head to his toes and set her hand on the back of his. "I believe it is, Lord Hodges," she said.

Even now, of course, they could not relax. For there would surely be scarcely a person in the ballroom who would not be remembering what had happened during the waltz in Netherby's ballroom less than a week ago. Was it possible that had happened so recently? It felt like forever ago.

They faced each other on the floor, and he took her in his arms when the music was about to begin.

"I really never expected to be notorious again," she said with a sigh.

Again. That broke his heart.

"This is why we came tonight," he reminded her. "To face the *ton* at one of the grand squeezes so that afterward we can put all the nonsense behind us. So that *you* can. But in order to complete the plan we must waltz."

So the *ton* could see exactly how they had looked just before scandal broke. So they could see how trivial and ridiculous it had all been.

The music began and he led her into the steps of the waltz, his eyes upon hers. He twirled her around one corner of the ballroom floor. She was gazing back at him and noticed he wasn't smiling.

"What is it?" she asked.

He raised his eyebrows.

"You are not smiling," she said.

Ah.

"With so many eyes upon us," he told her, "I am counting steps for fear of tripping over your feet or my own."

Her eyes laughed. His heart warmed and his feet somehow danced of their own volition, and they waltzed on, their eyes still upon each other.

And somehow the music and the dance wove their magic and seeped into every pore of his body and soothed his soul, while the colors of flowers and ball gowns and the light of innumerable candles swirled about the periphery of his awareness along with the hum of conversation and laughter. And he forgot for a few blessed minutes that they were on display, their every look and move food for speculation and possible censure.

Her cheeks were flushed and her lips slightly parted. Her eyes were dreamy. And she looked . . . Ah, Elizabeth.

"May I tell you something?" he asked her, and she raised her eyebrows. "You looked quite gorgeous in your gold and bronze gown last week with your elaborate hairstyle. But in your turquoise tonight with your hair dressed more simply, you are . . . Elizabeth."

And what sort of asinine comment was that?

Her eyes smiled and then laughed again. "Is that a compliment?" she asked.

"I used the word *gorgeous* of the other gown," he said, "and thus deprived myself of a greater superlative."

The laughter spread to her whole face.

"So I used the word *Elizabeth*," he said. "A superlative to outdo all superlatives."

Laughter bubbled over. "Oh, well done," she said. "Very well done."

"Language is the damnedest thing," he told her. "It lets one down just when one needs it most."

"But it did not let you down this time," she assured him. "I might have been pleased if you had used other superlatives like *stunning* or *glorious* or *incomparable*. But I like best of all being Elizabeth."

"Incomparable, yes," he said. "I did not think of that one. But I can never forget that you are Elizabeth." He grinned at her and then laughed. "You must be wondering if this is the quality of conversation you may expect of me for the next few decades."

"Is it?" she asked him, widening her eyes.

"Well," he said, "you will always be Elizabeth, you know."

"And you will be saying it for the next few decades," she said softly.

"Yes," he said, his eyes holding hers.

She smiled again and they waltzed on in a world that encompassed only the two of them.

The music ended far too soon. They stopped dancing and gazed at each other. And because there was a certain degree of familiarity in the moment, he was aware again of the attention that was still focused upon them from all parts of the ballroom. He moved his head a little closer to hers and was very tempted to kiss her. She made no move to pull away from him.

"Let us show everyone that we did *not* kiss, shall we?" he asked.

"Yes." And there was laughter in her face again and color in her cheeks and a twinkle in her eyes.

"Allow me," he said, stepping back from her and extending one hand while he made her a courtly bow, "to escort you back to your mother's side."

"Thank you." She set her hand on the back of his.

And quite suddenly and unexpectedly he wanted her. Good God, he wanted her.

Nineteen

Elizabeth waited until almost noon the next day before leaving the house, though it was irksome to have to wait so long. She was angry, a rare emotion for her. She was angry for herself, as who would not be? But even more she was angry for Colin. And for her family on both sides, all of whose members were using up their time here in town on her behalf, when they ought to be relaxing and enjoying themselves.

It simply was not fair. And it must not be allowed to continue. It *would* not be.

"No," she said to Wren when her sister-in-law offered to accompany her on her outing, though she had been deliberately vague about her purpose and destination. "No, thank you, Wren. It is just a quick errand. I will be back in no time."

"No," she said when her mother asked if she was at least going to take her maid with her. "No, it is quite unnecessary. I am a grown woman, Mama, and have been for many years. I do not need a chaperon dogging my heels wherever I go."

She had probably offended both of them, she thought as the carriage made its way along the street. It was unlike her to be so abrupt and ungracious. Both had looked at her with a slight frown, as though they would like to say something more but dared not. It was unlike her to come anywhere near to snapping. *That* Elizabeth had been left behind a long time ago.

They had all agreed at the breakfast table, Elizabeth included, that the ball had gone very well indeed. The Ormsbridges had received them with a particularly warm welcome and most of their guests either had been happy to see them from the start or else had thawed during the course of the evening. There had been a few who had not, of course, most notably Lady Dunmore and the rather large group of followers she had gathered about her and her daughter, but that was at least understandable and they had not made any sort of unpleasant scene. The unexpected appearance of Sir Nelson and Lady Elwood had surely been a good thing, even if the pair of them seemed lacking in obvious charm and had surely not smiled even once.

"It was kind of them for Colin's sake to put in an appearance," Elizabeth's mother had commented, reaching across the table to pat her hand. "And it was civil of Lady Elwood to walk with you, Lizzie, and of Sir Nelson to dance with you. Lady Hodges must have seen the announcement of your betrothal and encouraged them to go in person to acknowledge you and congratulate him. I can never quite forgive her for what she did to Wren, but perhaps she has redeeming qualities after all. People do change over the years, do they not?"

Wren had kept her attention on her plate, and Elizabeth

had not told them the truth of that surprise appearance of her future sister- and brother-in law. It was something she would deal with herself. However, she had been interrupted last evening when she had been talking with Wren, and what they had been talking about ought to be finished.

"Colin is hoping to establish some sort of civil relationship with his mother and Blanche," she had said. "We want to invite them to our wedding. But . . . But there is you, Wren. I do not know what happened when you called on your mother last year after your wedding, but my guess is that it could not have been good. Will you find it distressing—"

"This is your wedding, Elizabeth," Wren had said, interrupting her, "and Colin's. The two of you must do what you wish to do about Mother and Blanche without worrying about me. But if you invite them to the wedding, then you must invite them to the wedding breakfast too."

"Wren." Alexander had been frowning.

"No," she had said, holding up one hand. "I am not a fragile thing. I am certainly not going to force Colin and Elizabeth to choose between my mother and me. And this is not a matter for debate. Don't look at me like that, Alexander. Or you, Elizabeth. Not another word."

And not another word had been spoken on the subject.

When the carriage drew up outside the house on Curzon Street, Elizabeth was angry, though not in a way that was likely to erupt in uncontrolled fury. Only in a way that would carry her through the next half hour or so. It was past noon by then, but Lady Hodges was still not available to receive visitors. She would wait, Elizabeth informed the butler, stepping firmly over the doorstep to indicate to him that she was not to be trifled with.

"Kindly inform your mistress that Lady Overfield awaits her pleasure," she said.

He must have recognized her name, for he ushered her up to the drawing room to wait instead of keeping her standing in the hall. She awaited the lady's pleasure there for an hour. It was just after one by the ormolu clock on the mantel when the door finally opened.

Elizabeth had been directed to a love seat upon her arrival, but she had not remained in it after the first ten minutes. She had crossed first to a window to pull back one of the pink curtains. The light in the room was dim despite the bright sunshine outside, and it was distinctly pink hued. The butler had lit the candles in a gilded candleholder on the mantel next to the clock, but why see by candlelight when it was only just past noon and there was a world of daylight behind the curtains?

The curtains would not budge. Something held the two halves together, and something held them in place at the outer edges so they could not be moved. Extraordinary!

After that, Elizabeth had wandered about the room, noting that everything in it, from the carpet to the furnishings to the wallpaper, was either silver or gray or some shade of pink. There was a large number of chairs, sofas, and love seats in the room, enough to accommodate sizable gatherings. It was obvious, however, which chair belonged to Lady Hodges. It sat higher than all the others and was larger and more sumptuous. It dominated the room and looked more like a throne than a chair. The thought might have amused Elizabeth if she had been in the mood to feel amusement.

When the door opened at last, she was standing before the fireplace having a closer look at the clock, which was a magnificent piece. She turned.

Lady Hodges was alone. She looked like a fragile, hesitant girl, hovering in the doorway as though unsure whether she was permitted to enter. Like a girl, she was dressed in a white, high-waisted muslin dress with a low neckline and short sleeves, though Elizabeth could see that there was an inset bodice of fine gauze, which covered her bosom and ended in a small ruff about her throat. There were also sleeves of the same material covering her arms and shaped into frilled Vs over her hands. She was of medium height and very slender. Her blond hair had been curled and dressed with immaculate care. It was a remarkably realistic wig. The cosmetics on her face were easy to detect, but they had been skillfully applied to give the illusion of youth to a lady who must be sixty at the very least. She looked quite beautiful, but . . . Well, she looked more like a work of art than a real woman.

"Lady Overfield." She stepped lightly into the room and an unseen hand closed the door behind her. "How extraordinarily delightful that you have come to call upon me only a day after your betrothal to my son was announced to the world. Let me have a look at you." Her voice was that of a little girl. It made Elizabeth want to shiver.

She did not immediately take a look. First she crossed the room and ascended the two shallow steps to her chair. Seated on it, she seemed even slighter and more like a girl. It had been designed with that effect in mind, Elizabeth realized. Lady Hodges rested her arms along the velvet arms and turned her eyes upon Elizabeth, a slight smile upon her face. She took her time about looking her over from head to toe.

"My dearest Colin," she said. "It is hard to realize he is no longer quite a boy, though he still looks very young. And remarkably handsome. And easily influenced, I have heard. He has some growing up still to do. But of course you will help him with that, being a mature woman yourself. *How* old did you say you are?"

"I did not," Elizabeth said. "But you know very well how old I am, ma'am. You know a great deal more about me too than just that, and what you do not know you do not hesitate to invent. If you are aiming to embarrass me by looking me over and having me admit that I am significantly older than your son, you will not succeed. I do not embarrass easily when I have nothing for which to feel embarrassment."

"Oh, my dear," Lady Hodges said, picking up a monstrous peacock feather fan from the table beside her and slowly plying her face with it, "*has* someone been inventing stories about you? How very distressing for you. And how malicious of that someone. Perhaps it is untrue, then, that there are ten years between you and my son? Or nine years and five months, to be more precise. I do hope you were well received last evening. I sent Blanche and Nelson to lend you countenance and they informed me that you were very much enjoying yourself. I daresay any lady would who had such a young and handsome fiancé to show off to the *ton*, especially when she had stolen him from under the very noses of the young, inexperienced girls who were foolish enough to aspire to his hand. I was delighted to listen to Blanche's report, though I was sorry to hear that Miss Dunmore was there to mar your pleasure just a little. She is exceedingly lovely, is she not? It is being said that her mama was so determined that she marry my son that she tried to force him into it by implying there was already an understanding between them. Some even say she tried sending a notice of their betrothal to the papers, but I cannot believe she is capable of such blatant trickery. She is

not, however, a pleasant woman. I daresay you took no notice of either her or her daughter, who has been described
as a diamond of the first water."

There were several conversational starters that might
have led Elizabeth off into comment and protestation and
self-justification until she became like a dog chasing its tail.

"I have not come here to play games, Lady Hodges," she
said.

"I am happy to hear it," the lady said. "Games bore me.
I can never understand what is so amusing about charades
and blindman's buff and all the rest. Do come and sit on the
love seat close to me, and I shall tell you how I plan to welcome you into my family with a summer-long house party
at Roxingley. I already have the guest list drawn up—young,
high-spirited people who enjoy having fun in the outdoors,
and indoors too when the weather is inclement. You will
like them. They will make you feel young again. I daresay
you feel that your unfortunate first marriage robbed you of
your youth and that now, so many years later, you are too old
to recapture it. But it is never too late, Lady Overfield, and
with your second marriage, you know, you are going to have
to keep up or have Colin's eyes stray to all the beauties with
whom he will be constantly surrounded. Come. Sit."

Elizabeth remained where she was. She felt a little as
though she had been caught up in some sort of whirlwind,
unable to extricate herself or make her point. Except that
there was her anger, her point of calm at the center of the
storm.

"I will not be seated, thank you," she said. "I will not be
staying long. You began your campaign against me, Lady
Hodges, after my betrothal to Sir Geoffrey Codaire ended
and you feared that I might convince Colin that the honorable thing to do was to offer for me. He did, in fact, offer,

and I refused. You might have saved yourself the trouble. But the effect of your efforts was actually the opposite of what you intended. I did not either crumble or flee to the country, and Colin came back and persuaded me not only that I wished to marry him, but that he wished to marry me."

"Someone has clearly been telling lies about me," Lady Hodges said. "I—"

"I would be obliged if you would not interrupt," Elizabeth said. "We will be marrying, Lady Hodges, whether you like it or not, whether you decide to continue with your campaign or not. I would rather you did not continue, but I am prepared to deal with it if you do. Though I would warn you that running away is no longer how I deal with adversity. I will be Lady Hodges after my marriage, while you will become the dowager. I will be mistress of Roxingley and intend to make a home of it for Colin and myself and any children with whom we may be blessed. You will be welcome to continue to make it your home. But there will be room for only one mistress there, and I will be she. If there is to be a house party during the summer, as there very well may be, it will be planned and organized by Colin and me. The guest list will be one compiled and approved by us. I daresay we will pay you the courtesy of asking if there are one or two special friends you will wish us to invite."

"I wonder if my son will be so eager to marry an older woman, who, by the way, does not even have the saving grace of any remarkable beauty, when he learns that she has claws," Lady Hodges said. "I shall be obliged to warn him, you know. He may not like the prospect of not being the man in his own home. He was a lovely boy, Lady Overfield. Sweet and innocent and the most beautiful of all my children, though all of them were lovely."

"Except Wren, I have heard," Elizabeth said.

"Well." Lady Hodges made a dismissive gesture. "Rowena's disfigurement was unfortunate and quite grotesque. Impossible to look upon. She was a judgment upon me, I daresay. Though I did handsomely for her. I gave her to Megan and her wealthy admirer, and he married her and allowed Rowena to live with them and left his fortune to her. She has much for which to thank me, though she has proved ungrateful so far. I have yet to hear a word of thanks from her."

"I believe," Elizabeth said, "you will have to wait a long time, ma'am. Though I have heard Wren express a great deal of heartfelt gratitude to her aunt and uncle for the love they showered upon her when her life before they adopted her had been so devoid of affection from her own parents." But she did not wish to get drawn into open anger and spite. She would not give Lady Hodges the satisfaction of having discomposed her. "I shall bid you a good afternoon now. But before I do, I will add this. It is Colin's dearest wish that he have a family of his own to love and be loved by, just as I have on both my mother's and my father's side. And his dearest wish will always be mine. I hope you will come to our wedding. We will send invitations to you and to Sir Nelson and Lady Elwood. I hope you will all spend time with us at Roxingley. I hope you will be part of our lives and contribute to our happiness as we hope to contribute to yours."

Lady Hodges plied her fan and for once said nothing.

"Good afternoon, ma'am." Elizabeth inclined her head politely to her future mother-in-law and left the room. By the time she exited the house less than a minute later, her hands were tingling with pins and needles, her thoughts were spinning wildly in her head, and she felt short of breath. But she stood on the steps outside the house, pulling on her gloves and composing herself while she glanced across the pavement to where her carriage was awaiting her.

Except that it was not there. In its place was Colin's carriage. The door was open and Colin himself was leaning against the frame, his arms folded over his chest, one booted foot crossed nonchalantly over the other.

Colin had decided during last night's ball that the time had come to confront his mother. She had wreaked havoc in the lives of many people over the years, not least of whom were Wren and Justin and their father. He, Colin, had taken the path of least resistance after his father's death and stayed away from her. It was understandable. He had been only eighteen. But he had been feeling uneasy about it more recently, certainly since his discovery of Wren, alive and thriving, when for almost twenty years he had thought her dead. He had planned to do something about the situation this year and had indeed been trying, with mixed results. But though one of the most brilliant results was his betrothal to Elizabeth, that brilliance was overshadowed by the viciousness of the attack his mother had mounted against her and by what she had tried to do last evening when she had sent Blanche and Nelson to the ball. Meanwhile she had doubtless caused additional damage to Miss Dunmore, an innocent young girl.

Enough was enough, he had decided during the night. Yes, she was his mother, and one ought to honor one's parents and treat them with deference and respect. But there were limits to what one ought to overlook in exchange, and his mother had overstepped those limits long ago. Now she had gone after Elizabeth.

There was no point in calling upon her before noon, he knew, or even soon after. He went first to South Audley Street, where he asked for Wren and was shown up to the nursery, where she was bouncing the baby gently on her lap. Colin smoothed a hand over the child's head and leaned across him to kiss his sister on the cheek.

"Was last evening horribly upsetting for you?" he asked.

"The ball?" She raised her eyebrows. "Oh, I suppose you mean Blanche's appearance. What on earth was that all about, Colin? Disruption? I suppose our mother sent her to cause trouble. But poor Blanche was never of Mother's caliber. No, I was not upset."

"Elizabeth and I want to invite them to our wedding," he said, "and to the wedding breakfast. But we will not do so if you would rather we did not. No—" He held up a hand as she drew breath to speak. "You do not need to say what I am sure you think you ought to say, Wren. Say what you *want* to say. I know Elizabeth will respect your feelings and put your wishes first, as I do."

"She has already done so," she told him. "She spoke to me about it at breakfast. This is your wedding, Colin, and it must be just as the two of you wish it to be. Your relationship to our mother is necessarily different from mine. I can ignore her. You cannot, not if you plan to make Roxingley your home and Elizabeth's and exercise the full responsibilities of your position. Our mother is one of those responsibilities. You must by all means invite her to the wedding. But do you think she will come?"

"I have no idea," he said. "Where *is* Elizabeth?"

"She has gone out," she told him. "I daresay she will be home soon."

"In the meantime," he said, "may I hold my nephew? He

does not look undernourished, does he? Just look at those cheeks."

He left before Elizabeth returned home. He did not wish to be too late arriving at Curzon Street lest he find his mother's drawing room filled with guests and hangers-on when he arrived. He got there at one o'clock, only to discover that the carriage in which Elizabeth and her mother usually traveled about town was standing outside the door. Their coachman informed him that Lady Overfield had entered the house at noon—and yes, she was alone.

Colin's first instinct was to bound up the steps, hammer on the door, and dash upstairs to the drawing room to save his betrothed from being devoured whole by his mother. Fortunately, perhaps, he stopped to consider. She had come here quite deliberately, and she had come alone. And she was Elizabeth. He had assured her more than once that he trusted her to do her own living in her own way. He had told her—at least, he hoped he had made himself quite clear—that he would never play the heavy-handed husband and try to control her every move or rush to her rescue before she had appealed to him for help.

She was a woman with backbone and was perhaps—though not probably—even a match for his mother. She must be allowed to do what she had come to do, whether she succeeded or failed.

Sometimes it was not easy to be a man.

He flexed his hands at his sides, but there was no one to punch, except for two coachmen—hers and his own—who had done absolutely nothing to provoke him, and even if they had, he would have no excuse to resort to violence. So he resorted to waiting outside instead. After ten minutes he sent her carriage away. The coachman hesitated, but Colin raised his eyebrows, and the man, perhaps reading the desire to be provoked in his lordship's eyes, decided it was in his best interests to obey. Colin waited inside his own carriage and then outside, his arms folded across his chest, his feet crossed at the ankle, his eyes focused upon the door lest she slip away while he was not looking.

It was the hardest thing in the world to trust when the instinct to protect warred with it. It was very possible that she was being devoured in there, and how could she appeal to him for help when she did not even know he was at hand?

Perhaps she really *had* been devoured, he thought ten minutes later. How much longer would he wait before bursting in there without stopping to ply the door knocker first? But even as he asked himself the question, the door opened and she stepped out, looking cool and poised and perfectly in command of herself. Looking, in fact, like Elizabeth.

Until she noticed the change of carriage, that was, and him standing there waiting for her. Not that anything noticeably changed—nothing, at least that anyone else would have seen who did not know her. But he did. He knew her, and he *cared*. A great vulnerability gazed at him through her eyes, and he straightened up as she came down the steps, ready to open his arms and scoop her up and generally behave like the prince of fairy tales. But she recovered herself long before her leading foot touched the pavement, and she took his offered hand and got into the carriage without speaking.

Colin had a quiet word with his coachman, got into the carriage, and leaned past her to pull down the curtain over the window before doing the same on his side after the door had been closed. He took his place beside her and gathered her into his arms before saying a word to her. He pulled loose the ribbons of her bonnet and tossed the garment onto the opposite seat. He held her head against his shoulder and rested his cheek on top of it. He had no idea if she needed to be gathered in or not. But he needed to gather.

"Idiot," he said. "You precious idiot, Elizabeth."

"Thank you," she said.

"I would have come with you," he told her.

"I know," she said.

"I was coming anyway."

"I am not surprised," she said.

He sighed and rubbed his cheek against her hair. "You came alone."

"Yes."

"I suppose," he said, "she talked over you and under you and all around you and through you and had your head spinning on your shoulders."

"I told her not to interrupt me," she said.

That silenced him for a moment before he snorted with laughter. "And did it work?" he asked.

"Yes."

He wished he could have been an invisible spectator of that particular moment.

"I have invited her to our wedding," she said.

"Oh, have you?" he said. "And will she come?"

"She did not say," she told him.

"Because you would not let her get a word in edgewise, I suppose," he said, snorting with laughter again, though he felt anything but amused.

"But if it were genteel for ladies to make wagers," she said, "I would bet upon her coming."

"Oh, would you?" he said.

"She will have to call what she doubtless sees as my bluff," she told him. "She was planning a grand summer-long house party at Roxingley as a homecoming for you and a welcome for your bride. It was obvious that it was intended to be anything but, at least as far as I am concerned. Perhaps she believes—or believed—that even after our nuptials she could drive me away. In any case, I reminded her that after we are married *I* will be Lady Hodges and mistress of Roxingley, and that you and I will plan a house party if there is to be one, with a guest list we have prepared ourselves. I informed her she would be welcome to suggest a couple of guests of her own too. I made it clear to her that I will not dispute her right to consider Roxingley her home, but I added that there is room for only one mistress in any home and that after I marry you, I will be she. I actually used the word *dowager* to remind her of her coming role."

He was still holding her tight with one arm while his other hand was pressing her head to his shoulder. As though, like a frail female, she needed the support of an all-powerful male.

"She did not retaliate?" he asked.

"She talked," she told him. "I did not particularly listen. I went there to make a point and I made it. If I have offended you by talking thus to your mother, I am sorry. But if I *have* offended you, Colin, then I must decline to marry you. If I am to be your wife, I will not allow your mother to dominate either me or you."

"You would break off two engagements in one week?" he asked her. "You would be notorious all down through the ages, Elizabeth. You would be one of the few women to make an appearance in the history books. Boudicca would have nothing on you."

"*Have* I offended you?" she asked him, and her voice sounded a bit peculiar, as though she had spoken through clenched teeth. She was keeping them from chattering, he realized. She was not nearly as calm as she was trying to appear. Perhaps his sheltering arms were not so unnecessary after all.

He bent his head to hers, nudged her face away from his throat, and kissed her lips before moving his head back and gazing into her eyes. "I do not intend to allow her to live at Roxingley," he told her. "Not after the way she treated Wren. Not after the way she has tried to destroy you. Not after hearing that she will continue to try even after we are married. Or perhaps her threat about the house party was intended to make you change your mind about marrying me. Indeed, I am sure that must be it. But she does not know you, does she? Or me. I will not have it, Elizabeth. I shall return later and uninvite her to the wedding. I shall inform her that she may have the house here in town. I will make it over to her and purchase another for us. It is what I decided last night and came to tell her today."

She disengaged herself firmly from his arms and moved away from him to sit across the corner of the seat. She regarded him with a frown on her face.

"No," she protested.

"Elizabeth," he said, "she can only want to destroy us. It is what she does so that everything in her world is focused upon her. She cannot be changed. It is the way she is. You cannot draw her into our lives by simply expecting her to react like a normal human being. I have known her all my life, and she is now as she has been as far back as I can remember. She loves herself to the exclusion of all others, and such people cannot be redeemed. There is only one person in their lives who matters, and everyone else must be made to realize it and to pay homage to them. And she just happens to be my mother."

A truly ghastly thing happened then. He had closed up the carriage and given his coachman the direction to drive indefinitely until he was told otherwise. He had expected that Elizabeth would be upset and had thought to hold her and comfort her for as long as was necessary. Yet the tables had been turned on him. He felt a tightness in his chest and a soreness in his throat. He felt tears prick at his eyes and tried desperately to blink them back. He might have succeeded too if a determined swallow had not got all caught up with a sob—and then another.

"The devil!" he said. "Oh good God." He could cheerfully have died of mortification. And then she surged back across the seat toward him, and he held her to him again as her arms came about his waist, and he wept with his head pressed to her shoulder.

"She is my mother," he said when he could, and then wished he had kept his mouth shut. His voice did not sound like his own.

"Yes," she said.

It was all she said while he turned away from her, mopped at his eyes with his handkerchief, and blew his nose.

"The devil!" he said again. "I am so sorry."

"I am too," she said. "Sorry that there has to be such pain in your life. Unfortunately there is nothing I can do to change any facts. You have correctly identified her, Colin. She is absorbed in self-love. It must be a sort of disease, I believe, just as Desmond's drinking was. One cannot fight against it. One can only accept it or not. I abandoned Desmond because he was doing me physical harm and was largely the cause of my miscarriages. You do not need to abandon your mother, though. She can do us no real harm unless we allow it. I have no intention of allowing it. I will not give her power over us. But I do want her in our lives if it is at all possible. For your sake I want it."

"But why?" he asked. "Especially knowing as you do that she will never change?"

"But you can," she said. "You can forgive yourself for any way you believe you have mishandled your life since your father died. You can even forgive her—though you know she will never change. Trust me on this."

He looked at her, arrested for the moment. "Good God," he said. "That is it, Elizabeth. That is what we were talking about at that infamous ball, when we did not notice the waltz had ended."

"Oh." She smiled at him. "So it was. Well, I meant it then, and I mean it now."

He took her hand in his and laced their fingers. "But we could allow her a place in our lives only on our terms," he said. "It is something she would never allow."

"That choice," she said, "must be hers. If a door is to be shut permanently between you and your mother, Colin, she must be the one to shut it. I am not sure she will. Everything she has done this spring has been designed to bring you back to her—with a bride who is to her liking, it is true, and certainly not with the bride you have actually chosen. Nevertheless . . ."

"Elizabeth," he said, "she has put you through hell. For no reason at all except that you threatened her expectations of the future."

"And if I seek some sort of revenge," she said, "what do I make of myself?" He raised the back of her hand to his lips. "Besides, I care for you. And thank you for sending my carriage away and accompanying me home. Where is home, by the way? I had no idea it was so far."

"I told my coachman to keep driving," he said. "I thought you might need comforting."

"I did," she said. "And you have comforted me."

"By soaking your shoulder with my tears?" he asked.

"An exaggeration," she said, brushing her free hand over her shoulder. "It is scarcely damp. We will invite Sir Nelson and Lady Elwood to our wedding too."

"And I suppose," he said, "if it was genteel for a lady to place a wager, you would bet upon their coming."

"I would," she said.

He had little reason to feel any fondness for his eldest sister except that she had saved him from an unwanted marriage to Miss Dunmore. But . . . well, she *was* his sister, and his mother *was* his mother. And there was insufficient time to write to Ruby and Sean in Ireland and to have them come here in time for his wedding. In contrast, there were a number of Westcotts and Radleys currently in London, and the Marquess and Marchioness of Dorchester were on their way here, bringing Abigail Westcott with them. Abigail's sister and her family had been invited to come from Bath.

He had only Wren.

"But do I want Blanche and Nelson there?" he asked. "And my mother?"

"Yes," she said. "You do."

He laughed then, and because the curtains made them invisible from the outside, he wrapped his arms about her once more and kissed her. More slowly and thoroughly this time. And he wanted her. He wanted their wedding to be now, tomorrow, the day after. Soon. He wanted all that was Elizabeth in his life to stay.

Twenty

Replies—all acceptances—had come to the wedding invitations that had been sent out to a select few members of the *ton*, friends and friendly acquaintances. The church would be no more than half full, but they would know that everyone there wished them well, and what more could any couple ask of their wedding?

There had been no reply from Lady Hodges or from her eldest daughter and son-in-law. Colin might have accepted their silence as the shut door Elizabeth had referred to. If they did not answer their invitation or attend the wedding, then they had made their choice. He could not quite accept that sort of finality, however. He had set out to call upon his mother the day after the Ormsbridge ball but had been thwarted by finding that Elizabeth was there before him. Now he must go himself.

He did so on the afternoon before the wedding. His mother was, as he had half expected, entertaining. He bowed to her and his sister and brother-in-law when he was

shown into the drawing room and nodded distantly to Lord
Ede. He ignored the four young gentlemen visitors and the
three young ladies as well as the usual attendants about his
mother's throne chair. She did not attempt any introduc-
tions but waved everyone away with the explanation that
she wished to speak with her son. There were, of course,
the expected protestations of surprise from two of the
young men, who claimed that Colin could not possibly be
Lady Hodges's son but must surely be her younger brother.
Within a minute or two, however, the room emptied out,
leaving only Colin and his mother and Blanche and Nelson.

While he waited, Colin thought about the dream he had
had at Christmas when he had started to make goals for this
year—the dream of establishing a family of his own and
drawing into it the members of the old. Some of the dream
was materializing. He was about to marry. Ruby and Sean
had sent a hasty response to the letter he had written them
announcing his upcoming marriage and inviting them to
come to Roxingley for at least a part of the summer. They
were coming and bringing the four children with them. The
rest of the dream probably never would be realized. His
mother would never change.

"Mother," he said, "will you be in attendance at my
wedding tomorrow? It is my hope, and Elizabeth's, that
you will."

She picked up a large fan from the table beside her and
cooled her face with it. "You were quite right to reject Miss
Dunmore, dearest," she said. "She is a milk-and-water miss
and I never did think her more than tolerably good-looking.
She has the sort of prettiness that will not endure. Before
ten years have passed, she will resemble her mother to a
marked degree, and that will be unfortunate for her. End
this foolishness with the plain-faced widow, though. It is

not too late. Send her on her way. Pay her off if you must. Or I shall send Ede to do it if you wish. I shall help you choose the perfect bride. "

"I have already done that myself, Mother," he said. "Lady Overfield will be Lady Hodges tomorrow, and I will be the happiest of men." It was a horrible cliché. It also happened to be the truth.

She waved a dismissive hand. "Oh, do sit down," she said. "You look like a coiled spring."

Colin stood where he was.

"How droll it will be if you persist in marrying a dowdy older woman, dearest," she continued. "Everyone would see us all together and think you, Blanche, and I were brother and sisters. We would dazzle them. They would think the widow was our mother. How lowering it would be for you to have to correct them."

Colin clasped his hands at his back and gazed steadily at her. He would not dignify her taunts with a reply.

"Will you attend the wedding tomorrow?" he asked after a short silence, during which she fanned her face slowly and Blanche and Nelson did a fair imitation of statues. "You are my mother. I do not have a father to come."

"I was very vexed with your father," she said, resting her fan on her lap. "He deprived me of my youngest two children. First he implied I was incapable of looking after my own little Rowena when he sent for Megan to take her away and give her a home with that dreadfully dull older man who left Rowena a fortune she had done nothing to deserve when he ought to have divided it among all my children. I daresay *you* were chagrined. I know Blanche was, and I do not wonder at it."

"You are mistaken in that, Mama," Blanche said, speaking at last.

Her mother waved a dismissive hand at her. "And he sent you away to school, dearest, when I begged him not so to break my heart. He did it for that very reason. He could be very vindictive, your father, God rest his soul."

"I asked him to send me to school, Mother," Colin told her.

"Oh, you merely played into his hands by doing so," she said. "He was determined to send you anyway."

Was that right? Colin wondered. Perhaps giving him what he had asked for had not been such a gesture of love on his father's part after all. Perhaps it had been done primarily to hurt his mother. And had Aunt Megan been sent for specifically to take Wren away? Permanently? It must have been intended as a permanent thing or Colin would not have been told soon after that she had died. But that could surely not have been done to hurt his mother. She had never been able to bear to look upon Wren. She had never allowed her down from the nursery floor.

"Your father was a difficult man," his mother said. "But he adored me anyway. He would insist upon marrying me even though my dear papa could not offer anything for a dowry. He always told me that I was worth more than the greatest fortune in the world. Of course I could have done far better than a mere baron, but it would have broken his heart if I had said no, and I have ever been tenderhearted."

Colin left soon after that since it was clear he was not going to get an answer to the question he had come to ask. He still did not know if his mother would be at his wedding tomorrow or if Blanche and Nelson would be. When he had asked them as he took his leave, he had got a shrug from Blanche and the explanation that she did not know what her plans were for tomorrow.

Who knew what the future held? Would his mother

choose to live year-round in London at the Curzon Street House? Would he make it over to her and count his blessings? Would she decide to continue living at Roxingley during the summer and winter and even expect to continue organizing parties there? Would he feel compelled to build a dower house for her somewhere in the park? Would even that be workable? How would Elizabeth deal with her proximity? Meet the problem head-on? Insist that his mother be banished from Roxingley altogether? Somehow he could not see her doing that. Or losing the war against her future mother-in-law. He certainly would not wager against Elizabeth anyway. But this was his *mother* she would be dealing with, and no one had yet been able to stand against her.

Did all men feel a bit sick to the stomach on their wedding eve?

Ross Parmiter and John Croft were organizing a bachelor party for him tonight while Elizabeth was going to dine with some of her relatives. By this time tomorrow he would be married to her. He drew comfort from the thought.

Elizabeth Overfield was going to be *his wife*. If anyone had told him that six months ago, even one month ago, he would not have considered the prediction even worthy of comment.

But tomorrow she was going to be his bride.

Viola and Marcel, Marquess of Dorchester, had arrived in London in time for the wedding. But they had indeed been bewildered to discover not only that it was to be somewhat sooner than they had expected but also that the groom had changed.

"So you traded Codaire for a younger model of manhood, did you, Elizabeth?" Marcel said when she arrived at his home the evening before.

Viola tutted and the young people who had come into the hall with them to greet their visitor burst into peals of merriment.

"A vastly younger model," Elizabeth agreed. "Eighteen years younger, in fact."

"May I be permitted to hug the happy bride?" he asked.

"I will not be a bride until tomorrow," she told him. "This evening you may hug the bride-to-be."

Viola hugged her too. "You could have knocked me over with a feather," she said. "I was very prepared to be pleased for you, Elizabeth, for I remembered Sir Geoffrey Codaire as a very worthy gentleman—"

"As dry as dust," Marcel said, interrupting her. "You would have been having a coughing fit every time he moved, Elizabeth."

"—but not as a man of any obvious attractions," his wife continued with a speaking glance at him. "Now, Lord Hodges! Well, my dear, I did not see that one coming from a million miles away."

"I told you, Mama," Abigail said with a smile and a hug for Elizabeth, "that *I* did. While Jessica and Estelle and I were admiring Lord Hodges for his good looks and his lovely smile, I was fully aware that he sought out Cousin Elizabeth's company whenever he had the opportunity. And remember how gorgeous they looked when they were waltzing together on Boxing Day?"

"I believe your mother was too busy on that occasion noticing how gorgeous I looked waltzing with *her*, Abby," Marcel said while Viola tossed her glance at the ceiling and ignored his grin.

"I am very pleased for you, Lady Overfield," Estelle Lamarr said, offering Elizabeth her hand. "And I think it was very spiteful of the man to whom you were betrothed to embarrass you by accusing you in public of indecorous behavior. I cannot imagine anyone who is less capable of behaving indecorously."

"Thank you," Elizabeth said, smiling at the girl.

"Congratulations, ma'am," her brother, Bertrand, said as he shook Elizabeth's hand.

"Do come up to the nursery," Abigail said, slipping a hand through Elizabeth's arm. "Camille and Joel are up there with the children. They may not have heard your carriage arriving. Did you know there is another child now in addition to Winifred and Sarah and Jacob? They have just recently adopted Robbie from the orphanage. He is four years old and was a dreadful behavior problem. But Joel refused to believe he was a hopeless case, and then Camille refused to believe it and they are subduing him with love— with a great deal of help from Winifred, who keeps telling him that she will *not* under any circumstances call him a dreadfully naughty boy even if he keeps rolling his eyes at her forever and poking out his tongue as he pulls out the sides of his mouth."

"Oh dear," Elizabeth said.

"He is a sweet child, my newest grandson," Viola said. "And they went ahead with his adoption last week even though Camille had just discovered that she is with child again. Whoever could have predicted all this for Camille of all people, Elizabeth?"

Lady Camille Westcott had been the most humorless of high sticklers before the discovery was made that her parents' marriage had been bigamous and she was therefore illegitimate. Her world had been shattered, especially as it had included a broken engagement. But she had changed—

by sheer grim grit, Elizabeth had always thought—until by last Christmas she had become a young matron with three children, two of them adopted, always a little disheveled in appearance, slightly overweight, totally in love with her family, especially her husband, Joel, and as happy as a spring day when the sun was shining.

And her mother, Viola . . . Her world of quiet, humorless dignity as the loyal wife of a blackguard whom everyone had despised, had changed too beyond recognition. Her household now, even though she had the excuse that they had only very recently all arrived in town, seemed noisy and a bit disorganized and brimming with family warmth and affection and happiness. Who could ever have predicted it just a few years ago? And *what* a family. It included Viola's offspring and Marcel's and adopted children as well as those born to one or other of the family members.

Even Viola's younger daughter, Abby, seemed more cheerful than Elizabeth had seen her in the past three years.

Children came dashing and crawling toward them when they stepped into the nursery, all talking at once. But Elizabeth did notice one child at the far side of the room who was lying on his back and drumming his heels on the floor while Joel sat cross-legged beside him, talking to him with quiet unconcern. He waved cheerfully to Elizabeth.

What a wonderful way to spend her wedding eve, Elizabeth thought without any trace of irony, though it had become obvious that the dinner hour she had been quoted when she was invited had been a very rough estimate indeed.

She was spending it with family. Only a part of the

whole, of course, but a very precious part all the same. And the rest of it had been busy for half the spring, it seemed, plotting and planning and scheming on her behalf because she was one of them.

"What have you heard of Harry?" she asked Viola.

"His regiment was sent off to America," Viola said, "but he somehow missed going with them. I do not know how or why. I suspect he might have been wounded at Toulouse and has not told me about it, but Marcel keeps reminding me that even if he was, he is obviously not at death's door. He is in Paris. Oh, Elizabeth, I do hope the wars are really and truly at an end. I hope these past wars were wars to end all wars. Do you think maybe they were? No other wars ever? No other mother or wife or daughter to have to go through what I and so many others have been going through? But enough of that. He is alive and in Paris. You ought not to have started me on that particular theme. Tell me about the courtship and the proposal. Was it on bended knee? With roses?"

"It was . . . lovely," Elizabeth said.

But Sarah wanted to show her grandmama something and Winifred wanted to tell Elizabeth something else and Camille was coming toward them, the heel-drumming little boy astride one of her hips, scowling at Winifred, whose news was that she had a new brother whom *she would never stop loving no matter how hard he tried to make her do it.*

"For family is more important than *anything else* in the whole wide world, Cousin Elizabeth," she said. "Is it not?"

"It is indeed," Elizabeth said. She congratulated Winifred and smiled at Robbie and took the hand Joel was offering her.

Tomorrow was her wedding day, she thought. She could hardly wait to see Colin again.

To marry him.

Elizabeth wore a new high-waisted, cream-colored walking dress to her wedding. It was paired with a straw bonnet, the crown of which was trimmed with artificial primroses and tied beneath the chin with matching silk ribbons, and mustard-colored shoes and gloves. None of the garments were elaborate, and no one had influenced her choice, though Wren and her mother had tried when they went shopping with her. She had wanted to feel comfortable. She had wanted to feel like *herself*, as she had not at her betrothal ball to Sir Geoffrey Codaire in the gorgeous gold and bronze gown, her hair dressed more elaborately than she liked it. Today she had had her maid brush her hair smooth and knot it simply at her neck so that her bonnet would fit easily over it.

She picked up her reticule, took one last look in the mirror, glanced at the clock—she was a little early, though not by much—and made her way downstairs.

It was her wedding day, she thought, as though realizing it for the first time.

Memory washed over her. Of Anna, in this very house not long after she had come from Bath, still new to her role as the very wealthy Lady Anastasia Westcott, newly betrothed to Avery, bewildered and dismayed as the family planned a grand society wedding for them at St. George's. And of Avery arriving one morning while Elizabeth was sitting with Anna in the drawing room, and leaning over Anna's chair to invite her to come with him right then to be married quietly by special license. His secretary would meet them at the church, he had explained, and Elizabeth was invited to go along as the second witness.

She wished for a moment that her wedding could be just like it. But it could not. They had a point to make. Besides, they owed it to her family not merely to slip off to marry privately.

And she remembered Alexander and Wren's wedding last year. Wren had left for the church—also St. George's—from this house while Alex had stayed with Cousin Sidney the night before. Viola and Abigail and Harry had been staying here.

Today it was her turn. Her mother and Wren were to travel to the church with her, at her request. And Alex too, of course. He would be giving her away. They were waiting for her in the hall, and all three looked up to watch her descend the stairs.

"You were quite right, Elizabeth," Wren said when she was halfway down, "and Mama and I were wrong. You look beautiful as simplicity itself. You do it better than anyone else I know."

"You do have a style all your own, Lizzie," her mother conceded, "and are wise to insist upon keeping to it."

"I believe, Lizzie," Alexander said, "that despite my lukewarm response to the announcement of your betrothal, I am happy about it after all. I believe the two of you suit, and Wren agrees with me."

"I do." Wren had tears in her eyes. "I want the very best in life for Colin, and I want the same for you, Elizabeth. Why would you not find it together? It makes perfect sense that you would."

"If you make me weep before I even get to the church, you two," Elizabeth warned them as she joined them in the hall, "I will not speak to you for a month."

The sun came out from behind a bank of clouds as the carriage approached Hanover Square and drew up before St. George's. It was not by any means the largest or the most magnificent church in London, but it was the preferred venue for society weddings during the Season and always attracted a small crowd of the curious, who came to watch the bride arrive and, somewhat later, to see the newly married couple depart for the rest of their lives together.

"Five minutes late," Alexander said as he handed her down onto the pavement and consulted his pocket watch. "Maybe four and a half. Just right. Mama and Wren, we will give you time to go inside first."

Elizabeth could hear her pulse beating in her ears as she watched them ascend the steps and disappear inside the church.

"Nervous?" Alexander asked.

"But of course," she said, smiling at him and taking his arm. "Weren't you last year?"

"Of course," he said, grinning back at her. "And I have had not a single regret since. I wish you the same, Lizzie."

"Thank you," she said. "I am not marrying Colin just because I believe I ought, you know."

"I do know," he said, covering her hand on his arm with his own. And they climbed the steps together and stepped inside the church.

Doubts assailed her anyway at this most inopportune of times. What if she *had* agreed only because the plans she had made for herself had been dashed and the future had looked bleak? What if *he* had offered only because he believed he had compromised her and brought the wrath of his mother upon her? What if the gap in their ages *did* make a difference and would make true happiness impossible? What if . . . ?

But the arrival of her mother and sister-in-law must have been taken as a signal, and the great pipe organ had begun to play, and the congregation—looking larger than she had expected—was standing and turning to look back to watch her progress along the nave on Alex's arm. She saw friends and acquaintances and family, all smiling their encouragement. And . . . ah! She saw Lady Hodges, all in dazzling white with a delicate veil covering her face, Lady Elwood beside her with Sir Nelson, and Lord Ede on Lady Hodges's other side, next to the aisle.

They had come.

And she saw Colin, standing before the empty pew in front of his mother and sister, resplendent in fawn and dull gold, tall and slim and lithe and handsome, watching her come. He looked anxious and a bit pale, and then her eyes met his and he smiled. But how did she know that when she was still some distance away from him and the rest of his face was not smiling? But she knew. His eyes were smiling, and her own smiled back into them.

And suddenly all seemed right and she forgot doubts about the past and fears for the future, and everything became *here* and everything became *now*. It all turned magical, though that must be entirely the wrong word to use of solemn nuptials conducted within a consecrated church. *Mystical*, then. It all turned mystical—warm and intimate and wonderful and the rightest of right things she had ever done in her life.

The same conviction surely looked at her through his eyes.

Alexander gave her into Colin's keeping, and they stood before the clergyman in his formal vestments, and they were married. Just like that. In what seemed an extraordinarily brief span of time but with an eternity of consequences.

They were man and wife.

Oh surely, she thought, they had done the right thing. He had married her because he wanted to—he had said so and she trusted him. And she had married him because she wanted to. She had told him so and he knew he could trust her. What could be more perfect?

They were married.

His face beamed at her even though he was still not actually smiling. She smiled fully at him with all the power of her conviction that this was right, what they had just done.

It was time then to move to the vestry to sign the register, and Wren and Alexander rose to accompany them. Elizabeth signed the register as Elizabeth Overfield for the last time, and first Wren and then Alex hugged her while Colin signed his name. Wren hugged him tightly and held him close for several moments before relinquishing him to Alex's firm handshake and slap on the shoulder.

And then they were face-to-face again as man and wife, and he offered his arm to lead her from the vestry into the church and back up the nave. They bowed and smiled to family and friends and all who had come to celebrate the day with them—all except his mother and Lord Ede, who had left, it seemed. Sir Nelson and Lady Elwood had not, however, but were still seated in the second pew from the front.

A few moments later they emerged into sunshine to the applause of the people gathered outside. And to a few familiar faces—those of Mr. Parmiter and Mr. Croft and Mr. Ormsbridge, as well as Cousin Sidney and Bertrand and Estelle Lamarr and Winifred Cunningham.

"They left early for a purpose," Colin warned, turning a grinning face toward her. "Shall we make a dash for it?"

"They would be disappointed if we did not," Elizabeth said, setting her hand in his and running down the steps with him while they were showered with a veritable barrage of flower petals and the crowd applauded again and laughed. Someone whistled.

They were both laughing and breathless by the time they reached his carriage, though it was no sanctuary. It was an open carriage. Colin handed her in and took his place beside her a few moments before the vehicle rocked on its springs and moved forward.

The church bells rang a merry peal behind them, but the sound was all but drowned out by the ugly metallic rattle and screech of all the hardware that had been tied to the back of the carriage. They drove out of Hanover Square in all the din, their hands tightly clasped, their persons and the carriage seats and the horses' backs and the coachman in his immaculate livery liberally strewn with bright flower petals.

"If we look unconcerned," Colin yelled, "do you suppose no one will realize that we have just been wed?" They laughed into each other's eyes and she marveled yet again at the reality of it all. Her wedding day. *Their* wedding day.

They were married.

"Lady Hodges," he said.

"Yes."

And he leaned toward her and kissed her on the lips just before the carriage turned out of the square and disappeared from the view of those at the foot of the steps and spilling out of the church onto the square.

They could not hear the cheers and applause. Or even the whistles.

Twenty-one

The word *breakfast* as it applied to a wedding feast was always a misnomer. For one thing, the food that was served was anything but what one would normally expect of breakfast. For another, the celebrations continued for most of the day, for several hours in the ballroom while toasts and speeches were dealt with in addition to the meal, and then for a few hours longer in the drawing room, with a somewhat smaller gathering.

It was during the move from the one room to the other that Colin singled out his sister, who he sensed was about to take her leave with Nelson.

"Blanche," he said, touching her elbow, "come and stroll in the garden with me for a short while?"

She glanced through a window of the ballroom, but there was no excuse to be found there. The sun was still shining from a cloudless sky, and warm air was wafting through the open French windows. Nelson had been drawn into a conversation with John Croft and Sidney Radley.

Elizabeth was being borne off to the drawing room by her friend Miss Scott on the one side and the Dowager Duchess of Netherby on the other.

"For a very short while, then," Blanche said, taking his offered arm. "We are expected back."

"I was very, very pleased that you came to the church," he told her as they stepped outside. "And Mother. And even Lord Ede. And thank you for coming to the breakfast too. I suppose it was not an easy thing for you to do."

For this, after all, was Wren's home, and the two sisters had been estranged since Wren left Roxingley at the age of ten. Almost twenty years ago.

"No," she said after a small hesitation, "it was not. Would it have been better, Colin, if I had not come to warn you of that announcement and you had married Miss Dunmore? Did I drive you into contracting this marriage to spite Mother?"

"There are two things I cannot quite imagine," he said. "One is my wanting to *spite* our mother. I would like to have a relationship with her even if it can never be a close one. The other thing is that I would hardly marry just to spite a third party. Marriage is for life, and I hope for a happy one. No, Blanche. You did something for which I will always owe you a debt of gratitude. And I married Elizabeth because I wanted to. Because I hope and expect to be happy with her."

"She is *my* age, or very close," she protested.

"Yes," he said. "And I value and esteem her more than I do any other woman I have met. I thought she was beyond me, but she has assured me that she wants this marriage too. And I trust her word." Colin paused then for a minute. "But that is not what I wanted to speak with you about. I have something I need to ask you. Blanche, why have you remained with our mother all these years? Why has Nelson?"

"Someone had to," she said. "Rowena was gone and Ruby eloped and fled to Ireland when she was only seventeen. Justin killed himself and you completely cut yourself off from Mother. She needed us. All of us. But suddenly I was the only one left. And I was the one with a sense of responsibility. I was the eldest, after all."

"She *needed* us?" he asked, drawing her down to sit beside him on a rustic seat beneath a willow tree, which would shade them from the sun.

"Of course," she said. "She always needs other people, Colin, most notably her family. Her dream was that we would all surround her with our love—and our beauty—for the rest of her life."

He stared at her, feeling a bit aghast.

"Nelson . . . loves me," she added.

"I am glad you have him at least," he said.

"You think I am blind to the truth," she said, looking fully at him for the first time, two spots of color in her cheeks. "I am the *eldest*, yet there was always someone more favored than I. You most of all. No one else quite existed for her after you were born. But first Father treated her cruelly and sent you away to school, and then you left of your own volition after he was dead and Mother had planned a grand house party to welcome you as the new Baron Hodges. *I stayed.* I was the only one of us who stayed. I have given up my own life for her. But you are still the favorite."

Her voice was rather cold and expressionless, but he read a world of hurt in it. Had she never felt loved? And was she still hoping? How differently she had seen their world. Had he missed it all because he was young, and at school so much of the time? Had he run instead of trying to stay and understand? Was it too late to try now? It was what he had been telling himself since Christmas he must try to do. And Elizabeth did not seem to think it was too late.

"Blanche." He covered her hand with his own. "Will you be my sister?"

"Well, I already am," she said, and would have snatched away her hand if he had not curled his fingers about it.

"I do not know what your plans are for the summer," he said. "I suppose you usually live with our mother at Roxingley when she is there. Perhaps you fear you will not be welcome this year when Elizabeth and I take up residence. But we both want you to come. Ruby and Sean and the children are coming from Ireland, and we are going to invite all the Westcotts and Radleys. It is as important to Elizabeth as it is to me that my family be there as well as hers. Not just *be* there but . . . I want us to be a *family*, Blanche. I honor your devotion to our mother and I beg your pardon for forcing you to do it all yourself. That will change. Forgive me. Let me be your brother. Let Elizabeth be your sister-in-law."

She was silent for a while. "I am here, am I not?" she said coldly.

He squeezed her hand and released it. "I am realizing now there is so much I have not understood," he said. "I hope you will help me. Why do you say Father was cruel? I asked him to send me to school and he sent me. Did he do it because he loved me? Or because he hated me? And why did he send for Aunt Megan to come and take Wren away? I did not even know that fact until Mother mentioned it yesterday. Did he do it because he loved Wren? Or because he hated her?"

She looked at him warily. "I do not know," she said. "How would I?"

He felt a bit foolish for asking aloud. He had not meant to.

"Why would he hate you?" she asked. "Just because Mother loved you?"

"I do not know. I am only realizing there is much about us that I do not understand." He shook his head. "It is time I joined Elizabeth and our wedding guests in the drawing room," he said. "Will you stay for a while?"

"No," she said. "We must leave. Mother will be expecting us."

"And will you come to Roxingley during the summer?" he asked.

"I will talk to Nelson about it," she said. "But I expect we will. Mother will surely be there and she will have need of me."

Her answer would have to do. He wanted her to tell him she would come because of him and Elizabeth and because Ruby and Sean were coming—and Wren too, he hoped. But . . . *What* was it the Dowager Countess of Riverdale had said at Christmas time about the renovations to Brambledean? *Rome was not built in a day.* Yes, that was it.

He was going to have to be patient. Blanche clearly saw herself as a woman with a grievance. And perhaps in a sense she was right. She was the one who had stayed.

Perhaps he had more to learn about his own family than he had realized.

It was early evening before the last of the guests left the house. By that time they were mostly family members and took their leave with a great deal of noise and much hugging and kissing and hand shaking and back slapping and laughter. The house seemed very silent when the door closed upon them and Colin felt quite exhausted. Elizabeth,

standing in the hall beside him, looked at him with twinkling eyes.

"Welcome to our family," she said.

He laughed. "And what a welcome it was," he said. "Are
you ready to leave?"

There had been a spirited argument a few days ago
about where they would spend their wedding night. They
would, of course, spend it at this house, both Alexander and
Wren had insisted, just as *they* had last year, when everyone
else had stayed elsewhere so that the newlyweds could be
left to themselves. Elizabeth's various relatives on both
sides had added their voices to assure Colin that they actually looked forward to entertaining Mrs. Westcott and Alexander and Wren and the baby for the night. Indeed, they
were vying over who would have the pleasure.

Colin had remained firm, and all arguments had ceased
when Elizabeth had assured everyone that it was what she
wished too. They would go to Mivart's Hotel, where Colin
had reserved a suite of rooms. He had done it so they could
be alone together on their wedding night. Completely alone
in a place that was unfamiliar to both of them, waited upon
by servants neither of them knew.

Fifteen minutes after everyone else had left, Colin's
carriage—the closed one this time—drew up outside the
door, and five minutes after that it was in motion, being
waved on its way by a tearful Wren and Mrs. Westcott and
a more stoic Alexander.

And they were alone together at last.

He took Elizabeth's hand in his and leaned back against
the cushions while he allowed the reality of what had happened today to wash over him. He would no longer live in
the bachelor rooms that had been home to him—with the
exception of last summer and winter—since he came down

from Oxford at the age of twenty-one. He would never live alone again. He was now part of a couple. It was a sobering thought.

He was a married man.

Elizabeth was *his wife*.

"It is a strange feeling, is it not?" she said as though she had read his thoughts, and he turned his head to smile at her.

"Yes," he said, and squeezed her hand. Very strange. He had always valued the privacy his rooms allowed him. He had loved it too at Withington. There would be no more of that. Elizabeth would always be with him from this day on.

He kissed her briefly and they traveled the rest of the way in silence.

Their suite at the hotel consisted of two large, square bedchambers, both luxuriously furnished, each with a spacious dressing room, and a sitting room between. A fire crackled in the hearth there to combat the chill of the evening after a warm day, and candles had been lit in the wall sconces.

"What a cozy, welcoming place," she said after looking into each room and picking up a cushion from the couch to plump it unnecessarily. "I am glad we came here, Colin."

He had asked that his valet and her maid be sent up and that wine and sweet biscuits be brought to the sitting room.

"Shall we make ourselves comfortable before we sit down?" he suggested. They were still wearing their wedding finery.

"Yes." She smiled at him before entering the bedchamber to the left and closing the door. She was the poised, serene Elizabeth, he had noticed, and had somehow taken any awkwardness there might have been out of the situation.

It felt strange being married.

He retired to the dressing room of the other bedchamber and undressed before sitting for his valet to shave him. He donned a brocaded silk dressing gown over his nightshirt before dismissing his man for the night and stepping back into the sitting room.

Elizabeth was already there, pouring the wine into two glasses. She was wearing a long dressing gown of blue velvet that had a lived-in look about it, as though it had been a favorite for a long time. Her fair hair was loose over her shoulders and down her back.

She looked lovely.

He picked up the two glasses and handed her one after she had seated herself on the sofa. He offered her the biscuits too but she shook her head. He sat down beside her and extended his glass toward hers.

"There have been so many toasts today," he said. "But let us have a private one, shall we? Just for us. To a long and happy future together. And a mutual trust."

"To mutual trust and happiness," she said, clinking her glass against his before raising it to her lips.

And it struck him that the words were easy to say but would take a lifetime to honor. A lifetime of constant effort and awareness. It was hard enough to live up to one's ideals and dreams for oneself. But when one had to consider another person too? Was it even possible?

It would take a lifetime to find out. Well, the rest of a lifetime was exactly what he had.

"What a perfect day it has been," he said.

"It has," she agreed. "And one of the best parts of it was that your mother came to the wedding. You must have been terribly pleased."

"Yes," he said. "Even though she left the church before we did, I was pleased."

"Blanche and Sir Nelson came to the breakfast too," she said. "You talked with her for a while."

"I did," he said, and told her some of what they had talked about. "I believe she will come to Roxingley for the big family house party we are planning. She will come because she believes Mother intends to be there and she sees it as her duty to go where Mother goes. Whether she will allow any sort of relationship with Ruby or Wren or me remains to be seen. Or you. We can but try. I believe she is bitter because the rest of us escaped in one way or another and she, as the eldest, was left with the responsibility of giving our mother the support and audience she needs. She told me Nelson stays because he loves her."

"I hope she is right," she said. "I hope I can get to know them both better over the summer. I have much to thank them for. They came to warn you about that announcement. They came to the Ormsbridge ball but did not make any great effort to do what they had been sent there to do. They came to our wedding today but did not leave immediately after."

They smiled at each other.

"Tell me about your father," she said.

He stared at her.

"You never talk of him," she said.

He swallowed. "There is not much to tell."

She sipped from her glass and tipped her head to one side. She was waiting for him to say more, he realized. But she spoke again before he did. "If you would rather not," she said, "that is all right. We are not entitled to tear each other's souls apart just because we are married."

It was a strange thing to say. Was it true? He frowned.

"He provided for us," he said, "but he took no real interest in us. He rarely came upstairs to see us. I suppose he regretted his marriage. My mother was, by all accounts, extraordinarily beautiful as a girl, and she was much sought after. I daresay he fell headlong in love with her and married her without knowing her at all. By the time he did, it was too late. He spent a lot of time outdoors. When he was at home, he more or less lived in the library."

She set her glass down on the table before sitting back and picking up the cushion she had plumped earlier and holding it against her bosom, both arms clasped about it.

"He seemed to have held the worst of her excesses in check," he said. "Beyond that, he allowed her to do as she wished. I do not suppose he could do much else. I have sometimes thought of him as a weak man. Perhaps he was—as I have been weak since his death. He avoided confrontation, as I have. But I do believe my mother to be unique in the sense that she is almost impossible to control."

"Did you love him?" she asked after he had been quiet for a while.

"Yes," he said hesitantly. "Sometimes, especially after Wren went away and apparently died, I used to escape from the nursery and go down to the library and sit either under the desk or on the window seat with the curtain pulled far enough across to hide me. Occasionally I would read, but at other times I would just sit and breathe in the scent of leather-bound books and of his presence. He must have known I was there, but he never either acknowledged my presence or sent me away. Sometimes I would follow him about outdoors. I remember watching the sheep shearing with him once. I never asked his permission, and he almost never spoke to me, but again he did not send me away. I imagined he loved me in his own way."

"Imagined?" She reached out a hand to rub along his upper arm.

"I thought he had proved it when he agreed to let me go away to school," he said. "He had not allowed any of the others to go, though I know Justin had begged him. I suppose it is possible that he let me go because he believed he had made a mistake in keeping Justin at home and beginning a train of unhappiness that eventually led my brother to take his own life—though my father did not know of that outcome at the time, of course. However it was, he let me go even though my mother was vehemently opposed. It was the one time I know of when he held his ground against her. I thought he did it because he loved me."

"You *thought*?" she said.

"I think he did it to punish her," he said. "And to remove me from his sight. Just as he had summoned our aunt to take Wren away."

She patted his arm, and he frowned into her eyes.

"When Justin died," he told her, "I was brought home from school for the funeral. I went into the library afterward and curled up on the window seat even though I was fifteen. It was my first close encounter with death—and a suicide at that, though it was passed off as an accident. I had never been particularly fond of Justin, partly, I suppose, because he was ten years older than I was, but he *was* my brother. And he had been unhappy enough to end his own life. I did not understand why. I was young, and had been away at school But still, I was in a fragile state, though I held it all inside. My father came into the room while I was there. He brought the vicar with him. Apparently he wanted to show the vicar a miniature of Justin he kept in his desk. For once he almost certainly did not know I was there. While the vicar was looking at the painting, my father said words that haunted me long after. I suppose they still do."

He paused while she looked expectantly at him.

"No," he said. "I cannot say them. I am sorry."

She set the cushion aside and took the glass from his hand to set on the table beside her own. She moved closer to him and snuggled against his shoulder while she spread one hand over his chest.

"And I am sorry that quite inadvertently I raised a subject that is painful to you," she said. "You do not owe me the information. Let us not allow it to ruin our perfect day. It felt lovely at the church, did it not, to be surrounded by family and friends?"

His emotions felt raw. Memories that had been pushed deep for a long time after being explained away in any number of ways had been dredged up in the last few days to leave him aware of the fact that the wound had always been there, made worse by the fact that he had never let himself acknowledge there was a wound. And he could not share it with Elizabeth—even though not so long ago she had shared with him the deep hurt of the story behind the loss of her two unborn children.

Perhaps after all he was lacking in trust.

But at the moment he owed her her perfect day. And he owed it to himself too. They could never relive this day. Whatever happened today would forever remain a part of it, a memory they would both keep for the rest of their lives.

"I am so terribly unworthy of you," he said, raising one hand and setting the backs of his fingers against her cheek.

"You must take me off that pedestal you have constructed for me," she said. "I am not some superior being worthy only of your admiration and worship. I am a person. A woman. I want you to care for me, not worship me."

"Oh, I care," he told her.

"That is a very good thing to be told on my wedding day

even if I *did* have to prompt you," she said, her eyes twinkling at him.

"I love that expression," he told her. "That smile in your eyes. You were made for happiness and laughter. I loved to hear you laugh at Christmastime and I loved to provoke it. I intend to keep on doing it, you know. You would not have done much laughing with *him*, Elizabeth. You would have been expected to be eternally dignified. You would have expected it of yourself too. I do not expect any such thing. I want you to be yourself. Always. Every day. I want you to laugh and be happy."

"We could do worse than live on laughter," she said, her eyes incongruously growing bright with tears.

"And friendship," he said, getting to his feet and extending a hand to help her to hers. "We are friends, are we not? We always were and surely always will be. Can friends make love, Elizabeth? Is it time to find out?"

"Yes, indeed it is," she said, setting her hand in his.

Twenty-two

We are friends, are we not? Can friends make love?

His words felt like a cold dose of reality. But they *were* friends. They had a close, precious relationship. If she craved more, then she had only herself to blame. Though actually there *was* more, even if he did not realize it. He had a deep affection for her. She was quite sure of that. Deeper than one felt for a mere friend. It would be enough. She would make it enough.

She preceded him into the bedchamber she had chosen for her own and turned as he closed the door into the sitting room. He drew her into his arms and kissed her, and she leaned into him, very aware that she was no longer wearing her stays and he was without the usual heavy layers of clothing. She could feel all the warm, muscled firmness of his man's body pressed to her breasts and abdomen and thighs.

He stood back from her after a few moments to unbutton her dressing gown. He removed it and tossed it onto one of the chairs while his eyes moved over her white cotton nightgown. Despite some lace trimming, it was really a very plain, modest garment, made for comfort more than for sensuality. She had decided against shopping for something more bridelike. He took hold of the nightgown on either side of her hips and lifted it while she raised her arms. He tossed the garment to join her dressing gown without taking his eyes off her.

Oh my! She had been taken by surprise, and the flickering candles suddenly seemed rather bright. But she would not feel embarrassed. She was his wife, and this was who she was. This was what she looked like. She swallowed.

"You are awfully beautiful, Elizabeth," he said, his voice husky.

And without moving closer to her, he explored her lightly with his fingertips. She scarcely felt them, yet his touch raised gooseflesh of awareness and tautened her nipples and sent aches of longing stabbing down through her womb to her inner thighs. His eyes followed the movement of his hands, and he bent forward to kiss her featherlight at the top of her cleavage. He raised his head, took a step closer to her until she felt the silky brocade of his dressing gown brush against her breasts and stomach, spread one hand behind her head, angled his own, and kissed her lightly and lingeringly on the lips until she yearned for more. But he did not deepen the kiss. He moved his head back so that his lips merely brushed her own, and he looked very directly into her eyes.

"You are the most beautiful woman in the world to me," he said, "for your beauty comes from within and glows like an aura all about you. And you have admitted me within its light."

And *this* was *friendship*? Oh, Colin.

His eyes suddenly laughed into hers. "But it is not at all

a spiritual interest I feel for you tonight," he said. "I want you. In bed."

Oh. But she wanted him too. In an impersonal way because she had denied and pushed deep her needs for longer than seven years. In a far more personal way because he was Colin and her husband and he was knee-weakeningly attractive.

"Yes," she said.

He extinguished the candles on the dressing table as she lay down, and she heard him removing his nightclothes before joining her on the bed. She turned to him.

And he made love to her in a way that seemed to her very typical of Colin as she had come to know him. He was both gentle and thorough. He seemed to know what pleased her, whether by instinct or experience—it did not matter which—and he took his time about doing it. He made low, appreciative sounds when she caressed him with soft fingertips and light palms. And when at last he moved over her and came into her, there was all the heat of a slow passion burning between them, if those two words did not contradict each other. But she was not thinking with words. Indeed, she was not thinking at all, for there was only feeling and pleasure and pain/pleasure and the reaching for what lay beyond.

He took her there without haste, without demand, moving rhythmically in her until she clenched about him and then relaxed into the blissful oblivion that lay beyond pleasure. And he moved in her until he held deep and she felt the hot gush of his release deep inside as he sighed warm breath against her ear and his weight relaxed onto her.

They lay like that for a while as her fingers played gently through his hair, and she willed him not to move yet. It had been so long, and he was such a tender lover, her husband.

She verbalized the word in her mind.

He was her *husband*, this handsome, youthful, eager, kind, firm-willed man. He was her husband and she loved him. And she realized why the loving had been so good. For at every moment, even though he had not spoken, he had been making love to *her*. Not just to a woman or even just to his wife, but to her, Elizabeth. She did not know how she knew. She was not analyzing her thoughts, only allowing them to flow through her mind.

After a minute or two he murmured something, uncoupled from her, and moved to her side.

"I do beg your pardon," he said. "I must weigh a ton."

"Only half," she said. She felt light and a bit chilled with his weight gone, but he reached down and pulled the covers over them before turning onto his side and taking her hand and lacing his fingers with hers.

"You see?" he said, and there was humor in his voice. "It *is* possible for friends to make love."

"It is indeed," she agreed, laughing softly, for she felt she had a secret he did not know yet. But he surely would. "It is also possible for husbands and wives."

"It seems a bit unreal, does it not?" he said.

"That we are husband and wife?" she asked. "I hope it is *not* unreal. I would be living in sin."

"Ah, but I would do the decent thing and make an honest woman of you tomorrow," he told her.

"Well, that is reassuring," she said.

He squeezed her hand. "Am I expected to withdraw to the other room now?" he asked her.

"Are you *expected*?" She turned to face him. She could not see him clearly even though her eyes had grown somewhat accustomed to the darkness. "And what impersonal being might be doing the expecting? Do *I* expect you to withdraw? No. Do I *want* you to go? No."

He kissed her briefly on the lips. "The thing is," he said, and the humor was still there in his voice, "that I may want you again in the night. And you may not—"

"Or, on the other hand, I may," she said, cutting him off.

He chuckled. "I was not a complete failure, then?" he said.

She assumed the question was rhetorical. She smiled, settled her cheek against his shoulder, and promptly fell asleep.

Colin awoke when dawn was beginning to gray the window. Their fingers were still laced and her head was still against his shoulder. Some of her hair was tickling his face. Perhaps that was what had woken him. But he did not mind. He actually did not want to sleep. He wanted to savor the wonder of what had happened to him in less than twenty-four hours.

First there had been the euphoria of the wedding. That feeling had taken him a bit by surprise, actually. Ross Parmiter, his best man, had asked if he was nervous, if he was ready to run a million miles without stopping, if he was afraid he would drop the ring as Ross handed it to him, if his breakfast was sitting uneasily in his stomach, if his neckcloth was feeling tight enough to choke him. The answer to all the questions had been no. He had been exhilarated instead and impatient for the nuptials to begin. Even the church and the size of the congregation as it began to gather—somehow larger than it had seemed when they sent out invitations—had not cowed him. The arrival of his mother had almost brought him to tears. And the moment his eyes had alit upon Elizabeth . . .

Well. There were no words.

The rest of the day had passed in a happy blur with all the hugs and kisses and back slapping and speeches and toasts—and Elizabeth like his center of serenity in the midst of it all.

His wife.

Even their arrival at the hotel had been a part of a memorably wonderful day. As the door to their suite had closed behind them, he had felt that he was home, that they were. That anywhere they were together was home. It was a moment of realization that had warmed him to the heart.

He wished he had not called her a friend as he had suggested it was time they made love. It was not a very romantic word to use on such an occasion, was it? They *were* friends, especially as she had insisted that he take her down from the pedestal he had created for her and see her as a person on a level with himself. But surely they were more than just friends.

Of course they were. They were lovers. But even before they were, when they had still been out there in the sitting room . . . Even then he had loved her. And it seemed to him that she loved him just a bit too.

It seemed incredible that Elizabeth could *love* him. Did she? In *that* way, that once-in-a-lifetime way? That see-someone-across-a-ballroom-and-instantly-know sort of way? He smiled.

It was how he loved her. It was how he had loved her since Christmas Eve.

But inevitably he remembered something else. Something he had pushed ruthlessly from his consciousness for more than ten years. It had been bubbling back up recently and had broken into the forefront of his mind tonight.

Tell me about your father.

Innocent enough words. And he had begun to tell . . . until he could no longer do so. He had been unable to tell her or even, perhaps, himself. For he had always told himself, always believed, that it was his mother who was the chief source of pain in his life. And there was enough truth in that belief, heaven help him. But his father . . .

Did you love him?

Yes, he had. He had loved Wren first and foremost and then his father. After Wren had left and supposedly died, he had turned all his love upon his father and excused his unresponsiveness as just part of his natural reserve. He had interpreted his father's agreeing to his going away to school as an expression of love.

And perhaps he had been right. Perhaps he had been right about everything. And if it was true that his father had sent for Aunt Megan to come and take Wren away, perhaps he had done that too out of a sort of love.

Or perhaps he had been wrong about everything. Those words spoken to the vicar after Justin's funeral . . .

He would not think of them. He must think about them. He must confront his mother with his unanswered questions. Or . . .

Or someone else.

He would think about it tomorrow. Or later today, he supposed he meant. In the meanwhile, though this was no longer his wedding day, it was still his wedding night.

There had been sheer joy in the first part of it, in the disrobing and lovemaking and falling asleep in the certain knowledge that they had set the pattern for all the rest of their days—and nights. They had become each other's family yesterday and last night. It was up to them to make it a happy family even if there were only ever just the two of them.

He wanted her again, he discovered, just as he had warned her he would when he offered to remove to the other bedchamber. *Or, on the other hand, I may,* she had told him when he had started to warn her that he might want her again tonight if he remained in her bed. And he had been given the distinct impression that she meant it.

He moved her hair aside from her face and feathered kisses down from her temple to her jaw. She muttered and stirred and turned her head until their mouths met.

"Mmm," she said, and stretched, her body against his. She had a beautiful body—slim and shapely and perfectly proportioned.

"Mmm indeed," he murmured against the side of her neck beneath her ear, and he felt her waking up.

He moved over her and mounted her. She was warm and compliant and hot and relaxed in her depths. He loved her with quick, hard strokes as she awoke to the rhythm and matched it with inner muscles and the motion of her hips. And when he released into her, he knew that she was with him at the pinnacle and crested it with him.

He moved to her side, slid an arm beneath her neck, and turned her against him while he drew the covers over them.

"I warned you I might be troubling you again," he said.

"It was a great, vast trouble," she said, laughing softly and warmly into the hollow between his neck and his shoulder, causing him to shiver with contentment.

And for all his resolve to remain awake to savor his discovery of love and family, he sighed and slid back into sleep.

She was so glad he had been adamant about reserving the suite of rooms at Mivart's Hotel rather than agreeing to spend the night with her at the house on South Audley

Street. And she was glad she had backed him up when the rest of the family had tried to talk him out of it.

Having breakfast together at the small table in the sitting room felt cozy. It felt like being at home even though it was *not* home. They sat down late after lying in bed, talking, after they awoke. And they ate their meal in a leisurely fashion and ordered more coffee to prolong the meal while they talked and laughed over frivolities. They could put behind them the intense, wonderful emotion of yesterday and simply enjoy being together without any time constraints or the chance that they would be interrupted by the return home of relatives—*her* relatives.

"I need to go out," he said eventually. "I need to pay a call."

"So do I," she said, noting without guilt that half the morning was gone already, yet they were still sitting at the table in their dressing gowns. "I want to spend an hour or so with Araminta before she leaves her cousins' house to return to Kent. I will go now since you have something else to do."

He got to his feet and bent over her to kiss her—such a simple but lovely gesture of affection.

"You are going to call on your mother?" she asked. "You do not want me to come too?"

"No," he said. "This is best done alone."

Coward that she was, she was glad he did not want her company. She must call upon her mother-in-law, of course, before they left London, as they intended to do within a few days. They needed to go as soon as possible to Roxingley in order to make it ready for the onslaught of summer guests they had invited. Colin had not been there in eight years, and even then he had gone just briefly for his father's funeral. She had never been there. Very possibly there would be much to do. Indeed, if the drawing room at the house on Curzon Street was anything to judge by, there very probably would be much to do in order to make Roxingley *theirs*—hers and Colin's. But she looked forward to the challenge immensely.

Except for the looming problem of what exactly they were going to do about Lady Hodges—no, the *Dowager* Lady Hodges if she chose to move back to Roxingley in the summer. Colin had mentioned the possibility of building a dower house, but that would take time.

They left the hotel and traveled together in Colin's carriage to the house where Araminta Scott was staying. He came briefly inside with her to pay his respects to Araminta and then continued on his way to his mother's house. He would send the carriage back for her convenience, he told her.

"Oh, Lizzie," her friend said with a deliberately exaggerated sigh as the door closed behind him, "he is really quite delicious. Where may I find someone just like him, if you please?"

"He is one of a kind," Elizabeth said, laughing, "and he is mine. Now tell me what you plan to do with your life now you have had some time to give the matter some thought."

Araminta Scott was a year younger than she. But she had never married, mainly, Elizabeth was convinced, because her father had been determined to keep her at home to serve him. Now her friend was free to live a bit. Perhaps to live a lot.

They settled into a comfortable conversation.

Colin had not outright lied to Elizabeth, though he had not corrected her misconception either. It was not his mother upon whom he was calling. It was someone else. He hoped the man was at home. He would simply have to come back some other time if he was not. It was time he had answers.

Lord Ede was at home, as it happened, though it took him almost half an hour to come to the small visitors' salon off the main hall where Colin had been asked to wait.

Lord Ede entered the room and waited until his butler had closed the door behind him. He was tall and immaculately dressed. His silver hair gave him a distinguished look, though his handsome features had been somewhat ravaged by time and hard living. He stood a little way inside the door, a slightly mocking smile playing about his lips, one eyebrow partially raised as he regarded his visitor.

"Well, my boy," he said softly, "this is an unexpected pleasure. I trust you left Lady Hodges in good spirits this morning?"

"*Am* I?" Colin asked him. "*Am* I your boy?"

"Dear me," Lord Ede murmured, and both eyebrows went up to give him a look of arrogance. "Whatever gave you that idea?"

"And Wren?" Colin said. "Is she yours?"

Lord Ede took his time about withdrawing an elaborately enameled snuffbox from his pocket and flicking it open with his thumb. He examined the contents.

"Might I ask what has put such an extraordinary idea into your head?" he asked.

"Mother always called Wren's birthmark a judgment on herself," Colin said. "My father sent Wren away and made sure she was dead to the family. He sent me away to school when I was eleven and to Oxford after that. He did not do the same for Justin, yet Justin was the eldest son. I was always Mother's favorite."

Lord Ede closed the snuffbox without availing himself

of its contents. He looked at Colin for a few moments with lazy eyes.

"Perhaps, my boy," he said, "you should be having this discussion with your mother."

"I am having it with you," Colin said.

The half smile played about Lord Ede's lips again. "A discussion has to be a two-way thing," he said.

"You will not answer my questions, then?" Colin asked him. "But you will not deny that you are my father?"

"Ah," Lord Ede said, "but I will not confirm it either. Your evidence is quite flimsy. Your father did not disown either you or Rowena. Perhaps he sent her away for her own good. If that was so, then he did well by her. Perhaps he sent you to school because you asked it of him and he wished to please his younger son. You were a beautiful, good-natured child, and the youngest, a natural to be a mother's favorite. Your evidence is very flimsy indeed— my boy."

"If you *are* our father," Colin said, "then I believe it is time you did the honorable thing. You could not do so at the time because your wife was still alive and presenting you with children. And Mother's husband was still alive."

Lord Ede regarded him with almost open amusement. "You believe," he said softly. "Go on believing, my boy. It is your cheerfulness and optimism and the added streak of honor and stubbornness that have always endeared you to your mother. And to me—as her particular friend."

Colin nodded slowly. He was obviously not going to get any further with this man, who had always hovered in the background of his life, it seemed to him. Perhaps his father. And perhaps not.

He would probably never know for certain.

He would not ask his mother.

Perhaps it did not matter. Perhaps the mere asking of his questions would clear the burden from his mind at long last.

Perhaps it simply did not matter.

"Good day to you, sir," he said, inclining his head curtly and making for the door. Lord Ede stood aside to let him pass.

"Do give my regards to Lady Hodges," he said. "I believe you have done well for yourself, my boy. Despite the discrepancy in your ages, I believe she is the very one for you. Well done."

Colin paused a moment but did not either look at Lord Ede or respond. He continued on his way out of the room and out of the house.

Twenty-three

Elizabeth spent an hour with Araminta and then called briefly at South Audley Street to see her mother and Wren, who were in the nursery with Nathan. When she arrived back at the hotel, she found Colin already there and walked readily into his arms when he stood to greet her.

"This feels like coming home," she said with a laugh when she stood back from his kiss to remove her bonnet and set it aside with her gloves and reticule.

"It does now," he agreed, smiling at her. "You had a good visit with Miss Scott? She seems like a pleasant lady."

"She is and I did," she told him. "Did you thank your mother for coming to our wedding yesterday and tell her how much it meant to you? And to me? Did you ask if she really plans to come to Roxingley?"

"I did not call on her, Elizabeth," he said. "I never did intend to. I am sorry. I called on Lord Ede."

"Oh?" She looked at him in some surprise.

"I needed to ask him a question," he said. He examined

the backs of his hands for a moment and then curled his fingers into his palms before tapping them a few times against his thighs.

"I had better complete what I began to tell you last evening," he said. "When my father was in the library with the vicar on the day of Justin's funeral and showed him the miniature from his desk drawer, he spoke three words that have haunted me for eleven years, though I have sometimes pushed them deep enough to be almost forgotten. *My only son.* That is what he said. He sounded as if he was weeping."

Colin had been fifteen at the time. He had been brought home from school because his brother had taken his own life. He had been sitting on the window seat, where he had sat often as a child, drawing comfort from the presence of his father. The curtain had been half drawn so that he was hidden from the eyes of his father and the vicar as they came into the library. And his father, grief-stricken, had not chosen his words with care.

"You were young, Colin," she said, setting a hand on his arm. The knuckles of his clenched hands were white, she could see. "You were still a schoolboy. It must have seemed to your father at that moment as though the only son of his who was adult and ready to take over from him as his heir was gone at a moment's notice. He doubtless did not mean the words literally."

"It is what I have told myself more times than I can count," he said. "And of course the vicar reminded him that he had another son, who was a good lad and would make a worthy heir."

"What did your father say?" she asked.

"*Yes,*" he said. "He said yes. That was all."

Why had Colin been to see Lord Ede? She was not sure she wanted to know.

"My father arranged to have Wren taken away," he continued. "He sent for our aunt. She did not come by chance. I learned that only very recently. And he so willingly agreed to send me away to school that it seemed almost as though he had intended it all along. I was so happy that that latter possibility never occurred to me. Whenever I used to write to ask if I might spend holidays with friends, terrified that he would withhold his consent, he always said yes. He secured a place for me at Oxford before I even asked. I thought he did it all because he loved me."

"Oh, Colin." She leaned a little toward him. "Are you sure that was not the reason?" He might also have done it to rescue his younger son from the clutches of his mother.

"No," he said. "I am not sure. But he might have done it because he hated me. And Wren. Or at least because he wanted us out of his sight. I am not sure he was capable of hate. Just as I am not sure he was capable of love."

"Then you must think the best of him," she said. "You must not torture yourself with suspicions that cannot be proved." It was obvious what his suspicions were. It was equally obvious that his mother could not be trusted to tell him the truth.

He turned his head to look at her at last. His eyes were very blue—and very troubled. "My mother often said that Wren's strawberry birthmark was a judgment on her," he said. "On my mother, that is. A judgment for *what*? And I was always her favorite."

"You were the youngest," she said.

"And the prettiest?" he said with a fleeting smile. "I went to see Lord Ede this morning. I asked him if he is my father. And Wren's."

Her hand tightened about his arm.

"And?" she asked.

"He would not answer," he said, shaking his head. "He would neither deny it nor confirm it. He merely looked at me in that inscrutable, half-smiling, half-mocking way of his and kept calling me his *boy*. Why did he come to our wedding, Elizabeth?"

"He is your mother's friend," she said.

"Friend," he said softly.

"Colin," she said, "does it matter? I mean, does it *really* matter?" It was a foolish question. *Of course* it mattered very much to him to know who his father was. "You are who you are. You have grown up to be a man of principle and kindness. You have learned to stand alone yet have not cut yourself off from the dream of family and love. You have set yourself the task of building bridges and mending fences and whatever other analogy you care to cite. And with some success. Ruby and her family will be with us during the summer. So will Blanche and Nelson. And probably your mother. And all my family. All because of you. Start from today and discard what troubles you from the past."

It was always easier said than done, of course.

He gazed at her. "I would rather start from yesterday," he said.

"From our wedding?" She smiled at him. "Let us build a happy future, Colin. And let's do it by living a happy present whenever we possibly can. We are together here in these rooms that feel so much like home because we made them home last night. What more could we ask of the present moment? You are the man I chose, and I believed you when you told me I was the woman you chose. I love you, you know. With all my heart."

Why *not* be the first to say it? Why not make herself vulnerable by opening her heart to him? She trusted him.

She had trusted him with her person, and her heart was part of her person. He would not hurt her.

He moved then to take her in his arms and settle her head on his shoulder. She heard him sigh.

"I can remember telling you at the first ball of the Season we both attended," he said, "that the only time I had looked across the ballroom and found myself gazing transfixed upon a special someone, she was you. You laughed, believing I was joking. I laughed because I thought it too. Or, rather, I thought the truth inappropriate and therefore made light of it. And so I proceeded to look elsewhere for a bride, and you proceeded to make the way clear for Codaire to offer for you again. But I meant those words, Elizabeth. With all my heart I meant them even as I pretended to myself that I did not."

"Oh, Colin," she said, sighing against his neck. "And I knew it too when I saw you in the receiving line. But I refused to recognize it."

"We almost allowed nine years to come between us," he said. "When you look at me, Elizabeth, do you see a man nine years younger than yourself?"

She drew back her head and looked up into his face.

"No," she said, raising a hand to cup his cheek. "I see Colin. The man I love."

"And I see Elizabeth," he said. "The woman I adore."

"But not because I am on a pedestal," she said.

"What pedestal?" He stared at her blankly until his eyes crinkled at the corners.

He kissed her then, and they clung together as though the world were spinning away from them and they had only each other as an anchor.

"I love you," he murmured against her lips after a while.

"May I also *make* love to you? Or is that absolutely not allowed during the daytime?"

"Somewhere else in the world it is night," she told him.

"Ah," he said. "A good point."

And then he drew something of a shriek from her as one of his arms came beneath her knees as he stood up with her and carried her to the bedchamber they had used last night.

She was laughing by the time he had maneuvered the door open, stepped inside with her, and shut the door with one booted foot.

They remained in London for four more days before leaving for Roxingley. Colin looked forward to going with eagerness and trepidation. He had not really lived there since the age of eleven and had not been there at all since he was eighteen. There were no doubt all sorts of challenges awaiting them. There was no knowing what changes his mother had made to the house and park during those years the better to accommodate the parties she so often hosted. The letters of complaint he had received from the one neighbor did not reassure him—and that was just the man who had had the courage to write. There were perhaps a dozen more who would have liked to complain.

But he kept in mind Elizabeth's admonishment to think of the present rather than being bogged down in the past. Their suite at Mivart's Hotel really did feel like home in an absurd sort of way. But Roxingley was *really* home. It was where they would live for most of the rest of their lives. It was where they would bring up any children with whom they were blessed. They would put the imprint of their own personalities upon it, their own hard work and optimism and love and sense of family.

His mother might decide to live there too, of course, and that was a bit of a drag upon the spirits. But she could dominate their lives only if they allowed it. Not doing so was never as simply done as it sounded, not with his mother, but again it was a challenge he was prepared to take on—with Elizabeth by his side. If he did indeed have a dower house built at Roxingley, the problem would be at least partially solved. In the meantime, there were little-used apartments in both the east and west wings—at least, they had been little used in his time, and he could not imagine that that had changed. Elizabeth suggested they prepare a large and sumptuous suite of rooms in one of the wings for his mother's exclusive use.

His wife, he knew, was quietly excited about the move. She would be mistress of her own home again after a number of years of living in her brother's house in Kent with her mother. And, in Colin's estimation, she had been made to manage her own home and family. That aura of peace and serenity and competence he had noticed about her from his first acquaintance with her had been shaken in the last while but never shattered. It had returned in the days since their marriage until it enveloped him too and made him more content than he had ever dreamed of being. He would never admit it to her, but he still did place her on some sort of pedestal in his mind.

His bright, wonderful angel.

But when he tried to verbalize his feelings for her, he only embarrassed himself horribly and was very thankful he had not spoken aloud.

There were certain busy little tasks to accomplish during those four days and letters to write and a whole host of people to visit. He closed down the rooms that had been his home for five years and spent a few hours with his man of business. Elizabeth wrote to his mother and Blanche to thank them for coming to the wedding and making the day more memorable for them. She assured them that she looked forward to seeing them at Roxingley after the Season came to an end and to witnessing the reunion of all the Handrich family—for Wren, being one of the most courageous women Colin knew, had agreed that she and Alexander would be there.

They called upon all the members of her family—to thank those who had come from afar to help celebrate their nuptials, to thank the others for all the love and support they had shown in the past few weeks. They had all agreed to come to Roxingley for a few weeks of the summer, but farewells still had to be said now.

They called at the house on Curzon Street the day before they planned to leave, but his mother was not at home. It was unusual for her to be out, especially very early in the afternoon, and it did occur to Colin that perhaps she had simply chosen not to see them. But he did not argue the point. They would call tomorrow on their way out of London. Blanche had replied to Elizabeth's letter to inform her that she and Nelson would certainly be at Roxingley, since she had not seen Ruby or her husband for many years and would like to do so now—and to meet their children.

"She is thawing," Elizabeth said as she showed him the letter—a brief, rather cold little note. "We will give her time, Colin. As much time as she needs. And we must work on Nelson too. A stranger, more silent man I have never met, but I suspect that he really cares for Blanche. We will give them both time. You will have your larger family yet. I predict it with the greatest confidence."

"Oh, do you?" he asked, bending over the escritoire at which she sat to kiss the back of her neck. She looked back at him with twinkling eyes, his favorite expression of hers. Or perhaps a cofavorite with several others.

"I do," she said. "I have consulted my crystal ball."

They could not leave town quietly on the appointed morning. For one thing, there was no point in arriving too early on Curzon Street. It had always taken his mother several hours to prepare herself to face the day, even back in the time when she was naturally youthful and lovely. And she had never been an early riser. For another thing, Wren had insisted that they take breakfast at the house on South Audley Street and several of the Westcotts had promised to call there to see them on their way.

"I suppose," he said to Elizabeth, "we can expect a grand send-off."

"It is a little absurd, is it not," she said, "when it will be all of five days after our wedding? But one can expect no less of the Westcotts, you know. It would not surprise me if a few Radleys slipped in there too."

"I do love your family," he said, grinning. "Alexander's neighbors will doubtless lodge an official complaint about the noise."

"Not to mention several carriages plugging the street," she added.

All proceeded much as they had predicted until, late on the morning of their departure, the roadway outside Alexander's house was lined with carriages and the pavement before the door was clogged with people all talking at once and all insisting upon kissing Elizabeth and pumping Colin's hand.

"And here comes someone else," Jessica announced suddenly above the hubbub. "Oh . . . goodness."

"Oh look, Mama," Winifred cried. "Look, Papa. Look, Sarah. A fairy coach."

The white carriage drawn by the four white horses proceeded slowly along the street and came to a halt in the middle of the road while the family fell more or less silent in order to look.

"It must be your mother, Colin," his mother-in-law said unnecessarily.

Well, at least, Colin thought, drawing Elizabeth's arm through his and stepping off the curb with her to approach the carriage, they would not now have to delay their journey further by stopping at the Curzon Street house.

The white-and-gold liveried footman who had been seated beside the coachman had jumped smartly down from his perch in order to open the carriage door and set down the steps. His mother was going to get out, then, was she?

But it was Lord Ede who descended to the road first and looked unhurriedly at Colin and Elizabeth before turning to hand down Colin's mother, youthful and resplendent as usual in dazzling white with a fine lace facial veil falling from the brim of her hat. She stood beside him and looked benevolently from Colin to Elizabeth.

"My dearest son," she said, "and my dear Lady Hodges. You must understand that I really could not bear to be known as the *Dowager* Lady Hodges. Such a lowering, dowdy word. It would make me feel positively old and everyone would laugh and tell me how ludicrous it was and ask which Lady Hodges was the dowager. That would be tiresome for both of us. So I have changed my name. And my home. I daresay you planned to stuff me into a remote wing of Roxingley and to try convincing me that you were doing me a great favor. Pah!"

"Your mother married me by special license yesterday, my boy," Lord Ede said, looking very directly at Colin, a smile playing about his lips.

"Yes. I am Lady Ede," Colin's mother said. "Of course, everyone will marvel that I have chosen an older man and will whisper that I must have married Ede for his money. But that would be absurd, as your father left me a very tidy allowance, dearest. But marrying an older man is perhaps better than doing the opposite, though any number of young men have wooed me in the past eight years. I have always preferred experience to youth."

The hubbub suddenly resumed while everyone, it seemed, felt it necessary to congratulate the newlyweds and wish them well.

"Mother." Elizabeth stepped forward, both hands extended. "I am delighted for you. I do wish you happy."

"Yes," Lady Ede said. "I daresay you do."

Colin was gazing at Lord Ede, who looked back, one mocking eyebrow raised. "I suppose," Colin said quietly, extending his right hand, "this is not necessarily an answer to my question, is it?"

"Not necessarily," Lord Ede agreed. "But I will tell you this, my boy. If I were to have another son—I have two, you know—I could not ask for a better one than you."

Their hands met and clasped. His father? Colin wondered. Or not? He would probably never know for sure either way. But Elizabeth was right, he discovered. The past ought not be allowed to cloud the present or obscure the future. Really, it did not matter terribly much. The man he had always called father had never shown him much love or given him much attention, but ultimately he had done right

by him. And he had done right by Wren too. He must surely
have known that she had a better chance of a decent life
with a caring mother figure like Aunt Megan than she did
at Roxingley.

Wren was standing close to the door of the house with
Alexander close by. She was half smiling, though she made
no move to draw closer—or to duck back inside the house.
She was a woman who would surely always stand her
ground.

Colin took his mother's gloved hand in his and leaned
forward to kiss her cheek through her veil. "I wish you
well, Mother," he said. "We must not be estranged."

"Oh, hardly that," she said. "You have always been my
favorite, dearest. And you must know that you are a favorite
with Ede too. But how naughty of you to have suspected
that I might have been unfaithful to your father while he
was still alive."

"It is not true, then?" he asked her.

"Of course it is not true," she said. "Would I lie to you? I
abhor lies of all things." She looked around her, a queen
surveying her court. "I thank you all. You are most kind.
But Ede and I must be on our way. We are blocking the road
and everyone is already saying that I hold up traffic wherever I go."

Lord Ede handed her back into the carriage and followed her inside. The footman closed the door, took his
place on the box beside the coachman again, and the carriage proceeded on its way along the street.

"Well," the Dowager Countess of Riverdale said. "Well."

"Fairy," Sarah said, pointing after the carriage.

"That is not a fairy, silly," Robbie said from his perch
astride Joel Cunningham's shoulders. "That was an old lady."

Lady Jessica Archer and Lady Estelle Lamarr laughed

out loud before Viola shushed them and looked reproachfully at the Marquess of Dorchester, her husband, whose lips were twitching.

"Oh dear," Lady Matilda Westcott said. "Whatever has happened to the old rule that children are to be seen and not heard?"

Colin took Elizabeth's hand in his. "Are you ready to go?" he asked her.

"Home to Roxingley?" she said. "Oh, yes, indeed, Colin. I was never more ready."

Ten more minutes passed before their carriage finally drew away from the curb, and even then they both had to lean close to the window in order to wave to the family, who might have been seeing them off to the ends of the world for the next eternity or so if their lifted hands and fluttering handkerchiefs and even a few tears were anything to judge by.

And then they were alone. And on their way. Home.

Colin turned in his seat to look at Elizabeth and took her hand again and laced their fingers. She was gazing back at him with eyes that both shone and twinkled.

"The farce at the end of the drama?" he said.

The twinkle was very close to laughter. "Your mother's marriage to Lord Ede?" she said. "And her lovely sense of drama in arriving outside the house at that precise moment? It would be unkind to call it farce."

He grinned at her.

And then they were both laughing until they were helpless with it.

Would his mother lie? Well, of course she would. Did it matter? She was who she was, and his father—whichever of two men that was—was who *he* was. In the meantime, *he* was Colin Handrich, Lord Hodges, and he was going home with his new wife.

Whose face was filled with laughter and joy, just as his own must be.

He loved her, and she had told him that she loved him.

He trusted her word, and she knew she could trust his.

Life, at least in this precious present moment, was very, very good.

READ ON FOR AN EXCERPT FROM THE FIRST BOOK
IN MARY BALOGH'S WESTCOTT SERIES,

Someone to Love

AVAILABLE NOW FROM PIATKUS

One

Despite the fact that the late Earl of Riverdale had died without having made a will, Josiah Brumford, his solicitor, had found enough business to discuss with his son and successor to be granted a face-to-face meeting at Westcott House, the earl's London residence on South Audley Street. Having arrived promptly and bowed his way through effusive and obsequious greetings, Brumford proceeded to find a great deal of nothing in particular to impart at tedious length and with pompous verbosity.

Which would have been all very well, Avery Archer, Duke of Netherby, thought a trifle peevishly as he stood before the library window and took snuff in an effort to ward off the urge to yawn, if he had not been compelled to be here too to endure the tedium. If Harry had only been a year older—he had turned twenty just before his father's death—then Avery need not be here at all and Brumford could prose on forever and a day as far as he was concerned. By some bizarre and thoroughly irritating twist of fate, however, His Grace had found himself joint guardian of the new earl with the countess, the boy's mother.

It was all remarkably ridiculous in light of Avery's notoriety for indolence and the studied avoidance of anything that might be dubbed work or the performance of duty. He had a secretary and numerous other servants to deal with all the tedious business of life for him. And there was also the fact that he was a mere eleven years older than his ward. When one heard the word *guardian,* one conjured a mental image of a gravely dignified graybeard. However, it seemed he had inherited the guardianship to which his father had apparently agreed—in writing—at some time in the dim distant past when the late Riverdale had mistakenly thought himself to be at death's door. By the time he did die a few weeks ago, the old Duke of Netherby had been sleeping peacefully in his own grave for more than two years and was thus unable to be guardian to anyone. Avery might, he supposed, have repudiated the obligation since he was not the Netherby mentioned in that letter of agreement, which had never been made into a legal document anyway. He had not done so, however. He did not dislike Harry, and really it had seemed like too much bother to take a stand and refuse such a slight and temporary inconvenience.

It felt more than slight at the moment. Had he known Brumford was such a crashing bore, he might have made the effort.

"There really was no need for Father to make a will," Harry was saying in the sort of rallying tone one used when repeating oneself in order to wrap up a lengthy discussion that had been moving in unending circles. "I have no brothers. My father trusted that I would provide handsomely for my mother and sisters according to his known wishes, and of course I will not fail that trust. I will certainly see to it too that most of the servants and retainers on all my properties are kept on and that those who leave my employ for whatever reason—Father's valet, for example—are properly compensated. And you may rest assured that my mother and Netherby will see that I do not stray from these obligations before I arrive at my majority."

He was standing by the fireplace beside his mother's chair, in a relaxed posture, one shoulder propped against the mantel, his arms crossed over his chest, one booted foot on the hearth. He was a tall lad and a bit gangly, though a few more years would take care of that deficiency. He was fair-haired and blue-eyed with a good-humored countenance that very young ladies no doubt found impossibly handsome. He was also almost indecently rich. He was amiable and charming and had been running wild during the past several months, first while his father was too ill to take much notice and again during the couple of weeks since the funeral. He had probably never lacked for friends, but now they abounded and would have filled a sizable city, perhaps even a small county, to overflowing. Though perhaps *friends* was too kind a word to use for most of them. *Sycophants* and *hangers-on* would be better.

Avery had not tried intervening, and he doubted he would. The boy seemed of sound enough character and would doubtless settle to a bland and blameless adulthood if left to his own devices. And if in the meanwhile he sowed a wide swath of wild oats and squandered a small fortune, well, there were probably oats to spare in the world and there would still be a vast fortune remaining for the bland adulthood. It would take just too much effort to intervene, anyway, and the Duke of Netherby rarely made the effort to do what was inessential or what was not conducive to his personal comfort.

"I do not doubt it for a moment, my lord." Brumford bowed from his chair in a manner that suggested he might at last be conceding that everything he had come to say had been said and perhaps it was time to take his leave. "I trust Brumford, Brumford & Sons may continue to represent your interests as we did your dear departed father's and his father's before him. I trust His Grace and Her Ladyship will so advise you."

Avery wondered idly what the other Brumford was like and just how many young Brumfords were included in the "& Sons." The mind boggled.

Harry pushed himself away from the mantel, looking hopeful. "I see no reason why I would not," he said. "But I will not keep you any longer. You are a very busy man, I daresay."

"I will, however, beg for a few minutes more of your time, Mr. Brumford," the countess said unexpectedly. "But it is a matter that does not concern you, Harry. You may go and join your sisters in the drawing room. They will be eager to hear details of this meeting. Perhaps you would be good enough to remain, Avery."

Harry directed a quick grin Avery's way, and His Grace, opening his snuffbox again before changing his mind and snapping it shut, almost wished that he too were being sent off to report to the countess's two daughters. He must be very bored indeed. Lady Camille Westcott, age twenty-two, was the managing sort, a forthright female who did not suffer fools gladly, though she was handsome enough, it was true. Lady Abigail, at eighteen, was a sweet, smiling, pretty young thing who might or might not possess a personality. To do her justice, Avery had not spent enough time in her company to find out. She was his half sister's favorite cousin and dearest friend in the world, however—her words—and he occasionally heard them talking and giggling together behind closed doors that he was very careful never to open.

Harry, all eager to be gone, bowed to his mother, nodded politely to Brumford, came very close to winking at Avery, and made his escape from the library. Lucky devil. Avery strolled closer to the fireplace, where the countess and Brumford were still seated. What the deuce could be important enough that she had voluntarily prolonged this excruciatingly dreary meeting?

"And how may I be of service to you, my lady?" the solicitor asked.

The countess, Avery noticed, was sitting very upright, her spine arched slightly inward. Were ladies taught to sit that way, as though the backs of chairs had been created merely to be decorative? She was, he estimated, about forty years old. She was also quite perfectly beautiful in a mature, dignified sort of way. She surely could not have been happy with Riverdale—who could?—yet to Avery's knowledge she had never indulged herself with lovers. She was tall, shapely, and blond with no sign yet, as far as he could see, of any gray hairs. She was also one of those rare women who looked striking rather than dowdy in deep mourning.

"There is a girl," she said, "or, rather, a woman. In Bath, I believe. My late husband's . . . daughter."

Avery guessed she had been about to say *bastard*, but had changed her mind for the sake of gentility. He raised both his eyebrows and his quizzing glass.

Brumford for once had been silenced.

"She was at an orphanage there," the countess contin- ued. "I do not know where she is now. She is hardly still there since she must be in her middle twenties. But River- dale supported her from a very young age and continued to do so until his death. We never discussed the matter. It is altogether probable he did not know I was aware of her existence. I do not know any details, nor have I ever wanted to. I still do not. I assume it was not through you that the support payments were made?"

Brumford's already florid complexion took on a dis- tinctly purplish hue. "It was not, my lady," he assured her. "But might I suggest that since this . . . person is now an adult, you—"

"No," she said, cutting him off. "I am not in need of any suggestion. I have no wish whatsoever to know anything about this woman, even her name. I certainly have no wish for my son to know of her. However, it seems only just that if she has been supported all her life by her . . . father, she be informed of his death if that has not already happened, and be compensated with a final settlement. A handsome one, Mr. Brumford. It would need to be made perfectly clear to her at the same time that there is to be no more— ever, under any circumstances. May I leave the matter in your hands?"

"My lady." Brumford seemed almost to be squirming in his chair. He licked his lips and darted a glance at Avery, of whom—if His Grace was reading him correctly—he stood in considerable awe.

Avery raised his glass all the way to his eye. "Well?" he said. "*May* her ladyship leave the matter in your hands, Brumford? Are you or the other Brumford or one of the sons willing and able to hunt down the bastard daughter, name unknown, of the late earl in order to make her the happiest of orphans by settling a modest fortune upon her?"

"Your Grace." Brumford's chest puffed out. "My lady. It will be a difficult task, but not an insurmountable one, especially for the skilled investigators whose services we engage in the interests of our most valued clients. If the . . . person indeed grew up in Bath, we will identify her. If she is still there, we will find her. If she is no longer there—"

"I believe," Avery said, sounding pained, "her ladyship and I get your meaning. You will report to me when the woman has been found. Is that agreeable to you, Aunt?"

The Countess of Riverdale was not, strictly speaking, his aunt. His stepmother, the duchess, was the late Earl of Riverdale's sister, and thus the countess and all the others were his honorary relatives.

"That will be satisfactory," she said.

Anna Snow had been brought to the orphanage in Bath when she was not quite four years old. She had no real memory of her life before that beyond a few brief and disjointed flashes—of someone always coughing, for example, or of a lych-gate that was dark and a bit frightening inside whenever she was called upon to pass through it alone, and of kneeling on a window ledge and looking down upon a graveyard, and of crying inconsolably inside a carriage while someone with a gruff, impatient voice told her to hush and behave like a big girl.

She had been at the orphanage ever since, though she was now twenty-five. Most of the other children—there were usually about forty of them—left when they were fourteen or fifteen, after suitable employment had been found for them. But Anna had lingered on, first to help out as house-mother to a dormitory of girls and a sort of secretary to Miss Ford, the matron, and then as the schoolteacher when Miss Rutledge, the teacher who had taught her, married a clergy-man, and moved away to Devonshire. She was even paid a modest salary. However, the expenses of her continued stay at the orphanage, now in a small room of her own, were still provided by the unknown benefactor who had paid them from the start. She had been told that they would con-tinue to be paid as long as she remained.

Anna considered herself fortunate. She had grown up in an orphanage, it was true, with not even a full identity to call her own, since she did not know who her parents were, but in the main it was not a charity institution. Almost all her fellow orphans were supported through their growing years by someone—usually anonymous, though some knew who they were and why they were there. Usually it was because their parents had died and there was no other family member able or willing to take them in. Anna did not dwell upon the lone-liness of not knowing her own story. Her material needs were taken care of. Miss Ford and her staff were generally kind. Most of the children were easy enough to get along with, and those who were not could be avoided. A few were close friends, or had been during her growing years. If there had been a lack of love in her life, or of that type of love one as-sociated with a family, then she did not particularly miss it, having never consciously known it.

Or so she always told herself.

She was content with her life and was only occasionally restless with the feeling that surely there ought to be more, that perhaps she should be making a greater effort to *live* her life. She had been offered marriage by three different men—the shopkeeper where she went occasionally, when she could afford it, to buy a book; one of the governors of the orphanage, whose wife had recently died and left him with four young children; and Joel Cunningham, her lifelong best friend. She had rejected all three offers for varying reasons and wondered sometimes if it had been foolish to do so, as there were not likely to be many more offers, if any. The prospect of a continuing life of spinsterhood sometimes seemed dreary.

Joel was with her when the letter arrived.

She was tidying the schoolroom after dismissing the children for the day. The monitors for the week—John Davies and Ellen Payne—had collected the slates and chalk and the counting frames. But while John had stacked the slates neatly on the cupboard shelf allotted for them and put all the chalk away in the tin and replaced the lid, Ellen had shoved the counting frames haphazardly on top of paintbrushes and palettes on the bottom shelf instead of arranging them in their appointed place side by side on the shelf above so as not to bend the rods or damage the beads. The reason she had put them in the wrong place was obvious. The second shelf was occupied by the water pots used to swill paint brushes and an untidy heap of paint-stained cleaning rags.

"Joel," Anna said, a note of long suffering in her voice, "could you at least try to get your pupils to put things away where they belong after an art class? And to clean the water pots first? Look! One of them even still has water in it. Very *dirty* water."

Joel was sitting on the corner of the battered teacher's desk, one booted foot braced on the floor, the other swinging free. His arms were crossed over his chest. He grinned at her.

"But the whole point of being an artist," he said, "is to be a free spirit, to cast aside restricting rules and draw inspiration from the universe. My job is to teach my pupils to be true artists."

She straightened up from the cupboard and directed a speaking glance his way. "What utter rot and nonsense," she said.

He laughed outright. "Anna, Anna," he said. "Here, let me take that pot from you before you burst with indignation or spill it down your dress."

But before he could say anything more, the classroom door was flung open without the courtesy of a knock to admit Bertha Reed, a thin, flaxen-haired fourteen-year-old who acted as Miss Ford's helper now that she was old enough. She was bursting with excitement and waving a folded paper in one raised hand.

"There is a letter for you, Miss Snow," she half shrieked. "It was delivered by special messenger from London and Miss Ford would have brought it herself but Tommy is bleeding all over her sitting room and no one can find Nurse Jones. Maddie punched him in the nose."

"It is high time someone did," Joel said, strolling closer to Anna. "I suppose he was pulling one of her braids again."

Anna scarcely heard. A letter? From London? By special messenger? For *her*?

"Whoever can it be from, Miss Snow?" Bertha screeched, apparently not particularly concerned about Tommy and his bleeding nose. "Who do you know in London? No, don't tell me—that ought to have been whom. *Whom* do you know in London? I wonder what they are writing about. And it came by *special messenger,* all that way. It must have cost a *fortune.* Oh, do open it."

Her blatant inquisitiveness might have seemed impertinent, but really, it was so rare for any of them to receive a letter that word always spread very quickly and everyone wanted to know all about it. Occasionally someone who had left both the orphanage and Bath to work elsewhere would write, and the recipient would almost invariably share the contents with everyone else. Such missives were kept as prized possessions and read over and over until they were virtually threadbare.

Anna did not recognize the handwriting, which was both bold and precise. It was a masculine hand, she felt sure. The paper felt thick and expensive. It did not look like a personal letter.

"Oliver is in London," Bertha said wistfully. "But I don't suppose it can be from him, can it? His writing does not look anything like that, and why would he write to you anyway? The four times he has written since he left here, it was to me. And he is not going to send any letter by special messenger, is he?"

Oliver Jamieson had been apprenticed to a bootmaker in London two years ago at the age of fourteen and had promised to send for Bertha and marry her as soon as he got on his feet. Twice each year since then he had faithfully written a five- or six-line letter in large, careful handwriting. Bertha had shared his sparse news on each occasion and wept over the letters until it was a wonder they were still legible. There were three years left in his apprenticeship before he could hope to be on his feet and able to support a wife. They were both very young, but the separation did seem cruel. Anna always found herself hoping that Oliver would remain faithful to his childhood sweetheart.

"Are you going to turn it over and over in your hands and hope it will divulge its secrets without your having to break the seal?" Joel asked.

Stupidly, Anna's hands were trembling. "Perhaps there is some mistake," she said. "Perhaps it is not for me."

He came up behind her and looked over her shoulder. "Miss Anna Snow," he said. "It certainly sounds like you. I do not know any other Anna Snows. Do you, Bertha?"

"I do not, Mr. Cunningham," she said after pausing to think. "But whatever can it be about?"

Anna slid her thumb beneath the seal and broke it. And yes, indeed, the paper was a thick, costly vellum. It was not a long letter. It was from Somebody Brumford—she could not read the first name, though it began with a J. He was a solicitor. She read through the letter once, swallowed, and then read it again more slowly.

"The day after tomorrow," she murmured.

"In a private chaise," Joel added. He had been reading over her shoulder.

"*What* is the day after tomorrow?" Bertha demanded, her voice an agony of suspense. "*What* chaise?"

Anna looked at her blankly. "I am being summoned to London to discuss my future," she said. There was a faint buzzing in her ears.

"Oh! By who?" Bertha asked, her eyes as wide as saucers. "By *whom*, I mean."

"Mr. J. Brumford, a solicitor," Anna said.

"Josiah, I think that says," Joel said. "Josiah Brumford. He is sending a private chaise to fetch you, and you are to pack a bag for at least a few days."

"To *London*?" Bertha's voice was breathless with awe.

"Whatever am I to do?" Anna's mind seemed to have stopped working. Or, rather, it *was* working, but it was whirring out of control, like the innards of a broken clock.

"What you are to do, Anna," Joel said, pushing a chair up behind her knees and setting his hands on her shoulders to press her gently down onto it, "is pack a bag for a few days and then go to London to discuss your future."

"But what future?" she asked.

"That is what is to be discussed," he pointed out.

The buzzing in her ears grew louder.

New York Times Bestselling Author

MARY
BALOGH

"One of the best!"

—#1 *New York Times* Bestselling Author

Julia Quinn

For a complete list of titles,
please visit marybalogh.com/books

Do you love historical fiction?

Want the chance to hear news about your favourite authors (and the chance to win free books)?

Mary Balogh
Lenora Bell
Charlotte Betts
Jessica Blair
Frances Brody
Grace Burrowes
Gaelen Foley
Pamela Hart
Elizabeth Hoyt
Eloisa James
Lisa Kleypas
Stephanie Laurens
Sarah MacLean
Amanda Quick
Julia Quinn

Then visit the Piatkus website
www.piatkusentice.co.uk

And follow us on Facebook and Twitter
www.facebook.com/piatkusfiction | @piatkusentice

piatkus